CARLO KENNEDY

TIME SIGNATURE II
THE REGRETS OF OUR PAST

CARLO KENNEDY

220 Publishing

Chicago, Illinois
220 Publishing
(A Division of 220 Communications)

Time Signature II: The Regrets of Our Past
© 2016 by Carlo Kennedy. All Rights Reserved.
℗ 2016 by 220 Publishing.

This book is a work of fiction. Names, characters, places, and incidents either are products of the author's imagination or are used fictitiously. Any resemblance to actual events or people, living or dead, is entirely coincidental.

No part of this book may be reproduced, stored in a retrieval system, or transmitted by any means without the written permission of the author.

Published by 220 Publishing
(A Division of 220 Communications)

PO Box 8186
Chicago, IL 60680-8186

www.220communications.com
www.twitter.com/220publishing

For more information on the author, visit: CarloKennedy.com
Follow Carlo Kennedy on Twitter: @AuthorCarloK

Cover and Interior Design by Julie M. Holloway of JMHCre8ive.com

ISBN: 978-1-5136-1189-1

Printed in the USA

WHO'S WHO:
THE CHARACTERS FROM
TIME SIGNATURE

Augustine (Gus) Agnello: *Son of Rocco and Monica, husband of Colleen. Father of Sofia and Chris. Founder and owner of the Agnello Construction Company. Old school Italian-American family man.*

Christopher (Chris) Agnello: *Son of Gus and Colleen, younger brother of Sofia. Newlywed husband of Willow. Struggling college student, music major, failing songwriter, former leader of now-defunct 80s cover band. Spent a year in 1742/1743, where he met Willow O'Connell and her family.*

Colleen Delaney Agnello: *Wife of Gus, Mother of Chris and Sofia. Homemaker and part time bookkeeper for the Agnello Construction Company. Proud Irish Catholic, attends Mass every day, and volunteers at her church.*

James (Jimmy) Agnello: *Grandson of Rocco and Monica, nephew of Gus and Colleen, cousin of Sofia and Chris. Lost his parents when he was a boy. Also known as Jimmy the Fist, he has a mysterious past, including mob connections, witness protection, and the CIA. Now an agent for the newly formed TIA (the Temporal Intelligence Agency).*

Monica Agnello: *Immigrant from northern Italy. Widow of Rocco, Mother of Gus. Grandmother of Jimmy, Chris, and Sofia. Attends daily Mass with her daughter-in-law Colleen, and feels responsible for the spiritual well-being of the family.*

Rocco Agnello (deceased): *Immigrant from southern Italy. Husband of Monica, father of Gus, grandfather of Jimmy, Chris, and Sofia. Blues guitar player. Chris looked up to him, but he passed away when Chris was a boy.*

Willow O'Connell Agnello: *(Originally from the 18th century) Daughter of Patrick, sister of Fergus and Colum, newlywed wife of Chris.*

Armando Fernandez: *Son of Puerto Rican immigrants, U.S. Marine. Newlywed husband of Sofia.*

Sofia Agnello Fernandez: *Daughter of Gus and Colleen, older sister of Chris. Newlywed wife of Armando. She is working on her Ph.D. in astrophysics, and she is the one who built the time machine.*

Carrig Hannon: *(In the 18th century) Childhood schoolmate of Fergus and Colum. Sidekick to Aedan. Employed as a Dublin city watchman until he and Aedan helped Chris and the O'Connells escape. Left Dublin to avoid the consequences. Never head from again.*

Aedan MacCluin: *(In the 18th century) Childhood schoolmate of Fergus and Colum. Employed as a Dublin city watchman until he and Carrig helped Chris and the O'Connells escape. Left Dublin to avoid the consequences. Never heard from again.*

Nero the Cockapoo: *The Agnellos' family dog. Part cocker spaniel, part poodle. The world's first time traveler.*

Colum O'Connell: *(Originally from the 18th century) Son of Patrick, brother of Fergus and Willow.*

Fergus O'Connell: *(Originally from the 18th century) Son of Patrick, brother of Colum and Willow.*

Mary O'Connell (deceased): *Wife of Patrick, mother of Fergus, Colum, and Willow.*

Patrick O'Connell: *(Originally from the 18th century) Father of Fergus, Colum, and Willow.*

Nancy Pugliese: *Wife of Peter, adoptive mother of Sara. Next door neighbor to the Agnellos.*

Peter Pugliese: *Husband of Nancy, adoptive father of Sara. Next door neighbor to the Agnellos.*

Sara Pugliese: *Adopted (African American) daughter of Peter and Nancy. Sofia's best friend since childhood. Attending dental school.*

The Resonator: *The time machine that runs on music. From the outside, it looks like a large wooden crate.*

Donald Wordman: *Scientist turned politician. Chair of the government subcommittee that is looking into recent events which suggest the possibility of time travel. He is preparing to run for the nomination as the democratic party's candidate for president.*

PROLOGUE

Back in the Puglieses' garage – in August of 1999 - Jimmy emerged from the wooden crate, stepping around the puddles of vomit all over the floor. And since, for him, throwing up was contagious, he joined in on the puking. But eventually, everyone finished wiping their mouths, and got to hugging, and crying, and laughing. And a little more puking. But mostly hugging, and crying, and laughing.

By the time Jimmy could catch his breath and look around at the assembled group of confused and happy time travelers, Sofia was already wearing the engagement ring. Armando had proposed the minute she returned from 1743. One month later, Sofia and Armando were married in a double ceremony along with Chris and Willow. Six hours after that Sofia was pregnant.

CHAPTER 1
A WHO A SAY?

Jimmy Agnello found himself standing alone on a train platform. He had said goodbye to his parents, and watched them climb up into the graffiti-covered train car. He couldn't bring himself to walk away, so he just stood there on the platform, his overcoat moving with the wind, watching the train pull away from the station. He kept his eye on the car where his parents were sitting, straining to see them through the dirty windows. As the train sped by him, it seemed to go on forever, kicking up litter and debris along the tracks. And as Jimmy started to wonder just how long this train was, it seemed to pick up speed, suddenly going dangerously fast for a train that was still partly in the station. Jimmy wondered at the length and speed of the train, but he didn't notice that he was now seeing the train from high above, as it raced along at ludicrous speed, rocking side to side on the tracks as though it might jump the rails at any moment. A signpost up ahead said Velo City. *What's that? Another train on the same track? Stop the train! Stop!!* Jimmy thought he had screamed it at the top of his lungs but there was no sound. His mind yelled again, *Mom! Dad!* but the two trains collided in a devastating explosion. There was nothing he could do to stop it. Then Jimmy woke up with a shudder.

As his whole body tingled from the shock of the dream, he realized he was lying in a strange bed, and it took him a second to remember where he was. *Oh yeah. New York. Plaza Hotel. New Year's Day. Today is January First, Two Thousand. So much for Y2K. Today is the day I save my parents.*

    Jimmy was in a hurry, and it felt like it took forever to shower, put on his trademark jeans with mock turtle neck, leather sport coat and Italian shoes, gather up his thirty-year-old twenty dollar bills, his ear plugs and Dramamine, and an 8-track tape, and finally get down to the lobby and into a cab. He was not interested in wasting any time, so he popped the Dramamine in the cab as it took him downtown into the financial district. Even at such an early hour, with New York traffic it was impossible to tell if he was being followed, so he got out of the cab a couple blocks from his destination and looked over his shoulder as he walked the rest of the way. He circled the block twice just to be safe, and then he made his way to the secret laboratory of the Temporal Intelligence Agency, where the time machine was being held under lock and key. Of course, he had the key.

    Letting himself in, Jimmy locked the door behind him and walked directly over to the Resonator, the sound of his shoes echoing in the mostly empty industrial loft. The 8-track tape was Steve Miller's *Book of Dreams*, released in 1977, the year of the train wreck. It was easy enough to grab the tape from his aunt Colleen's collection before leaving home. But Jimmy had no illusions about dropping in at just the right time. He didn't know when or where any of the songs on the album were first written, so he could only hope to get back before the time of the accident without going too far back to be able to do anything about it. With Chris' adventure in the eighteenth century looming in his mind, Jimmy got into the Resonator and inserted the tape. He put in the ear plugs, and without a second thought, pushed the green button. The song *Sacrifice* began to play, and the Resonator's computers processed the sound waves, multiplying the harmonics, and sending out the vibrations to reach back into the past to the origin – to the time and place of the original performance of that song.

Before he knew it, Jimmy and the wooden crate materialized on the loading dock of a San Francisco recording studio, in the year 1976. When he figured out where he was, he thought to himself, *At least I'm in California. That's good. I'm close.* A quick trip past the newsstand, and he realized he was a year too early. *Damn. How can I warn them without risking they will forget all about the warning before next year rolls around?* But it turned out to be a moot point because Jimmy couldn't locate his parents. He made several phone calls, and then a bus ride down to Los Angeles, all the time worrying that something might happen to the Resonator and he could be stuck in the 1970s. But Jimmy's parents were nowhere to be found. So he decided to try another angle. *If I can't prevent them from getting on that train, maybe I can prevent the train wreck altogether.*

Jimmy had read articles about the accident, and although his parents were never mentioned, the articles all gave the name of the man who was eventually blamed for the crash. The switchman's name was John Paul Richards, and the train collision, whether it was really his fault or not, had ruined his life. *Maybe this is better*, Jimmy thought. *If I can pull this off, I can save a lot of lives.*

It wasn't hard to find John Richards. He worked for the railroad, at the LA switchyard. Jimmy asked around and found out where he was, and then waited until quitting time. Sure enough, Richards made his way to a neighborhood bar, and Jimmy followed him in. The next morning, when Richards woke up he was in a lot of pain. When he looked in the mirror, he couldn't believe his eyes. There was a tattoo on his chest that wasn't there the day before. The letters were large, bold, and backwards, so he could read them in the mirror – in fact, he would read them in the mirror every day for the rest of his life – and he would never know just how much that tattoo had saved him. The tattoo said:

March 23, 1977 – Watch Out For Track #6

Back in the year two thousand, Jimmy first checked the railway records for any evidence of the 1977 train crash. There was none. Then he checked the newspaper archives. The crash never happened, because he had prevented it. Now it was time to find his parents. *Where would they be?* Jimmy decided that his best bet was to call his Uncle Gus and Aunt Colleen, and see if they knew where his parents were. When the phone rang at the Agnello home in the suburbs of Chicago, Gus fumbled with the receiver as the coiled cord got caught on his large gold crucifix.

"Hel- Hello? Dammit. Hello? Sorry. Almost dropped the phone. Hello?" He fumbled with the CD player on the kitchen counter and turned down the volume of his Roberta Flack disc.

"Hey Uncle Gus. Maybe it's time you got a cordless phone."

"Jimbo! No, this phone's fine. I don't need the latest damn thing. How's it going out there in the Big Apple?"

"Okay." Jimmy tried to figure out how to ask about his parents without letting on that he wasn't sure whether they were alive.

Gus went on with a barrage of questions. "How's Sofia doing? When's the hearing?"

"She's fine. Haven't seen them yet today, they're still at their apartment. The hearing is supposed to be soon, but Wordman is stalling, trying to get Sofia to make some improvements on the machine before they… um… anyway… uh…"

"Jimmy, what's up?" Gus could tell something else was on Jimmy's mind.

"Uncle Gus… um… tell me about my parents."

"Oh, geez. Um, well… you know, your dad, he was my brother, and…"

Was? Jimmy's heart sank. *Damn, they're still dead. But how? I prevented the accident.* Jimmy decided to press for more information. "Yeah, but what happened?"

Gus paused. It was painful for him to talk about it. "Well, you know there was the accident – the train…"

"In California."

"No, Jimmy, it wasn't in California. Don't you remember? It was in Brazil. They were on a train going from Buenos Aires to Rio – no one knows why, exactly – but anyway the train derailed. A defect in the tracks, apparently."

Colleen jumped in, "Let me talk to him." Gus handed the phone to Colleen.

"Hi Jimmy."

"Hey Aunt Colleen."

Gus walked out of earshot, and Colleen spoke in a lower voice. "James Agnello, you'd better not be trying to use that time machine to change the past!"

"What?" Jimmy tried to fake a protest.

"I know what you're up to." She sounded seriously angry. "You stop it right now! Jesus, Mary, and Joseph, we almost lost Christopher, and we can't afford to risk losing you. You can't save them. You can't change the past. Just leave it alone." She crossed herself.

At this point Monica walked by and shouted for Jimmy to hear, "You don't want to know what's in the past!"

Now Jimmy was outnumbered, and so he had to let it go. But he had no intention of giving up on trying to save his parents. *Why are they still dead? I prevented that accident, so why did they die in a different train wreck?*

Before Jimmy could think about it any more, the door to the lab swung open and Sofia and Armando walked in, talking loudly and struggling to manage the door while carrying the coffee and bagels they had bought on the way from their new apartment in Greenwich Village. As Sofia took off her coat, Jimmy could see that she had given up on dressing up, and had gone to wearing sweat pants every day. He could also see that her baby bump was beginning to show. Jimmy noticed that

Armando seemed to stand a little taller since the wedding. He had let his hair grow out a bit, but he still looked like a soldier – he still wore his military Velcro watch, and kept a pistol at his side under his suit jacket.

"Hey Jimmy," Sofia chirped.

"Hey Sof-. Hey 'Mondo." Jimmy nodded to Armando, who nodded back. "What's on the agenda today?"

Sofia hung up her jacket and adjusted the scrunchie on her pony tail. "Wordman's got me working on the auto-pause function, you know, so the Resonator can be sent back in time without anyone in it. If we ever have to pick anyone up again, that would come in handy, but I could never get it to work before." She turned on the stereo and put on *The Joshua Tree* by U2. "Anyway, it's taking up all my time and I can't work on my new project." Then she reached into her purse and pulled out a card, handing it to Armando. "Happy four month anniversary!" she smiled. "It's a few days early, but I couldn't wait."

Armando looked like he was about to get misty, so Jimmy jumped in. "What's this new project?"

Sofia's dark brown eyes flashed wide with excitement. "It's something for the dreams – and the headaches," Sofia replied. But she was distracted, and wasn't ready to talk about it. "Jimmy," she said tentatively, "I've been thinking about what we talked about. About you using the Resonator to try to save your parents. Maybe it's not such a good idea. Anyway, I don't think it will-"

Jimmy was suddenly indignant. "Not a good idea? To save my PARENTS?" Sofia looked surprised at Jimmy's outburst, and then looked at Armando. Armando looked disappointed.

"Jimmy, calm down." Then she whispered, "You know Armando looks up to you."

"Yeah, well I don't want to be anybody's role model." Both Jimmy and Armando avoided eye contact with each other as Jimmy kept talking, half under his breath. "I just want to be somebody's son. Anyway, I already tried."

"What?" Sofia and Armando said in unison.

"I already tried. First thing this morning I got in the time machine, and I went back to California in the 1970s, and I actually prevented the train wreck that killed my parents."

Sofia looked confused. "But Jimmy, your parents died in Brazil."

"Yeah, you think that *now*. But for the last twenty-three years, we all believed that they died in a train accident in California. And then I prevented that train accident from ever happening. And now I get back here and everyone tells me they died in a *different* train accident, this time in Brazil. I mean, isn't that weird?"

"So wait," Armando made the "stop" motion with his hands. "You're saying that you prevented the accident that took your parents, and now that accident never happened, but they're still dead?"

"Yep," Jimmy nodded. "And *you* don't even remember the original accident."

"Yeah, that *is* weird." Armando agreed.

"I have to try again," Jimmy said. "I have to."

"What are you going to do, go to Brazil?" Sofia was skeptical.

"Look," Jimmy pleaded. "You always said you wanted your inventions to help people, right?"

"Yeah." Sofia admitted.

"Okay, so this is one way to do that. You can't take this away from me. I need your help."

"Alright," Sofia agreed reluctantly. "Alright." She rubbed her belly and looked down. "I do want my inventions to make the world a better place."

†††

Donald Wordman was awakened by a familiar dream. He dragged himself out of bed, and put a bookmark in his Richard Dawkins book, and set it on the nightstand. He straightened up his hotel room, putting away the VHS tapes of *Frankenstein* and *Forbidden Planet*, but in the wrong boxes, and then he cleared the browser history on his computer. He took his heart medication, and lit a cigarette. Then he decided to skip the shower and get right to work. He threw on one of his many expensive, but ill-fitting suits and half-assed his way through putting on a tie, all the while struggling to maneuver the tie around the cigarette hanging out of his mouth. After calling for a limo, he made the driver wait for him while he got his coffee and donut. In the limo, the speakers pulsed with Ziggy Marley's song, *A Who A Say (There Ain't No*

Jah?), that is until Wordman complained about the music, and asked the driver to turn it off.

As soon as Wordman arrived at the lab, the whole atmosphere changed from relaxed to tense. Wordman took charge, telling Sofia what to do and then pacing around the floor, chain smoking, saying things like, "We have to strike while the iron is hot," and "time is money." He continually pressed Sofia for progress reports on the auto-pause.

"And I don't want you working on anything else until you get that perfected," he barked. "Also, you need to get rid of the 8-track player. Replace it with that new mini-disc. That's got to be better, it's digital."

Sofia chose her words carefully. "Dr. Wordman, the digital recording is a compressed file. It doesn't retain all the harmonics needed for the Resonator to work. If anything, we should be replacing the 8-track with a turntable. But it's like I've told you before, I don't think that will make any difference. There are just too many variables for time travel to be accurate, or even stable. We still don't understand how the song writing process and rehearsals factor into the equation. We haven't really defined what constitutes the first performance of a musical piece."

Wordman's voice softened and took on a condescending tone. "Sofia, honey, I just want you to succeed here. I want you to finish the project, and get your Ph.D. so you can move on with your life. I know being here in New York can be overwhelming, and even a bit confusing, but you have to put away anything that's distracting you from moving toward your goal. I mean, look at me. My work in research, though underappreciated, opened doors that led to a career in politics. And now I'm going to be running for president. At the end of the day, I'm living my dreams. And you can, too. But you just have to understand that everything's different now that you've invented a time machine. It's like… time itself is now a commodity."

Sofia didn't like it when Wordman talked about the monetary value of time travel. She worried what might happen if the wrong people got their hands on a time machine. But Wordman had been given the authority to oversee the time machine at least until the hearing, and now he was acting as though he was Sofia's mentor. So Sofia just kept quiet as Wordman spoke to her chest. "You need me to guide you here. Remember what happened to your brother – you almost didn't get him back. You don't want to make a mistake that costs someone close to you their life, do you? I can help you be successful in this project. I can help you get your Ph.D. …Or not."

Armando squinted at Wordman. Sofia swallowed her initial reaction, and took a deep breath before she responded. "Thank you Dr. Wordman. Though I think that if the goal is to finish my Ph.D., then I ought to be working on the FTL Transmitter."

Jimmy jumped in to try to break the tension, "What's FTL?"

Sofia, Wordman, and Armando all answered at once. "Faster Than Light."

"Oh," Jimmy elongated the word with sheepish sarcasm.

"It's my original Ph.D. project," Sofia explained. "But it's also the transmitter that goes with the receiver – the one that will allow us to send messages back in time."

"That's fine," Wordman said, "but the hearing is coming up soon and we need to have the time machine running with no glitches by then… in case we have to demonstrate how it works." Then he added, "And no side projects. I don't want to find out you're wasting your time with that dream catcher idea."

"Dream catcher?" Jimmy was curious.

†††

Sara sat motionless on the plane, waiting for it to take off for New York. She was staring out the window, but she was really just staring off into space. In her mind she was replaying the last thing her adoptive father had said to her.

Your mother and I are splitting up.

Sara had walked out of the house without responding, and she could still hear the slam of the front door echoing in her head. Her shoulders shuddered a little, so she decided to retreat into her headphones and listen to some Maxi Priest. She zipped up her sweatshirt as far as the zipper would go and slumped down into the seat a little. As she looked in her purse for the headphones, she panicked just a little as she remembered that the airport security officers had taken away her pepper spray. But at least they let her keep the whistle, pocket knife, and baton keychain. *I will not be a victim*, she whispered. Suddenly she was startled by the shadow of a man leaning over her. The steward told her she had to put her big purse in the overhead bin. Sara didn't want to let her purse out of her sight, and when the steward saw that the prospect of being parted from her purse almost made her cry, he relented and let her stuff it under the seat in front of her.

She turned the music on, and started straightening the magazines in the seat pocket. Next to her sat a disappointed Colum, fumbling with his carry-on, trying to get comfortable in the midst of all of his belongings in the tight space. He was disappointed because he was hoping to use the time on the flight to talk with Sara. But now he could see that she wasn't interested in talking. So he turned around to give a look toward Chris and Willow, seated in the row behind him. He winked at his sister, who had just looked up from her fashion magazine. "We're gonna fly! Can you believe it?" Willow just squeezed Chris' hand.

Chris pushed up the sleeves of his sweatshirt and tried to hand his headphones to Willow. "Ok, listen to this one. This is the original version of the song I played on my guitar in the pub in Dublin. It's called *Take On Me*. You have to hear the original."

But Willow wasn't interested. "Sweetheart, I'd rather just remember it the way you played it. Besides, I don't really like your nineteen eighties music." Chris' frowned a little. Willow continued, "Don't you have any *new* music? I want to hear more music from *this* year."

Chris just sighed. "*Et tu*, Willow?"

"Oh, sweetheart." The lilt of her Irish accent always made Chris melt a little when she called him "sweetheart." "Don't worry about me, just enjoy yourself. This trip is going to be like our honeycomb."

"You mean honeymoon?"

"Right. What did I say? Anyway, we should take the opportunity to have some fun."

"Well, that works for me. I'm ready to live in the moment."

A little while later, Colum found himself walking down the aisle of the plane, trying to keep his balance as turbulence made the plane sway from side to side. Colum could see clouds out the windows, and he knew that he was very high up in the air. Suddenly he noticed that the emergency door was slightly open, and the wind was whistling through the crack. He looked around in panic, but no one else noticed that the door was open – or if they did notice, they didn't seem to care. Colum struggled to move himself over to the door, as the plane swayed more wildly. He tried to close the door, but it wouldn't close, and his efforts only made it open wider. Then Colum screamed as the wind took him right out of the plane, and he lost his grip on the door. He tried to scream again as he fell, but he couldn't catch his breath. His heart pounded as he plummeted toward the earth. He could see the green fields of Ireland below him – they were rushing up to meet him as he fell faster and faster and faster. And just before he hit the ground, he awoke with a start, and made a grunting sound that made everyone around him turn to look.

Colum was embarrassed, but Willow reached up and put her hand on his shoulder. "Another bad dream?" she asked. Colum just nodded. He had been excited to fly for the first time, but now he wasn't so sure. The only thing he was sure of, was that they were past the point of no return, and there was no getting off the plane. He could feel the force of gravity as the wheels left the ground and the plane tilted up into the sky. He reached for the airsickness bag, and got to it just in time.

†††

When Sofia had finished for the day, Armando came to the lab to pick her up. "Hey Jimmy," he said. "Have you seen the picture from the latest ultrasound?"

"Seriously? About a hundred times, bro."

"Oh, yeah. I forget who I've shown it to." As Sofia cleaned up her workbench, Armando changed the subject. "I don't get why you don't like Clinton."

"What, in addition to the blue dress?"

"He's not the enemy, Jimmy. The enemy is out there. Outside our borders. We need to stop worrying about what our president is doing behind closed doors and protect this great country from its enemies."

Jimmy smiled and shook his head. "Spoken like a good immigrant. Look, 'Mondo – in the big picture, you either trust the government, or you don't. I don't." Wordman gave Jimmy a dirty look, but Jimmy continued. "You know what the Jamaicans call it? Poli*tricks*."

Armando shrugged. "Well, I have to trust the government. That's where my orders come from. And I like being on the front lines protecting America from everything that's not American – especially now that I have a family."

"Look, don't get me wrong. I want to protect this country, too. I just think sometimes the enemy is closer to us than we think. You have to assume the worst, then you'll be ready for anything."

Armando nodded. "I can agree with you on that. Are you carrying?"

"Always."

"I gave Sofia a pistol. Just a little Bursa .380. She didn't want it, but I made her take it."

Jimmy looked over at Sofia. "Sof's packin' heat, eh?" he said with a smirk.

Sofia scrunched up her nose and stuck out her tongue at Jimmy. As Armando and Sofia left the lab, Sofia turned back to give Jimmy a look. She knew what he was going to do, and she had left the Resonator ready for him to make another trip into the past to try to save his parents. But this time Jimmy had to figure out how to stop a train wreck in Brazil. There was no way to locate his parents to warn them, no one even knew why they had been in Argentina or why they were traveling to Brazil. The job seemed infinitely harder than last time. But Jimmy was not about to give up. He had a plan, and it didn't even require that much precision in timing. He just had to get there before the accident. Jimmy waited as patiently as he could, while Wordman finished up a phone call and a cigarette.

"We have to strike while the iron is hot," Wordman repeated to whomever was on the other end of the line. "I'm counting on you… I need it before the hearing, because after that…" Wordman glanced at Jimmy. "Yes, I told you… Don't you mean *whom*? And stop saying 'youse' – you sound like a damn fool. As everyone knows, the proper second person plural is 'y'all'." Wordman's well-hidden southern accent came back for just a second. "Now get on it. Time is money. Now more than ever."

When he hung up the phone, he turned around and was startled to see Jimmy standing there. Even though he knew Jimmy was there a moment before, Wordman always seemed to startle easily. Jimmy promised to lock up, and Wordman finally left the lab. As soon as the door closed behind him, Jimmy made his move. All that day, while Sofia had worked and Wordman supervised, Jimmy had been researching the train accident in Brazil, and then searching for just the right 8-track tape. Eventually he found a vintage music shop on Bleecker Street that had some 8-tracks of classic world music. He bought a recording called *Africa Brasil*, by Jorge Ben, released in 1976. Then he had exchanged his old twenties for Brazilian currency, but he couldn't get his hands on any bills from before 1976. Nevertheless, he knew he had to risk it. Within a few minutes, Jimmy was looking up at Rio de Janeiro's massive statue of Christ.

"I need your help on this one, bro," he said to the huge Jesus.

One stolen motorcycle later, Jimmy was at the site of the train derailment. He looked at the tracks, but couldn't see anything wrong with them. The reports had said that the derailment was caused by a defect in the metal of one of the tracks, and the repeated stress of trains going around the curve had finally resulted in a broken rail. But at this point Jimmy couldn't see where the track would break, and he didn't know how to get anyone to fix it. So he did the only thing he could. He would break the track now, when no train was on it, and that would force the rail company to fix it before his parents ever got on board. He reached into his backpack and took out a block of explosives, and a remote detonator. After placing the C-4 on the tracks, and making sure there were no trains coming, he went off to a safe distance, and triggered the explosion. There was no question that the train company would know the tracks were damaged, since the once deserted stretch of rails quickly became alive with the sounds of yelling and people running to see what had happened. For Jimmy, their voices were drowned out by the sound of the motorcycle speeding away.

When Jimmy returned to the year two thousand, he couldn't wait to try to contact his parents. This time Colleen answered the phone. Jimmy decided not to waste any time beating around the bush. "Aunt Colleen, I know you said not to try to go back in time to save my parents, but I did. Are they alive?"

Colleen was silent for a moment. "No, Jimmy, they're not. They died on that train. I'm sorry." Jimmy didn't say anything. "Jimmy, are you alright? You're back safe and sound? I really wish you wouldn't play around with time travel. What if something goes wrong?"

"I'm fine, Aunt Colleen. I'm just... I don't know. I don't understand why I can't save them. I went all the way to Brazil, and I'm sure I must have stopped that train derailment from happening."

"Brazil? Why would you go to Brazil?" Colleen was confused. "Jimmy, your parents died in Spain. And it wasn't a derailment. It was a terrorist's bomb that caused the train to crash."

"I gotta go." Jimmy hung up the phone without waiting for goodbyes. He closed up the lab quickly and walked out to the street, not knowing exactly where he was going to go.

Normally, Jimmy loved Manhattan. *It's a city with energy*, he would say. Jimmy liked the excitement, but he also liked the ability to be where the action is and still be anonymous. It was as if, as a city, New York was an introvert – like an introvert at a party. It wants to be at the party, but it also just wants to be left alone to go about its own business and observe. *I'll mind my business, and you mind yours. That's why people look down when they walk. They don't want eye contact. New York favors people who don't have to ask for directions, not because New Yorkers are rude, but because they don't want to be vulnerable. To stop on the street and talk to a stranger is to be vulnerable to pickpockets, or whatever. If you stop and stay in one place too long, you're a target. New York is a city full of good people with nobody to be good to – it's a city full of turtles, or hermit crabs – full of people going through life hardening their shells.* On this day, Jimmy couldn't enjoy the energy of the city. He could only harden his shell.

As he walked along in no particular direction, Jimmy constantly checked his surroundings. He made sure no one was following him, and he made sure he wasn't walking into an ambush. At every moment he was hyper-aware, and the self-protective habits he had picked up over the last decade were in full force. Even though his appointment to the newly created Temporal Intelligence Agency (the TIA) was a well-kept secret, just being back in the States meant that his friends from the old days could find out he was around. And that could be… awkward.

Eventually, Jimmy ended up in Little Italy, on Mulberry Street. And after self-pityingly eating two cannoli, he wound up in front of Old St. Patrick's Cathedral, on the corner of Mulberry and Mott Street. Tentatively, he walked in, and sat down on one of the pews toward the back. After reassuring himself that no one else was around, he let down his guard a little, and closed his eyes to pray. But after a while, Jimmy sensed that someone was watching him. He looked around, but only a statue of Saint Teresa of Avila was looking down at him. Then Jimmy saw some movement out of the corner of his eye. Someone was there, but he couldn't see who it was. He quickly exited the pew and moved off to the side of the church where he could get a better view of anyone coming toward him. Someone was lurking in the shadows. Then that someone spoke.

"Pssst. Jimmy. Is that you?"

"Who is that?" Jimmy whispered.

Emerging into the dim light, the lurker said, "Jimmy, it's me. Joe."

"Crazy Joe! You big fanook, how the hell are ya?" Jimmy was happy to see a friend, but a bit unnerved that someone from the old days could find him here in New York. Jimmy and Joe hugged and slapped each other on the back.

"Not good, Jimmy. They know you're back. They sent a few of the boys here to try to track you down. If I could find you, they can find you." Joe backed up a step and looked Jimmy up and down. "Look at you, all grown up! Jimmy the Fist!"

"Yeah, I don't go by that name any more. Anyway how *did* you find me?" Jimmy thought he had been so careful.

"Ha. I just staked out that cannoli place you always used to talk about. I knew you couldn't come to New York without going there. And sure enough, I made you when you showed up there just now. Really Jim? Two cannolis?"

"You know the word 'cannoli' is already plural, right? Anyway, I had to get the chocolate covered one. But I couldn't *only* have the chocolate covered one. So… what about Dante? Does he know I'm back?"

"The Bastard? He wants you dead most of all. Thinks you betrayed him."

"Shit. Thanks, bro. I gotta get out of sight." Jimmy started moving toward the front door.

"Yeah you do." Joe agreed. "I wish we had time for a real reunion, but I can't be seen here either. But I had to tell you. I couldn't let 'em clip you."

"Yeah, I appreciate that." As Joe ran out the side door, Jimmy started to say, "Can we get together later?" but he was startled by two gunshots that echoed in the vestibule. Jimmy couldn't see who the shooter was, but by the time he ran to where he had last seen Crazy Joe, he was lying dead in a river of blood. Jimmy backed away putting his hand on his gun, and then, looking around, turned and ran for the front door, and out into the street.

Jimmy ran as fast as he could away from the church, and then around the block. When he thought he had put enough distance between himself and the shooter, he slowed to a walk, and turned another corner, hoping to look inconspicuous. As he walked, he thought about Crazy Joe. He thought about the old days on Rush Street. And he thought about Dante. Dante Corona was mob muscle, and a fixer, which meant he was a hit man. But when Jimmy first met him, he seemed like the coolest guy in Chicago. He was only 5'2", but tough as a railroad spike. Martial arts expert, and bodyguard to the boss, Dante had shown Jimmy the ropes. Taught him everything he knew, really, and Jimmy looked up to him, and wanted to be like him. Now Jimmy was sickened by the thought of ever wanting to be like *that douchebag Dante*, but he wondered just how much he had turned out like his old teacher after all. Then he started thinking about his family. *Coming back was a huge risk. I hope I'm not putting everyone in danger. I have to try to save my parents, but it's only a matter of time before the old crew catches up with me.*

As Jimmy walked, he kept checking over his shoulder, and soon it became clear that someone was following him. A guy in a pea coat and a black knit cap. Hands in his pockets, head down. Jimmy turned a corner, and so did the guy. *Definitely following.* Jimmy could watch his reflection in the store windows he walked past. The guy was closing the gap between himself and Jimmy. If Jimmy wanted to keep his distance, he would have to run, but that would give him away. Then Jimmy could see in the windows that the man was reaching up to his knit cap, and pulling it down over his face. It was a ski mask, and Jimmy knew what was coming next. As Jimmy came to the corner, a van pulled up right in front of him, blocking his way. The side door opened, and the man behind him dove at him to tackle him and throw him into the van. But Jimmy was ready, and at the last moment, he stepped to the side, and the man in the mask fell face first into the running board of the van. He cried out with a barrage of expletives and held his mouth as blood flowed through his fingers. There was a lot of yelling and confusion from the men inside the van, but Jimmy just kept on walking as they pulled their injured partner in, closed the door and sped off.

That was close, Jimmy thought. *But they'll be back. Time is running out.*

†††

"We're going to Mass," Sofia said.

"Is that you, Colleen?" Armando joked.

"I'm not asking. I need to go, and I need you to go with me. Anyway, I want to see the cathedral."

"No, not the cathedral. It's going to be crowded, which means they won't give us wine. They'll just give out the host because it's quicker. I like to get the wine."

"Sounds like you like to whine."

Armando sighed. "Okay. Whatever you want."

"Happy wife, happy life."

"Yeah, now you really sound like your mom."

"I know you're teasing, but you know what? I do want to be like my mom. I mean, I know she's only a housewife and all, but she was always a really great mom. And now I'm going to be a mom. I want to be a good mom, like her. And I want her to be proud of me."

"You will be a great mom. But also, we'll be a team. Together we outnumber this kid."

"Until the next one comes along." Sofia smiled.

After receiving communion Sofia went back to her seat, knelt down, and prayed. *God... I don't want this. I don't want to be in charge of a time machine. I don't want to send people through time. Or dogs. I feel like I've already screwed this up, and it can only get worse. Can't I get out of this? Can't you get me out of this? I just want to work on my new invention. The Resonator isn't even mine, really. I didn't invent it. I only put it together from someone else's plans. Jesus, I don't even know where those plans really came from. Whose plans are they? Whose plans have I been following? This is too much cosmic responsibility. Maybe I should just quit and hand the whole thing over to Wordman. I need to be a wife, and mother, I can't be messing with the space-time continuum. I don't want to be famous. I do want to make the world a better place for my baby, but I'm afraid that if I keep going like this, I'm going to make everything worse.*

†††

Chris and Sara had been subpoenaed to appear at the hearing, along with Sofia, Armando, and Jimmy. Willow and Colum came along to New York for moral support, and because Colum was trying to get to know Sara better. But the committee had no intention of interviewing Colum or Willow, because that would be an admission that the time machine was successful and time travel actually exists – and as it turned out that was something the committee was determined not to admit. So everyone gathered at the hotel and waited for the call that would summon the "witnesses" to the hearing.

Colum spent much of the time watching television – his new favorite pastime – but he had to keep a garbage pail close to him at all times because if the camera moved too fast or the editing was too quick, he would lose his lunch. In fact, everyone who had traveled through time was experiencing a heightened sense of motion sickness, headaches, and especially disturbing dreams. The O'Connells couldn't even ride in a car without the risk of car sickness and migraines. Sofia called it *Resonator Lag*. "It's like jet lag," she would say, "but multiplied by about a thousand. Because you didn't just travel across time zones, or over the international dateline. You traveled across over two hundred and fifty *years* of time zones and datelines."

As the group sat around in one of the hotel rooms, Jimmy brought up the subject of everyone's curiosity. "You said something about a new invention, one that could fix that... Resonator Lag, as you called it - can you fix it?"

"I think so," Sofia said thoughtfully. "I think so. I think the dreams are caused by latent anxiety left over from traveling faster than the speed of light. Our brains are not wired for that kind of travel – it's not natural – so our minds are having trouble dealing with it, even though we can understand it logically."

"Maybe *you* can understand it," Colum interrupted. "Could it *be* more confusing?"

Sara let out a laugh in spite of herself. She thought Colum was funny.

But Jimmy was impatient. "Alright, *Chandler*, let the lady talk."

Sofia continued, "I'm working on a new invention that will allow us all to process our dreams, and hopefully that will release the anxiety, and get rid of the problem. You see, most dreams are basically excremental."

"Excremental? You mean like... poop?" Chris was ready to ridicule whatever Sofia was trying to say, but Armando gave him a look that told him he'd better be quiet.

"Yes, *moron*. Like poop. Mental excrement. Waste from the mind. Most dreams are leftover anxieties, or unfinished thoughts from the day before, or fragmented feelings of regret – like things from the past we wish we could change, but we can't. You know like when someone says something nasty and you think of a perfect comeback, but only when it's too late to say it. Anyway, our minds need to work through that, and get rid of that waste. It's one way we deal with trauma or anxiety, and it keeps us sane. In fact, dreams can be a little like time travel. You can go to the past, be in the present, even dream of the future, all for the sake of sanity. But all of us who have *actually* traveled through time are suffering these side effects, and it's coming out in our dreams. It's a vicious cycle because the disturbing dreams are actually preventing us from getting enough sleep, which means our minds can't process our anxieties through normal dreaming. But we keep having these… velocity dreams, and they're waking us up and keeping us out of REM sleep. If it keeps up, we're all going to start getting really crabby."

Now Chris was concerned. "Wait, what do you mean by crabby? Do you mean *crabby* crabby, or do you mean, like, *crazy* crabby? Could we lose our minds?"

"No… No. I don't think so… Maybe, yes. But don't worry, I'm working on a solution to the problem. Kind of a cure, I guess, that will tame our dreams, and hopefully get rid of the headaches, too. It's a totally new invention – finally one I can really be proud of - I call it the Lucidator." The announcement was met with blank stares all around. "You know, like, as in *lucidity*." More blank stares. "When you're dreaming, but you *know* you're dreaming?" Sofia sighed. "The Lucidator will capture our dreams, and allow us to process them."

"Why don't you just call it the Dream Catcher?" Sara asked.

"Because that name is already taken," Sofia said impatiently.

"It sounds great," Armando said. "I'm sure it will work. No problem."

When the day of the hearing finally came, two black SUVs pulled up to the hotel to pick up Chris and Sara. Sofia and Armando were already in one of the cars, and since no spectators were allowed at the hearing, Colum and Willow had to stay back at the hotel. The hearing was held in a nondescript conference room on the second floor of a nondescript government building. When Sofia, Armando, Chris, and Sara were ushered in, the committee members were already seated at a long table in the front of the room. Donald Wordman sat in the center, and directed the proceedings. In the back of the room there were a few men in formal military uniforms, sporting what looked like an uncomfortable number of medals on their chests, along with a couple of men in tweed jackets with elbow patches.

Jimmy wasn't there yet, so they started without him. After taking Sofia's testimony about her research, Chris was asked to tell the story from his point of view.

"Just start at the beginning," Wordman prodded.

"Well…you know… no one likes to come home to chaos… When I came home that day, the house looked like a cross between a crime scene and a rummage sale."

A senator from Wisconsin interrupted, "And what year was this, for the record?"

"It was 1999. I was twenty-one."

Just then Jimmy interrupted the proceedings by walking in late, accompanied by two unknown men in dark suits, with dark shirts, and dark ties. All three of them had security badges on. Wordman looked annoyed, but chose not to say anything to Jimmy and his fellow TIA agents. The committee members waited politely for the three men to sit down. In the break caused by their arrival, one committee member leaned over to another and whispered, "You'd think, of all people, *they* could be on time." Then he just snorted in that half laugh-half exhale that acknowledged an irony without making too much noise.

After an uncomfortable silence, Wordman encouraged, "Please go on…"

Once everyone had told their versions of the story, the committee members conferred with each other, and then with the TIA agents. Eventually, they broke their huddle, and Wordman banged his gavel to get everyone's attention. He cleared his throat. "Having heard the testimony of the parties involved… I hereby declare that these proceedings are concluded. We have not recommended that any criminal charges be brought, as it is unclear what relationship the actions of certain individuals have to the law as it stands now. No doubt this incident will inspire new laws limiting the experimentation with new technologies. Furthermore, this committee will not comment on the truth or accuracy of the statements given, nor will it admit to, or acknowledge, the actual existence of time travel. However, in the interest of national – and global – security, we have determined that the device known as the Resonator is to be dismantled, and destroyed."

Jimmy stood up, and raised his hand. Wordman acknowledged him with a gesture. "The chair recognizes the representative of the newly formed Temporal Intelligence Agency, Special Agent James AG-nello."

"It's *Ahn-yello*," Jimmy corrected. Wordman nodded like he didn't care, so Jimmy continued. "The TIA agrees that the device is to be dismantled, however, according to the articles of the charter of the Temporal Intelligence Agency, it is within our jurisdiction to take possession of the device, and all of its accompanying equipment, and take responsibility for dismantling it."

"Agreed," Wordman admitted. "But you *will* destroy it, correct?"

"We will," Jimmy confirmed. "But first… we just need to use it one more time."

†††

Chris stood on a street corner on the edge of Times Square, looking up at the twin towers of the World Trade Center. New York in January was bitter cold, but there was no snow on the ground. The sky was grey yet somehow it was still bright out. Chris scanned the skyline with all of its man-made marvels – concrete, steel, and glass - as he thought about the fact that just six months earlier he was running for his life in the year 1743. It seemed impossible. But here he was in the middle of all this traffic and noise, horns and sirens. Chris smiled. He was feeling grateful for being able to get back to his own time, and especially for being able to bring Willow back with him. He swore to himself he would never get back into a time machine ever again.

Suddenly Chris became very aware of the fact that he was standing still, as New Yorkers rushed past him in all directions, bumping into him as though it was his fault for taking up space and slowing them down. They didn't say they were sorry. They didn't say anything. They just kept on walking, never knowing that this regular guy from the Chicago suburbs had been to the 1700s and back. *New York thinks it's the center of the world,* he thought. *But it's more like it's on the edge of the world. This city is like a fancy restaurant. It's all sparkle and shine, until you go into the kitchen and look close. After you're here for a while, you start to see the industrial side. The grease and the dirt, the exhaust and the garbage, the rats and the roaches, and the dog pee running in little rivers from the sidewalks into the gutters. Hmm. It's a great place to come and eat, but it's better if you stay out of the kitchen.* Chris watched his breath condense in the air, and he thought it looked like a spirit leaving his body. He felt the cold in his lungs and the crystals forming in his nose. And then he heard an unfamiliar sound. At first he didn't recognize it, but then he realized it was the sound of his brand new cellular phone ringing inside his coat pocket. He pulled out the phone, and struggled to unfold it and push the right button before the caller could hang up. "Hello?"

"Christopher!" It was Jimmy. Chris could barely hear him over the traffic noise, and to make it even worse, a train whistle blew at just that moment. Chris pressed the phone to his ear.

"Oh, hey Jimmy! This is great, you're the first call on my new cell phone."

"Chris, you have to come right away. The time machine was stolen!"

CHAPTER 2
MANY RIVERS TO CROSS

"There's a blizzard coming!" Colleen was calling out to Gus from the front door as he, Patrick, and Fergus climbed into the Suburban. "It's all over the news." Nero thought about running out the door, but after hearing the howling of the wind, he decided against it.

"S'blood!" Patrick rubbed his head where he bumped it on the car's door frame.

Fergus stifled a laugh. "Jaysus, Dad, when are you gonna remember that you're tall?"

"I know," Gus yelled back to Colleen. "We're gonna make it a short day. Be back before it gets dark." But as they pulled out of the driveway, Gus could see that the sky was already getting dark, even though it was still morning. *But I'll be damned if I'm gonna let the weather stop me from getting work done*, he thought.

When they arrived at the construction site, the three men hurried into the shell of a building to get out of the wind. It was cold in the building, and they rubbed their hands as they walked among the wall studs and stepped over piles of wire and pipe. They took the construction elevator up to the fifth floor, and stepped out onto a wall-less and windy open space overlooking the Chicago skyline. Gus liked to walk out close to the edge and look out over the city.

"Well if it isn't Saint Augustine." Gus turned around to see three men coming up from behind him. One was wearing a cashmere overcoat and gloves, but the other two wore light jackets, much too flimsy for the winter weather. Of the two with light jackets, the taller one tried not to look like he was shivering. The shorter one wasn't shivering at all. His anger was keeping him warm. Gus recognized the one in the cashmere overcoat right away. He was the last person Gus ever wanted to see again in his life. And now this man and his companions blocked the way to the elevator.

"Do I know you?" Gus pretended not to remember the man in the overcoat. Patrick and Fergus turned to face the men, and Fergus took a step forward, as if to protect Gus.

Fergus spoke with authority. "You're not supposed to be here. This is a closed construction site. Hardhats required."

"You don't remember me?" the man in the overcoat made a sad face. The three trespassers walked toward Gus, Patrick, and Fergus, backing them up toward the open edge of the fifth floor. "That hurts my feelings, Gus. 'Cause I remember you. Yeah I remember *all* about you." Then he looked Fergus straight in the eyes and squinted at him. "Oh, where are my manners? Forgive me. My name is Al. Al Tallone."

"Al the Frog," Gus said under his breath.

Al continued, "And these are my associates, this is Vince, and this is Dante – we call him The Badger."

Gus glared at them. "You mean The Bastard. I've heard of you. What do you guys want? Why are you here, after all this time?"

Al forced a laugh. "Right down to business, eh?" He looked at Patrick and Fergus. "You fellas might not know this, because you weren't around back in the old days, but I used to be a business associate of old Gus here."

Patrick and Fergus looked at each other. Gus interrupted. "And that's why I don't do city contracts any more. I'm strictly private commercial and residential. So I got nothing I can help you with."

Dante spoke through gritted teeth. "Not so fast. We ain't lookin' for your help. You got something we want. And if we don't get it, we can make your strictly private whatever whatever… very… not so private."

Al put up a hand to silence Dante. "But if we do get what we want, we can make it worth your while. Maybe even another sweet deal, like in the old days."

"Not interested." Gus said, shoving his hands into his coat pockets.

"You misunderstand," Al said, with emphatic sarcasm. Then his voice got suddenly serious. "We're not asking. There's a computer at your house. Left there by your daughter. Sofia." He enunciated Gus' daughter's name slowly as Gus clenched his fists in his coat pockets. Al waited to see if Gus would say anything, but he didn't, so Al went on. "We just need that computer." Al and his associates all took a few steps forward, until Gus, Patrick, and Fergus felt compelled to take a few steps back, toward the edge of the building.

"Ya know," Vince spoke up. "If a person should fall down dere from dis height, a person might die. But then again, a person might not.

A person might just break his neck, or his back, and end up in a wheelchair for the rest of his life – maybe even be a vegetable." Vince looked right at Gus, "Drooling on yourself, so your wife has to wipe your ass when you shit your pants."

†††

Chris threw open the door to the lab and ran in, expecting to see an empty loft. But the wooden crate was there, right where it had been before, and everyone else was standing around it. "I thought you said the time machine was stolen," Chris said with a tone of annoyance in his voice. But as he moved closer, he could see that the crate was wet and dirty, and covered with dents and scratches.

"It was," Sofia said. "But now it's back. It wasn't taken out of this room. Someone *used* it. And you can tell by looking at it – it's been through a lot."

"Who used it?" Chris looked at Jimmy.

"Wasn't me," Jimmy said. "I mean… okay, I did use it. But this is not from me. Someone else used it – someone who's not in this room – someone who has no business using it."

"And we think we know who it was." Armando was just coming in, and Chris realized that he hadn't noticed Armando wasn't there until now. Armando was still wearing the security badge from an intelligence briefing. He took off his red tinted sunglasses, and paused before speaking.

"Well, Agent Fernandez, what did they tell you?" Jimmy figured that at this point it didn't matter if the others knew about Armando's new role as the liaison between military intelligence and the TIA.

Armando took a deep breath. "You were right, Jim. It was Wordman." He looked to Sofia to see her reaction, but she didn't seem surprised. "Of course we can't be sure, but everything points to him. He's nowhere to be found. Dammit, I should have kept an eye on him. I should have guarded the machine better."

"It's not your fault, honey," Sofia reassured him. "I should have known we couldn't trust him. But I don't get it – why would he use the time machine?"

Sara jumped into the conversation. "And why is he missing? If the time machine came back, didn't he come back with it?"

"Well, that's what the TIA has to figure out," Armando said, looking at Jimmy. "They want *you* to go after him." Jimmy nodded, and Armando continued. "But I learned something about our friend Donald Wordman that may tell us what he's trying to do."

"What's that?" several of them asked at once.

"Well you know that Wordman is trying to get the Democratic Party's nomination for president, right? Seems there's this reporter who started digging into his past to find some dirt on him. And she found out that back when he was in college in Georgia, he was driving drunk. He ran a red light, and he hit and killed a woman walking in a crosswalk. A cop's wife, in fact. And she was pregnant. Wordman was arrested, but never charged. Oh, and the reporter I mentioned… she recently turned up dead."

"Holy shit," Chris said. "If he's willing to kill a reporter, he's sure as hell willing to steal the time machine."

Armando continued. "Right. We think he used the time machine to try to go back to his own past and prevent himself from hitting that woman, so it can't come back to haunt him when he's running for president."

Willow spoke up. "So where is he now?"

"I think we can answer that," Sofia said, looking at Jimmy. "I had just gotten the auto-pause working, and I told him that. For some reason, I think he was waiting for that before taking the machine. As you know, you don't need the auto-pause if you're going back in the time machine, but I think he was afraid he would get out and forget to push the pause button, or get sick and not be able to push it, so he wanted to use the auto-pause to make sure he didn't get out and have the machine come back and leave him there. But what he didn't understand is that the auto-pause function also has a built-in failsafe. If you send the machine back without anyone in it, you have to have a way for it to come back by itself if something goes wrong. So I installed a trigger. Kind of like the tilt sensor in a pinball machine. If someone were to try to move or damage the time machine, it will trigger the failsafe and send it back to where it started from. Judging by the dents and scratches, something happened to the Resonator after he got out of it, and that automatically sent the machine back here. Wordman must still be in the past."

"Right," Armando confirmed. "That's the working theory. And Jimmy, you have to use the time machine to go back and get him. Now the drunken hit and run happened in 1974, at the University of Georgia, in Athens. Wordman was 20 years old, and his father was a state senator. We figure it was his father who was able to cover it up at the time."

"Yeah, but he's not in Georgia," Jimmy said, sticking his head into the crate. "Check it out. Geez, smells like wet plywood in here. Look, there are bits of palm leaves inside the crate, along with a bunch of garbage, including this pop bottle. See the brand? Ting. There's only one place I know of where you can get Ting. Jamaica."

"So, wait," Chris said, trying to process all the information. "If he's trying to undo an accident in Georgia, why did he go to Jamaica?"

Sofia smiled. "If you were trying to go to the 1980s, why did you go to the 1740s?"

"Well, I wasn't *trying* to go to the…" Chris began with heavy sarcasm in his voice, but then he got it. "Oh."

"Yeah," Jimmy continued. "The tape in the 8-track is Eric Clapton's album *461 Ocean Boulevard*. It was recorded in Miami in 1974. Clearly it's a used tape, so Wordman must have gotten it second hand. He probably figured he would arrive in Miami, leave the machine on pause, and take a bus up to Georgia to fix his mistake – maybe warn his younger self. Problem is, when he pressed play, the tape was wound to track five, which is the song… wait for it… *I Shot the Sheriff*. Yep, Clapton's cover of the Bob Marley song."

"What do you mean by 'cover'?" asked Colum.

"Oh," Jimmy answered, "a cover song is when you record a song written by someone else at an earlier time."

"I see," Colum nodded. "Like when that old guy and his rock band made a recording of the Devo song *Satisfaction*."

Jimmy rubbed his eyes with his palms. "Um, 'that old guy and his rock band' are the Rolling Stones, and that was *their* song. But yes, Devo covered the Rolling Stones song *Satisfaction*. That's a cover song."

"The point is," Sofia added, "that we've never really understood how the Resonator locks in on the vibrations of a song, so we don't know why it would pick the original recording over the cover version on the tape, and not, for example, an earlier demo tape or rehearsal session. The problem is that we just can't count on it being predictable, let alone accurate."

Jimmy said, "But what we do know is that Wordman ended up in Jamaica. *I Shot the Sheriff* was on Bob Marley and the Whalers' album *Burnin'* which was recorded in Kingston in 1973. He must have been sleeping in the crate, trying to figure out how to get to Georgia, until something happened to it and it came back here without him."

Willow asked, "How do we know for certain he didn't come back with the time machine?"

"Because if he did," Sofia said, "he would have at least tried to clean it up so we wouldn't know he took it."

"Oh, of course." Willow looked at Sofia with admiration. She secretly hoped Sofia would guide her as she tried to navigate the twenty-first century.

"Wordman must still be in 1973, trying to make his way to Georgia," Jimmy concluded.

"And you have to go stop him," added Armando. "You have to find him, and bring him back in handcuffs."

"Not me alone," Jimmy said. "I'm going to need some help."

"Count me out," Chris said quickly. "I'm never getting in that time machine again."

Jimmy took a moment to respond. "Actually... I wasn't thinking of you. I was thinking I need someone who will... how do I say this? Someone who can come with me to Jamaica and... blend in." Jimmy looked at Sara.

At first Sara was shocked, and a little afraid. But then the thought of going back to the house in Chicago flashed through her mind. She smiled and said in a near-perfect Jamaican accent, "Yah, mon. Me a go dat ends wit ya. When I an I go deh?"

†††

Patrick was in pain. As he lay in the bed, he couldn't open his eyes, but he could feel that every part of his body hurt. He tried to turn onto his side, but it was difficult to move, like something was holding him down. Finally, he gathered up his strength and turned his body over hard. But the bed was even harder. Patrick tried to force his eyes open, but everything was blurry. He felt around and he realized that his bed was made of rough, cold concrete. He turned his head and it slammed into a concrete pillow. *Why is this bed made of cement?* he thought, and then he awoke, and sat up to find himself in a normal bed. The same bed he'd been sleeping in for the last six months at the Agnello house. He laid back down and as he settled into the soft, warm sheets he felt grateful.

Downstairs, Gus was in his office looking at the Apple computer Sofia had left behind. *This is what they want.* He stared at the computer, listening to the crack and snap of a fire blazing in the fireplace. It made the room extra warm, just the way Gus liked it. As he took a stack of ledgers out of his safe, he saw his old pistol: a Colt 1911, .45 caliber that was issued to him by the United States government shortly after he graduated from high school. *Hmpf. 1965. The Pope came to the US, and I went to Nam.* Gus took the gun out of the safe, and checked it over, making sure the magazine was full.

"Jesus, Mary, and Joseph, it's warm in here." Colleen stopped in her tracks and changed her mind about coming in. She continued talking to Gus from the doorway. "All you need to do is get your books out of the safe, and put them in order, from oldest to newest. I'll do the rest – I'll get started when I get back from the shelter. Oh wait. After the shelter I'm going to the gym. I'll do it when I get back. I'll put everything in the computer, and then we just use the computer from now on. And you didn't even have to spend any money buying a computer. See how that worked out?"

Gus nodded absent-mindedly as Colleen walked away. *Being married to a smart woman isn't easy… but it is worth it.* He stacked the ledgers on the desk, but the oldest one he set aside. He picked it up and held it in his hand for a moment, feeling the weight of it. Then he threw it into the fire.

Fergus awoke with a shout, which made everyone in the house look up toward the bedrooms, and then shrug their shoulders. The dreams were common enough now that no one talked about them much anymore. As Fergus came down the stairs, Colleen gave him a compassionate look. "Another dream?" she asked.

"We were on the boat, on Lake Micheline," he began.

"Michigan," Colleen corrected. "Lake Michigan."

"Right. What did I say?" Fergus continued, "We were on the boat, going fast. And then we were going faster, and faster. And the wind was blowing at us, and it was burnin' our faces. And then people's heads started coming off."

Colleen chuckled, but quickly covered her mouth. "Oh," she said through her hand, "that *would* be disturbing." Then she walked to the closet to get her coat, turning away from Fergus to avoid laughing.

Patrick came into Gus' office and closed the door behind him. "Is that it? Is that the computation machine?" he asked.

"Computer, yeah." Gus acknowledged.

"You're not going to give it to those thugs, are you?"

"I don't know. I mean, I could just buy another one. But so could they – so obviously it must have something on it that they want. And that something is probably information that could put Sofia in danger."

"What are you goin' to do?" Patrick asked.

"I'll tell you what I'm gonna do." Gus said with new determination. "I am going to buy a new one – but I'll give them the new one. That will buy us some time. Then if they ask about the information, I'll say it must have been erased."

Later that day, Colleen was entering Gus' old financial information into the computer and singing random pieces of classic rock songs to herself. In the middle of a Moody Blues medley, she stopped abruptly and called out to Gus. "We're going to the early Mass tomorrow because I promised to help out at the shelter again after that!"

"But it's my only day to sleep late," Gus called back. "Can't we skip Mass tomorrow? We go every week, we can take a break."

"Take a break? You need to pray more, not less. You know what I say, prayer uncoils the spring."

"I pray every day," Gus responded. "Most of my prayers are short petitions asking God to damn things."

"Very funny. I'm sure God is laughing his beard off."

"You know I don't take sides," Monica chimed in, "but Colleen is right." Monica had finally stopped wearing all black when Chris and the others returned from the eighteenth century, but she still wore her hair in a bun, and she was still on a mission to save the family. "*Ma, che sei grullo?*"

"Geez, Ma." Gus decided to try another approach. "Anyway, Col, I can't match you no matter what I do – you're so holy it's ridiculous."

Colleen crossed herself and muttered under her breath, *If you only knew, my love. I'm not better than you. Truth is, it's probably too late for me. But it's not too late for you.*

The next morning, Gus was up for the early Mass. Colleen noticed him putting on his cufflinks and asked, "Why do you still wear those things? I can hardly find new shirts for you that take cufflinks."

"I wear them because my father wore them." Gus looked at the letter A engraved in the gold of one of the cufflinks.

After receiving communion, Gus knelt and spoke to his father, Rocco. *Hey Pop. If you're up there, watching over me… I need some help. Some… protection. The old crew is crawling up my… well, you know. I tried to put that behind me, I really tried. I thought I was out, but they're trying to pull me back in. And now that they're back, I don't know how to make them go away. So if you could put in a good word for me…*

After the service, Monica and Colleen made their way to the shelter to prepare lunch for the homeless, and Gus walked out of the church alone. He was met in the courtyard by Dante Corona. Gus looked Dante up and down. He didn't say anything, but just stared at Dante with contempt.

Dante broke the silence. "Nice garden."

"Mm hmm." Gus was impatient.

"Gus, do you know what periwinkle is?"

"Can't say that I do," Gus answered. "I'm not much of a green thumb."

Dante looked down at the plants. His voice was deceptively calm. "You know… da thing about a garden is, sometimes one particular plant, like periwinkle for instance, it just keeps on growing until it gets too big for said garden. In fact, it seems like it wants to have its own garden. But it doesn't own dat garden. Somebody else planted it in dat garden. Somebody else gave dat plant its start… in dat garden. And everything it has in dat garden, it owes to da one who planted it dere. And it doesn't matter how much da gardener likes dat plant, when it gets to dat point, dere's only one thing to do. The plant dat gets too big for da garden, it has to be pulled up."

"Is there a point to this gardening lesson?"

"I am afraid, Mr. Augustine Agnello, dat *you* are the periwinkle." Dante pointed at Gus with his index finger and pinky, making the *cornuto* horns with his hand.

"I'll give you the computer," Gus said.

"A wise move," replied Dante. "But now dat is no longer enough, my friend. I need you to look around your house, maybe in your garage, or your basement, and see if you can find something that looks like dis." Dante showed Gus a photo of Sofia's receiver. "And of course when you find it, I will need you to give it to me."

"What is it?" Gus was trying to stall for time.

"Fuck if I know, just find it!" Dante threw the photo at Gus and walked away, muttering to himself.

†††

"No. No. No. No. NO!" Sofia's face was getting red. "You cannot take her!"

"Well, it's her decision," Jimmy said.

Sara jumped in, "I'm right here. You don't have to talk about me in the third person."

"But you don't get it," Sofia pleaded. "It's too dangerous. The machine is unreliable."

Armando put his hand on Sofia's shoulder. "Honey," he said, "I trust what you say. But I also have more faith in you than you have in yourself most of the time. We have to catch Wordman, so *somebody* has to use the time machine to go back and get him. It has to work."

Sofia took his hand and held it in hers. "But we almost lost Chris." She looked away from Chris, avoiding making eye contact. "I can't put Sara in that kind of danger."

"Again with the third person!" Sara complained. "Look, it's like Jimmy said. It's my decision. And I'm willing to do it."

"Ugh," Sofia sighed and put her face into her hands. "I never wanted to invent a stupid time machine, and I never wanted to work for the stupid government. I just wanted to make something that would help people. To make the world a better place. I don't want to be famous. I just want to be... harmless."

Chris said, "I hate to say it, but she's right. It's too risky to go back in time. If you could go into the future, that might be a risk worth taking, but the past is... well, it's too dangerous. And if something goes wrong, you could end up going so far back in time that there are no songs you can play to get back. You could be stuck in the past forever."

"Or worse," Sofia said softly.

"Wait, what would be worse?" Sara asked.

"Well," Sofia began thoughtfully. "If something goes wrong and the Resonator dematerializes in the present, but can't lock onto a signal in the past, you could spin off into the void."

"What does that mean, 'spin off into the void'?" Jimmy asked. "And why is this the first we're hearing about it?"

"Well, I mean, it's purely theoretical," Sofia said. "It's not like we know for sure. But imagine… Imagine a circle. Like a clock, but not with a minute hand and an hour hand. A clock with a season hand and a year hand. And the hands on the clock, they trace a line from the center of the circle to the outside, right?"

"Ok, slow down." Armando said. "So there's this clock, with a season hand and a year hand."

"Right." Sofia continued. "Time on a grand scale. Now, imagine that you are *on* one of the hands of this clock. The closer you are to the center, the shorter the trip around the circle, right? That's what time travel is, moving toward the center of the circle to shorten the path of travel around the circle. And in the case of the Resonator, the hands move backward, so you're traveling back in time. Now you can't go all the way in to the center, because that's the infinity point. If you were at the center, you would be traveling infinitely fast, and you would effectively be in all times at once. You would be eternal. You would be

God. Or, to put it another way, only God exists at the center point. Like if you could somehow play a recording of the sound of Creation, you would travel back in time so far that you would hit the edge of omnipresence. So theoretically, the closer you get to the center, the closer you get to God. Which means that the farther away from the center you go along the hands of the clock, the farther you move away from God."

"What?" Several of the others expressed confusion and annoyance.

Sofia went on, "If you think that's confusing, we haven't even gotten to the paradox yet. So here it is. As you approach some multiple of the speed of light – and I don't know what that multiple is, it could be warp two, or warp ten, or warp ten thousand, I don't know – the force of it would be enough to break the hold of all gravity, including the gravity that holds matter together. It would be like spinning so fast on a merry-go-round that the centrifugal force throws you off. But in this case, you would be thrown off of the circle completely. You would be thrown out of the universe and into the void – as far away from God as you can get – you would be in hell."

"The outer darkness," Willow whispered, remembering her gospel lessons.

"Right, Willow," said Sofia. "You would find yourself banished from the presence of the omnipresent God."

"I *knew* it!" Chris shouted. "Before any of this happened, I thought, I wonder if time travel is a sin. I wonder if time travel is like trying to play God."

"Relax, Kierkegaard," Jimmy said sarcastically. "Science is not a sin."

"Not all science," Chris said. "But this is like the Icarus of science. Flying too close to the sun – kind of literally."

"Kind of literally?" Sofia chided. "Nice oxymoron, *moron*."

"You're missing the point," Chris protested. "That could have happened to me. And it could happen to Sara, or Jimmy. Fuck Wordman. Leave him in the 70s, and let him rot there. No one should ever get into that thing again."

Willow folded her arms and leaned back in her chair. "And I suppose ya wish *you'd* never gone back in time?"

"No, of course not," Chris said quickly. "I'm glad I found you, and I'm glad we could bring you back here. But I had no idea this could have happened to us."

"We have to dismantle it," Sofia said in a monotone. "Destroy it. Make sure no one ever uses it again. There are just too many variables. Even if nothing goes wrong with the time travel itself, you could never know that you wouldn't change something in the past that will change history – or ruin the present."

"Now wait a minute," Jimmy said. He was thinking of his parents, and how his attempts to save them had been unsuccessful. And in his mind he was defending his intentions to keep deliberately trying to change the past. "We still have some work to do." Everyone looked at Jimmy, waiting for him to admit what they all already knew. "Okay, yes, I need to use the time machine to save my parents. So sue me."

"Hold on there," Colum said. "If you go back and arrest this Wordman fellow before he can prevent himself from killing that woman, then aren't you letting her die? Aren't you participating in her death?"

"That's two deaths," Armando said. "Remember, she was pregnant."

Colum paused, waiting for Jimmy to answer, but he didn't say anything, so Colum went on. "So why do you get to save your parents, but nobody saves the woman Wordman killed? And you know what I'm going to say next, don't you? What about our mother? Why aren't we going back to our time to save her?"

At this point the room erupted into everyone talking over each other, with escalating volumes as everyone tried to be heard over the other voices. "Why do you get to save your parents, but what Wordman is doing is wrong?"

Chris yelled the loudest, and eventually everyone else stopped talking and looked at him. "ARE YOU PEOPLE NUTS? No one should go anywhere in that time machine. Don't you remember that I almost got stuck in the past?"

"Yes, Christopher, we remember," Jimmy said. "We don't have Alzheimer's."

Everyone looked at Jimmy, confused.

"What?" Chris barked. "What's *alls-heimers*?"

"You know, Alzheimer's," Jimmy said impatiently. "The thing some old people get, when they lose their memory. Like dementia. Anyway, that's not the point."

"Oh yeah, I remember reading about that," Sara said. "Nobody's heard of it because they cured that, like, twenty years ago. A couple of doctors from Brazil…"

"Wait!" Jimmy interrupted. He looked at the group. "You mean you have never heard of Alzheimer's disease?" He looked back to Sara. "And you're saying it was cured by *Brazilian* doctors?"

"Yeah." Sara looked confused. "So? Haven't we gotten off on a tangent here?"

"The train." Jimmy said, looking at the floor. "The train in Brazil. I prevented the accident. Those doctors must have been on that train – and they didn't die in that accident with my parents, and they cured a disease. You see – this is exactly my point!"

"Whoa, Jimmy." Armando said. "You might have saved a couple of doctors, but you also might have saved a couple of serial killers. You don't know."

"Playing God!" Chris shouted. "Even if you could kill baby Hitler, you can't do it without changing other things in the past. My fingerprints are all over the seventeen hundreds, in Dublin, London, Bristol…"

Sara gasped. "You were in Bristol?"

"Yeah," Chris answered. "Uh, we had to take a boat from Dublin to Bristol, and then get a carriage to get to London. Didn't I tell you that part?"

"Um, noooo," Sara said, with a suddenly acquired attitude in her voice. "So did you happen to notice that Bristol was a major hub for the slave trade?" She felt her muscles tighten all over her body.

Chris became careful with his words. "No, I didn't see anything. But we were kind of running for our lives, you know. We just got off the boat and got out of town." Chris turned to Colum and Willow. "Did you guys notice anything?"

"Could you *be* more oblivious?" Colum smirked as he said it. "Yeah, there were slaves. Chained up and everything. I can't believe you didn't notice."

Chris looked at Sara. "Hey I'm not racist. I was just a little preoccupied."

Sara put her hands on her hips. "Mm hmm. You're not racist. Maybe you're not actively racist, but you're passively racist – because you have the luxury of being blind to it, and still benefitting from it."

"Wait a minute," Chris protested. "That was over two hundred and fifty years ago, and like I said, I was running for my life." Willow took Chris' hand as an act of solidarity. She knew Sara had a point, but she was also a little bit happy that Sara was mad at Chris. It reassured her that Sara wasn't interested in her husband.

Sofia spoke up to break the tension. "All right you two. We can all agree that Chris is an idiot."

"Hey!" Chris protested.

"But I think he's less of an idiot since he got back from the past. So maybe we can give him some credit for improvement."

Armando spoke up. "I think we need to try to do all the good we can. I don't think the time machine should be destroyed. I think Sofie's created something that can be used to save lives, so we need to try to save all the lives we can."

Jimmy responded, "Well, as far as the TIA is concerned, the Resonator is a weapon of mass destruction – or it could be, if it fell into the wrong hands. And Wordman is the perfect example of the wrong hands. If he manipulates the past, he could do something, or blackmail someone, to ensure that he gets elected president, and that would start us down a path to disaster. Do you know that if he's elected he plans to militarize the IRS? Yeah, he wants to give all IRS employees uniforms *and guns*, and give them the power to rat on anyone who doesn't step up to pay for all his expensive promises. He says Europe is doing great with fifty percent income tax, and we should do the same. And if anyone doesn't like it, the IRS would be like the Inquisition – guilty until proven innocent."

"This is all my fault," Sofia put her face in her hands. "I should never have built that damn thing."

"But that's not the worst of it," Jimmy continued. "Wordman is drafting a secret bill that would make it a crime to travel to the present from another time. He calls it the *Temporal Immigrant Isolation Act*. That means anyone who came here from the past…" Jimmy pointed to Colum and Willow, "would be arrested, and spend the rest of their lives in prison."

Colum balled up his fists, and Willow tried hard not to cry.

Chris held Willow tight and said, "Look, let's get someone else to do this. Can't the TIA assign some other agents to go back into the past and pick up Wordman? Why should Jimmy and Sara be the red shirts?"

Jimmy answered, "Thanks Chris, but I like to think of myself more as the Captain Kirk of the group. Anyway, the TIA assigned me, it's my job. And no one is making Sara go." Jimmy gestured toward Sara, which made her shift in her chair.

Everyone looked at Sara. "Well, now I'm having second thoughts. I mean, I don't want to start having the dreams or the headaches. And I don't want to get thrown out into the void, or whatever."

"Either way, I have to do this," Jimmy said. "And if I don't, the TIA will destroy the Resonator anyway. Look, the committee agreed to delay the destruction of the machine so that we could drop off the receiver to twenty-nine year old me, otherwise I wouldn't be there to help build the Resonator in the first place. But I never told Wordman that I've already done that. I did it before he ever took over the project, so when he started asking about the receiver, I told him we left it back in Chicago. Anyway, we can use that excuse to stall for a little more time, but then we have to make a move. We have to stop Wordman, and I have to save my parents."

†††

Gus looked everywhere, but he couldn't find the receiver. He had no intention of handing it over to Tallone and his crew, but at least he could honestly say he had no idea where it was. As he was finishing up looking in the garage, Patrick came from the kitchen, and closed the door behind him.

Without even saying hello to Gus, Patrick got right to the point, "We need to get more locks on the doors. Let's go to the hardon store and get some."

"You mean the hard*ware* store," Gus said, still looking into a box.

"Right," Patrick replied. "What did I say?"

"You said hardon," Gus chuckled. "Which is what that mean little bastard has for that equipment. I got a new blank computer to give him next time he shows up, but I couldn't give him the other thing if I wanted to. It's not here."

"We also need some guns," Patrick added. "Where can we get some guns?"

"We don't need more guns."

"*More* means you have some?"

"I have one. It's enough. Anyway, if we get into a gun battle with these animals, then we've already lost. But you're right about the locks. We can go to the hardware store, and then stop by the deli for a meatball sandwich."

"Ugh," Patrick couldn't hide it any longer. "Does it have to be Italian food? Always with the Italian food."

"You don't like Italian food?" Gus looked up at Patrick for the first time since he came into the garage.

Patrick's voice softened. "It's just that we eat it *all* the time. Anyway, forget I said it. I'm very grateful…"

"No," Gus interrupted. "We can get something else. We can go to the Irish pub. Get some Irish stew."

Patrick paused and wrinkled his nose. "What I'd really like is Mexican."

As Gus, Patrick, and Fergus pulled out of the driveway, they didn't see the black Lincoln parked down the street. They also didn't see it follow them to the hardware store. It was in the aisle with the locks that Al, Vince, and Dante confronted Gus, Patrick, and Fergus.

Al Tallone walked up behind Gus. "Thinking of increasing security around your place? Probably a good idea. You never know when there are bad people around."

Patrick took a step toward Al and pointed his finger in his face. "Listen here you guinea dago…"

At this, Al, Vince, Dante, and Gus all took a step back, put up their hands, and said, "Oh!"

Patrick looked surprised, and Gus said, "You know your son-in-law is a guinea dago."

"Sorry," Patrick looked down at the floor. Then he looked up at Al. "You leave this family alone, or I'll be the bad people you need to worry about."

Al dismissed Patrick and turned to Gus. "You better keep your Irish setter here on a leash. If he gets off the leash, he could get run over."

Gus tried to calm the situation. "The computer is in my trunk. You can have it now." He looked at Dante. "But I couldn't find that other thing. Whatever it is, it's not in my house."

Dante took a step toward Gus. Even though he was much shorter than Gus, his attitude and bulky upper body projected unpredictable danger. "I don't believe you."

Al put up his hand to stop Dante. "Let's wait and see what's on the computer. If we're happy, maybe we believe you. If we're not, maybe we don't."

As the men walked to the parking lot, Al tried to talk to Gus like he was a friend. "I could do you a favor, you know. I could get the boss to send some work your way. Could be very lucrative for you."

"And what's in it for you?" Gus asked with skepticism in his voice.

"Not much," Al shrugged. "Coupla no-show jobs for my crew, a little kick-back. The usual."

"Not interested," Gus said.

Fergus spoke up. "Maybe we should think about it, Gus. For the extra money."

"Yeah maybe you should think about it, Gus." Al mocked.

Gus barked, "I said I'm not interested."

Gus had put the new computer in the old computer's box. It was enough to keep up the hoax for the moment, but Gus had to admit to himself that it was only a matter of time before they realized this was not Sofia's computer. As the three men walked away with their prize, Dante turned back and said to Gus, "Say hello to your nephew for me."

"What?" Gus was angry. "Jimmy? You don't talk about Jimmy. And you don't talk about my daughter. You leave them out of this!"

Dante only smiled. "Heh. You think *you* know Jimmy? I know him better than you. I know him like he's the back of my hand. Jimmy the fuckin' Fist." Dante spit on the ground, raised his eyebrows, then turned and walked away.

Vince put the computer into the trunk of Al's Lincoln, and said, "You gonna call him?"

"No," Al answered. "Not yet. I don't trust that dick-head any farther than I can throw him. But at least maybe with whatever's on this computer he can pay off his markers."

Once back at home, Gus pulled Fergus aside by the lapel of his coat, and spoke to him quietly. "Never speak when you should listen. Never tell anyone outside the family what you're thinking."

Fergus avoided making eye contact with Gus as he pulled away from Gus' grip. "I'm just trying to make my way in the world. And that takes money. Money is safety. Jaysus, the world is bigger than ever, and the really powerful people... I mean from what I can see it seems like the real money is in demolition, and here I'm trying to be a builder! What am I thinking?"

Gus took Fergus by the shoulders and turned him to look into his eyes. "I get it. I do. Once upon a time, I was you. And I gave in to the temptation to do their shady deals to sock away some extra money. But what they want from you is more than you get. You're never even with them. You always owe them. Look, Fergus. You, and your dad, and your brother. You're part of my family now. And you will always have a place in my family. I will make sure you never go hungry. But you have to trust me, and follow my lead. You have to do things my way, because I've been doing this a long time. I've already made my mistakes. You don't have to make them too."

Colleen was in the kitchen stirring the sauce. Gus wandered in, still shaking his head from his talk with Fergus. He tried to dip a piece of bread in the sauce, but Colleen took the bread away from him before he could get to the pot. "Hey!" he protested.

"Hey, yourself," Colleen answered. "You can wait. Did you call the kids?"

"No, not yet. But I'll be glad when they get home, so Christopher can get back to school, and maybe I can take him around a bit and show him more of the business."

"Honey," Colleen said lovingly, "I just don't think he wants to go into the family business. It's not his thing."

"It's not his thing?" Gus was annoyed. "Well I'm just afraid that earning a living might not be his thing, either. You know, you work your ass off to be a self-made man, and to try to make things better for your kids. But if you make things better for your kids, then your son can never be a self-made man. We sacrifice for the next generation. But if we suffer so they don't have to, then they don't get the benefit of learning from the suffering."

"You can't suffer in their place, dear. And you can't prevent them from suffering, no matter how hard you try. Like Mary at the foot of the cross. You can only suffer along with them."

"Well, that's my point. Security is good, but you can't protect them from everything – I mean you shouldn't. Does the sword maker protect the steel from the hammer? Does the diamond cutter protect the diamonds from the… the thing that cuts the diamonds?"

"Nice analogies, honey."

"And what if there's no one I can trust to take over the business after I retire? If I just sell it to someone else, or worse if I close up shop, it'll be like it never existed. And after I'm gone, it'll be like I never existed."

"No one who has ever met you could possibly forget you," Colleen reassured him. "That's what life is about – living the kind of life that means you'll be missed when you're gone. That's all you need."

"No, you don't get it." Gus was getting frustrated. "I've got to leave a legacy. That's how the family name continues on. Dad's gone, and my brother. I'm the only one left, and when I'm gone, it will be just Christopher."

"And Sofia."

"Yes, I know. But I want to leave behind something… permanent. Something with the family name on it. Not just on a sign, but really… a landmark… the way they used to do, you know, like some big building that says AGNELLO on the side of it, built right into the brick of the building, so no one could ever take it down – you would have to tear the whole building down, you know what I mean?"

"Yes, I do, but…"

"And I feel like it can't wait. Like I've got to get moving on this. You know, time is money."

"No!" Monica's voice came from the living room. "Time is not money! Time is much more valuable than money. Look at me, I'll be dead soon…"

†††

"Let's go shopping!" Sara said. "Just us three girls. Jimmy and Armando have their TIA meeting, so there's nothing else we can do."

Willow smiled. "Can we go out to lunch, too? I've heard all about this Italian restaurant in Times Square. It's called Sz-Barro."

"No!" Sofia said. "We can go out to lunch, but we're not going to that place. We'll get some good New York pizza."

"Pizza Hut?" Willow asked with excitement.

"Sister," Sofia put her hand on Willow's shoulder. "Trust me. I'll pick the place."

"Okay great," Sara said. "I also want to stop by this book store."

"Why what's at the book store?" Sofia asked.

"Well," Sara stalled. "There's a book signing." Sofia gave her an impatient look. "Ok, it's Harriet. Harriet is reading from her new book, and I just want to stop by and say hello."

"Okay, well why didn't you say so?" Sofia scolded. "We'll go."

"Who's Harriet?" Willow asked.

"Harriet is Sara's ex-boyfriend's mother," Sofia answered.

"Yeah," Sara said, "but she's more than that. She's like a mentor to me. She's given me a lot of good advice in the past."

"You can't tell her about the time travel," Sofia said.

"I know, I know." Sara thought a moment. "But I feel like I need to talk to her."

The sign on the bookstore window said,

>MEET THE AUTHOR!
>HARRIET T. LEWIS WILL BE HERE IN PERSON
>READING FROM HER NEW BOOK OF POETRY.

Sara, Sofia, and Willow went in just as Harriet was starting to read one of her poems. "I call this poem, 'You Can't Speak for Me'." Harriet cleared her throat.

>"You Can't Speak for Me.
>'You can't speak for me,' said the woman to the man...
>'You can't speak for me,' said the black woman to the white woman...
>'You can't speak for me,' said the poor black woman to the rich black woman...

'You can't speak for me,' said the Muslim poor black woman to the Christian poor black woman…

'You can't speak for me,' said the disabled Muslim poor black woman to the non-disabled Muslim poor black woman…

'Who will speak for me?' asked God."

The audience clapped politely, and then lined up with their books to get Harriet's autograph. Sara got in at the back of the line. Sofia and Willow waited patiently, and when Sara got to the front of the line, Harriet was so happy to see her that she gave her a big hug, and then signed her copy of *Who Will Speak for Me?*

After the crowd dispersed into the bookstore, Harriet and Sara could talk with some privacy. Sara took a small velvet box out of her pocket. She opened it, just to give it one last look. The diamond sparkled in the fluorescent light. "Will you give it back to him?" Sara asked.

"Oh, child," Harriet said with compassion. "I so wish you would have worn it all the way to the altar. But I know my son. I understand."

"Will you take it?"

"Sara, honey, I think you have to give it back to him yourself. But you're in luck. He's in town right now. Doing his act at the Comedy Cellar. I've got some VIP passes for tonight's show– you can take all your friends. Then you can see him after the show and give it back to him."

Sara sighed. "Can I ask you for some advice?"

"Of course, Sara," Harriet smiled. "Tell me."

"I've been asked to do something..." Sara began. Then she had another thought. "Have you ever done any genealogy, you know, looked up your ancestry?"

"Well, you know black folks looking up the family tree can be a painful experience. Often as not that tree has a noose hanging from it. So, no, I never looked into that. All I know is that my mother named me after Harriet Tubman, and that's good enough for me. Is this about being adopted by white folk?"

"No, not really," Sara said, though she wasn't sure. "I mean, I'm happy to call myself Italian and play along with the whole Italian pride thing, but every time I look in the mirror I'm reminded that I don't know who I really am. And sometimes white people try so hard not to make me feel uncomfortable around them... it makes me feel uncomfortable around them, you know what I mean? With their, 'I don't see you as black' nonsense. It's like I have to be a minority within a minority – a subset of black people who don't make white people feel uncomfortable - like I have to be different from my own people just to fit in with other people. Trouble is, I'm not even sure who my people are. I've heard folks say they would die for their family, but I don't know who my family is. I don't have anyone I would die for."

"Do you have friends?" Harriet asked.

Sara glanced back at Sofia and Willow. "Yeah. Good ones."

"Greater love has no one than this, that he lay down his life for his friends. That's Scripture." Before Sara could respond, Harriet went on. "Speaking of that, I want you to have something. It's meant a lot to me for many years. But I want you to have it. And when you use it, you can think of me as part of your family." Harriet opened her purse and dug to the bottom, and pulled out a small brown leather book. She handed it to Sara, who took it and held it as though it were the most valuable thing she'd ever held in her hand.

Sara turned the book over, running her fingers over the soft textured leather. She looked for a title, but there was nothing printed on the outside. "What is it?" she asked.

"It's a prayer book," Harriet explained. "The prayers in that book got me through some hard times, that's the truth. Something tells me you're going to need this now."

"Thank you," Sara said, holding the book tight to her chest. "Thank you."

Harriet put her hand on Sara's shoulder. "Wherever you travel, take this with you, and you'll always have an anchor."

Harriet recommended a restaurant for lunch, and Sara took the lunch as an opportunity to tell Sofia and Willow what she was thinking. After the food was placed in front of them, and the waitress walked away, she said, "I'm not looking for emotional reparations. I hate when people are overly nice to me out of their liberal guilt. Or worse, when they're nice to me because they're objectifying me as a sex object. I never thought I would complain about people being nice to me, but what I really want is for people to be real with me. I feel like I'm at a crossroads, here. I could go bitch, or I could go zen. And I'm trying really hard to go zen."

"I really don't think there's any risk of you becoming a bitch." Sofia was trying to lighten the mood.

"Oh but there is," Sara said. "You don't know what it's like to live in two completely separate worlds. To have to function in one world where you know you're different, but everyone around you is falling all over themselves to pretend you're not."

Willow, for her part, was a bit uncomfortable with the other women using the word "bitch" so much. She was also anxious to contribute to the conversation. "Well, I was a Catholic in eighteenth century Ireland."

Sara looked up from neatly separating the food on her plate and her eyes met Willow's. She could see that Willow's comment was sincere, and that there was some truth in it. But Sara said nothing.

Finally, Sofia broke the tension. "I know what you mean. Being a genius living among idiots is really difficult." Sara nearly spit out her food, and as soon as Willow realized it was okay to laugh, the atmosphere was relaxed again.

"So I hear you're going to be a barber," Willow said to Sara.

"A barber? No, a dentist."

"Isn't that the same thing?"

While the young women were on Fifth Avenue, and Armando and Jimmy met with the TIA to go over the information they had on Wordman and to create a plan for capturing him, Chris and Colum took the opportunity to go to Ellis Island. There, Colum stared at the many anti-Irish signs in the museum. "Help Wanted: No Irish Need Apply" was a common theme. He saw sign after sign, and it made him turn melancholy. "So apparently they didn't have it much better after they came here," he said.

"Apparently," Chris agreed. "Italians, too. And Armando's got relatives who came here on a raft made of garbage."

"Shite."

When the seven of them regathered that evening, they met at the St. Lawrence Grill for dinner. Sara broke the bread and passed the basket while Jimmy and Armando filled in the rest of the group on their meeting. "The TIA is convinced it was Wordman who took the time machine," Jimmy began. "Armando, have the Cuban sandwich, it's great here."

"I don't eat pork," Armando stated matter-of-factly, as he scanned the room for possible threats and mapped out an exit strategy. "A Cuban has two kinds of pork." He touched the gun under his coat to make sure it was easily accessible. "Our superiors think Wordman was trying to get his hands on the time machine all along, from the minute he heard about it. If he could use it, he could theoretically go back in time and give himself the plans for the Resonator, and he could even pretend he invented it."

"For all we know, he did," Sofia said with a look of resignation on her face.

"What?" Jimmy couldn't understand why she would say such a thing. "And what kind of Puerto Rican doesn't eat pork?"

"A pig's a filthy animal," Armando explained.

"Well, *I* sure as hell didn't invent the time machine," Sofia was raising her voice. I just got the plans handed to me. I don't know who invented it."

"Are you quoting Samuel L. Jackson?" asked Chris. "You don't eat pork because of *Pulp Fiction*?"

"Look you guys are missing the bigger picture here!" Sofia was trying to get everyone's attention. "Just because we *can* do something doesn't mean we should."

"That's part of it," Armando explained. "But also my parents always grossed me out with their whole pig roasts, and the pig's head just laying there on the table staring at you, and the *chicharrones*, ugh." He stuck out his tongue.

Chris raised his voice to talk over the increasing volume of the conversation, "Sof-, now *you're* quoting *Jurassic Park*?"

Sofia gave Armando and Chris a stern look, and everyone stopped talking. "Look," she said. "I don't know how I can say this any more clearly. WE CAN'T DO THIS! Are you forgetting that the Resonator only holds one person? How the hell are two of you going to travel back in time, capture Wordman, and then bring him back in the time machine – that's three people! It can't be done." She adjusted the scrunchie in her hair. "And don't even get me started on the dangers of time travel again!"

"Well we just have to figure out a way," Jimmy said. "And when I say *we*, I mean *you*. You're the time lord."

Sofia looked down at her belly. "I do have two heart beats." She put her hand on Armando's hand to reassure him she wasn't mad at him.

Armando looked at her lovingly. "You can do this. For you, it's no problem."

"There's one more thing," Sofia said, looking down at her hands. "I think Wordman took my gun."

"What?" Armando barked.

"I'm sorry, honey, but I told you I didn't want it. I left it in the drawer under the workbench. It's not there now."

Chris' cell phone rang, and the conversation was interrupted by a call from home. "Hey, Mom… Yeah… Yep, everyone's fine. They're all here, we're at a diner… Uh huh… Okay…" Chris handed the phone to Colum. "It's your dad."

Colum took the phone. "Hi Dad… Yeah… Yep, everyone's fine. They're all here, we're at a diner… Uh huh… Yeah, we're still having the dreams. How about you?"

Sofia said, "Tell him I'm going to fix that!"

Colum handed the phone back to Chris. "Hello? Hi Nonna." He put his hand over the phone, "It's Nonna." He took his hand away from the phone. "Yes, Nonna, we're going to Mass." He shrugged as Sofia pointed at him and mouthed the word *liar*. "She wants to talk to you."

"Hi Nonna," Sofia said sweetly. "What? But it's my new invention, why wouldn't I want to…"

Monica interrupted her. "You don't want to know what people dream."

There was a pause, and then Colleen got back on the phone. "Hi honey."

"Hi, Mom," Sofia said. She was trying to be upbeat, but her frustration with the time machine and now with Monica's disapproval of her new invention, her voice sounded depressed.

"What's the matter, honey? Colleen asked.

"Oh, just science stuff," Sofia said.

"Sofia," Colleen said softly, "I know what it's like to just want to retreat into a quiet life. Just be a homebody and not have such responsibilities on your shoulders. It's dangerous out there, I know that. Believe me, I know that. Your father thinks he can make life safe by providing financial security and putting bigger locks on the doors, and Sara tries to protect herself with all those gadgets, and pepper spray. But sometimes… sometimes, to protect the ones you love… sometimes to have to go after the bad guy. Sometimes you have to play offense."

Sofia ended the call and handed the phone back to Chris. Everyone just looked at her for a moment. Then she surprised them. "Fuck it," she said. "We're going to get that mother fucker Wordman."

†††

That night, when Sara and the rest of the group went to the comedy club, Sofia stayed behind at the lab to work on her new project, the Lucidator. She thought that working on that project would clear her head and help her prepare to send Jimmy and Sara back in time.

Colum was apprehensive about meeting Sara's ex-fiancé. "His name is Maurice? A French fellow?"

"Not exactly," Sara said, a bit self-conscious.

"Why did you break it off?" Chris asked.

"Well, not that it's any of your business, but he just wasn't the right guy for me. He's a good guy, deep down, I think, but he's not my soul mate."

It was the 10:30 show at the Comedy Cellar, and by the time the group was ushered in, Maurice Lewis was already into his act. He stood tall on the stage, with six-pack abs and biceps stretching out a t-shirt that was a size too small for him, and he wore an equally small fedora perfectly perched on the top of his head.

"I think white people are jealous of the N-word, am I right? They want to say it, but they know they can't because it's our word. So I think white people need their own N-word. Then they wouldn't be so jealous, am I right? How about we give them the word 'Nilla' – you know, short for vanilla, like those cookies. Then white people can talk cool, and say things like, Are you my Nilla? Nilla, please! Do I look like a Nilla to you? Do I have a sign on my lawn that says *Dead Nilla Storage*?"

The audience emptied their lungs with laughter, energized by the mandatory two drink minimum. Jimmy, Armando, and Chris especially thought Maurice was hilarious, but Colum was a bit distracted by the fact that the woman he loved had a tall, strong, black ex-fiancé.

Maurice went into a new bit. "My ex was so OCD…"

Sara's heart sank into her stomach. *He's talking about me*, she thought. *That jerk is turning me into a comedy act!* For the rest of Maurice's act, Sara wished she was invisible.

After the show, Sara brought her friends back stage to introduce them to Maurice. Colum shook Maurice's hand and said, "I thought you were going to talk about the pompatus of love."

Maurice laughed and said, "I like this guy." He looked at Sara. "Is he your boyfriend?"

Sara said, "No," so quickly that it broke Colum's heart. Then she saw several of Maurice's friends whom she knew from college, and the awkwardness was displaced by an entirely new awkwardness – the awkwardness of everyone realizing that Sara had a whole group of black friends they had never met. Eventually, Sara was able to take Maurice aside and talk to him alone.

"So you're ex is so OCD?" Sara folded her arms and tapped her foot.

"Well, I didn't know you were going to be in the audience."

"Doesn't matter. You shouldn't use me in your act."

"But it's funny stuff. And it's not really about you. It's just based on you. You know, like, 'inspired by historical events,' am I right?"

"No, it's not fair. It's not right to use me like that."

"Look, Sara, it's a sad world, and I'm just trying to get the world to cheer the fuck up. Some people write songs, or poetry, or whatever. I tell jokes. They're just funny stories."

"It's too public for something so private."

"Okay, okay. I'm sorry. I'll take that stuff out of the act."

"Thank you. Anyway, I came here to give this back to you. I tried to give it your mom today, but she said I needed to give it to you myself. I guess that's closure or whatever."

Maurice took the ring box. "Yeah, I guess it is. But are you sure? We were good together. Even though you were pretty OCD." He smiled, hoping he could get Sara to smile too.

Sara didn't smile. She remembered how Maurice used to seem safe because he was funny. But it wasn't funny any more. "No, I need to move on. And you need a woman who doesn't mind being part of your act."

†††

The next morning, the group prepared to send Jimmy and Sara into the past. They hoped the trip would be easy. They hoped that from the perspective of Sofia, Armando, Chris, Willow, and Colum, the whole mission would take less than a moment, and that Jimmy and Sara would be back right after they left. But they still had so many unanswered questions.

When they gathered in the loft, there was silence at first, as several members of the group just stared out the window that faced the Brooklyn Bridge. Armando was the first to speak. "Tell them how this is going to work," he said to Sofia. "She told me, but I can't explain it."

Sofia took a deep breath. "Our two biggest problems are that the Resonator only holds one person, and you can only use a song once. So we can't put two people in the crate, but we also can't just send them back to the same time and place one at a time, because we can't use the same song a second time. But we can send two people back using two different songs on the same album, and hopefully that will put them close enough together that they can meet up and get the job done."

"What about getting them back?" Colum said. "If they catch Wordman, there will be three of them. How will they get back?"

"That's even trickier." Sofia's hands were shaking as she adjusted her scrunchie. "When the first person goes, he will have to send the Resonator back empty so we can send the second person. When the second person goes, that person can leave it paused in the past so it's ready to return – but again it only holds one person. To get the second person back we would have to use another song. The problem is that we don't know how long it will take to find and capture Wordman, so we won't know what song to use until the first person comes back here and tells us where and on what date the second person is waiting."

"But what about Wordman?" Chris asked. "You have three people to get back here."

Jimmy said, "Well, if we can't get all three people back, we're prepared to leave Wordman's body behind."

"You mean you would kill him?" Willow was shocked.

"Those are the orders," Armando confirmed.

Everyone fell silent again. Sofia sighed and went on. "Now if something goes wrong, we need a way to communicate with the people in the past."

Willow spoke up. "I know! If someone gets stuck in the past, they could write a new song, and play it right then and there, and then the time carriage could use that song to find them."

Sofia smiled at Willow. "That's what I thought at first. But if you wrote a song in the past, we wouldn't have the music here, unless you got it published and the sheet music was preserved. And even then we would have to find it among the millions of songs that have been written. Then we would have to get it performed and recorded, and we couldn't be sure that the recording would be enough like your performance in the past to make it work. So this is the plan." She looked at Jimmy and Sara. "If you get stuck in the past, you put an ad in the newspaper. Something with keywords we can look for in the computerized archives. Like the word 'resonator.' Then you include the place where you need to be picked up. We'll know the date from the date on the newspaper, and hopefully we'll be able to get some music that will send the time machine back there, and with the auto-pause function, it will stop and wait for you to get in. I wish I had a better plan, but that's the best I could come up with." Willow crossed herself.

Now there was nothing left to do but to send Jimmy and Sara back to 1973. The Resonator was prepared, as Jimmy and Sara put on their bell bottoms. Sara wore a tie-dyed shirt, and Jimmy put on an African dashiki shirt. He found a leather sport coat with wide lapels, and brought that along as well, just in case. "Who's going first?" Sofia asked, as she inserted an 8-track tape of the Bob Marley album *Burnin'* into the Resonator. "The first song is *Get Up, Stand Up*."

"I'll go first." Sara wanted to get it over with. Jimmy shrugged his acceptance. As Sara got into the wooden crate she held her breath. The trap door was closed and Sofia picked up the remote control. She held it for a moment, procrastinating the responsibility, and then pushed play. Everyone was startled by the ear-splitting sound of the tape fast-forwarding. Sofia almost panicked, but she pulled herself together and pressed the play button again. The tape stopped and then started playing somewhere in the middle of the song, *Rastaman Chant*. The Resonator dematerialized. It was gone for a second, and then it reappeared empty.

Everyone looked at Sofia with anticipation as she spoke slowly. "Okay... um... everything's okay." Sofia was thinking it through. "It played a song from the album. Wasn't the song I meant to play, but it was a song from the album. So it should have worked just the same. It went to Jamaica... Sara got out of the crate... and sent it back to us. So far so good."

Now everyone looked at Jimmy. "I guess it's my turn," he said. Jimmy got into the crate while Sofia took the 8-track tape over to her workbench and checked it over. When she was satisfied that the tape was undamaged, she fast-forwarded it back to the beginning. This time the tape played just fine. *Get Up, Stand Up*, and Jimmy was gone.

When the wooden crate rematerialized, everyone expected someone to get out. They thought it meant the mission was over, and they could work on the problem of getting two more people back to the present. They figured Sara would come out of the time machine, and tell them that Jimmy was holding Wordman in the past, and was ready to be transported back. But no one got out. The crate just sat there as the group stared at it. After a moment, Sofia and Colum both ran toward the trap door, and almost bumped heads. Colum deferred to Sofia, and she opened the door. The only thing inside the Resonator was a small piece of paper. As Sofia took it out, she realized it was a note from Jimmy. She read it out loud:

I'm in Jamaica, in 1973. I've been here for several days. Sara is NOT here. I've looked everywhere and she's nowhere to be found. Wordman has left Jamaica and is on his way to Georgia. I'm going after him. Since I can't take the machine with me, I'm sending it back to you. You will have to figure out a way to get us back from Georgia. I hope you can find some music to bring us home. Pray for me. And find Sara.

– JA

Sofia's voice broke when she read the words, "Sara is not here." By the time she got to the end of the note tears were streaming down her face. The others were trying to hold back their tears, and their panic. Willow covered her mouth, and Chris hugged her. Armando went over to Sofia and she collapsed into his arms.

Colum's fear was mixed with anger. "How the fook are we going to find her?"

Armando gave him a stern look. "Calm down, Colum. Sofia will figure it out. It's no problem."

"It seems like a pretty fookin' big problem to me," Colum yelled.

Armando's attitude softened. "Okay, we get it. We will find her." Armando pulled Sofia's face up to look at him. "Honey, I know you can solve this problem. Tell us what to do."

Sofia tried to wipe her eyes. "Um… check the newspapers. See if Sara placed an ad."

Armando was able to use the computer to access a database of newspaper archives. He searched on the word 'resonator' and the search returned a lot of ads for people selling metal guitars. But the oldest one stood out. It was in the Savannah Morning News, and the date was July 1st, 1876:

Three-legged horse for sale. Inquire of Miss Sara Resonator, Savannah Georgia.

"That's her!" Colum shouted.

"No shit, Sherlock," Chris chided.

Sofia's eyes glazed over. "Oh my God. 1876. Oh my God. Oh my God."

"No problem," Armando said. "We just have to find the right song."

"No, you don't get it," Sofia's heart was breaking with guilt. "I sent a young black woman into the south, alone, in 1876. Oh my God!"

"Don't panic, Sof-," Chris said. "We'll get her back. We'll send the time machine back there, and she'll just jump in and then bada-bing-bada-boom, she'll be back here before you know it."

"No," Colum said. "It's not good enough. She's in danger. Chris, you know what it was like being a Catholic in Ireland. I think this is worse. And anyway, she won't know where to find the machine when it gets there. She won't know where it is. Someone has to go back and find her." The group looked at Colum, but no one said anything. Then he said, "I'll do it. I'll go back and get her. Let me go, and I'll bring her back."

"Really?" Willow was surprised that her brother would volunteer to travel through time again.

"I love her, Willow." Colum said. "I want her to be my wife. If I can prove myself to her – I can save her – and then she will know. Anyway, I can't imagine not spending the rest of my life with her, even if that means my life is short."

"No, Colum," Willow protested. "It's too dangerous. Dad wouldn't want you to."

Armando spoke up, "I think you're both right. Someone has to go after her. But it's too dangerous for just one person to go. I'll go with Colum, and we'll bring Sara back."

Sofia started to cry again. "No! I can't lose you. I need you! Your baby needs you!" She looked around the room. "Chris can go with Colum!"

"Oh, hell no!" Chris said. "Don't you remember me saying I would never get into that thing again ever?" Willow made her feelings clear by shaking her head.

Armando took a breath. "Chris, you're the one with the most time travel experience. After all, you survived in the eighteenth century for a year – who better to spend a day or two in the nineteenth?"

Sofia tried some psychology. "I know you're afraid, Chris, but Sara is family. We have to help her."

"I'm not afraid, that's not it," Chris lied. "I'm just… I don't know. The dreams, and the headaches."

Then Chris remembered something his grandfather Rocco used to say. *Being a man means doing what you know is right, even if you're afraid of the consequences.*

Willow could see that Chris was getting ready to give in. "But you still don't know how to get them back," she said through her tears. Her fear was turning to anger toward both Sofia and Chris, along with a bit of jealousy toward Sara. But she knew these feelings were selfish, and so she gave up and just looked down at the floor and wiped her eyes. Chris tried to hold her hand, but Willow pulled her hands from his and turned away from him.

"Trust me," Sofia said. "I will get them back. I'll be damned if I'm going to lose Chris again, let alone my best friend." She gave Armando a look to reassure him that he was really her best friend.

It took the group a long time to do the research on music of the 1870s, as well as gather some recordings. Over the course of a couple of weeks, tension and frustration ran high. When they were finally ready, it was at the end of a long day and the sun had gone down, but no one was in any mood to wait until morning. The windows in the loft looked ominously dark.

Sofia took an 8-track tape out of a bag. "This is a tape of songs by the nineteenth century songwriter Henry Clay Work. Who's going first?" Both Chris and Colum hesitated. "C'mon, someone has to go first." Colum stepped forward. "Okay," Sofia continued. "The first song is called *My Grandfather's Clock*, written in 1876. But it wasn't written in Georgia, it was actually written in the north, so when you arrive in 1876, you'll have to send the time machine back here, and then make your way down the east coast to Savannah. You guys will have to meet up in Savannah. So you'd better check your maps now and decide on where to meet."

After going over the maps, Colum gathered his supplies, and his nerves, and got into the crate. "Well… you can't learn to swim on the kitchen floor," he said with a smirk. He closed the trap door, Sofia pushed play, and the song took the time machine and Colum to the year 1876.

The crate returned empty, and Chris got ready to get in. Sofia fast-forwarded the 8-track tape. "This is a recording of a song called *Marching Through Georgia*. It was written by Henry Clay Work in 1865 – a decade too early - but this arrangement is for a marching band, and it was copyrighted in 1876. That's the best we could get, but I think it will work."

"You *think*?" Chris said. "Shit."

Sofia gestured toward the crate, and Chris kissed Willow and got in. Sofia locked eyes with him as he closed the trap door. From inside, he said, "All right. Push the damn button." Willow wiped her cheeks.

Sofia pushed the button and the loud music of a marching band started up. The time machine started to fade from view. But after just a few phrases of the music, there was an audible *snap* as the tape broke in the machine. Sofia and Willow both gasped. The wooden crate disappeared as it played its randomly generated computer melody.

Armando, Sofia, and Willow all looked at each other without saying a word. The time machine was gone for what seemed like forever. When it finally reappeared, it was accompanied by a louder version of the same computerized melody it had played when it dematerialized. As soon as Sofia heard it, she screamed, "Noooooo!"

"What? What?" Both Armando and Willow were alarmed.

Sofia crumpled to the ground and buried her face in her hands. "Nooooo! Noooo! Nooo! Noo! No." The last one was just a whimper.

Armando bent down to hold Sofia. "What's wrong? What happened?"

Sofia forced her words through the sobs. "The failsafe. The auto-return. It came back on its own!"

"What does that mean?" Willow demanded.

Sofia could hardly make herself understood. "It means it came back on its own. It means Chris didn't send it back. Look inside."

Willow ran to the crate and opened the trap door. It was empty.

"I told you!" Sofia screamed. "I told you it was too dangerous!" She slapped Armando on the arms repeatedly.

"Okay, okay, calm down," Armando said, grabbing Sofia's arms so she couldn't keep hitting him. "Didn't he go where you sent him?"

"No!" Sofia's frustration was coming out as anger. "No he didn't! The tape BROKE! The process was aborted. He left here but he never arrived there… or anywhere… don't you see? He's gone! He spun off into the…"

"The outer darkness?" Willow choked on her tears.

Sofia winced in pain, grabbed her stomach, and collapsed on the floor.

CHAPTER 3
BABYLON TOO ROUGH

Sara was still holding her breath when the Resonator materialized. After the sound died down, she stayed perfectly still as long as she could, and then finally she took a breath. The air was hot and humid. Stuffy, even. She opened the trap door and looked out as a warm ocean breeze brushed across her face. Getting out of the crate, she could see the water. *Wow*, she thought. *I'm really here – in the past. It really worked. That Sofia... she's really something.*

A thick fog prevented Sara from seeing very far into the distance, but she could see the coastline, and she could see the vague outline of ships docked in the harbor. Nothing looked familiar, but she had only ever been to the western side of Jamaica, never to Kingston, so she assumed all was going according to plan, and sent the time machine back to the year two thousand. Once it was gone, she walked toward the ships. She could hear the rhythmic sounds of the workers on the docks: the pounding of hammers, the squeaking of pulleys, and men chanting and shouting.

As Sara walked closer to the docks, she could see the closest ship through the fog. She read the name, *Neptune*, but when the fog cleared a bit more she knew something was wrong. This was not a ship from the 1970s. This was an old-time wooden sailing ship. Sara started to panic, and as she looked around, her fears were confirmed. The dock workers were all black men, most of them covered with scars, some of them were branded, and a few were missing their right arms. The cargo they were loading was cotton. Sara gasped and covered her open mouth with her hand. She looked around her to see if anyone was aware of her presence, and quickly ducked into the shadows behind the nearest stack of shipping crates. She slumped down with her back against a crate and put her face into her hands. *Please God…*

†††

When Jimmy arrived in Kingston, the time machine materialized in a junkyard next to an empty lot. There, Bob Marley and the Wailers were playing an outdoor concert. When Jimmy opened the trap door, the song *Get Up, Stand Up* was just finishing – and the sound was deafening, coming from a speaker very close to the Resonator. Jimmy realized that a lot of people had seen him arrive, but no one seemed very phased by it. They all just shrugged their shoulders and took another drag of the ganja. *Hmm – there he is, the man himself. Bob Marley. This is so cool. No time to hang around and listen, though.* He checked the gun tucked behind his back, and felt for his wallet.

Jimmy tried to look inconspicuous as he wandered through the audience looking for Sara. The hot air was a welcome feeling on his face and arms after New York in winter. He closed his eyes for a moment and soaked in the warmth. When he opened his eyes, he noticed for the first time that the island was alive with colors, and in the silence between the songs, he could hear the buzz of the bugs in the trees. But the longer he looked, with no Sara in sight, the more he started to worry. *Where the hell is Sara? What if I can't find her? And how am I going to find Wordman without Sara to help me get in good with the locals?* He walked the perimeter of the empty lot, looking into the trees, hoping to see Sara hiding in the bushes. "Sara!" he called out in his loudest whisper. "Sara!" Eventually, the concert was over and the crowd dispersed. Jimmy felt he had no choice but to leave the vicinity of the junkyard and go looking for Sara. He put a padlock on the trap door of the Resonator, and set out along the road into town.

†††

Sara knew that she was in danger. She lost track of how long she sat against that shipping crate, alternately crying and praying. Eventually she heard men's voices. The voices sounded like they were in charge, and they were coming toward her. She knew she had to gather up the courage to move, and get out of sight. She crawled along the ground at first, but then mustered the strength to stand up and walk along the boardwalk that followed the coastline. She could see warehouses up ahead, so she kept walking, hoping to find her way to someplace, or someone, who could help. As she walked she realized she was not on the coast at all, but on a river or inlet of some kind. And as she came near to the warehouses, her whole body cringed and her skin crawled when she saw the shackles and chains attached to the walls.

These were slave pens. Sara couldn't even bring herself to think about what year this might be. But she knew her situation was bad.

Is this Jamaica? If it is, I'm a lot farther back in the past than 1973, she thought. Sara decided to turn inland, hoping to find some trace of civilization. She turned away from the river and walked along a dirt road that led to a group of buildings. The road itself was almost tranquil. As she moved farther from the river it got very quiet, and for a moment Sara almost felt a sense of peace. There was a tavern, and a hotel. There was an open square with a tree in the middle of it. Hanging from the tree was a frayed noose, the rope grey from a long time of exposure to the elements. Sara looked away. She tried to focus on the buildings, to see if any people were around. But the tears came back, and she just ran farther down the road, looking for a place to hide.

After a while, Sara got tired and slowed to a walk again. She worried that the road was going nowhere, and thought it might be best to turn back toward the river to stay close to the port. If there is a town here, she reasoned, it would be near the port. After stopping for a moment and looking in all directions, Sara turned right onto another dirt road, and soon it seemed like this one was more well travelled. As she walked, a horse-drawn carriage passed her. Sara thought the driver gave her a curious look, but she couldn't be sure. She knew that her 1970s clothes would make her stand out here, wherever she was. Soon she came to a cemetery surrounded by a high brick wall. It felt like a dead end, literally. Sara broke down again and sat down in the grass at the base of the wall, and surrendered to the tears. After a while, not knowing what else to do, Sara opened her purse and dug to the bottom. There she found the small leather prayer book that Harriet had given her. She opened the book, and let the pages fall to a place where the book had been opened many times before. Then she started reading, and praying, as she shut out the dangerous world around her.

After a while, Sara felt a bit of emotional strength returning to her, and she finally looked up from the book, and turned her head to look at the cemetery wall. "I hope I don't end up in there," she said out loud.

"Of course you won't, silly!"

Sara jumped from the surprise, and turned around quickly to see a young white girl standing over her. The girl was about sixteen years old, and was wearing a dress that looked like something out of *Gone with the Wind*. "Oh! I didn't see you," Sara sputtered. "I guess I didn't realize I said that out loud."

"I'm sorry I startled you," the young girl said.

"That's okay." Sara was skeptical about the girl's intentions. "So why won't I end up in here?" Sara gestured toward the cemetery.

"Because that's a white cemetery," the girl said matter-of-factly. "Negroes get buried in the negro cemetery, next to Potter's Field."

"Ne-? Uh, okay." Sara thought about how to respond, but realized she had better be careful about what she said. Saying the wrong thing could be dangerous. "My name is Sara. What's yours?"

"Sara? That's my grandmother's name. She spells it with an 'H.' Do you spell it with an 'H'? I'm Daisy Gordon. I was born on Halloween. Pleased to meet you."

"I'm pleased to meet you, Daisy Gordon. And no. No 'H', just S-A-R-A." As Sara tried to pull herself to her feet, she cut the palm of her hand on a sharp stone in the wall. "Ow!"

"Oh dear!" Daisy could see blood seeping from the cut. "You've gotten yourself a nasty gash. Please come to my house, and we'll get you bandaged up. I only live around the corner, on Oglethorpe Street."

"You would take me to your house?"

"Of course, silly. My mother raised me to be charitable."

"Yeah, but you're white. And I'm black. You did notice that I'm black?" Sara joked.

"Yes, I noticed. But you're clearly a refugee in need, dressed as you are. It wouldn't be Christian to let you suffer. I think it's best to… to help people at all times… no matter who they are."

Sara held her bleeding hand as she followed Daisy down Oglethorpe Street. "Thank you, Daisy. Um, this is going to sound like a silly question, but as you said, I am a refugee – and I'm a bit lost. Can you tell me what town this is?"

"Why it's Savannah, of course. Savannah, Georgia. The only town General Sherman could not burn to the ground. Though we've had our share of fires since then."

When they arrived at the Gordon house, Daisy passed by the front door, and ushered Sara in by a side door that led into the kitchen.

"Mother! Mother!" When Nellie Gordon came into the kitchen she was surprised to see Sara there with Daisy. "Mother this is Sara. She cut her hand, and I said we would get her a bandage."

"And so we shall," Nellie said. She looked Sara up and down with her dark eyes, while fanning out her dress. Then she noticed the silver sitting out in plain sight on the sideboard and said, "Juliette you stay here with our guest while I get the bandages. Sara, you say? Hmm."

When she left the room, she could be heard muttering to herself, "I will never understand that girl… why she would give a cussed fart about a…"

Sara raised her eyebrows at Daisy.

"My given name is Juliette. But I like to be called Daisy."

Just then the door swung open and another young girl came in. "Daisy! Daisy, I saw you with a… oh hello."

Sara nodded. "Hello. I'm Sara."

"Sara, this is my friend Margaret Thomas," Daisy was excited to introduce her new charity case to Margaret. "Their house has hot running water, and flush toilets!"

"Juliette Gordon!" Nellie was annoyed to hear talk of toilets, and just a little bit jealous of the Thomas' modern conveniences. "Here." She handed the bandages to Daisy. "Be a nurse, not a chambermaid." Daisy took the bandages and curtsied to her mother. "And you'll need this." She took a bottle of whiskey out of the cupboard, and handed it to Daisy. "And after you finish bandaging her wound, you can take her… well, outside."

Sara gritted her teeth and gripped her forearm over the sink while Daisy poured the whiskey over her hand. Then Margaret helped Daisy wrap the hand. When it was done, Daisy said, "Mother wants us out of the house now. But maybe someday I'll show you my paintings."

"You're an artist?"

Daisy nodded enthusiastically. As they walked out into the sun, they met Daisy's father coming toward the house. Margaret and Daisy curtsied to Daisy's father. Sara tried to curtsy as well, but somehow it felt awkward.

"Father, this is my new friend, Sara." Daisy turned toward Sara. "Sara, Father is a general."

"United States General William Gordon, at your service." He bowed politely. "My dear mother's name is Sarah." He smiled at Sara, but she wondered if it was sincere. "What troubles are you girls getting into today?"

"No troubles, Father. Just going for a stroll," Daisy smiled and curtsied again. "Come," she said to Sara, "Margaret and I will show you the town."

Since Sara had nowhere to go, she decided to go along and learn as much as she could about her surroundings. Her mind was already on the newspaper ad she would have to place to let Sofia and the others know where she was. But for now, Sara thought, it was time to say as little as possible, and listen as much as possible. As they walked through the town, Sara began to allow the warm weather and blue sky to relax her. She was enchanted by the antebellum architecture, and the tree-lined squares. Spanish moss hung from the trees, giving the whole town a look of charm and antiquity.

"Savannah is the last true city of the South," Daisy explained as they walked along. "It truly is the glory of the South - but we're not just living in the past, oh no. We're embracing the future, too. Take my father, for instance. He was an officer in the confederate army. Now he's a general for the Union. We're very progressive."

"Uh huh," Sara was looking up at the trees.

"And there's Mr. Crown," Margaret added.

Daisy nodded. "Yes, that's right. Mr. Crown is leading in the rebuilding of the South, and he's doing it from right here in Savannah. He's a great man."

"A great man," Margaret echoed.

"Why is there no moss on these trees?" Sara was still looking up.

Daisy and Margaret looked at each other, but didn't say anything.

"Yeah," Sara was scanning the skyline of Savannah. "All the trees have that moss hanging from them, but not the ones on this side of the square. Why is that?"

Margaret cleared her throat, but said nothing. Finally, Daisy spoke up. "That's hanging square. It's built over the first cemetery in Savannah, and it's the place where… well, you know." Daisy's voice got very quiet. "Folks say that a long time ago they hanged a young girl just about the same age as we are… for *murder*. She was with child, as well, and they had to wait until she gave birth to hang her. The men were so unnerved by the thought of hanging a new mother, that they built the scaffold so high that she was way up in the trees when she... No one knows what happened to her baby. But now her ghost haunts the trees. That's why they don't grow the moss."

Sara gave Daisy a skeptical look. "Really?" she said sarcastically. "I don't believe in ghosts."

"You don't believe in ghosts?" Margaret was incredulous. "That's the surest way to get the ghosts to come after you! They're going to want to prove themselves to you. You should take it back."

"I'm not taking it back." Sara was getting more comfortable with her new friends, and she was letting a little attitude come back into her voice. "But you know what? I'm hungry." She thought of the contents of her purse. Money from the 1970s was not going to be of any use here. "What year is it?" she blurted out.

"Why... you don't know what year it is?" Daisy put her hands on her hips. Then she softened. "I'm sorry. I suppose they didn't teach you numbers, did they?"

"Who?"

"You know... when you were a... slave."

"I was never a slave!" Sara's voice was starting to harden. "And I did learn numbers. And letters. And chemistry. And biology. Hell, I majored in premed."

"Well, I *am* sorry," Daisy responded. "I'm afraid we're not acquainted with this Major Preemhead. Was he your master?"

Sara gritted her teeth and resisted the temptation to say what she was thinking.

"You said you were hungry," Margaret was trying to ease the tension and get back to being philanthropic. "We'll get you some food from my mother's pantry."

Sara was almost angry enough to refuse to take food from the girls. But she was hungry, and after all, she reassured herself, they were only a product of their environment. They might be racist. They might be treating her like a charity case. But they were all she had. So she accepted the bread and cheese they offered, along with a small glass of warm sweet tea. It wasn't until Sara started eating that she realized just how hungry she was. While she ate, the girls told her ghost stories to try to convince her that she should believe in ghosts.

"Once the mayor of Savannah…" Daisy began.

"Mayor Jones…" Margaret added, enthusiastically.

"He moved into a house on State Street. But very soon after he moved in, he just moved right out, and left town for good. And do you know why?"

Sara shook her head.

"Because the house was haunted! And that house is still empty to this very day. No one can live in it, because the ghosts don't want anyone to live in it."

"Another family moved into a house on Perry Street. Just a few years ago, this was. The first night in the house they heard running and screaming in the upstairs. But no one was there. Then they heard a woman's voice, clear as day, screaming, and screaming. And they moved out the very next day. And that house is also empty to this day."

"And then there's the Willink house," Margaret said. "Old Mrs. Willink drowned in the river, and now her ghost haunts her house."

Daisy jumped in, getting excited. "The orphanage, on Houston Street."

"Yes!" Margaret agreed. "Two little girls – sisters - died in a fire there, and now they haunt the building. Oh, and the Telfair House on Saint James Square."

"Old Mary Telfair died just last year," Margaret said with wide eyes. "But she never left the house."

"And the old Curiosity Shop," Daisy's voice was starting to squeak.

Sara finally swallowed her last bite. "Okay! I get it. Are there any houses in Savannah that are not haunted?"

The girls giggled. "Do you want to see it?"

"See what?"

"The Old Curiosity Shop, silly!"

Sara couldn't think of a reason to say no, and she didn't want the girls to leave her alone, so she decided to stall for time and try to gather more information. "Sure. Why not."

The girls led Sara down another dirt road, lined with homes and punctuated by squares. This part of town was alive with activity, and people walked in every direction. Some of them stared at the unlikely trio walking along, and a few men tipped their hats to the white girls as they passed. After a time of silence, Daisy said, "Eighteen Seventy-Six."

"It's 1876?" Sara thought for a moment. *After emancipation. That's good. Reconstruction. Still very dangerous.*

When they reached Monterey Square, Sara could see a building on the corner, dark and boarded up. The exposed windows were broken, and the sign was hanging by one side. It said, *The Curiosity Shop. Theodore Meves, Proprietor.*

Daisy got close to Sara so she could whisper. "When we were little girls, Mr. Meves came to town, and opened his shop. It was the most wonderful place, with the most amazing oddities. There were glass cages that held serpents with feet on them, just like the serpent that tempted Eve in the Garden of Eden. There were two real live leprechauns who worked for Mr. Meves, and there was even the skeleton of a half man-half monkey."

"The missing link!" Margaret whispered. "We didn't even know what that meant at the time, but we sure thought it was exotic."

"But it turns out the missing link is a blasphemy to the Bible, so the townsfolk shut the Curiosity Shop down, and Mr. Meves and his leprechauns just disappeared, never to be seen again."

"And now it's haunted," Margaret concluded with a shudder. And with that, the two girls backed away from the square. "Let's go home," they both said in unison.

"Um, I don't exactly have a home to go home to."

"Oh, where are our manners?" Daisy said. "Of course, you're a refugee. We will take you to…"

"To the boarding house on Bryan Street," Margaret finished her thought.

"To the boarding house on Bryan Street," Daisy confirmed. "My father will pay for your lodging."

"No *my* father will be happy to pay for your lodging," Margaret insisted.

"But I'm sure *my* father will insist," Daisy said with polite condescension. "After all, he did take note that Sara has the same name as Grandmother."

As the girls politely argued over who was going to be the more philanthropic with their fathers' money, Sara just about had a panic attack. She clutched her purse close to her and looked around, surveying her surroundings. She had no idea where she was, let alone where Bryan Street was. So she had no choice but to accept the hospitality of two younger girls who treated her like a pet project. If she didn't, she was sure she would be sleeping under the stars that night.

When they reached the boarding house, Sara had to wait in the street while Daisy and Margaret went up to the house to speak with the owner, a confederate army major's widow named Mrs. Lillibridge. Sara couldn't hear the conversation, but it seemed like it took a while for the girls to get Mrs. Lillibridge to consider letting Sara stay there. Even with financial pledges from both the Gordon and Thomas families, Mrs. Lillibridge kept looking at Sara and shaking her head. Finally, the widow went back inside, and Daisy and Margaret walked over to Sara. "She has agreed to let you stay here for a short span," Daisy explained. "But before she allows you in, she feels the need to ask her current guests if they don't mind her renting a room to a negro woman. She's afraid they might leave if they prefer to stay among white people, and she says she cannot afford to lose their business. You see, the boarding house is nearly empty on account of the coming fever season."

Sara just sighed in resignation, and hated herself for hoping that she would be allowed to stay in the boarding house.

"The men are out for the day," Daisy went on. "She won't make a decision until they get back, so there's no point standing here in the street. Let's go see if my mother will let you... will let us sit in the parlor."

When they returned to the Gordon house, Sara sheepishly followed Daisy and Margaret in through the servants' door. As they moved from the kitchen into the hall, the three of them were surprised by Nellie Gordon sliding down the banister of the great staircase. Nellie landed perfectly and with great flourish, both feet on the wooden floor. "Oh, it's you." she said, disappointed. "Well, crap, I thought it was Mrs. Anderson. She's coming over for tea." Nellie sighed. "Now I have to go back upstairs and get ready to make my entrance again."

"Mother, may we sit in the parlor?"

"All of you?" Nellie looked at Sara.

"Yes, mother."

Nellie sighed even louder.

"Mother, you can play the piano, and we'll listen ever so quietly, and when you finish a song we'll clap ever so loudly!"

"Oh all right."

As it turned out, the two other guests of the boarding house didn't much care who else stayed there. But Sara was expected to eat her dinner in the kitchen with the cook, rather than at the table with the white folk. That is, until a young teenager named Tom Kennedy found out about it.

"So where's the negro girl?" he said, stuffing potatoes into his mouth.

Mrs. Lillibridge stammered. "Well, she's in the kitchen… eating her supper."

"But isn't she a paying customer?" Tom pressed.

"No she is not. Her room and board are being paid by some generous families of the town, but she is a refugee. Or so I'm told."

"What's her name?"

"I believe it's Sara."

"Sara," he repeated in a whisper. Tom paused to catch his breath. Then he called out toward the kitchen door, "Oh Sara! Sara, come in here, into the dining room!"

Mrs. Lillibridge was mortified. Sara opened the door a crack and peeked in. She could see the horrified look on Mrs. Lillibridge's face, which only made her want to join the men at the table all the more. Tom was gesturing for her to come and sit down. Sara looked at the other guest. Dirty clothes and hands. Clearly a working man. She made eye contact, and he shrugged. So Sara came in, and brought her plate with her.

"Thank you," she said. "I was getting tired eating at the counter. It feels good to sit down."

"I'm Tom Kennedy. From Hanover, Illinois. My uncle is Frank Kennedy. Do you know of him?"

"No, I'm afraid not. I'm not from Savannah, so I don't really know anyone. Except Daisy and Margaret, that is." Sara looked toward Mrs. Lillibridge, who gave her a disapproving look. "My name is Sara Pugliese."

The other guest spoke up. "You have a last name! And a mighty fancy one at that, especially for a… a refugee. Is that a creole name? I'm Solomon Gleason."

"Mr. Gleason is an architectural ironworker," Tom said the words slowly, looking at Gleason to make sure he got it right. "He did those great balconies on that huge house on Broughton Street."

"The Marshall House. Now that was a grand old house! Until it was used as a hospital by the Union Army. Men went in with all their limbs, and came out… well, now folks just call it the Saw House."

"And now it's haunted by all the soldiers who died there!" Tom added with excitement.

Gleason looked impatient. "Now I'm working on the railings for the double staircase leading up to the Davenport House."

Sara wanted to change the subject away from amputations and hauntings. "So Tom, you came here all the way from Illinois? I'm from Illinois, too. From Chicago."

"You're from Chicago? Did you also leave to get away from the typhoid?"

"Uh... no. Is that why you came here?"

"Yes. We got the typhoid real bad in Hanover. I had two sisters, Mary, and... and Sarah..." he gestured toward Sara, acknowledging the name and suppressing his emotions. "And a brother, Willie Junior. We lost them all in one year. I was the youngest, and now I'm the last."

"I'm sorry for your loss," Sara mumbled.

"So my mother made my father send me here to his brother Frank. But he says I can't stay with him because he's..." Tom switched to a whisper, "divorced." Mrs. Lillibridge blushed and fanned herself, but Tom just went on. "But it looks like I'm going to have to leave Savannah soon anyway. My uncle tells me that everyone who can go leaves the city and moves farther inland for the fever season. And where are you from, Mr. Gleason?"

"Oh, actually I live here in Savannah – my shop is over on Liberty Street. But ever since my wife passed away last year, our house just seems too big for me. So sometimes I stay here at the boarding house, and help out with odd jobs for Mrs. Lillibridge. Tom, I am sorry for your loss. Matter of fact, I lost my oldest son to typhoid about seven years ago."

Sara's mind had wandered, and she was lost in thought. *Fever season? I thought that sounded familiar. Of course! 1876! I knew that date was significant. The yellow fever epidemic. In 1876, over a thousand people died in a matter of two weeks. When was that? What month? Damn, I can't remember. I have to get out of here before the epidemic hits!*

†††

As Jimmy reached the edge of Kingston, he came to a roadside stand made of scraps of wood and tin. A Rastafarian man was sitting on a stump behind the stand, carving a design into the side of a hallowed out gourd. The word "Food" was painted across the top of the stand, so Jimmy stopped and waited for the Rasta man to look up.

"Greetins an reespek," Jimmy said. "Wa'ppun, mon?"

The Rasta man just squinted at Jimmy without saying anything.

"Wa ya hab?" Jimmy asked. But he knew that whatever was for sale, he was pretty sure it wasn't going to be sanitary.

"Ackee an saltfish."

"Irie, mon." Jimmy put five Jamaican dollars down on the rough wood. "Dey call me Jimmy. Wa ya name, me dread?"

"Dey call me K-Ron. But me nuh ya dread, informa."

"Informa!" Jimmy acted insulted at the accusation that he might be a narc. But he couldn't blame K-Ron for thinking so. "Nuh fi me informa. A true. Me name be Jimmy – me lass name be Agnello."

"Italian?"

"A true."

K-Ron spit on the ground. "Italians downpress Zion."

Jimmy had forgotten that before World War II, Italy invaded Ethiopia. Apparently K-Ron had not forgotten. Jimmy thought fast. "Long time pass. Grudge is sin, me brudda."

"True, true," K-Ron admitted. "Catholic?"

"Me baan dat weh. Now jus seekin' livity."

"Ya know nuff truth fa a baldhead."

"Nuh fi me baldhead!" Jimmy protested again. "Me a cleanface. Me hate Babylon, and all dey politricks, same as ya do, star. Rastaman, I an I be downpressed. I an I mus be link up."

"Hush," K-Ron apologized. He tentatively decided to accept Jimmy, and served him his ackee and saltfish.

"Feel no way," Jimmy reassured him. Then he decided to risk asking about Sara. "K-Ron, me dread, di ya see a shorty gal gwaan dis road? 'Er be walkin' alone."

"Nuh, when dis dawta come deh?"

Jimmy realized he had no idea when Sara would have arrived, so he just shrugged. It could have been earlier that same day, but it could have been much earlier. Theoretically, she could even arrive later than he did. With time travel, just about anything was possible. Jimmy didn't want to think of how far apart they might actually be. So he decided to ask about Wordman. "Di ya see a mon, a baldhead Jake, him look like da professor fram *Gilligan's Island*?"

"Nuh, mon. Neba ben ta dis Gilligan Island."

†††

Sara found herself in a comfortable bed. Allowing herself to wake up slowly, she kept her eyes closed to enjoy the feeling. She let her body sink into the smooth sheets and down pillows of the boarding house brass bed, savoring the warmth of the soft blankets. It felt as though she were surrounded by satin. She turned to her side, but her hand bumped against the wall. *Wait, that's not the wall. It's hard, but it's covered with satin, too.* She turned to the other side. Another satin-covered wall. Sara tried to open her eyes, but she could only open them a little bit. It was still dark, and she tried with all her strength to force her eyes to open and focus on something. When they finally did, Sara screamed, and pounded her fists at the sides and lid of the coffin that she was in. She yelled for help, as loud as she could, but her screams were muffled. She pounded and kicked at the coffin lid. *Oh my God! I've been buried alive! Help me! Help me! Look for the wire, Sara. Look for the wire.* Sara felt around her frantically searching for the wire that would be attached to a bell on the surface of the graveyard. *Dead ringer. Dead ringer. Pull the wire.* Sara found the wire and pulled it, but the wire broke and went slack in her hand. Sara closed her eyes and cried out, *Nooooo!* Suddenly she found herself surrounded by rough plywood. She pounded at the walls, and realized that she was inside the Resonator. She tried to open the trap door, but it was locked from the outside. There were voices outside, and Sara could hear that they were talking about her. She tried to get their attention, but they just kept on talking. She kicked at the door and yelled for help, and when she became so exhausted that she could no longer kick or yell, she woke up in the boarding house bed.

Sara cried for over ten minutes straight. Eventually there was a loud knocking on her door, and the voice of Mrs. Lillibridge, "Whatever are you doing in there, girl? Are you ill? This is a boarding house, not a hospital!"

"I'm... It's okay. I'm fine. I'm sorry." Sara wiped her eyes and cheeks on the sheets. *So that's what they mean by disturbing dreams. Holy Shit.* Sara sat up, and forced herself to put her feet on the cold floor. Eventually she stood up, but just stood there still on the hard wooden floor, wondering what to do next. Her mind procrastinated dealing with her reality, so it focused on the feeling of bits of dust and dirt under her feet. *Newspaper ad. Have to put an ad in the paper, so Sofia knows where I am and she can come and get me.*

Sara washed her face in the china basin and got dressed, but before she could gather the courage to leave her room, there was another knock on the door. She opened the door to see Mrs. Lillibridge holding a folded dress.

"This is from those girls, the Gordon girl and the Thomas girl."

"Oh. Thank you." Sara took the dress and closed the door. After a few minutes she realized she would not be able to get the dress all the way on by herself. She could get into it, but she wouldn't be able to tie up the back. But another knock at her door revealed two young philanthropists who were eager to help. As they were dressing Sara, she tried to warn them about the coming yellow fever. "Girls…"

"Now Sara" Margaret said. "The proper way to address us is, *ladies.*" Both girls giggled.

"Ladies," Sara went on, rolling her eyes, "Do you know about yellow fever?"

"Of course, silly," Daisy answered. "That's why we go to the country house every summer in July. Sometimes we don't come back to town until October. Mother is already packing our things for the trip. We're leaving next week."

"So are we!" Margaret was delighted by the thought that they were all leaving town at the same time.

Sara tried to think of what else to say. *Do I tell them it comes from the mosquitos in the rice fields? What difference would it make?* "Okay, well, make sure you get out of town in time." *Good advice. I hope I can follow it myself.* "Yellow fever is really serious. Some people went – uh, some people could go into a coma, that is, a faint, and you might think they're dead, and they can get buried alive."

"We know all that," Daisy was impatient. "That's what the bells are for. That's why we have the expression, 'saved by the bell.' That's why the undertaker puts a man on watch overnight in the cemetery - the graveyard shift. Now let's change your bandage."

"Okay, well, I wouldn't want that to happen to you." *Or me.* "So if you ever think someone died… Just make sure before you bury them, okay?"

A smile crept across Margaret's face. "I heard that people who are buried alive make especially angry ghosts!"

"Could you imagine... waking up in a coffin... underground?" Daisy shuddered.

"I think I can." Sara was quick to change the subject. "Could you help me place an ad, um, advertisement in the newspaper?"

"An advertisement?" Margaret scrunched up her nose. "Now what would a refugee need with an advertisement?"

"Well... I have to... I mean... I just need to do it. I'm keeping a promise."

That was good enough for Daisy. "Father says we must always keep our promises. And the easiest promises to break are the ones you make to yourself. We'll help you. We can take you to the newspaper office this morning. But it's going to cost money. Do you have any money?"

Sara's heart sank. "No, I don't."

Both girls frowned. "Our fathers were very cross with us for promising that they would pay for your room and board."

"Yes. We're so very sorry, but if you don't have any money... well, I'm afraid you cannot stay here at the boarding house any longer."

"That's okay," Sara sighed. "I'm grateful for the one night. I just don't know what I'm going to do now."

Daisy's eyes lit up. "Mr. Crown! We'll take you to Mr. Crown. He'll help you. He's such a good man."

"We couldn't!" Margaret protested. "His is a good man. But he's a very busy man."

"We can and we will. After the newspaper office, we will take you to see Mr. Crown."

Sara was apprehensive about doing anything that would raise too much awareness of her presence. "I don't know. I was kind of hoping to keep a low profile."

"Nonsense," Daisy's voice carried the tone of a stubborn child.

"But we've never even met Mr. Crown," Margaret said. "We need an introduction. It's not proper for two ladies to simply… arrive unannounced at the office of Mr. Crown."

"Never mind all that." Daisy waived her hand in the air. "When we tell Mr. Crown about Sara, he will want to help her. Now," Daisy stared at Margaret, "how much money is in your purse?"

The sign on the building said, *Savannah Morning News*. Daisy and Margaret went in first, and then gestured for Sara to come in. They were directed to the editor's desk. Sara noticed the name plate on the desk. *Joel Harris. That name sounds familiar.*

"Mr. Harris, I am Daisy Gordon."

"I know who you are, Miss Gordon. What can I do for you?"

"Miss Thomas and I would like to place an advertisement in your newspaper." She motioned for Sara to come closer, and whispered, "What do you want it to say?" When Sara told Daisy what she wanted the ad to say, Daisy just stared at her with an indignant look on her face. Sara realized that the girls might think she was trying to take advantage of them. "Miss Sara," Daisy almost sounded angry. "You do not own a three-legged horse. How is it that you can claim to have one for sale?"

Sara thought fast. "It belongs to a friend. I told you, the ad fulfills a promise."

Daisy said nothing for a moment, but just looked at Sara. Finally, she pursed her lips and turned back to Harris. She took a deep breath and looked him right in the eye. "Three-legged horse for sale…" Harris wrote it down without a second thought. Daisy and Margaret pooled their purse money and paid for the ad, and the young women walked out into the Savannah sun. Harris looked at the three of them as they walked away. An unusual group: two sixteen-year-old wealthy, white girls, and a twenty-six year old black girl in a dress she clearly didn't own. They seemed like they were friends. Harris smiled at the thought of it.

The three of them walked along in silence for a while, until Daisy spoke. "Well, Miss Sara Resonator, that's a funny name."

"Thank you for placing the ad for me. I don't know how to repay you."

"Ahhhhhh!" They were startled by a large, old, black woman coming around a corner. She was wearing a ragged mumu, with a lot of home-made necklaces and jangling bracelets, and she waved her arms in the air and yelled at the girls. "Ahhhh la la ma ga ga YOU! Get out my way! Get out my way! Don't you know who I am?"

Daisy and Margaret were paralyzed. Margaret whispered, "The Boo Hag."

"Ah! Ahhhhhh!" The old woman took a step toward them and made threatening gestures. Daisy and Margaret turned and ran. Sara didn't know what else to do. She was more startled than afraid, but she didn't want to get separated from the girls, so she ran, too, and followed them. After a while, the old woman went on her way, and the three young women were able to regroup and catch their breath.

"What the hell was that?" Sara demanded.

"Your curse is fitting," Daisy said. "That was the Boo Hag."

"What's a Boo Hag?"

"It's old Annie Flax," Margaret whispered. "She's a kitchen maid. She used to work at the City Hotel, but now that it's closed down, she works at an inn. But she hates everyone, especially ladies. She's very uncouth, and she has even been known to slap a person in the face!"

"And she has voodoo powers," Daisy added.

"Eee-vil powers," Margaret's voice was even softer now.

"You must stay away from her," Daisy continued. "If she drinks your blood, she can steal away your soul!"

"All right, that's enough," Sara broke the spell by speaking in her regular voice. "Enough with the ghosts and witches. Let's go see this Mr. Crown."

The girls made their way to the John Wesley Hotel, and the office of Dickey-Jim Crown. Sara could sense that the closer they got, the more nervous and apprehensive Daisy and Margaret became. It was apparent that they didn't really know this Mr. Crown. They only knew *of* him. But Sara had little to lose at this point, and she needed a place to stay and something to eat while she waited to be rescued. She shook off the thought that Sofia might not be able to find her, and she might be stuck in nineteenth century Savannah indefinitely. As they climbed the stairs of the hotel, she took a deep breath and followed close behind her young benefactors.

"Mr. Crown is a pillar of the community," Daisy whispered.

"He only has the South's best interests at heart," Margaret agreed.

"Some people say Mr. Crown *is* Savannah," Daisy concluded.

They walked through the hotel lobby and were met at a pair of enormous double doors by a black man in a tuxedo. "May I help you?" he asked.

"I am Miss Da-" Daisy cleared her throat. "I am Miss Juliette Gordon. This is Miss Margaret Thomas. Mr. Crown will know of our fathers. We would like a word with him, please."

The butler said nothing, but went through the double doors, closing them behind him. A few minutes later, he came out and ushered the three young women into a spacious wood-paneled office. Sara looked around and took in her surroundings. Red carpeting. Velvet chairs. A large, hand-carved, wooden desk. And behind the desk was Dickey-Jim Crown, the most powerful man in Savannah. He looked like a fat Colonel Sanders, complete with the white linen suit and beard, and a panama hat.

Crown was in the middle of a conversation with another man who was leaning over the desk. He wore a long coat, open to expose his gun belt, one side of the coat tucked behind a gold-plated revolver that flashed in the sunlight that was coming in through the tall windows. Crown smiled as he talked, with a smile that seemed like it should be too large to leave any room for words. In a heavy southern accent, he drawled, "We strayed from the formula, and we paid the price." As the young women approached the desk, Crown turned to acknowledge them. "Why, hello ladies. Welcome to my hotel. The John Wesley is honored by your visit."

Daisy and Margaret curtsied, and Sara tried to do the same. *Damn, I really need to learn how to do this right,* she thought. Then, *Wait a minute. What am I thinking? I don't want to keep having to do this.*

Margaret was too nervous to speak, so Daisy raised her chin, and began, "Mr. Crown, thank you for taking the time to see us today, we apologize for arriving unannounced, however we are confident that when you hear of the plight of this poor refugee… well, based on your reputation, sir, we just know that you will want to help relieve the suffering of this unfortunate creature."

Creature? Sara's mind was in a whirl. *What have I let myself get into? Are they mocking me? Are they setting me up for something dangerous? Why have I just been going along with all this? I don't even know these people, or why they're being nice to me – maybe it's all a trick!* Sara could see Crown looking her over. Something didn't feel right.

Crown thought for a moment, then smiled his wide southern smile. "Ladies, thank you for coming here and bringing this tragedy to my attention. But where are my manners? Allow me to introduce my good friend, the Reverend Edward Meyers. Perhaps you already know him, if you are Methodists." Sara wondered why a Methodist preacher would need a gold-plated revolver. Crown continued, "Now, as I see it, any refugee who makes his – or her – way to our fine city," Crown was looking at Sara while he talked, "well, we are obligated – wouldn't you say obligated Reverend?"

"I would indeed, sir."

"We are obligated to do all we can to help. You ladies have performed a commendable act of charity, and I am certain that God himself is smiling on you as we speak, isn't that so, Reverend?

"It is indeed, sir."

Daisy and Margaret smiled with pride, and curtsied.

Crown got up from his desk chair, and adjusted his pants. As he pulled on the belt under his overhanging belly, Sara could see the glint of a gold belt buckle. "Now you ladies have done enough. I will be most gratified if I can take on the Christian burden of caring for this poor creature."

I'm right here, Sara thought, suddenly annoyed at people speaking of her in the third person again. But then her annoyance turned to panic as it became clear that Daisy and Margaret were being asked to leave her there. After a few more polite words, the pleasantries turned to goodbyes. *Oh shit. They're leaving me here! How do I know I can trust this guy?* And before she knew it, the two young girls were gone, and Sara was face to face with Dickey-Jim Crown.

"You have nothing to fear, my dear," Crown was finally speaking to Sara, but Sara wasn't sure she liked it. "I am here to rescue you." Turning to the butler, Crown spoke quietly. "Bring Esther here." Then Crown went back to his conversation with the Reverend as if Sara wasn't there at all. "Are you still reading Mr. Wellhausen, Reverend?"

"I am indeed," Meyers answered. "Fascinating insights, the man has. Although his name is pronounced *Vellhausen*."

"Yes, I know. Remember I went to Harvard," Crown bragged. "I know German. I simply detest it."

"And are you still reading Mr. Darwin?"

"I am indeed," Crown answered. "And I often think that Mr. Darwin's theories about animals could be applied to humans."

"How so?"

"Well, just as we know that whites are more highly evolved than negroes…"

There it is, Sara thought. *I'm still right here! Damn, this can't be good.*

"I believe that some whites are more highly evolved than others. For example, why did some of us survive the war of aggression, while others did not?"

"Well, I'm sure I do not know. Because we're of better stock?"

"That is exactly right, Reverend. You see, war, whatever its faults, is a form of natural selection. It weeds out the weak, and those of us who are more evolved, are more able to adapt to the… situation we find ourselves in now. Shall we say, the post-war realities."

Reverend Meyers changed the subject. "Will you be going to the theater? Tonight is the premier."

"Unfortunately, I have no time for the arts," Crown answered. "Though I have gained a new appreciation for the theater since 1865." Both men laughed. "Did you know that I met Mr. John Wilkes Booth once? When he played here at the Savannah Theater."

"So you've told me many times."

"If I could speak to him today I would congratulate him for his performance on April the fourteenth." The men laughed again.

"That's my birthday!" It was a small, joyful voice in the doorway.

Sara turned around to see a small black girl of about eleven years old, wearing a tattered canvas dress, with her hair tied in tight braids. Next to her was a tall, slender black woman, holding the little girl's hand.

Crown looked up at the woman and the smile disappeared from his face. "I done told you a thousand times. Keep that one out of my sight!" The little girl moved behind the woman to hide from Crown's gaze. Then Crown looked at Sara. "This is... What was your name, girl?"

"Sara."

"This is Sara. She's a *refugee*." The word curdled on his tongue and came out with contempt. "Take her upstairs and... make her feel welcome."

The tall woman walked over to Sara, who was now paralyzed with fear. The woman took Sara by the arm, and walked her out of

Crown's office. As the double doors were closed behind them, Sara could hear Crown's voice. "Oh, did I tell you? I've got a new bulldog. I'd like to try him against the sheriff's mastiff. If you bet with me, I think we could both make a lot of money."

The tall woman tried to calm Sara. "I'm Esther. And this is my daughter, Rosie."

"Sara. Nice to meet you. I think." Sara turned to look back toward the double doors to Crown's office. "What's his deal?"

"Do you mean… playing cards?" Esther was confused by the expression. "Yes, he likes to play cards, and he likes to gamble, but he doesn't like to lose. Losing drives him into a fury."

"No, I mean… Never mind. It's pretty clear. I just don't know why he would help me."

Esther sighed and looked down at her feet. "Sara, the John Wesley is not really a hotel. Not the kind where respectable people stay. He doesn't want to help you. He wants to put you to work."

Sara looked around, and realized what Esther meant. It was now midday, and yet the lobby was full of women in lingerie, overflowing their bodices. In the parlor she could see a roulette wheel spinning, and a pool table. "I need to get out of here," she said, her eyes wet with desperation.

"Yes, I know. But you can't leave now. Let me get you some lunch, and later I'll take you to some of our people." Sara hesitated, but Esther reassured her. "You can trust me."

Esther walked Sara up the stairs, and Sara became more nervous with each step. But there was no way out, and little Rosie looked so happy as she followed close behind. Esther brought Sara into a room, and shut the door.

"Do you… work here?" Sara asked.

Esther avoided eye contact. "I did. I used to. But now he keeps me for himself."

Sara was at a loss for words. After an awkward silence, she turned to Rosie. "Happy birthday."

"It's not my birthday today."

"But I thought you said…"

Esther spoke up. "Rosie heard Mr. Crown say April the fourteenth. That's her birthday. She was born the night…" Esther took a deep breath. "The night Mr. Lincoln was shot."

✝✝✝

Jimmy noticed a beat-up old guitar leaning against a tree. After eating his ackee and saltfish, he asked K-Ron, "Dat you axe? Me go play pon it?" K-Ron shrugged and gestured toward the guitar, so Jimmy picked it up, sat down on the stump, and played a soulful rendition of Bob Marley's *Redemption Song*.

"'Ow ya know dat sahng?" K-Ron was impressed.

"Me tol de trut, mon. I-ya Rasta - sight?"

"I an I overstand. I an I be bredren." And with that, K-Ron shook Jimmy's hand.

Right. We're brothers. Jimmy knew he was in. Now it was just a matter of finding someone who knows something and finessing the information out of them.

"Ya mus come to da nyabingi meetin," K-Ron said. "It begin dis evenin."

"Ya, mon. All fruits ripe," Jimmy said, indicating that he would go. Being invited to a nyabingi meeting was more than he could have hoped for. All the local Rastas would be there, and chances were good that someone would know something about the whereabouts of Sara or Wordman.

As the sun began to go down, Jimmy followed K-Ron through the Kingston shanty town. The nyabingi meeting was to be at a place called the Pinnacle yard, in the hills of St. Catherine, overlooking Kingston. It was a commune back in the 1940s and 50s, until the police shut it down. Now the Rastas would meet there for their gatherings, and some of them lived there. As K-Ron and Jimmy walked up the road into the foothills, the diminishing sunlight became increasingly blocked out by the trees, and the poverty became more and more desperate. A group of people were bathing in a small waterfall that ran off of a rock and onto the road. A baby screamed from inside a tin-roofed hut, and no one seemed to answer its cries. A woman butchered a goat on a tree stump. And on they walked, deeper into the forest. Both K-Ron and Jimmy walked in silence, except when K-Ron said, "I an I nuh say dem you Italian, truss me, mek dem vex."

"Jah know," Jimmy agreed. He knew he couldn't use his last name any more, which he admitted to himself was probably a good idea anyway. *What if someone asks?* he wondered. *I know. I'll use the name from Chris and Sofia's Irish side. I'll be Jimmy Delaney.*

When they reached the Pinnacle yard, K-Ron led Jimmy into a clearing, where a bonfire was already burning, and a drum circle was starting to form. There must have been over a hundred men and women there, as well as some children. Many people sat around the outside of the circle smoking the ganja, and some of them were talking to themselves with an animated, rhythmic babbling. As they noticed Jimmy coming into the clearing, a few of them shouted, "Babylon! Babylon!" and pointed. Jimmy looked around, scanning his surroundings for any possible escape routes. But when he sat down next to K-Ron in the circle, the group focus went back to the bonfire, the drumming, and the smoking. Still, Jimmy could see that many eyes were on him, and all those eyes were suspicious.

"De shepherd! De shepherd!" someone shouted. "Him have a prophecy!"

Jimmy watched as an old man struggled to his feet, and moved toward the bonfire, to the middle of the circle. His body looked frail, but his voice was strong and loud.

"'Ow did I an I come hya?"

"Slav'ry!" everyone shouted in unison.

"An 'oo bring I an I hya?"

"De white mon!"

"An 'oo is de white mon?"

"Goliath!"

"An 'oo is de black mon?"

"David!"

"An weh do I an I waan go?

"Zion!"

"An 'oo downpress Zion?"

"Babylon! Babylon!" Jimmy could feel the stares.

"Marcus Garvey!" The mention of the name was met by cheers from the crowd. "Marcus Garvey, him spoke to I an I, him say Jah Ras Tafari is de king of kings, an de lion of Judah!"

Shouts of "A true! A true!"

"'Him say de black mon inherit de eart' - an de white mon is de syatan!"

As the crowd cheered, Jimmy was aware that a lot of people were looking at him when the preacher said "satan." Those with drums beat on them as a form of applause, and the others chanted something Jimmy couldn't quite understand. Out of the corner of his eye, he saw a small rock flying in his direction. Without turning his head, he caught it in the air, and everyone around him gasped. The drumming stopped, and after a moment, the preaching went on.

As Jimmy looked over the crowd of Rastas, something caught his eye. He noticed another white face. A girl, in her early twenties, with blue eyes and blond dreadlocks. *Well, you don't see that every day,* Jimmy thought to himself. He decided he would have to keep an eye on this girl.

After the preaching wound down, someone shouted, "Ossie!" and a man got up, produced a saxophone seemingly out of nowhere, and said, "Me call dis sahng, *De Light of Saba.*" As the song began, everyone with a drum joined in, and many of the people chanted along. The crowd seemed to go into a trance, as many of them got up and danced.

It was now pitch dark except for the light coming from the bonfire. Jimmy pretended to take a hit from the coconut pipe every time someone passed him the "chalice." It was pretty easy to fool the Rastas, since they were all high, but that made Jimmy realize that he wasn't going to get much information out of them like this. At one point he noticed the white girl looking at him. *If I go over to her now, she'll think I'm hitting on her. Actually, she is kind of hot. Focus, Jim.* So he let some more time go by before meandering over to her. "Wa'ppun, me gal?"

"Move ya backside, rude boy!" the girl replied.

Jimmy put up his hands in a surrender gesture and backed away. "Hush." He thought it better to give her some space than press for an introduction. To his surprise, the blond girl got up and followed him as he walked away. Jimmy walked to the edge of the clearing, and turned to face her.

"What are you doing here?" she asked, shedding her Rasta accent.

"I should be asking you that question," Jimmy said. When she just stared him down, Jimmy said, "Look I think we got off on the wrong foot here. I'm Jimmy. Jimmy Delaney."

The blond woman seemed taken aback for a moment, but then shook Jimmy's hand. "Irish, eh? Me too. My name's Molly. Molly Mallone."

"Really? Molly Mallone? Like the song?"

"Far as you know," she answered. "I saw you when they passed the bong. You didn't take a real hit. So what's your story? Why are you here?"

"I'm just walking the earth, looking for peace, but instead I find only violence."

"Uh huh." Molly folded her arms. "That's the TV show, *Kung Fu*."

"Oh, you know about that?"

Jimmy and Molly both got very quiet when they heard the sound of someone walking through the brush. Molly put her finger up to her mouth in a *shh* gesture. Then she walked off without saying another word. *That was weird,* Jimmy thought. His attention turned back to the Rastas gathered around the bonfire, and how he might be able to ask them for information. But they were all just too stoned. *I'll have to wait until morning.* Jimmy looked around to figure out where he would sleep. Some of the Rastas were already passed out on the grass, and Jimmy knew the others would follow suit and just fall asleep anywhere at all. They were used to being homeless, but Jimmy didn't like the idea of sleeping under the stars. Actually, it wasn't the stars he hated. It was the bugs. And spiders. And snakes. On the other side of the clearing there were some old, run-down shacks. *Maybe I could sleep in there. At least there might be a floor.*

Jimmy made his way over to the shacks, trying to look nonchalant. As he moved away from the bonfire, he could hear the sound of water running by. So he kept walking past the shacks, and down to the bank of a small river. In the glow from the fire, he could see a wooden bridge over the river, and two people on the bridge. One of them was Molly. The other was a large man wearing a knit tam over his dreadlocks. They seemed to be talking, but then the conversation became heated, and Jimmy was shocked to see the man attack Molly, and grab her throat. *Shit!* Jimmy ran for the bridge at top speed, hoping to save the young woman from her attacker. As his feet hit the wooden planks of the bridge, he arrived just in time to see Molly knock the man to his knees with a quick palmstrike to the chin and an elbow-knee combination. The man tried to hold himself up with one hand on the ground, while holding his throat with the other, but Molly knocked him out cold with a right hook to the jaw. Molly tried to pull the man up by his dreadlocks, but his dreadlocks came off. He was wearing a wig. Molly grabbed him by his real hair, and then around the neck as she put him in a headlock. Jimmy just stood there looking on in horror as Molly twisted her body, breaking the man's neck. She let his limp body slide down onto the wooden deck of the bridge, and then she kicked him over the side of the bridge and into the river.

†††

Esther gave her own lunch to Sara, and then led her out of the hotel through the kitchen. They hurried away from the main streets, and walked along a deserted, dirt road for what seemed like hours. Rosie skipped along behind them, sometimes stopping to pick wildflowers along the road. Eventually they arrived at a small group of log cabins. "This is where I used to live," Esther said, indicating the old slave quarters. "Some of our people still live here. You can stay here for a while."

"Are you going to get in trouble?" Sara asked. "For helping me?"

Esther looked to see that Rosie was out of earshot. "Most likely. But I know how to make him forget his anger."

Sara shuddered, and then hoped Esther didn't notice. Esther opened the door to one of the cabins, and motioned for Sara to go inside. Inside it wasn't much more than a hut with a dirt floor. "The wind and the rain come in, but at least the smoke can't get out," Esther smirked. "Used-to-be slaves stick together by what they used to do. This camp's all used-to-be pickers, jinners, and packers. Now the men are blacksmiths, brick layers, carpenters. They're the lucky ones. The ones who worked the rice fields are too bent over to do much at all. Bosses whipped 'em if they stood up even for a second. If they didn't get shot runnin', or the fever didn't take 'em, well they can't do much now. Least these folks have a trade."

Sara's mind was reeling, overwhelmed by her own situation combined with thoughts of slavery and whippings. At that moment another woman came in, and Sara could see scars covering her arms. "Sara this is Naomi. She's going to watch over you."

"They whipped the women, too?" As soon as she said it, Sara was self-conscious, worried that she shouldn't have drawn attention to Naomi's scars. Naomi looked down, embarrassed.

"Women too," Esther answered. "Even if they were with child, though that often took care of that."

Naomi spoke up, "Worst part wasn't the whipping, neither. The worst part was the salt and red pepper they rubbed in after."

"Jesus," Sara was starting to feel sick.

There was a knock at the cabin door, and a deep male voice, "It's me - John Brown."

Esther opened the door to reveal a tall, muscular man in a course cotton shirt and pants, carrying a bow and a quiver of arrows in his two large hands. But before John Brown could speak again, he had a coughing fit, and turned away from the door. Esther turned to Sara with a sympathetic look and said, "It's from the jinning and packing. Gets in the lungs."

"I'm sorry, what's jinning?" Sara asked.

Esther looked at Sara confused. "I know you're young enough maybe you don't remember what it was like to be a slave, but how do you not know what jinning is?" Sara didn't answer, so Esther continued. "It's when they pick the seeds out of the cotton. John Brown used to be a jinner and a packer. But now he's a hunter." Esther smiled at John. "He's going to get us some supper."

"You're going to hunt for our dinner with that?" Sara pointed at the bow.

"Hunt. Steal. It's all hunting of a kind." John smiled back at Esther.

"We all became good at thieving during our time on the plantation," Naomi explained. "It was the only way to get enough to eat. The bosses taught us to steal by starving us."

That evening, Naomi and John Brown shared their supper with Sara. Black-eyed peas and bacon rinds. Hoe-cake and something called "lob-lolly mush" which seemed to Sara like a bland potato soup. And one small rabbit. Sara tried to organize the food on her wooden plate, but it kept running together. They drank hard cider, which made Sara light headed, and made John Brown talkative. "Freedom ain't easier than slavery," he said. "But at least we get meat that ain't spoiled. Only time we got meat back then was in the pen, when they wanted to fatten us up to get a good price. Or we ate what we stole. I remember when we use to go lying out. We would run into the woods for a night, or sometimes even a week."

Naomi nodded her head. "Once we all lay out for almost two weeks. When we came back, boss made us wear bells around our necks for a month."

"You came back?" Sara asked.

"We always came back," John answered. "Because runaways get shot. And we always got beat, but it was worth it for a few days of rest. Now, ain't no one to run from, ain't nowhere to run to, ain't no rest, no how."

After their meal, Sara asked to keep a candle burning so she could read. Both Naomi and John were impressed that she knew how, and agreed to spend the wax. Opening the small leather prayer book, Sara tried to concentrate. She struggled to hold back the tears as best she could, but she was sure that John and Naomi heard her when she let a whimper escape. She thought about how she was going to get back home. She prayed that Sofia and the others would see the ad she placed in the newspaper. She was ashamed of herself for ever thinking that she could protect herself with a little whistle and some pepper spray. *I would have to pepper spray this whole damn world! I can't protect myself here. This one town alone is more dangerous than all the hijackers and bombers back home – I can't protect myself from it. It's built into people's souls. I can't protect myself from everyone. Someone has to be on my side. Someone has to...* Her own words failed her, so she retreated into the words of the prayers in the book.

When the candle was blown out, Sara lay on a blanket on the hard dirt floor. The cold came right through the blanket, and felt like it was draining the warmth from her body. Her muscles ached from the combination of the emotional tension and the contact with the ground.

But she knew that she was safer there in the cabin than anywhere else in Savannah.

†††

Jimmy found himself below the surface of the water. He checked the gauge on his SCUBA tanks. *Plenty of air.* He dove down deeper into the Caribbean waters, surveying his underwater surroundings. It was warm and serene. The water was clear, and the colorful fish swimming by made everything beautiful. Jimmy swam farther from the shore, toward some coral that looked interesting. All of a sudden, it became hard for him to breathe. *Something's wrong. Why I am having trouble breathing? Why am I losing oxygen?* He checked the gauge again, but it was cracked. *No air! Can't get to the surface in time!* Jimmy started to panic, but then remembered that panicking was the one thing that could prevent him from getting out of this alive. He held what little breath he had left, and swam for the surface. He could see the sunlight reflecting off of the top of the water, but the more he swam, the farther away the surface seemed to be. His arms and legs were getting tired. *Can't go on. This is it. I'm going to die here.* Then a sense of peace washed over him. The silence of being under water became a peaceful quiet that drew him in, and fought against the ache in his lungs. He considered giving up and just letting the quiet overtake him. But the intense pressure in his chest won out, and his hands finally broke through the surface of the water. He ripped the mask from his face and gasped for air. As the air filled his desperate lungs, he could see that he was not in the Caribbean at all, he was in that small mountain river, and all of the Rastas were looking at him pointing. Then they started to call out, *Jimmy the Fist! You're Jimmy the Fist! Jimmy Agnello is Jimmy the Fist!* Jimmy shook his head and tried to deny it. *No! No!* And then he woke up in a sweat. He was alone, on the floor of one of the broken-down shacks of Pinnacle yard.

Jimmy rubbed his eyes and sat up, wishing he had thought to bring a toothbrush. Suddenly Molly came in, moving quickly, and closing the tin door behind her. Jimmy raised his eyebrows. He wasn't sure if she posed a threat, so he got to his feet quickly and took a step back.

"You have to go," she said. "Police are here to raid this place."

"Shit! Wait! I need some information. Maybe you can help me."

"Why should I?"

"Because we're both… Irish?"

Molly squinted at him and said nothing, then she ran out the door. Jimmy moved to follow her, but by the time he came out of the shack, she was nowhere in sight. Jimmy could hear the shouting of Kingston police, as Rastas ran in all directions, confused. Jimmy ran for the edge of the clearing, checking for his gun. It was gone. He stopped in his tracks and felt around his belt behind his back. *Shit, no! It's gone.* He looked back toward the shack. *Did I leave it in there?* He ran back to the shack, and looked all around, scanning the floor, but his gun was not there. He turned and pushed his way out through the tin door, and ended up face to face with four Kingston police officers, guns drawn.

†††

Sara was disappointed to find out that former slaves didn't eat breakfast. They only got two meals a day on the plantations, so they never got into the habit of eating before noon. She tried to kill some time by organizing the contents of her purse. Before long, Esther showed up with Rosie. Sara was glad to see them, especially Rosie, since she always brought an air of joy wherever she went.

"Was he mad?" Sara asked, not really wanting to hear the answer.

Esther said nothing, but showed Sara a fresh bruise on her arm.

"That Son of a-"

Esther made the *shh* gesture and tilted her head toward Rosie.

"Sorry."

Esther looked down and pulled at a lock of hair behind her ear. "Truth is, I thought I could calm him down. I thought the worst would come to me. But he likes his negro girls. One was never enough for him. Back on the plantation… when he would take our women… he would make our men watch, just to show 'em who's boss." Esther was lost in thought for a moment, then she snapped out of it. "Sara, he sent some men out to look for you. They're searching the camps, so it's just a matter of time before they come here. I'm sorry, but you can't stay here."

Rosie spoke up. "Where will you go, Miss Sara?"

"I don't really know, but I hope that my friends are looking for me. I just don't know where they'll be."

Sara had to sit down for a moment to collect her thoughts. She didn't know where to go, but she also didn't want to stay long enough to think about it too much. She thanked Naomi and John Brown, and walked out of the cabin clutching her purse close to her chest. Walking along the road, Sara was alone, and felt more lonely than ever before. *I don't know where to go… I guess I've got until I get to the center of town to think about it. I can't go back to the boarding house without money. Anyway, old Mrs. Lillibridge hates me. And Crown is looking for me. Will the girls help me again? Is that too much to ask?*

Sara was snapped out of her conversation with herself by the sound of approaching horses, their hooves pounding on the dirt road. She looked up to see a group of men on horseback coming right toward her. Her heart seemed to stop for a moment, and when it started again, all she could do was look around desperately, but there was nowhere to go. Only more deserted dirt road in each of the four compass directions, and open fields in between. Nowhere to run that might provide a place to hide. With no other options, she turned down a side road that she hoped would lead to a less deserted part of town. But the horses were much too fast, and soon she heard them turning the same corner behind her and closing in fast. The next thing Sara knew, she was forced to stop running, surrounded by four horsemen. Their leader was Chatham County Sheriff George Bartleby, and the others were three brothers with a nasty reputation: Bernard, Blaise, and Brant De la Croix.

Sara fumbled with her oversized purse. *Pepper spray!* But the bandage on her hand caught on the zipper of the purse, and she couldn't move her hand around enough to dig through the purse. Tears streamed down her face as she pulled at the bandage, and finally pulled her hand free. Then she remembered that she didn't have that pepper spray. The airport security guards had taken it from her back in Chicago. She stopped, and looked up from the purse to face the men.

"Is that her?" Bernard was unwinding a rope from his saddle.

Sheriff Bartleby nodded. "Yep. That's her. Mr. Crown says bring her back in one piece."

"But he said we could break her in, right?"

"Yep. He said we could break her in."

CHAPTER 4
NO WOMAN NO CRY

The hard metal of the handcuffs felt especially cold on this hot August Jamaica morning. Jimmy cringed under the merciless hands of the Kingston police as they shoved him forward. They shoved and pulled and pushed as he stumbled down the mountain path to the nearest road and the waiting police jeeps. Then the bumpy and bruising ride down into the city, and before he knew it, Jimmy was in a cage. *At least the cuffs are off*, he thought as he rubbed his wrists. He sat on the concrete bench, looking around at the stark cell, wondering how he was going to get out. Others who were arrested at Pinnacle yard were being brought in, but no sign of K-Ron or the white girl. As Jimmy sat there, thinking about the passing of time, with no information on Sara or Wordman, he started to feel the nervous tension of a mission that was slipping through his fingers. He stood up and paced the floor. After a while, he went to the bars and stuck his face through as far as it would go. "Hey! Hey you!" Jimmy waved his arms in the direction of an officer with his feet up on a desk.

The desk officer didn't look up from his Dick Francis novel. "Quiet you!"

"Hey! I'm American!" Jimmy exaggerated his Chicago accent just a little. "I was just going on a hike, and they arrested me. I'm sorry if I was trespassing, I didn't know that was private land."

"Not private. Restricted."

"Restricted, then. I didn't know. I'm very sorry, but it was just a mistake. I didn't mean to break the law."

"Let's see your passport, then."

"I left it at my hotel."

"Which hotel?"

"The Half Moon." Jimmy knew that if he could get them to believe he was a wealthy American staying at the most prestigious hotel in Kingston, they might let him go.

The officer sighed. "Alright then. Wait a while, and as soon as we can spare a couple of men, we'll take you to your hotel. Show us your passport, and we'll drop the charges."

Of course Jimmy didn't have a passport from the 1970s, but he was one step closer to freedom. After an hour or so, two officers came to the holding cell, opened the door, and put Jimmy back in handcuffs. Jimmy frowned. "Is that really necessary? I don't want my associates to see me like this. Could be bad for business."

The officers looked at each other and shrugged. "Alright. Just 'til we get to the hotel, then." They ushered him out to a four-door jeep and helped him into the back seat.

All the way to the Half Moon Resort, the two officers fired questions at Jimmy. Questions meant to check his story. "Are you here on holiday, or business? With family, friends, or colleagues? What business are you in? How long are you staying?" They meant to see if Jimmy hesitated in his answers, or got tripped up in any way that would tip them off to something fishy. But Jimmy just casually fired back the answers he was making up as he went along. Eventually they arrived at the hotel. But although Jimmy knew about the hotel, he had never actually stayed there. So when they were taking the handcuffs off, and the officers gave it one last attempt at trying to figure out if Jimmy was lying, he knew he was at the mercy of a 50-50 chance. "Nice to be so close to the beach, but too bad they don't have a swimming pool."

Damn, Jimmy thought. *If this is a trick question, and they do have a pool... But if it's an innocent question, and they don't have a pool... Or if it's a trick question, and they don't have a pool, but they're thinking ahead and expecting me to be ready for a trick question...* Jimmy stepped down out of the jeep and made his decision. "Oh, that's okay. Who needs a pool when you have the Caribbean."

It was clear he had made the wrong choice when both officers drew their guns and ordered him back into the jeep. But there was no going back to that cell. Jimmy kicked the jeep door wide open, which knocked one of the officers down. The other hesitated just long enough for Jimmy to run in front of a group of tourists, preventing the officer from shooting in his direction. Then Jimmy ducked behind a cabana, and around to the other side of the building, with the two officers in close pursuit.

✝✝✝

Sara stared at the four horsemen surrounding her, gripping her purse tight to her chest, and fighting to hold back tears.

Brant, the youngest of the De la Croix brothers, fidgeted with his reins. "Are we gonna do her right here?"

Sheriff Bartleby shrugged. "What the hell, there's nobody around."

Blaise laughed loudly. "You go first, Brant. If we're gonna break her in, the smallest one should go first." The other three men laughed while Brant muttered curses under his breath.

"I'll go first." Bernard started getting down from his horse. Sara could feel her whole body starting to shake. She did her best to stand still, but she couldn't control the trembling.

BAM-BAM-BAM, BLAM-BLAM-BLAM-BLAM-BLAM-BADDA-BAM-BADDA-BAM

Sara nearly jumped out of her shoes, but then she quickly recognized the sound. It was firecrackers - lots of them. All four of the horses bucked and jumped, throwing the men to the ground, and then running off in random directions. Bernard landed on his head and was knocked unconscious, and the other three were sucking air from getting the wind knocked out of them. Then another man on a horse rode right up to where Sara was standing. It took all her courage to look up at the man. He was wearing a cowboy hat and smoking a cigar.

"Colum?"

Colum smiled. "Howdy Ma'am."

Now she couldn't help it, the tears streamed down her face, as she sobbed loudly.

Colum reached down and pulled her up onto his horse, and they galloped away down the road toward the town. Sara held Colum tight around his waist and pressed her face into his back, her tears soaking his shirt. They didn't even turn around to look at the sheriff and his men, left behind in the dust. Colum just kept on kicking the horse until they were in the center of town with plenty of people around. Then Colum let the horse walk, and continued on going north through the center of town up to Bryan Street.

When they reached Mrs. Lillibridge's boarding house, Colum pulled back on the reins and brought the horse to a stop. Sara jumped off as quickly as she could, happy to be on familiar ground again. She took a step back to look at Colum. "Is it really you? How did you find me?"

Colum smiled and looked around. "You know… this place – this time – feels almost like home. Horses and carriages. It's like there's this peace and quiet that I didn't even know I missed."

"But how did you find me?"

"Yeah, that took some doing. We saw your newspaper ad. Three-legged horse, ha! That was funny. But that infernal machine dropped me off in a place called Conneck-tickut. In case you don't know, it's nowhere near here. I had to stow away on a ship that brought me down the coastline as far as a place called Charles-town, South Carolina. Then, I walked. And I've been walking for four days. I finally got to Savannah yesterday. Have you seen Chris?"

"No, I haven't seen him – did he come, too? And where did you get those firecrackers?"

"In a very confusing place called Chinatown. We had to walk through there on our way back from the big statue of freedom because Chris wanted to buy some numb-nuts."

"Num-chucks?"

"Right. What did I say? Anyway, I got here and started asking around if anyone knew you, or knew where you were. But no one could tell me anything. So I decided to stay in this boarding house for the night, and I met Mr. Gleason and Mr. Kennedy – I believe you know them?"

The door of the boarding house opened, and young Tom Kennedy stepped out. He was looking back toward the inside, finishing a conversation with Mrs. Lillibridge. "Yes, ma'am, we do need rain, indeed. Oh, hello Mr. O'Connell. And Miss Sara! I'm so glad you found her."

"What is this, an Irish family reunion?" Sara was annoyed that Colum still hadn't gotten around to telling her how he found her on that road. She turned and whispered to Colum, "It's like *Gone with the Wind* around here, with all the Kennedys and O'Connells – when is Scarlet O'Hara going to show up?" The volume of her voice began to increase. "And now that I think about it, why is it that so many slave owners were Irish? And Catholic?" Sara's whole body tensed as the realization sunk in that Colum – and everyone now around her – came from a world in which slavery was legal. Her stomach turned a bit as she looked at Colum and took another step back, farther away from him.

"Don't look at me," Colum said. "The Popes said slavery was a sin two hundred years before I was born, so if Catholics owned slaves, it wasn't because the Church said it was okay."

Sara squinted at Colum.

"So I got that going for me." Colum gave Sara a weak smile.

"Look, right now we've got bigger problems," Sara gestured for Tom to come closer so she could talk to the two men in a low voice. "I happen to know that a terrible yellow fever epidemic is coming here very soon." She looked at Colum, "We have to get out of here." Then she looked at Tom, "I mean, we have to get out of town as soon as possible."

"How do you know this?" Colum asked.

"Trust me. I learned about it in college. I majored in pre-med."

Tom was confused. "Who is Major Preemhead?"

Sara just went on. "We can't stay here. Crown is not going to give up looking for me. We need to disappear until we can find Chris and get back home."

"You need to become a ghost." Solomon Gleason had come out of the house and joined the group on the porch. When they responded to his comment with confused stares, he explained himself. "What I mean is, you need to hide with the ghosts. Hide in someplace that's supposed to be haunted. Crown would never go there – no one who ever owned slaves would go there." More confused stares. "Look, everyone knows that anyone who ever had slaves is terrible frightened to die, because they're sure they will be tormented by the souls of the slaves they beat and maimed. Many a powerful man has called his former slaves to his deathbed to beg for their forgiveness, so he can die in peace."

"Really?" Sara was surprised at the combination of superstition and guilt.

"Yes indeed," Gleason continued. "The irony is, the only ones who ever forgive their former masters are the ones who got religion – even though those same masters tried to prevent them from learning to read the Bible."

Sara's voice took on a tone of urgency. "What's the closest haunted house?"

"Now wait a minute," Colum objected. "I'm not really-"

Gleason chuckled. "In Savannah? Can't swing a dead cat without hitting a house that's supposed to be haunted. But if you want an empty one, I would suggest the Willink House. Corner of Price and Perry, near the Brick Wall Cemetery." Gleason pointed down the road in the direction of Price Street.

"Yeah, I heard about that one." Sara said absent-mindedly digging through her purse. "The lady drowned, and now she haunts the house."

"That's what they say. But before the war it was used as a secret school for slave children. You should be able to get in through the root cellar. Door's in the back."

Sara grabbed Colum by the arm and started leading him in the direction that Gleason had pointed.

"Wait a minute!" Colum protested. "A haunted house? Are you serious? Can't we talk about this? Are there no other options? Aren't we taking the horse?"

†††

K-Ron was happy to see Jimmy show up at his food stand, and quickly agreed to help him find a place to hide among the Rastas of Kingston's Trenchtown. Jimmy followed K-Ron through the makeshift shacks and lean-tos, around the tree stumps and garbage, to a place where several Rastamen were sitting in a circle around a fifty gallon drum. It was clear that at night there would be a fire in that drum, but for the moment, it was nothing more than a landmark, a place for people to gather. Jimmy knew the police would be looking for him, but hoped they would at least buy the lost American story enough to assume he wouldn't be hiding among the Rastas.

Soon Jimmy noticed that two of the men stood out from among the others. They were "nubbies," just beginning to grow their dreadlocks, and they were drinking from a bottle in a paper bag. Since Rastafarians didn't usually drink alcohol, it all seemed a bit out of place. Jimmy raised his voice to get everyone's attention. "Greetins and reespek. I an I give tanks to de Almighty! Me waan aks uno you - Di ya see a mon, a baldhead Jake? Him Babylon fa certain – 'im called Donald Wordman. Me mus find 'im, or kill me dead, ya nuh see it?" A few of the Rasta men looked at Jimmy for a moment, then looked away. Most of them ignored him, and no one said anything. "Di ya see a brownin' gal? Har name she called Sara. Me need find har, too." Still no one said anything. Frustrated, Jimmy sat down on a cinder block to think.

After a while, one of the nubbies walked up to Jimmy and stood over him. "Wa ya dween hya? Yan nuh b'lang hya. Wa ya nuh gwaan?"

Without looking up, Jimmy spoke softly, in perfect American, "Judging by your nubbies, and the fact that you're drinking rum, I'd say you don't belong here either. So I could ask you the same question." He looked up at the pretender. "What are *you* doing here?"

The fake Rastaman reached into a pocket and produced a switchblade knife. Jimmy was on his feet in a split second and the instant the knife snapped open, Jimmy grabbed the attacker's wrist, pushing the knife hand away from himself. Then he stepped in and spun his elbow into the man's head, stunning him long enough to catch him in a headlock. Still holding the knife hand by the wrist, Jimmy held the attacker in a choke until he passed out. His fellow nubbie watched the whole thing in shock, and then ran off. As Jimmy released the headlock and let the man's body drop to the ground, he noticed the white girl with the blond dreadlocks standing there watching him. K-Ron directed a few Rastamen to drag the would-be stabber's unconscious body off somewhere out of the way, while Jimmy picked up the switchblade, closed it, and put it into his own pocket. Then he walked over to where Molly Mallone was standing with her arms folded.

"Not bad," she said. "You've had some training."

"Why do you think he came at me like that?"

"Same reason his pal came at me last night on the bridge. His cover was blown."

"Who were those guys?"

"I couldn't say."

"Okay then. Who are you? I mean, who are you really?"

"I told you. The name's Molly."

"Mm hmm." Jimmy's voice was heavy with skepticism. "I noticed you fold your arms without crossing them. Same as I was taught. So you're ready for any surprises?"

"Nah, I just fold my arms like this to keep from wrinkling my sleeves."

"You didn't seem to be worried about wrinkling your sleeves last night." Jimmy tentatively moved a bit closer and lowered his voice. "You killed that guy. Just snapped his neck."

"Had to be done."

"Because *your* cover was blown?"

"The more important question right now is whether I can trust you to keep what you saw to yourself. Or do I have to break your neck, too?"

Jimmy didn't say anything for a moment, then shrugged. "Who am I gonna tell? I'm on the lam myself."

In the evening, the Rastas cooked some small fish over the fire in the fifty gallon drum. Jimmy tried to make small talk with Molly, hoping to get more information and figure out whether she could be trusted. "I thought Rastafarians were vegetarians. I guess they eat fish, though, huh?"

"They eat small fish, but not the bigger ones. Big fish are predators, like Babylon."

"Oh." Quickly running out of small talk, Jimmy noticed that people were watching him closely, and with suspicion, so he brought a few of the Rastas sitting nearby into the conversation. "Jahmekya hab a black prime minister, no?"

One of the Rastas took the bait. "Had. New one a white baldhead. An I an I nuh Jahmekyan. I an I Nazarite. I an I a David, and Babylon a Goliath."

"A true," Jimmy said. "But layta David craven. Even David sin. All dutty politricks. So, repatriation, sight? Or reform Jahmekya?" Jimmy knew this would start a debate among the Rastas that would take the focus off of himself. The younger Rastas were more aware of the poverty in Africa, and wanted to reform Jamaica. The older ones idealized Ethiopia as Zion and longed to "return" there. The younger men chanted their slogans, *Liberation in Jamaica*, and *Liberation before Repatriation*. By this time Molly had wandered off away from the circle around the fire. Jimmy took the opportunity to follow her. At first, he couldn't see where she went, but after moving to the outskirts of the shantytown, he saw a flash of white skin in a telephone booth on the corner under the lights of a liquor store. Jimmy was able to move close without being seen, and so he snuck up behind Molly to see if he could hear what she was saying.

She was leaving a message on an answering machine. "Hey, Mike. It's me. Did you check out the blues at Kingston Mines, like I told you? I'm seeing a comedy trio, but one of them got fired from the show. But I still don't know the day and time of their performance. Also, there's a new act in town. Calls himself Jimmy Delaney. Weird, right? I don't know if his act is good or bad. I'll call in again tomorrow." Then she hung up. Jimmy knew a coded message when he heard one. He knew she was telling her handler that she was in Kingston, but things weren't going so well. That's why she mentioned the blues. No doubt if things were going according to plan she would have recommended jazz. The comedy trio must be the nubbies and their friend in the tam, pretending to be Rastas. Molly was telling this Mike person that there were three of them, and the one who got fired is the one she killed. Jimmy wondered what their "performance" might be. Clearly Molly wasn't sure if Jimmy could be trusted, and Jimmy wondered whose side she was on.

When Molly turned around to exit the phone booth, she saw Jimmy standing there, and she could tell that he had been listening. She pushed her way past him, and then, without warning, turned around and shoved him into the phone booth. Surprised, he stumbled backward, and she closed the glass doors. Before Jimmy could get back on his feet, Molly had picked up a broken piece of wood from the ground and shoved it through the door handles of the phone booth. Jimmy was locked in, and Molly just turned and walked away.

✝✝✝

Sara and Colum didn't speak at all for a long time. They each settled into the least uncomfortable spot they could find in the basement of the Willink house, and just waited in silence, listening. What they were listening for, they didn't really know. Maybe they were listening for the sound of Crown's men out looking for Sara. Maybe they were listening for the sound of old Mrs. Willink haunting the place. As they looked around the root cellar, they took note of their surroundings. Dirt floor. Stone walls. Wooden cabinets on one side. A single small window above them. And the wooden steps leading up to the angled door. As the sun moved across the afternoon sky, the light dimmed. Their stomachs ached with hunger and their thoughts began to turn to what they were going to do next. Colum spoke first, in a low whisper. "Chris wasn't at the meeting point. We agreed to meet at noon at the railroad station, but I have no idea if he's already here, or if he hasn't arrived yet. I'm going to have to keep going back there every day at noon until we find him."

"What if he doesn't show up?" Sara whispered back. "We have to get out of town before the yellow fever epidemic hits or we could die a horrible death here – we don't belong here!"

"I don't know what else to do. If we don't know where Chris is, we also don't know where the time machine is. We can't get back without him, even if we wanted to."

"How did you find me on that road?" Sara was mindlessly sweeping the floor around her with her hand, pushing the dust and small pieces of debris against the stone wall.

"Mrs. Lillibridge introduced me to those girls you met, and they sent me to the John Wesley hotel – which is not the kind of hotel a respectable girl like you should be going to, by the way. Anyway, at the hotel I met a very nice man named Dickey-Jim Crown. He gave me this cigar, in fact."

"Colum, Crown is not a good man!"

"Relax. I know what he is. A man you can trust doesn't have his office in a whore house. Anyway, I could tell he was anxious to find you, which meant he didn't know where you were. He said I should let him know if I found you, so he could feel better about your safety. Hmpf. When I left, I just followed his men."

After a while Sara noticed that she could no longer see the dust and debris on the floor. The room was now quite dark. Although they didn't say it, both Sara and Colum were constantly reminded that the house was supposed to be haunted. The conversation got progressively louder, in a subconscious attempt to make their surroundings feel more normal. "It's getting dark."

"Yeah."

"How long do you think we should stay here?"

"Long enough to be sure Crown's men have quit for the day. A little while longer."

Sara began to feel a bit claustrophobic in the root cellar. "I really don't want to stay down here any longer."

Neither one of them dared to say it, but they both started to feel as though they were not the only ones in that basement. "Just a little longer," Colum said, fighting the urge to stand up. "Here, I'll light a match so it's not so dark." He pulled a small box of matches from his pocket and scratched one across the stone wall. The flame flared up a light that flickered shadows all around them. In the light of the match, Sara and Colum could see that the cabinet doors – all of which had been closed a moment ago – were now open. Without a word, Sara ran for the door, and Colum followed close behind, lighting the way with his match. The root cellar door swung open with a bang, and the two of them ran out into the humid Savannah night air. They didn't look left or right, but just kept running in a straight line away from the Willink house. But after running only one block, they found themselves at the high brick wall of the old cemetery.

Sara recognized the road. She grabbed Colum's hand and pulled him to the left and without a word just started running south toward the camp of former slaves and their log cabins. After a while, they got tired and slowed to a walk. It was pitch dark now, except for a sliver of moonlight. Both of them started to worry that they might get lost, but neither one spoke. Eventually, they could see faint lights coming from the fires in the cabins. They walked to John and Naomi's cabin, and Sara knocked on the door.

"Hello? It's Sara. Um, I need some help."

The door opened to reveal a shirtless John Brown.

"Oh, I'm sorry." Sara looked away.

"Nothin' to be sorry about," John answered, and he turned away from the door to motion for them to come in. As he turned, Sara saw his back. The scars looked like a huge tree across his back. Sara gasped and covered her mouth. Her eyes started to fill up with tears. "Oh, that." John said. "That's from the chinkey-pen switch."

Sara tried to regain her composure. "What's a... chinkey...?"

Colum whispered, "Like a cat-o-nine-tails, but with metal chinks on it."

"Least I still got both my arms," John said.

Sara gasped again. "I saw men without their arms. They cut off people's arms?"

"If you raised your arm against your master. Yes, they took it."

"That's enough talk of those times," It was Esther. She was seated near the back of the cabin, next to Rosie, who was lying on a mat. "I'm trying to get Rosie to sleep. Now go to sleep little girl, or old Rene will come and get you."

"Oh mama," Rosie said. "I'm not a little girl. I'm too old to be scared of Rene."

"Who's Rene?" Sara whispered.

"You don't know the story of Rene?" Naomi said. "He was a giant, a monster who killed children. Townsfolk rose up and lynched him. But he came back from the grave, and kept right on killing." Naomi's eyes widened, and Rosie pulled her blanket up to her eyes.

Naomi ushered Sara and Colum all the way in, and closed the door behind them. Then she looked Colum up and down, and Colum became uncomfortably aware of his minority status as the only white person in the cabin.

Sara noticed everyone looking at Colum. "Oh, sorry. This is my… friend, Colum."

"You'll stay here for the night," Esther said, still staring at Colum. "But Crown's men will be out looking for you again in the morning, so you'll have to find somewhere else to go. It won't be safe here."

John put on his shirt, and brought out three tinplated cans, and a can opener. Two of the cans contained condensed milk, and the third contained biscuits.

As he opened the cans, Sara smiled at him and asked, "Did you hunt these yourself, Mr. Brown?"

John smirked and said what he always said. "Stealing is a kind of hunting."

Sara thought about Wordman for the first time since she arrived in Savannah. *He's a politician who lives on the assumption that the end justifies the means. But the sad thing is, by treating their slaves worse than their livestock, slavers taught these people to live by the same assumption. They had to steal to survive, so they came to believe that stealing was acceptable. Why is it that so many people believe that the only thing you can do that's wrong is get caught?* Sara broke her biscuits into perfect quarters before eating the sections one at a time. She looked around the one room cabin. *I'm going to sleep here again. With all these people in the same room. Hmm. So much for privacy.*

Colum could see that Sara was staring off into space again. He wanted to reach out to her, to be strong for her. He wanted to rescue her. But he was in no position to be anyone's savior. He might feel more comfortable in the nineteenth century, but in reality he was just as lost as she was. All of a sudden, Sara noticed Colum staring at her. "What are you looking at?"

"Nothing. I mean, not nothing. You, actually. I was just looking at you."

"Why?"

"I, um. No reason."

Esther smiled and looked away from the scene as she twisted her hair behind her ear.

Colum could see John take Naomi's hand. For a moment, he felt inspired. "Alright. Um… there is a reason." John Brown's eyebrows went up, as Sara turned to face Colum. "I like you, Sara."

"Oh, for God's sake," Sara was embarrassed.

"Just listen to me for a moment," Colum went on. "I know I joke a lot, but this is serious. A man needs a woman. I mean… a wife. I used to think a man had to make his fortune before he could find a wife, but now I think…"

"Whoa, just stop right there," Sara put up her hands. "You *like* me? And you need a *wife*? You don't even know me. I've been wondering if I can even have white *friends*, let alone a white... oh never mind. This is crazy."

Colum looked around the room. "I don't think it matters, your skin color... my skin color. People are all the same, no matter what color they are. There's good people and bad people of any color. And I think you're one of the good ones."

"ONE OF THE GOOD ONES?" At this, Rosie woke up, and Esther gave Sara a look. But Sara just went on, "Are you kidding me? You expect me to fall for you because you say I'm one of the good ones? Well forget it, Colum! I won't thank you for saying I'm an exception to my people! I won't betray my own people just to be called acceptable by you."

"I didn't mean it like that! I meant... you know, there are good black people and bad black people, just like there are good white people and bad white people."

"Save your excuses!" Sara got up from the table as if to walk away, but the cabin was so small there was nowhere to walk. She paced the length of the front wall, keeping her face turned away from Colum.

"Sara, I'm sorry." Colum got up to follow her pacing. "That came out wrong. I really didn't mean... look I was trying to say that I really like you." His voice lowered to a whisper. "I thought maybe we could go on a couple dates, then after our third date we could have some sex, and you know, see how it goes."

"WHAT?"

"What's the big deal? I mean, I'm sure I wouldn't be the first white guy you…"

"Stop right there!" Sara growled through gritted teeth.

Esther spoke up, "Yes, both of you please stop this talk. Rosie's awake." Immediately both Sara and Colum felt self-conscious for having their argument in front of the others.

Sara lowered her head and looked down to avoid Esther's eyes. "I'm so sorry," she said. Then she looked at John and Naomi. "I'm sorry. I'm very thankful for a place to sleep tonight." Then she looked at Colum. "We aren't done with this conversation. But if you think I'm going to fall for a racist who calls me a slut… well, you've been watching way too much TV."

Colum buried his face in his hands. "No. That's not what I meant."

John spoke up. "I think you've said enough, boy. Better hold your tongue for a while."

Colum took the advice and didn't say anything more for the rest of the night. Eventually, when Esther got Rosie back to sleep, the adults sat around the table wondering what to do next.

John Brown said, "I wish we could help you more, Miss Sara. But it won't be safe to stay here."

"Thank you. I know you're putting yourselves at risk to hide us here," Sara said. "But we'll be going tomorrow. We have to find our other friend, and then we can go home. I hope."

"Where is this friend of yours?"

Sara looked at Colum, but he didn't answer. "He's supposed to meet us at the railway station. But we don't know what day he's getting into town."

"Railway station's haunted, you know."

"Oh, for crying out loud, is anything not haunted in this town?"

John, Naomi, and Esther just looked at each other and shrugged. Naomi said, "When a town has seen as much suffering and death as this one… and the railway station, well that's built on over a battlefield from the revolution. A thousand people died there in just one hour. After the battle, they buried 'em so fast, a lot of 'em were buried alive."

Sara shuddered. "Well, we don't believe in ghosts, do we Colum?"

Colum didn't say anything, but just raised his eyebrows and shrugged, as if to say, *Don't ask me.*

Esther spoke up. "Socrates. He'll know what to do."

Now Colum spoke, "The philosopher?"

"The barber," John answered.

"He's a root doctor," Naomi corrected, giving John a disapproving look. "Yes, he is a barber, but he's also a root doctor. Used to be a tobacco sorter – they have the *knowing* powers – now he deals in root."

"Root?" Sara thought it sounded like superstition.

"Yes, root," Naomi continued. Then seeing the confused expressions on Colum and Sara's faces, she whispered, "Conjures."

Esther joined in on the whispering. "Last fall, the Boo Hag put the mouth on Mrs. Anderson, the police chief's wife. But Socrates got rid of the conjure with the dirt from a preacher's grave."

John looked disgusted. "Oh, that old Boo Hag ain't nothin' but a bitty. She couldn't cast a spell with a fishin' rod."

"Yeah, I met her," Sara said. "She seems pretty crazy, though."

"Socrates is a wise man," Naomi said. "He'll know what to do. You go see him tomorrow. First thing."

"Well, we have nowhere else to go at this point," Sara said. "We just need to check for our friend at the railroad station at noon."

As the fire died down, so did the talking. Colum took a spot near the fire to lay down. *Heaven's hearth is reserved for the poor*, he muttered to himself.

Sara was beginning to feel the weight of an oppressive thought. *What if we don't find Chris? What if the time machine never comes back here? What if Sofia can't get us back? She got my message in the newspaper ad, but the decision to send two people back to find me means we don't know where the time machine is. If Colum had come back for me alone, at least he would know where he left it. Now we're running out of time. Crown's men are looking for me, and the epidemic is coming. We have to move, but all we can do is wait.*

Esther was sitting over Rosie, watching her sleep. Sara walked over to her and sat down. After a while, Sara whispered, "Is he her father? Crown, I mean."

"No, thank the Lord. But that's why he can't stand to see her. She reminds him that someone else had me first. But I suppose if he was her daddy, that might make things better for her." After a while, Esther whispered, "I had another one."

"Another one?"

"Another daughter." Esther's expression was blank, her eyes and her thoughts were far away. "I had my first little girl. But days were long then. Folks slept hard. Too hard. One morning… I woke up, and she was underneath me… I tried to wake her… but she was already with the Lord." Sara's eyes filled with tears as Esther went on. "I like to think he was saving her from…" The two women clung to each other and cried silently.

†††

The iron door slammed into place, leaving Jimmy alone in a padded room. He had tried to get out of that phone booth. He even tried breaking the glass. But the more he tried to escape, the more attention he attracted, and it was only a matter of time before the police showed up. And this time, there was no chance of tricking them into thinking he was a rich tourist out for a hike. He had tried to talk his way out of being arrested again by telling the police the only thing he could think of that might interest them. In three years' time, someone was going to try to assassinate Bob Marley. But Jimmy's plan backfired. The only reason the police could accept that Jimmy would know about the assassination attempt was that he was in on it. But since they couldn't put him on trial for a crime they thought he might commit in three years, the judge had him committed to the hospital's psychiatric ward. It had all happened so fast that Jimmy didn't have time to make a plan to try to escape. All alone in the cell, he punched the padded wall out of frustration. He paced around a while, and then put his face up to the small opening in the door to try to see down the hallway.

Then he heard a voice. "Psst! You dere!" Jimmy could hear the voice, but couldn't tell where it was coming from.

"Are you talking to me?"

"All depends. You a political prisoner?"

Jimmy thought for a moment. "I suppose I am."

"What be you name?"

"Jimmy. Jimmy Delaney."

"Bah. Neba 'eard of you."

"Okay, what's your name?"

"Howell. Leonard Howell."

"Well, I never heard of you Leonard Howell."

"Then ya nuh fram 'round hya."

"True true. Any weh a go step out a hya, Leonard Howell?"

"Eff so, I an I nuh be hya all dis time."

"A true."

Jimmy pulled his head back into his cell, and sat on the floor. He tried to drown out the sound of Howell preaching into the hallway so he could make a plan for his escape. Since there was no chair or bench in the cell, all he could do was lay back and stare up at the ceiling, while Howell went on about kingdoms, and the coronation of Haile Salassie of

Ethiopia, and Nazarite vows, and about all the characters in the Bible who were black, including Jesus.

Soon Jimmy found himself face to face with a young Dante Carona. There he was, in his bell bottom pinstripe pants, his leather vest with fringes on it, and his Village People moustache. Dante spoke, "Kid, you can't dish out what you haven't gotten. You have to take it before you can give it."

"You're not my father!" Jimmy woke himself up. *Shit. Still in the loony bin.* The hallway was quiet, and Jimmy realized that he was exhausted. So even though he still didn't have a plan for escape, he gave in to the desire for sleep, and drifted off.

†††

Colum found himself in Dublin, standing on a bridge. He looked down at his hands and saw that he was holding a rope. The rope went over the edge of the bridge, and Colum could tell that something heavy was hanging at the other end of that rope. He looked over the edge of the bridge and saw the Roman priest hanging by his neck. He jumped back away from the edge of the bridge and the rope slipped through his hands. He instinctively tightened his grip on the rope, but as he held onto it, he looked down again and in his hand was a torch. When he looked up, he could see the family cottage, engulfed in flames. In the doorway, he could see the vague outline of his mother, Mary. *Mother! Mother!* he screamed. *Come out!* But instead of coming out of the burning cottage, she slowly turned around and went inside, closing the door behind her as the fire overtook the whole cottage. *No! Mother! I'm sorry! I'm sorry!* Colum looked down again at the torch in his hand, but it was gone. He looked up to see the Whitefriar Chapel. He knew it was about to explode, but he could not stop it from happening. He stood there staring at the church and waiting. Even though he knew it was coming, when it happened he was startled. As the wall blew outward, he woke up yelling, "I'm sorry!" and woke up everyone else in the cabin. "I'm sorry," he repeated, this time softly. "I had a, um, a dream."

"What was your dream about?" Rosie asked.

"Now Rosie, that isn't polite," Esther scolded.

"No, it's okay," Colum said, rubbing his eyes. "I was dreaming about my mother. You see… she died a long time ago."

"Oh," Rosie said sadly, looking down at the floor. Esther put her arm around her daughter.

Sara sat up slowly. "Funny. I had a dream about my mother, too. But not Nancy. My birth mother, I guess. I was back home, in my room, and I was rearranging the furniture, and there was a knock at the door. I asked who it was, and there was this voice I've never heard before, saying she was my mother. I tried and tried to open the door, but I couldn't get it open. It was locked or something. I finally yanked it open, but there was no one there."

"Let's get you to Socrates," Naomi said. "It's almost dawn. You need to be gone from here before Crown's men start their search again."

John Brown agreed to take Colum and Sara to see the root doctor. He took his bow and arrows, and led them away from the cabins, and into the woods. They stayed in the trees to avoid being seen by Crown's men, as they circled around the southern edge of Savannah. Eventually, John led them out of the trees and into the open, not far from the railway yard. "Follow this road a ways up. You'll know Socrates' house by the haint blue door. After you meet him, you can see about your friend at the railway yard, just over there." And then he disappeared back into the woods.

"Wait, don't you need to introduce us?" Sara yelled as he disappeared into the trees.

Colum squinted in the bright dawn sunlight. "What's hate blue?"

"It's not *hate* blue, it's *haint* blue," Sara answered impatiently. "It's a ghost thing. Supposedly, evil spirits can't cross over a threshold that's painted to look like water."

"Then I'm gonna get me a haint blue suit."

"Mm hmm." Sara shook her head and started up the dirt road.

Colum walked fast to keep up with Sara. "Look we don't really have to go see this root doctor. I mean, if it's all a bunch of superstition, we can just forget about him and go try to find Chris."

"We could." Sara stopped walking, and Colum almost bumped into her. "But then if we see Esther again, if we need her help again, she'll ask about it, and if we didn't go, that will seem like we don't trust her. If she takes it personally, she might not help us anymore. And so far, she's about all I've got." Sara started walking again, and Colum followed, but kept a bit of distance. He knew he was still getting the cold shoulder from her after their conversation the night before.

When they came to the blue door, neither one of them wanted to knock.

"Do you think he's even up yet?" Colum said, hoping to postpone their meeting with the root doctor.

"How should I know?" Sara didn't bother to hide the annoyance in her voice. "I suppose John wouldn't have brought us here this early if he thought the guy was still in bed." Sara stepped up to the door and knocked hard. Then she ran around the corner of the little house, leaving Colum standing alone on the doorstep.

An older black man with a white beard answered the door, and when he saw that his visitor was white, he stood up as straight as he could, and smoothed out his shirt and pants. "What can I do for you, sir?"

"Are you the... uh... barber?"

"Yessir, I am at that. Best in town. Clean you up real good, if you don't mind me sayin' so, sir."

"No, I don't mind at all." Colum was glad to have a reason to be there other than roots and conjures. "I would like a, uh, haircut... I guess."

"Well, then, step inside, sir." At that moment Sara came around the corner, but Socrates didn't seem surprised. He just held the door for her to enter. Once the door was closed behind them, he said, "Haircuts cost money. You got money?" Colum and Sara looked at each other. "Didn't think so."

"Esther and Naomi sent us," Sara blurted. "John Brown brought us here. They thought you could help us."

"D.J. Crown is a powerful man," Socrates said.

"How did you know…?"

"Now if you could get me a toenail of his, or even a fingernail, I could cast the roots on him, but you'd still have to bury the sack in front of his house – I won't do that for you."

"No… um, thank you, sir. That's okay." Colum tried to find the words to ask for some kind of non-magical help.

"Thank you for the offer," Sara said, "but we really just need some advice. Or at least our friends thought you might be able to help."

"You're in luck. Advice is free. But I don't know what wisdom I have that will help you folks. Except that you shouldn't rightly be seen together."

Sara and Colum looked at each other again. Sara turned away. "That would be fine with me," she huffed, "but we need to find our friend. Another white boy, like him. He was supposed to meet us at the train station. You haven't heard of anyone like that around, have you? Someone looking for me, maybe? Or looking for him?"

"Can't say that I have. But you don't want to hang around the railway station. Too many angry shades there. Too many buried alive."

"Yes, we heard."

"All I can say is, most of the black folks in town will be at the tent meetin' tonight. If this fellow is lookin' for you, he might show up there."

"Okay, where is this tent meeting going to be?"

"Out at the meetin' grounds. Northwest of the railway station."

"What time?"

"What time, you ask? What time, indeed. At meetin' time. After sundown, whenever it starts. Until whenever it ends."

Sara and Colum said their goodbyes, and thanked the old root doctor, all the time wondering if seeing him had been a waste of their time. They made their way to the railway station, but when they got there they realized they were too early. As they wandered through the station, it seemed eerily vacant. They walked around looking for some sign that Chris had been there.

"Do you think he's been here, looking for us?" Colum asked, trying to draw Sara into a conversation.

"I don't know. If he was here, he could have left some kind of sign. Something we would recognize. Let's just keep looking."

"We could leave a sign for him." Colum was encouraged that Sara was willing to talk to him.

"True. What kind of sign?"

At that moment, Colum saw someone out of the corner of his eye. He could see the person's shadow moving out of sight around a corner. He tried to follow the person, to ask if anyone had seen Chris, but he stopped abruptly and fell to one knee. Sara could see that he was having trouble breathing. Colum gasped for air.

"I have to get out of here," he said, trying to inhale. Sara helped Colum to his feet, and they moved out of the station and sat down on a bench near the platform. There, Colum was able to catch his breath. "It was like I was suffocating. Like I was…"

"Buried alive?"

"You don't really think…?"

"No, but we can't stay here." Sara and Colum moved away from the railway station, and found a place to hide where they could still see the station, but wouldn't be seen from the road. They waited there for over two hours, hoping to see Chris appear at the station. But no one came. Conversation was sparse and tense, as both Sara and Colum worried that they might be stuck in the nineteenth century for good. Each of them wondered whether they could survive here, even without a coming yellow fever epidemic. When it was clearly well past noon, Colum finally said, "What do we do now?"

Sara thought for a moment. "We have to lay low until night. Then we can go to the tent meeting and see if Chris shows up there. But in the meantime… all I can think of is… well, you won't like it."

Colum and Sara found Solomon Gleason at the Davenport house, working on the railings. They didn't call out to him, for fear of drawing attention to themselves, so when they sidled up to him, he was startled at first.

"Oh! Oh, forgive me. Hello Miss Sara, Mr. O'Connell. What can I do for you?"

Sara looked at Colum and gestured for him to speak, so Colum started. "Mr. Gleason, can we trust you to keep our whereabouts a secret from the men who are looking for us?"

"I don't like Crown, or his men," Gleason answered. "I have no loyalty to him."

"Well, I guess that's good enough for us. We need a place to hide. Like the last place, but maybe not quite as haunted."

Gleason smiled. "You started at the bottom. The Willink house is only a little haunted. Nowhere to go from there but more haunted."

Sara spoke up. "We don't believe in ghosts, Mr. Gleason."

Colum interrupted her, "Speak for yourself."

Gleason's smile left him and his voice got serious. "I can get you into the Marshall House Hotel."

Colum took a step back. "Isn't that the one they call the Saw House?"

"Yep. They say the doctors ran out of places to dispose of all the amputated limbs, so they just buried them in the house under the floor boards."

"Don't tell him that!" Sara didn't want to hear it herself.

Gleason walked with Sara and Colum toward the Marshall House. They stayed off of Broughton Street to avoid being seen, and moved along the smaller streets, cutting through yards and between houses. They came up to the Marshall House from the back, and Gleason got the back door open. He poked his head in and looked around but he didn't step over the threshold. "Yep. This is where they would have to bite the bullet."

Sara pushed Colum through the doorway, and then followed him in. When she turned around to thank Gleason, he was gone. Sara shut the door and whispered, "Stay away from the front windows."

There was some furniture, covered in sheets, in what must have been the parlor of the hotel. Sara took the lead to uncover a couch and chair, and move them away from the windows and out of sight. The movement of the couch made a terrible sound on the wooden floor, breaking through the silence with a great heaving and scraping. Then, more silence. Sara sat down. Colum wasn't sure what he was more afraid of, the ghosts or the possible conversation with Sara. He promised himself he wouldn't speak unless spoken to. He sat down in the chair farthest from Sara, as dust was thrown up from the cushion, making him cough. The cough echoed in the mostly empty rooms of the hotel's ground floor. In the silence that followed, the ticking of a clock seemed to get louder and louder. Sara and Colum ignored the ticking, until they realized they were listening to it. *Tick. Tock. Tick. Tock. Tick. Tock. TICK. TOCK. TICK. TOCK. TICK…*

"Sara?" Colum mentally kicked himself for breaking his vow and speaking first.

"Yeah?"

"You hear that, right? The ticking sound?"

"Yeah, duh."

"It's a clock, right?"

"What else would it be?"

"Yeah, except... where's the clock?"

Sara looked around, but quickly realized that Colum had already done that, and there was no clock. Her body shivered and she could feel a chill on the back of her neck. She stiffened in her seat, and Colum also sat up in his chair. They both looked around the room, then strained their necks to see into the hallway and entryway. No clock.

"Well it has to be somewhere," Sara said.

Colum got up and moved slowly across the room. Now they could focus on nothing else but the sound of TICK. TOCK. TICK. TOCK. Colum moved out of the room and scanned the walls for a clock, but there was no clock. He checked the mantle above the fireplace. No clock. When he moved out of sight, Sara got up and followed him, deciding that the unknown was better than being left alone. They walked together slowly throughout the first floor of the hotel. The floorboards in the dining room creaked under their feet, which made them stop in their tracks and look down, as they remembered Gleason's words about the amputated limbs. Eventually they had looked over the entire first floor with no sign of a clock, and they came to the foot of the stairs and looked up toward the second floor. Neither of them wanted to go upstairs. They looked at each other, each one hoping the other would go first, when both realized that the house was silent.

"Shh!" Colum said.

"I wasn't saying anything," Sara whispered.

"Right. But don't say anything for a minute… You hear that?"

"No ticking."

"It stopped. I mean, you heard it, right?"

"Yeah, I heard it."

Then they both heard a loud creaking sound. Colum gripped the banister, and Sara grabbed onto Colum's shirt with both hands. *Footsteps.* Sara let out a little squeal. *Coming closer.* Sara tightened her grip on Colum's shirt.

"Hello? Miss Sara? It's me, Tom Kennedy."

Sara's shoulders relaxed as she loosened her grip on Colum's shirt.

Colum turned to face Kennedy. "How did you know we were here? We're supposed to be in hiding."

"I saw Mr. Gleason, and he told me you were here. He said you might be hungry, and he said I should bring you something to eat."

"You didn't tell anyone we're here, did you?" Sara asked.

"No. Just Mrs. Lillibridge. I had to get the food from somewhere."

Sara and Colum looked at each other. Sara shook her head as if to say, *We can't trust her.* But they were hungry, and the food provided a welcome diversion from thoughts of their haunted surroundings, the dangerous men who were after them, and the fact that they were stuck in 1876 with a yellow fever epidemic coming.

As Sara and Colum ate, Kennedy couldn't take the silence. "There are a lot of good people in Savannah." His comment seemed to come out of nowhere.

"Of course," Sara was caught off guard and realized she was speaking with her mouth full.

"I just mean that this Crown fellow, he's not what Savannah is. I've met some good people here. It's hard to tell sometimes, because they're so tense all the time. Trying to be polite, but always with the guilt of their past. Manners… are important to them."

Colum wasn't so sure. "Crown's men have no manners."

"But there's good men, too, like Mr. Gleason, or my uncle."

Colum gestured toward Sara. "Sara here is going to be a dentist. Sara, how do you know which teeth are the good teeth, and which teeth are the bad teeth? The ones that need to be pulled."

Sara thought for a moment. "So we're using teeth as a metaphor for people? I guess you can't just go by the part you can see. A tooth can be all polished on the top, but underneath, it can be rotten. You have to look underneath. Seems to me Savannah is like a mouth full of pearly white teeth, but if you look at the roots, some of those teeth are rotten. Crooked teeth can be straightened. Crooked people… I don't know."

After Kennedy left, the hotel was more quiet than ever. Now the sun was getting low in the sky and the light coming in the windows was making strangely shaped shadows. Colum and Sara sat in silence, periodically perking up at the sound of creaking coming from nowhere in particular. They couldn't bring themselves to talk, so they waited and prayed for sundown as the shadows grew longer and the parlor grew darker. Suddenly, Colum sprang to his feet and ran toward the dining room. Sara jumped to her feet, but was too afraid to follow him. A moment later, Colum came back walking slowly, with his head hanging down.

"What?!" Sara demanded.

"Didn't you see him? Tell me you saw him."

"Him? Who?!" Sara was becoming more nervous.

"The... guy. The... he was right there!"

"Colum what are you saying, there's someone else here?"

"I thought so, but now I... I mean, no, I checked. I thought he went into the other room there, but I ran after him, and there's no one there. Nowhere he could have gone."

"Who did you see?"

"I don't know, some... man. Looked like a soldier. Only had one arm. I didn't see where he came from, I only saw him out of the corner of my eye – right there – he turned that corner, and then he was gone." Colum moved quickly back into the parlor and sat back down in his chair, throwing up another cloud of dust. "Shite." Sara just stood looking at him, wondering what to say or do next. The house was quiet again, and Sara sat down on the couch.

Just when Sara started thinking about the possibility of lighting a candle, she and Colum were startled by the sound of someone running in the hallway above them. The footsteps were loud, but they were close together, like the footsteps of a child. Now Colum was less willing to run after the sound. He looked at Sara, who had a terrified look on her face. He felt he had to do something, so he got up slowly, and walked over to the stairs. He looked up toward the second floor, but couldn't see anything. By this time the running had stopped. Colum decided not to go upstairs. He looked at the back door, then walked over to Sara.

"We should leave," he whispered.

Sara looked toward the front window and the street. She thought about Crown's men on horseback searching for her. "If anyone comes down those stairs," she whispered, "we can be out the door before they get to us. But if we go outside, and they see us, there won't be anywhere to run. I think we have to stay here for a little while longer."

Colum didn't want to seem less brave than Sara, so he sat back down in his chair. After a while, Sara lay down on the couch to get more comfortable. The hotel remained silent, and soon both Sara and Colum were asleep. *Tick. Tock. Tick. Tock. Tick. Tock...*

"Ahhh!" Both Colum and Sara were startled awake. "What?"

"What?" They stared at each other and Sara repeated, "WHAT?"

"I felt something... on me."

"Me too, like a hand, someone touching me on the arm."

"I felt it on the forehead. Like someone was, you know, checking to see if I had a fever."

Suddenly there were voices outside. Men calling to each other, "You go around back, we'll go in the front."

"Shite!" Sara and Colum jumped to their feet. Colum peeked out the front window, strangely glad to be facing a living threat. Crown's men were in front of the house, getting down from their horses. "C'mon!" he whispered. He grabbed Sara by the hand and they ran out the back door and across the yard. They almost made it to State Street before Crown's men spotted them. When Colum and Sara heard the men yelling, they turned on State Street and headed west. Cutting in between the buildings and running in a zig-zag pattern prevented Crown's men from keeping them in view, so they were able to keep going until they came to the railroad tracks. From there they could see the lights of the tent meeting. They crossed over the tracks and headed for the crowd gathered around the tent, and before Crown's men could catch up with them, they had disappeared into the crowd.

As they moved through the crowd, they scanned the faces, hoping to see Chris somewhere among the people. But most of the people there were black, which made Colum nervous that he might stand out. To make matters worse, everyone was standing still, all reciting the Lord's Prayer in unison, so Sara and Colum were the only ones moving around, and not praying.

"We have to hide," Colum whispered. They crouched down as they moved along the edge of the crowd. Soon the prayer was over and the preacher started making the invitation for people to come down to the front and confess their sins.

Colum felt vulnerable. *Don't call on me, don't call on me.*

A man raised his hand, and walked toward the podium. Colum could see that he was white. *So I'm not the only white guy here.* The man turned and Colum was surprised to see that he only had one arm. At that moment the crowd got quiet, and the man spoke.

"I know what you see when you look at me," he began.

Someone in the crowd yelled, "Old Sam!"

"Old Sam, indeed," the man went on. "I was the devil to you. I bought and sold your mothers and fathers, your brothers and sisters, I did." Gasps from the crowd. "I put 'em to work, and when they didn't work hard enough, I put 'em to the whip. And sometimes, when they raised their arm against me, I cut it off." More gasps from the crowd. "But God has punished me, as you can see. For when I went to war to fight for my right-" The man's voice caught in his throat as he suppressed his emotion. "To be able to own another human person, well, God took my arm. But he didn't take it quick. No, that would have been too good for me. He took it slow, first with a bullet, then with the gangrene, and then with the saw. And now I can't but walk past the old Marshall Hotel without feeling pain in the arm that ain't there no more. It hurts me just to walk by that house, and yet every day I do. I could avoid it, but I don't. And I'm not even sure why. I just know that I need some peace. So I stand before you now to ask for your forgiveness."

The black preacher hesitated for a moment, and then raised his head. "Brothers and sisters… let us lay hands on this man and pray for peace in his soul."

Colum and Sara could see Crown's men on their horses circling around the edge of the crowd on the opposite side of the tent. Then they started moving through the crowd. This time Sara took the lead and grabbed Colum's arm. "Let's go," she said. "It will take them a while to search the crowd. That will give us a head start."

As quickly as they could, Sara and Colum crouched their way out of the light from the tent meeting and made their way toward the railway station in the shadows. From there they followed the road past the root doctor's house, and headed for the woods on the south end of town. They got a bit turned around, though, and started to worry that by now Crown's men would know that they were not still in the crowd at the tent meeting. But they kept moving, and eventually they came to a cemetery with no wall around it. In the moonlight, they could see the outlines of a few old gravestones under a dead tree.

Sara had an idea. "Let's cut through the cemetery. Even if they catch up to us, they won't follow us through a cemetery at night."

"Are you joking? *I* wouldn't follow us through a cemetery at night."

"You gotta be a twenty-first century man, Colum. Let's go."

"Shite."

Colum was looking behind them when he almost fell into an open grave. "Shite!"

Sara looked around. "There are a lot of open graves here. I wonder why. Are they getting ready for something? No, it looks like these were graves that were dug up. That's weird." They kept walking among the graves, and a few times the moonlight revealed a name on a gravestone. "Slave names. This must be the ne-." Sara sighed. Soon there were fewer open graves, and the headstones became a little nicer and more expensive-looking. Sara started walking more slowly, straining her eyes to read the names in the dark. "All those people. So many of them buried alive because of the wars, or the epidemics."

Colum was getting anxious about how slowly they were moving through the graveyard. "If the living are buried like the dead, it's no wonder that later the dead walk like the living."

A voice came from behind them, "Those aren't shades."

Sara and Colum jumped with fright, and spun around to see a priest standing there, like he'd been there the whole time, just strolling around casually with his hands in his pockets. Colum took a step back, and stumbled, landing down on one knee. Sara gasped, "Oh, you scared us!"

"Sorry about that. I'm Father Murphy. You're in the Catholic section of Potter's Field – the strangers' cemetery."

"Oh, uh, we didn't mean to trespass," Colum said. "But we are Catholic."

"You're not trespassing. This is holy ground. No need to fear here."

"What did you say?"

"I said no need to be afraid."

"No I mean, when you first snuck up on us."

"Oh, I said, they're not shades."

Sara asked, "What do you mean?"

"Well," the priest looked at Colum, "You said something about the dead walking like the living. But those aren't the shades of the dead. The hauntings, all of it. They're not ghosts, they're demons."

"What?"

"When people die, they don't stay here. They go… wherever it is they're meant to go. Heaven or hell. No, when people think they've seen a ghost, they're being tricked by the devil's angels. Demons mean to trick people into putting their faith in superstition, or just to spend more time thinking about them than about God. What they really want is to steal people's joy, and trick them into despairing. When people say Savannah is haunted, what they really mean to say is that Savannah is under demonic oppression. It's the result of all the evil that's happened here. The wars, the slavery, the torture. It attracts 'em, and brings 'em out. The Church is here to reclaim this place for Christ."

Sara and Colum just stared at the priest, not knowing how to respond. But Father Murphy just shrugged his shoulders and turned to walk away. Then he stopped and turned back. "The angel of death will put away the sword of plague when the people of Savannah truly reject the culture of suffering and death. But even though slavery is over, too many still cling to the old ways. There's a saying on one of these gravestones, one of the old ones. It says… well, let me show it to you." Sara and Colum still didn't know what to say, so they followed the priest as he led them through the maze of graves. "Here it is, I'll read it. It says, 'Where the sign of the cross is, evil is weakest.' I like that. It's a saying from the early days of Christianity."

When Colum saw the name on the grave, he fell to his knees and put his face into his hands. "What?" Sara insisted. Colum said nothing, so Sara moved closer to see what had affected Colum so much. The name on the headstone was Carrig Hannon.

"What?" Sara repeated.

Colum regained his composure, and without explaining, read the stones out loud. "Carrig Hannon. Born 1722, Died 1789. Shannon Duffy Hannon. Dutiful Wife. Born 1730, Died 1770. Aedan MacCluin. Loving Husband, Faithful Friend. Born 1722, Died 1779. Maria Rossi MacCluin. Beloved Wife. Born 1725, Died 1745." Colum paused. "Jaysus, she was only twenty."

"Probably died bringin' a child into the world," Fr. Murphy said. "In those days, medicine wasn't as advanced as it is now."

"Why so many empty graves?" Sara asked.

"As the war was coming to an end, and Sherman was marching toward Savannah, those who still had family in town got moved to private land or plantations. To prevent desecration by the Union soldiers. But these graves are so old…"

"So they came to America," Colum smiled a little. Then the smile went away. "Poor Carrig was alone the last ten years of his life. That's why no one was there to put 'loving husband' or 'faithful friend' on his gravestone. Just this saying, he must have asked for it in his will. 'Where the sign of the cross is, evil is weakest'."

The priest crossed himself, and Sara and Colum followed his lead.

"Hold it right there!" It was Crown's men, holding torches, and pointing their revolvers at Sara. Sara and Colum were surrounded.

†††

Jimmy could hear the voices in the hallway. They were coming closer. "Move it! Open the door!" Then the sound of a key in the door of his cell. The door swung open, and there Jimmy saw one of the Rasta impostors holding a gun to the orderly's head. "Who is he?"

The orderly's voice was shaky. "Nobody knows who he is, he had no ID."

The nubbie turned the gun toward Jimmy. "So who are you?"

Jimmy smirked. "I'm Jimmy the Fist." Then he quickly stepped to the side and backed up to the wall just inside the door, where the gunman couldn't see him. Jimmy crouched down just in time as three bullets came through the wall above his head. He waited for the gunman to peek around through the doorway, and then he sprang upwards, grabbing the gun and pushing it out of the way as his elbow came up into the man's chin. The gun went off, and the bullet ricocheted off the cement floor under the padding. Jimmy twisted the man's arm, forcing him to let go of the gun, and when he had control of the gun, he kicked the man in the groin, to keep him down long enough for Jimmy to get away. He pushed past the frightened orderly and ran out into the hallway, checking the gun as he ran. The slide was all the way back. That last bullet was the last bullet. Jimmy dropped the gun and broke into a sprint. He could see daylight up ahead and ran for the door at top speed. He hit the door hard, and shoved at the locking bar to open it. The door swung wide and Jimmy ran out of the building, only to stop in his tracks as he faced the other Rasta impostor. The nubbie was holding a large silver revolver, and pointing it at Jimmy. His hands were shaking, but he was close enough that he wasn't going to miss. Unfortunately, he was just far enough away from Jimmy that he couldn't jump him and take the gun away. Jimmy looked right and left. Nowhere to hide. Nothing to dive behind, and no time to make a move. Shaky hands pulled back the hammer on the revolver, and closed one eye to aim.

BAM, BAM... BAM

The fake Rasta jerked backward from the impact of two bullets to his chest, and then he slumped forward, and the third bullet hit him right in the top of the head. He was dead before he hit the ground. Jimmy turned around to see who the shooter was.

"Hmpf. Molly Mallone. You gonna shoot me, too?"

"With your own gun? That would be so uncool." She turned the gun around and handed it to Jimmy. Then she pulled an extra magazine out of her back pocket and handed that to Jimmy as well.

"This *is* my gun! Where did you get this?"

"I took it from you while you were sleeping in that shack up at Pinnacle. You were so sound asleep you didn't even stir."

Jimmy was embarrassed. "Look, thanks, I guess. I mean, I get it, you had to shoot that guy. But geez, right in the top of the head, I've never seen anything like that. I thought I'd seen everything, but that was… disturbing."

"Oh, I'm sorry. I didn't mean to *disturb* you, Mr. Delaney. But I can't afford to leave anything uncertain. This is not a game. This world is violent and dangerous and you can either let evil win, or you can fight back. But you have to make your decision about which one you're going to do ahead of time. 'Cause when the danger presents itself, you won't have time to decide. You will only have time to act." At that moment, the last remaining Rasta impersonator came stumbling out of the doorway, and Molly pulled her own gun from a holster behind her back and shot him twice in the chest. She hesitated for a moment, and when he didn't go all the way down to the ground, but tried to hold himself up on one knee, she shot him again in the top of the head. He slumped to the ground. "Now it's time to go."

Molly ran to a car waiting at the curb and got in behind the wheel. "Yes, you too," she yelled out the open window. "You gotta get in."

Jimmy got in the car. As they sped away, he was silent. He couldn't get the image of what had just happened out of his head.

Finally, Molly spoke. "You know, it's your fault I had to kill them. I would have liked to get those two alive and take them to Gitmo for questioning."

"You mean torture?"

"Potato, potahto."

"What are you, CIA?"

"What are you, a talk show host?"

"I mean if you're supposed to be with the good guys, how can you…? I mean, it seemed so… easy, like you enjoyed it."

"Look, Jimmy. Unless you're a priest, I'm not making a confession. Anyway, you have to fight fire with fire. The world is full of violent, brutal animals. And you have to be *more* violent than the bad guys or you're just going to be a victim. *Ignis pugna igni*. Fight fire with fire."

"So who were those guys?"

"Bombers. Hijackers. We think they were planning to bomb the prime minister's office, and then hijack a plane to Cuba, framing the Rastas for the bombing. Of course now we'll never know."

"Well, you still stopped it."

"Yes, I did. And although you might think it was done in too casual a fashion, I may have also avoided an escalation of the war into a whole new arena. Coulda been another Cuban missile crisis, or worse. Better three assholes die than a whole lot of young soldiers. People get all bent out of shape by the thought of political assassinations, but let me tell you, assassination is a legitimate alternative to war. And the best part is, you civilians never have to know you were in danger. Now, where do you want me to drop you off?"

"Uh, back at Trenchtown, I guess." Jimmy couldn't risk Molly seeing the time machine. He would have to walk there to play it safe. "Hey, have you seen a black girl, about twenty-four, maybe looked like she was lost. Not a Rasta, but with a pretty good fake Jamaican accent?"

"No, but that white guy you're looking for isn't on the island anymore."

"Wordman?"

"Yeah, the sleazy fuck was able to schmooze some rich tourists, and talk them into taking him to the mainland on their yacht. A big one, called the *Narragonia*. They're headed for Savannah."

"Thanks. How do you know all this?"

"Never ask a magician how she does her tricks, my friend."

The car came to a stop along the edge of Kingston's shanty town. Jimmy got out of the car, and stood there watching as Molly wiped off the steering wheel and dashboard with a torn up t-shirt. She wiped down the area around the fuse box under the dash, and then got out of the car, and wiped around the front edge of the hood. Then she went around to the back of the car, and wiped down the trunk. Jimmy didn't walk away, he was mesmerized by the methodical process. Then Molly took a duffle bag and a can of gasoline out of the trunk. She poured the gas over the car, and in through the windows, dousing the front and back seats. Then she calmly lit a cigarette.

Jimmy wondered if he should thank her. "So, goodbye, I guess."

Molly looked at Jimmy hard for a long moment. She took a long drag on the cigarette and pulled something out of her pocket. She closed her eyes and took another drag. "Damn, I should never have quit these." She held out her hand and Jimmy could see that she was holding a switchblade knife. He jumped just a little when she pushed the button and the knife flipped open in Jimmy's direction. Then Molly flicked the cigarette into the car, and the gas burst into flames.

Jimmy took a step back, looking back and forth between the burning car and the knife in Molly's hand. "Shouldn't we go?"

"Not so fast. See this knife?" Jimmy nodded. Molly closed the switchblade and continued. "I took this knife from a guy who wanted to kill me with it. Then I used it on him. That was in Rome. One of my first gigs. The first time I ever killed a man, actually. So I go to the Vatican, where Pope Paul the sixth is having an audience. And when the Pope has an audience, he always blesses any rosaries, or crucifixes, or other religious articles, whatever you might be holding in your hand at the time. I went, and I was holding this knife. So this might be the only switchblade in history ever blessed by the Pope. I guess you could say it's my lucky knife." She handed it to Jimmy.

"What do you want me to do with it?"

Molly looked at him hard again. "I want you to have it."

"Why?"

"I... I don't know. I just do. Take it before I change my mind and stab you with it." Molly smirked and Jimmy took the knife.

"Thank you. For saving my life. And for the knife."

"Don't thank me for doing my job. Just take that and... protect your family. By whatever means necessary. Fight fire with fire." Then she picked up her duffle bag and walked away as the car continued to burn.

Later that night, Jimmy sat alone in the last pew at Holy Trinity Cathedral in Kingston. He looked up at a statue of Saint Sebastian, patron saint of martial artists. Sebastian looked utterly defeated – his hands tied behind him, his body stuck with the arrows of a fourth century firing squad. *How can I leave without Sara? What if she's here on the island? If I leave, I could be stranding her here. Getting her involved in this was wrong. I didn't think it through. But now I can't let Wordman get away. And I can't stay here and keep looking for Sara when there's no sign of her. And I can't take the time machine with me to Georgia. I'll have to send it back and hope Sofia and the others can find both me and Sara and bring us back.*

Jimmy looked down at the piece of paper in his lap, and the pen in his hand. He started to write.

I'm in Jamaica, in 1973. I've been here for several days. Sara is NOT here...

CHAPTER 5

I SHOT THE SHERIFF

Jimmy found himself on a racing boat speeding toward the mainland. The captain was nonchalant as Jimmy clung to a side rail. The captain shouted, "She's the fastest boat in the Caribbean!" Jimmy could hardly hear the captain's voice over the roar of the twin engines and the thunder clap slapping sound the boat's hull was making against the water. Jimmy looked around and wondered how this could possibly be the fastest racing boat around. It looked like it was being held together with duct tape and rope. And it was so dirty, he hardly wanted to sit down on the cracked vinyl seat, let alone touch anything. The captain pushed the throttle all the way forward.

"Are you sure you want to go full speed?" The captain didn't hear Jimmy yelling. Or maybe he ignored him. "We don't need to go this fast!" The slapping was deafening now as the boat rocked back and forth in a rhythm alternating between the boat equivalent of a wheelie and then crashing back down onto the surface of the water. Then the boat started to waver from side to side, and all those disaster films of racing boats flipping over backward flashed through Jimmy's mind. And then, sure enough, the boat flipped. The wind caught it just right, and the boat turned over in the air, and came crashing down on its top, splintering into a million pieces. The next thing Jimmy knew, he was under water, but he was so turned around that he didn't know which way was up. He couldn't see more than a few inches in front of him because of the churning water and bubbles. *What's that? A Rope!* Jimmy grabbed the rope and held on. It was the anchor. He held on tight to the anchor rope, and tried to pull himself along, but then he realized he was pulling himself downward toward the bottom of the bay. When he looked at the rope in his hands, it was not a rope at all, it was a snake. He recognized the black and white stripes of the deadly sea snake. He jerked his body back and held the snake away from him with his left hand, trying to keep it away to prevent it from biting him. He looked at his right hand, and he saw he was holding the switchblade that Molly had given him. He opened the blade and swung it at the sea snake. The snake's head was cut off clean, but in its place another head grew up. It was the head of a cobra, and it looked Jimmy right in the eyes and hissed at him. And then Jimmy woke up.

  Jimmy rubbed his eyes quickly, forcing himself to get up and get going before anyone might see him. After all, a white man among the Rastas would still stand out, no matter how well he was able to speak the part. He walked through the slums toward the beach, hoping to feel a little cleaner after a swim, and also hoping to find a boat to take him to Savannah. Swimming in the salt water was no good substitute for a shower, but it would have to do. He came out of the water dripping wet, and walked along the beach toward the marina, drying in the hot morning sun. The smell of salty humid air and seaweed on the sand awoke a thousand thoughts in Jimmy's mind, which made him anxious, so he picked up his pace and ran along the beach toward the docks. As he ran he came up to a group of people sitting around a fire that had clearly been burning all night. Some of them looked like Rastas, but some of them didn't. One had a guitar, and was half-heartedly strumming some chords. As Jimmy walked closer he recognized the song. Anyone would have. It was Bob Marley's song, *Jammin'* which wouldn't be released for another four years. As Jimmy came up to the group, he could see that the man with the guitar was Bob Marley himself. Jimmy smiled to himself.

"Greetins. Dat sahng a say won – dat a bashy jam, mon. Wa ya call it?"

"Dun know." Marley answered.

"It be jammin'." Jimmy smiled to himself again.

"Jammin' it be, den." Marley looked Jimmy up and down. "Siddung hya." Another man looked annoyed that Marley should ask Jimmy to join the group. Jimmy recognized that man as Peter McIntosh, better known as Peter Tosh.

Jimmy decided it was safe to let go of the Jamaican accent. Not everyone around the fire was a Rasta, and it would be better to gain Marley's trust as an outsider than to be found out and shunned as a pretender. "My name's Jimmy. I know who you guys are. I caught part of your concert the other day. I really love your music."

No one was surprised that Jimmy wasn't really a Rasta. Peter Tosh just shook his head, but Marley gave him some friendly ribbing. "Well, look who be all speaky-spokey now, eh?"

Jimmy smirked sheepishly. "And what's wrong with being bilingual?"

"You like dat sahng?"

"Yeah, it's great. I mean I'm sure it's going to be great when you put some words to it."

"It a sahng about good times. But Peter, hya, 'im nuh like good times."

Peter spoke up. "I an I like good times as much as da neks mon. But I and I muss be playin' sahngs dat change da world, sight? None dese bomboclot lovey-dovey sahgns."

Marley handed the guitar to Jimmy without saying another word. Jimmy hesitated a moment, but then took it. *What could I possibly play? Nothing reggae, I'll either look like a poser, or I'll risk playing something that hasn't been written yet and it could get me in trouble.* Then Jimmy had an idea. He thought of all the Irish songs he had learned from Chris and the O'Connells, and he played *The Star of the County Down*, but with a reggae beat. The group loved it, all smiles as they clapped casually. All except Peter Tosh, who just rolled his eyes. When Marley and some of the others encouraged Jimmy to play another one, he looked right at Marley and said, "This one is for our Catholic mothers." Bob Marley's eyes got a little watery as Jimmy played a reggae version of *The Curragh of Kildare*. When he finished, the group just looked at him in silence. "You know, Ireland is an island, too. So that makes Irish music just another kind of island music. All island music is written by people who are downpressed by Babylon."

There was general agreement from the group. "A true. A true."

"Hey, uh, maybe you could help me. I'm kind of in a bind, and I need to get to the mainland. Preferably Savannah, Georgia. Do you know how I could get a boat over there – maybe work for my passage?"

Marley looked Jimmy up and down. "Nuh get strong money?"

"I have some money. Not sure it's enough."

"Easy, den. Ya go ta da marina. Link up wi Gabriel. First mate a da tug boat. Tell him I and I sent ya. Him get ya dere."

After a while, and a few more Irish reggae songs, the group broke up, leaving Jimmy and Bob Marley sitting in front of a now extinguished fire. Jimmy endured an awkward silence, and after rehearsing what he was going to say in his head, he spoke up. "Bob?" Marley nodded. "Do you ever… go to the doctor?"

"Babylon doctors quattie, mon. I an I use herbal medications."

"Yeah, but what if something was, you know, wrong with you? Something bad. You'd never know. Then it might be too late."

"Money can't buy time, me yute."

"Hmm. Money can't buy time. True true. But if you could avoid something you might regret later…"

"I an I all have regrets in the past," Marley interrupted. "But ya can't undo da past. Only cover it with better tings in the present and future."

"Love covers a multitude of sins?"

"A true. Da fix for da past is nuh in da past. Jus' be 'appy 'bout what is saved radder dan gloomy 'bout what is lost."

As Jimmy walked away from Marley and toward the marina, Marley's words echoed in his head. When he got to the marina, he asked around for the tug boat's first mate, Gabriel. But what he didn't know was that Wordman had gotten to Gabriel first, and paid Gabriel to stop anyone from following him to Savannah. So when Jimmy finally found Gabriel, he could tell his guard was up. "Are you Gabriel?"

Gabriel looked at Jimmy hard and said, "Maybe. 'Oo waan ta know?"

"I'm Jimmy. Bob Marley sent me, told me I should talk to you." Jimmy turned a bit to gesture in the direction of the extinguished fire down the beach. As he turned back to face Gabriel, he could see the mooring hook in Gabriel's hand, and it was coming down fast toward his head. But Jimmy remembered Dante's training. *Don't trust your instincts,* he would say. *Just when your brain wants you to back away – that's when you need to move in close.* Jimmy lunged forward and swung his elbow into Gabriel's throat before the hook could come down on him. It swung past the back of his head and slammed into the railing of the pier. Jimmy's head came down on the bridge of Gabriel's nose, which caused Gabriel to pull his head back. Jimmy then grabbed the back of Gabriel's neck and proceeded to put his knee into Gabriel's stomach and chest until Gabriel crumpled into a ball on the dock. Jimmy threw the mooring hook into the water and then ran for the shelter of the boat house to get out of sight.

Now what? That guy was supposed to be my ticket to Savannah, but obviously that's not going to happen.

"May I help you?" Jimmy turned around to see a well-dressed ship's captain facing him. He was obviously not Jamaican, judging by his British accent. When the captain saw Jimmy's shirt, covered in blood from the head butt to Gabriel's nose, he took a step back and said, "Bloody hell."

"Um, that's not what it looks like."

"It looks like blood."

"Well, it is blood. But it's not mine. The other guy attacked me. I was just defending myself."

"Mm hmm. And who might you be?"

Jimmy was still so flustered from the attack that he answered without thinking. "Jimmy Agnello." *Oh, shit. I'm supposed to be Jimmy Delaney. How could I be so stupid!*

The captain tilted his head as he looked at Jimmy. "Did you say your surname name is Agnello?"

"Yeah, why?"

"Have you ever heard of the Merchant Venturers?"

"Merchant Venturers? Yeah, actually I have. Are you one of them? You know you guys helped my cousin in Bristol."

"Your cousin? Indeed. But that was over two hundred years ago."

"Right... Um, listen. I know you don't know me, but I need your help."

"The fact that you are an Agnello is all I need to know about you. What can I do to help?"

Two days and one cargo ship ride later, Jimmy was standing on a different pier - in Savannah, Georgia. Walking away from the docks, he ended up in front of a restaurant called "The Pirate's House." *Seems like as good a place as any to start looking for Wordman.*

†††

Crown's men left Colum and Fr. Murphy standing helpless in the cemetery while they marched Sara away. Colum shouted threats at them until they fired a couple of shots over his head. But the ambiance of the cemetery and the presence of the priest meant that Sara was safe for the moment, at least until they got her back to Crown.

Back at the hotel, she was locked in one of the rooms. As the door closed, she could hear the key turn from the outside, and a voice saying, "We'll leave you alone as long as you don't make a fuss. But if you call out or bang on this door, we're comin' in there to shut you up." Sara got the message and stayed quiet. But she also stayed awake all through the night. She expected something to happen soon after the sun came in through the windows, but it seemed like a long time before someone opened the door. It must have been ten o'clock when she heard the key in the lock. She backed herself into the far corner of the room, expecting the worst. When the door opened, Sara was relieved to see that it was Esther. Immediately Esther put her finger up to her mouth to keep Sara from speaking. "I'm so very sorry," she whispered. "I never thought they would find you."

"It's okay," Sara whispered back. "I know you did your best to help. Is there any way out of here? Can you help me escape?"

Esther sighed, and looked around to see if anyone was in the hallway. "Yes, but not now. Too many people around. We can't trust the other girls. They all think they want my situation. If they only knew. I'm sorry but now I have to take you to Mr. Crown." Esther walked Sara down the stairway and through the lobby. The eyes of the other women were all on Sara as she was escorted into the office.

Dickey-Jim Crown was seated at a poker table with four other men, playing cards. The Methodist preacher was there, along with two other men Sara didn't know, Thomas Ballantyne and Francis Blair. Crown's eyes stared into his cards, and his fat face made him look like a huge angry baby. His hands twitched as everyone waited in silence. Then he forced a smile as he put his cards on the table. "Gentlemen, I believe this hand belongs to me – full house." Sara looked at the cards. A pair of jacks and three kings. But all she could see was KKK. Crown looked at Sara and got up from the table, adjusting his pants and pulling on his belt, revealing the flash of the gold belt buckle for just a moment until his flabby belly dropped over it again.

Crown stared at Sara. "My dear, have I done something to offend you? Because that is the only reason I can think of for you to refuse my hospitality in such a discourteous way." He turned to the men at the table. "As I see it, gentlemen, this kind of behavior is exactly why we must preserve the dignity of Savannah before it is gone forever. Before the war, this great city was in her glory and the plantations hummed with prosperous activity, but now I am reduced to a less glorious occupation, and you can see here the proof that those with no rights of pedigree have become uppity, as if they can rise to the level of well-bred society." He turned back to Sara. "You must learn that you cannot rise to our level. And we will not sit idly by and allow you to bring the best people down to yours!"

"I don't want to work for you… in your *hotel*." Sara made air quotes around the word "hotel" with her fingers.

Crown squinted at her. "Why are you doing that with your hands?" Crown tried to imitate the air quotes but his hands were too shaky. "Is that some sort of rude gesture meant to offend me? Well, as I see it, *refugees* like yourself are a significant part of the problem, and I will be doing you and everyone a great service by giving you gainful employment. Isn't that right, gentlemen?" The other men laughed and grunted their agreement. Crown turned back toward Sara and went on. "And your good fortune is only increasing today, my dear, because I have decided to personally avail myself of your services, as your first customer." Crown motioned for Esther to take Sara back to the room, and turned to rejoin the men at the table. "As I see it, gentlemen, negro women are like horses. They exist for us to ride them!" The men at the table laughed, all except the Reverend. He glanced at Sara for a split second, and then looked down at his cards.

Sara gave Esther a panicked look that said, *Get me out of here!* But Esther's saddened look in response told Sara that she would not be able to help her escape at the moment.

Crown saw the look of panic on Sara's face. "Cheer up," he said to her, touching her arm. "A girl like you – if she knows how to keep to her place - can become quite successful working at my hotel."

Ballantyne spoke up, "Just don't expect Dickey-Jim to pay you!" The others broke into laughter for just a moment - until they saw the scowl on Crown's face.

Sara's fear turned to anger in a flash. She took a step toward the table of men and glared at them. "You men. You talk about women like they're your pets. And you talk about women in parts. You take us apart so you can pretend we can't hear you, so you can separate our hearts from our bodies – so you can break our hearts and still use our bodies. A man has the luxury of seeing his body as a tool, something he uses to get a job done. But a woman doesn't have that luxury – a woman sees her body as her very self, as much as her own soul, and if you turn it into something to be bought and sold, then you've taken away her humanity, and you've made her like an animal. Well, I won't be your pet!" Then she turned to face Crown and looked him in the eyes. "I won't be your servant. I won't be your victim."

Esther listened to Sara's speech with awe, and a decision came into her mind. She vowed to herself that the path to the future was now clear; that the key to her future was Sara. But her thoughts were disrupted by the shock of Crown's fist punching Sara in the face. Sara fell to her knees, holding her cheek and gasping for air. The pain was too great to cry, and all she could do was crawl back a bit away from Crown.

He just looked at Esther, waved her off, and went back to his poker game.

As Sara was walked out of the office, she could hear Crown address the other men. "Now, gentlemen, as far as the matter of this new carpetbagger who has come to town. We will have to call the brotherhood together to take care of him, just like the last one. He has no right to the glorious sun of a Savannah morning, so he must not awaken to it tomorrow, do you understand? Now, what was that carpetbagger's name?"

The Reverend replied, "His name is O'Connell. Colum O'Connell."

Sara stopped walking when she heard Colum's name.

Crown called out, "Esther!"

"Yessir?"

"Once Miss Sara is secure in her room, come back down here."

"Yessir."

When Esther returned to Crown's office, she soon realized that this was the day she had been dreading for a long time, the day that her worst fears would begin to materialize.

"Yessir?"

"How old is that girl of yours?"

"Rosie? Um. Why, she is only just ten."

"Don't lie to me. I know for a fact that she is eleven. And I believe it's high time we put her to work."

"No, sir... please, she's just a little girl."

"Don't worry, we'll start her off easy. Baths, massages, first-timers. Until she gets used to it."

"But sir…"

"Now you listen here! As I see it, you are in no position to tell me about my business. We need all the girls we can have on our roster, and your girl will fetch a grand sum – more than most of the girls - for the right customer." Crown smiled his forced smile. "And her share of that money goes to you, of course."

"You would have me sell my daughter?"

"Don't pretend to be shocked by it. It's nothing new. I want that new girl, Sara, and Rosie, both put to work as soon as possible. Now I have a luncheon I must get to. If anyone asks for me, I'll be at Mr. Hamilton's house, with the mayor and the sheriff."

Esther turned away so Crown wouldn't see her tears. She wiped her face with her sleeve as she walked out of Crown's office. Crown put on the panama hat that covered his bald spot and headed out of the hotel and down Abercorn Street toward Samuel Hamilton's house. Hamilton was the president of the electric company, and so he had one of the first houses in Savannah that was wired for electricity. The house was only a few years old, and Hamilton was so afraid of burglars that he kept the outside electric lights on even during the day, and hired an off duty police officer to stand guard on his roof. Crown muttered to himself about the showiness of it, but in reality he was jealous. Crown tipped his hat to the officer on the roof as he made his way up the steps to the front door. Once inside, he greeted the sheriff.

"Sheriff Bartleby, good day to you."

"Good day to you, Mr. Crown. I believe you know my deputy, John Ronan."

"Indeed I do. Good day to you, Mr. Ronan." The deputy nodded, but was too intimidated by Crown to speak.

Hamilton came into the room. "Gentlemen, we are still waiting for the mayor and chief Anderson. Once they arrive, we can make our way into the dining room. While we wait, I propose we have a drink." Glasses of whiskey were poured, and everyone looked at Crown, waiting for him to make his usual toast.

"To our departed friend, Charles Lamar, gone but not forgotten. He kept the dream of the south alive as long as he could. We miss his flaming red hair. We miss his nasty disposition." Chuckles and, "Here, here," from the men. "And most of all we miss his business! He kept the plantations humming long after they tried to take our livelihood away." The crystal glasses clinked and the men savored their whiskey. When the chief of police arrived, Crown addressed him immediately, using his military title. "General Anderson, I do wish you would tell that wife of yours to disassociate herself from that woman Nellie Gordon. As I see it, we cannot trust the Gordon family, and I do believe that William Gordon was a Union spy during the war."

Chief Anderson took a deep breath and counted to three in his head. "Thank you for your advice, Mr. Crown. But as an *unmarried* man yourself *I do believe* that you overestimate a husband's ability to control his wife's behavior." The other men muttered their agreement.

At this, the mayor of Savannah entered the room. "We have a larger problem than that, I am afraid." All the men looked at him, waiting for him to elaborate, but he turned to the sheriff. "Tell them sheriff."

Sheriff Bartleby put down his glass. "Gentlemen. We have a serious problem. We're seeing the first cases of the fever, and doc Arnold says it could be the beginning of a real epidemic." The normally well-composed men expressed their shock and disgust with a variety of expletives.

"Damnation!" Crown downed the rest of his whiskey. "Time was, a man could get out of town for fever season. When enough income came from the plantation. But now, I can't leave the hotel." The other men agreed that getting out of town was not an option for them, and that there was too much business to take care of, and too many loose ends to tie up. "Besides, if we are absent, the carpetbaggers will fill the void, and we cannot let that happen, gentlemen. We have to be diligent to guard our fair city against the intrusive laws of the federal government. Furthermore, we need to discuss my idea for a law that would allow us to arrest anyone who presumes to rise above his station, and have them committed to the asylum."

The mayor spoke up. "There will be time for that later, Mr. Crown, but at the moment we need to decide on a plan of action for dealing with the victims of the fever. I defer to the wisdom of the Chatham County Sheriff."

"I say we use the tunnels." The sheriff had clearly thought about this and was prepared to present his plan. "We take the fever patients out of the hospital through the slave tunnels, so we don't stir up a panic. Then we get rid of them, so they don't spread it."

Deputy Ronan was horrified. "What will we tell their families?"

The sheriff looked at him sternly. "We tell them that they died."

†††

It was a strange juxtaposition that swirled around in Jimmy's mind. Classic Savannah architecture and early disco music. Jimmy walked along Bay Street, looking for the Antebellum Club, but he heard it before he saw it. The bass was pumping out into the humid night air, and he could almost smell the combination of sweat and cocaine. Jimmy turned a corner, and there it was. Just the kind of place where Wordman would hang out. Jimmy already knew what it would be like inside before even going through the door. He had spent his share of time in places like this in Chicago. Dark, low ceilings, colored lights under a transparent dance floor, private rooms in the back. This is where all the big money players of Savannah would be, along with any celebrities who might be in town. He pushed the door open as the music enveloped him and pulled him in.

Jimmy went to the bar and ordered a drink. "Disaronno. Neat." The music was pounding, so it was difficult to talk, but Jimmy decided to try anyway. "Ever meet a guy named Donald Wordman?"

The bartender smiled. "You mean Doc Wordman? The professor? Yeah. He's the senator's cousin or something, right?"

"Something like that."

"Yeah, he's in town. I've seen him with Mr. Williams. You can check the VIP rooms in the back, they might be back there."

"Thanks." Jimmy paid for his drink and moved toward the back of the club. He didn't want to move too quickly and seem like he was on a mission, but if Wordman was back there, he didn't want to let him get away. A large man standing at a velvet rope put up a hand to stop Jimmy from walking past. "Just want to see a friend. The bartender told me I might find him with Mr. Williams."

The bouncer smiled. "Oh you must mean the Professor. I don't think he's here now, but Mr. Williams is in there." He unclipped the velvet rope from its bronze post and let Jimmy walk through. But Jimmy didn't get very far before he was stopped by a southern gentleman in a very expensive suit.

"May I help you?"

Jimmy hesitated for a second. "I'm looking for a Mr. Williams."

"Then you have found him." The man in the suit gave a wide smile and turned on the charm. "What can I do for you?"

"I'm looking for a friend of mine. Donald, uh, Doc Wordman. The bartender said you know him."

"That I do. That I do. I haven't known him long, mind you, but I do consider him a friend. And what is your business with the Professor?"

"Well, it's a personal matter." Jimmy thought fast. *How do I get this guy to tell me where Wordman is without him tipping Wordman off that I'm here? There is no one who should be looking for a forty-six year old Wordman in 1973. If he hears that someone is looking for him, he'll know something is up and disappear.* "Actually, we haven't seen each other in a long time. I'm not sure he'll even recognize me. So I was kind of hoping to ease into the reunion, you know? I think it would be fine if I could just talk to him, but if he knows I'm looking for him before I meet with him, it might be awkward. You would be doing him a favor as well as me, if you could just, um, not tell him that you met me."

Williams looked at Jimmy with suspicion. "Tell you what. I'm having a party at my home tomorrow night. The Professor will be there. Consider yourself formally invited. There will be a lot of people there. You can mingle with the guests, and you can see Dr. Wordman in a... relaxed environment." Williams handed Jimmy a card with his address on it, and turned to walk away. "The party begins at eight o'clock sharp, Mr..."

"Delaney."

"The party begins at eight, Mr. Delaney. And folks around here know better than to arrive late to one of my parties." Williams smiled, then turned and walked through a velvet curtain and out of sight. Jimmy could tell that was his cue to leave. He gave the bouncer a nod and walked away, still holding his drink in his right hand. He looked at the drink and realized that he and Williams never shook hands. Jimmy wondered if Williams could be trusted.

Behind the velvet curtain, Williams walked to a circle of plush couches surrounding a low table. Wordman was sitting on one of the couches, his head bent over the table, his nose greedily following a line of cocaine. When Wordman came up for air, Williams was standing over him, shaking his head.

Wordman startled. "Jesus, Jim. Don't sneak up on a guy."

"I just met a man who says he's an old friend of yours."

Wordman's eyes widened. "Nobody knows I'm here. Who was he?"

"Says his name is Delaney. Do you know him?"

"Doesn't sound familiar. But like I said, no one knows I'm here. So if this Delaney is looking for me, he knows something he shouldn't know. You didn't tell him I was here did you?"

"Do you see him here now? I did tell him, however, that you would be at the party at my house tomorrow night. You can wait upstairs, and when he arrives I'll point him out to you – you'll see him before he sees you."

"Good." Wordman took Sofia's gun out of his coat pocket, and made sure there was a round in the chamber, ready to go.

"There's no need for that, Professor."

"Let's hope not."

Jimmy walked out onto the street, and the lower volume of the music was a welcome change from inside the club. *Gotta find a place to sleep.* He walked down Drayton Street toward the historic center of town, and came upon the Marshall House Hotel. *Looks like as good a place as any.*

He went in, and felt a chill as he realized the place seemed deserted. The reception desk was empty, but a ring of the bell brought someone out. "Hi. Um, I know it's late, and I don't have a reservation, but I don't suppose you have a room?"

"Have lots of rooms. Any preference?"

"No, I'm just gonna crash here for a night or two. Any room is fine."

"Here you go. Sign the book." The clerk handed Jimmy the key to room 214, and Jimmy signed in. Then the clerk disappeared around a corner. Jimmy shrugged and walked up the long staircase to the second floor. He opened the door to the room and went in, locking the door behind him. He flopped down on the bed, just grateful he wasn't sleeping in a shack any more, and he thought his last thoughts of the day before falling asleep. *Why are those people letting their kids run through the halls in the middle of the night? I really have to get a toothbrush.*

Hours later, Wordman was settling into his room at an inn called The 17Hundred90. He had stumbled in after all the staff was gone, but he had the munchies. So he decided to walk down to the kitchen and raid the refrigerator. The inn was quiet and dark. Security lights gave off a yellowish glow, and as he made his way into the kitchen he could hear the hum of the industrial sized refrigerator and freezer. The more alone he felt, the more he sensed that he had to be as quiet as possible. He looked around the kitchen, just to make sure there would be no witnesses to his crime of hunger. Shadows in the corners of his eyes made him want to get his refrigerator raid done as soon as possible so he could get back to his room. Slowly, he made his way over to the large chrome fridge. As he reached out his hand toward the handle of the door, he stopped to listen. The hum was gone. He listened some more. Nothing at first, but then, a sound, like the jangling of keys, or jewelry. Wordman spun around, but no one was there. He listened again, but there was no sound. Eventually he turned back toward the refrigerator door. As he turned, he felt a hard slap across his face. He jumped back in shock and backed himself into the corner of the kitchen to see who had slapped him. But there was no one there. He wanted to run, but he would have to cross the length of the kitchen to get to the door. He listened. Silence, and then the jangling sound. Wordman ran for the door, and that jangling sound followed him out of the kitchen and didn't stop until he was halfway up the stairs. Wordman kept running, no longer caring who heard or saw him, and he didn't stop until he had locked himself in his room. He quickly searched the room to make sure he was alone, even checking behind the shower curtain.

It took him a long time to fall asleep, and when he did, any real rest he might have gotten was prevented by vivid dreams of driving a car at dangerous speeds, tunnel vision images of hitting the young woman he killed, and the sound of jangling jewelry following behind him. The last thing he dreamed before waking up in a sweat was a vague memory of being in a limo in New York. In the dream, Wordman was complaining to the limo driver, who just ignored him and turned up the music. The song was Ziggy Marley's *Have You Ever Been to Hell?*

†††

Ascending the steps to the John Wesley Hotel, Colum had no idea what he was going to say to Dicky-Jim Crown. He was supposed to let Crown know when he found Sara, and Crown would know that he hadn't done that. But he didn't care. The time it would take to come up with a plan would be too much time wasted, and Sara was in danger. Colum swallowed his fear and forced himself to put one foot in front of the other. As he moved toward the door, he was stopped by the three De la Croix brothers. He hoped they didn't recognize him from the firecracker incident. "I need to see Mr. Crown."

Bernard spoke for the three brothers. "Mr. Crown ain't seein' no one. Least of all some no account carpetbagger."

Colum looked confused. "I don't know what a carpetbagger is, but I can assure you I am not one."

"If you don't know what a carpetbagger is, how do you know you're not one."

"Well, I think I would know."

"What are you then?"

"I'm an Irishman."

"What if carpetbagger means Irishman?"

"Well, then I would be proud to be one."

"So you admit you're a carpetbagger."

"No, I didn't say that."

"I think you did."

"Look, can I see him, or can't I?"

"You can't." With that, the three men shoved Colum back making him stumble down the hotel steps, until he fell backwards onto his butt in the dust of the street. Then the brothers went inside the hotel and closed the door.

Colum paced in front of the hotel, not knowing what to do next. But he couldn't bring himself to leave knowing Sara was inside. He started moving around the side of the building, trying to see in through the windows, to see if he could catch a glimpse of her.

"It's not polite to look in windows."

"Oh I'm not peeping. I'm just…" Colum turned around. "Daisy! I'm glad to see you. Sara's in trouble, and I need help." Soon Colum was back at the boarding house with Mrs. Lillibridge, Daisy, and Margaret. He explained to them what was happening, and the young girls were horrified to hear what kind of establishment the John Wesley Hotel really was. Colum racked his brain for some way to get Sara out of the hotel, but it was Mrs. Lillibridge who came up with the plan.

A loud knock at the boarding house door broke up the conclave, and the widow innkeeper opened the door. "Oh, Reverend Meyers! Well, this *is* a surprise. If I had known you were making a visit today, I would have dusted off my Bible."

"I'm afraid this isn't a pastoral visit, Mrs. Lillibridge. I come with a message for Mr. O'Connell. Will you deliver it?"

"I certainly will, Reverend."

Meyers handed her a letter sealed with wax. "Thank you. I'll see you on Sunday."

"Yes. Sunday." Mrs. Lillibridge closed the door and Colum was already right behind her. She handed him the letter, and the three women gathered around him to see what it said.

To Mr. Colum O'Connell

Sir, Since you are not known in this town nor this county, and nevertheless you are known to be a carpetbagger, a scoundrel, a rascal, and a scallywag, your behavior and your very presence here demands satisfaction. Therefore I insist that you meet me tonight at the Brick Wall Graveyard, at sundown, with whatever friend you may think proper, to settle this business according to the laws of honor.

Yours sincerely, Mr. D. J. Crown.

"I'm a scallywag? What does that even mean? What does this letter mean?"

The widow Lillibridge sat down and fanned herself. "He's challenging you to a duel."

"A duel? With swords?"

"Pistols, I imagine."

"Wait." Colum thought for a moment. "This could be the key to our plan. But I need someone who can tell me more about how this duel thing works."

"You're not really going to accept the challenge?" Daisy was afraid for Colum's life.

Colum didn't say anything. He was working things out in his head. "Who knows a lot about duels?"

"Well, they're always in the newspaper," Margaret observed. "So Mr. Harris would know about them."

"Can you take me to him?"

Soon Colum and the girls were standing in the office of the *Savannah Morning News*. Joel Harris wasn't looking up from his desk, so Daisy cleared her throat and spoke up. "Mr. Harris, this is Mr. O'Connell."

"Ah, yes. The scallywag."

Colum was annoyed. "How do you know about that?"

"From the announcement in today's edition." Harris shuffled through the papers on his desk, and then picked one up to read from it. "The honorable Mr. D. J. Crown has written and published a challenge to one Mr. Colum O'Connell, who is a carpetbagger, a scoundrel, a rascal, and a scallywag, demanding satisfaction according to the laws of honor, et cetera, et cetera." Harris put down the paper and looked at Colum. "Do you have the letter?" Colum handed him the letter and Harris read it over. "Hmm. As I thought." Harris paused and looked Colum in the eyes. "You understand that you must not meet him. You must not accept this challenge. You see, most of these letters of challenge will say that an apology will suffice to avoid a duel. But not this one. Most duels nowadays end in a handshake, but Crown - he means to kill you. And don't think for a moment that you have a sporting chance. The last carpetbagger who came to Savannah went out to duel with Crown. He's dead now. Curiously shot three times - from three different angles. I know that because I had a reporter who wrote about it. I say, 'had,' because he's dead, too. Klan got to him. Make no mistake. This is not a duel, it's an ambush." Harris handed the letter back to Colum.

Colum thanked Harris and turned to walk out of the office. He muttered to himself as he left the newspaper office. *So when Crown and his men show up for the duel… I have to be somewhere else.*

Back at the boarding house, Colum found out that he was about the same size as the widow's deceased husband, Major Lillibridge. And once Colum was wearing his confederate army uniform, Daisy was able to convince her mother to introduce Colum to Mrs. Anderson, the wife of the chief of police.

"This is Major Preemhead. Doesn't he look damn fine in that uniform?" Mrs. Anderson blushed at Nellie Gordon's language. But Colum was able to play the part well enough to ask for an introduction to chief Anderson. When they walked into the police station, the chief was nowhere to be found, but seeing Colum with Mrs. Anderson convinced the sergeant in charge to write a note of introduction to Dickey-Jim Crown. And with that note in hand, Colum bid good day to the ladies, and headed for the house with the haint blue door.

Sundown came, and Crown stood among the desecrated graves of the Old Brick Burial Ground. He stared at the open holes where Union soldiers had dug up the graves looking for valuables, and used the coffins as firewood. Some had scratched jokes and obscenities on the tombstones with their bayonets. Crown's hatred for the north, born during his time at Harvard and nurtured during the march of General Sherman, had burned his heart to a crisp. But the fire never went out, and now he found it flaring up again. He gave a nod to his fellow klansmen who were in hiding, waiting to kill Colum. Somewhere, deep down, Crown believed that seeing Colum die would douse that fire of hatred just a little bit. He looked at the dueling pistol in his hand. One of a set of two – the only one his father left to him after he had died in a duel. He remembered his father's words – words that he knew his father had failed to live by: *Never bet on anything but a sure thing.*

As Crown impatiently chewed his cigar in the graveyard, Colum made his way to the John Wesley Hotel. There, dressed in Lillibridge's uniform and with a fresh haircut, he made his way up the steps to the front door. This time there was no one at the door to stop him, so he walked into the lobby as though he had been there a hundred times. He scanned the lobby, and slowly, deliberately, made his way over to the office door. Just as he expected, he was intercepted before reaching the door. It was Ballantyne and Blair. Fortunately, they had not been with Crown when he first met Colum. Ballantyne spoke up, "May we help you, sir?"

"Yes, I hope that you can. My name is Major Preemhead."

"Major. Your reputation precedes you. We have heard of you. Allow me to introduce my associate Francis Blair. And I am Thomas Ballantyne. We are at your service."

"Why thank you gentlemen. I was hoping to meet with Mr. Crown. I have here a letter of introduction."

Blair and Ballantyne looked at each other. "Forgive me, Major, but from where do you hail?"

"From... what now?"

"Where are you from? You see, you don't sound like you're from around here."

"Ah. Yes, well, I am not from Georgia, that's true. I came to these shores, not very long ago, from Ireland, you see. That is a bit of an Irish accent you are hearing."

"Right. Well, you are not the first Irishman to wear that uniform, I daresay. But I am sorry to say that Mr. Crown is not here at this time."

"Oh, that is unfortunate. But I do have important business. Would it be possible for me to wait for him?"

After examining the letter of introduction, Blair and Ballantyne opened the door to Crown's office and led Colum in. They invited him to sit and wait there, and then they said their goodbyes and left. Colum waited a few minutes, and then pretended to be pacing the floor in Crown's office. As he went by the door, he would look out to see if anyone was in the lobby. When the path to the stairs was clear, he made his move, and snuck up to the second floor of the hotel. All the doors were closed. *Shite. This is going to take a lot longer than I thought. How am I going to find her? I need to stay out of sight of the lobby.* Colum went to the far end of the hall and started looking through keyholes. *Wow. No way to unsee that.* And then he saw her. Through the fourth keyhole he could see Sara sitting alone on the brass bed with her head in her hands.

Colum put his mouth up to the keyhole and whispered as loud as he could whisper. "Psst! Sara! Psst!" Sara looked up, but she looked scared. "Sara, it's me! Colum!" Sara ran to the door. "Can you hear me?"

"Yes!"

"Open the door."

"It's locked."

Colum frantically looked around for a key, but there were none to be found. *Time for desperate measures.* He went back to the first room at the end of the hall and tried the door knob. It was locked. He tried the next one. Also locked from the inside. He tried the next one. The knob turned and the door opened. Colum opened the door just a few inches, ignoring the angry shouts from the couple inside the room. He reached around the door to the keyhole on the inside, but the key was not in the door. Colum closed the door, and looked around. He would have to try the other side of the hall, but the ticking of the grandfather clock reminded him that time was passing quickly. He crept to the other side of the hall, trying to stay out of the line of sight from the lobby. He went to the first door and tried the knob. Locked. The second door. Locked. At the third door, Colum was acutely aware that he could now be seen from the lobby, if anyone should look up the stairway. He tried the doorknob, and it turned. He opened the door a bit and reached in, in spite of the objections of the room's occupants. His hand searched the inside of the door for the keyhole. Then he felt the hard metal of the key sticking out of the lock. He worked it out of the keyhole and shut the door.

Fortunately, the room keys were all the same, and a moment later, Colum was in the room with Sara, locking the door behind him.

"What are you doing? Locking us in?"

"I just want to make sure no one saw me, and no one is coming after us. We'll just wait here for a couple minutes." Colum saw the bruise on Sara's face. "Jaysus, what happened?"

Sara turned away. "I didn't need you to save me, you know."

"Maybe not. But I had to find you. I couldn't stand losing you."

"What do you mean you couldn't stand losing me?"

"I mean… it took almost losing you to realize… that I love you."

"You love me? You hardly know me."

"Sara, how well do you think a man would have to know you to love you? How many months, or years, would a man have to know you to know he loves you? Because whatever amount of time you say, you would be selling yourself too short. Do you think it's hard to love you? Do you think it takes work to love you? Let me tell you it's as easy as falling into a hole. And not loving you is about as easy as stopping yourself from falling when you're already in midair. You act like you think you're not lovable, like loving you is some big event that can only happen under rare circumstances. But I'm living proof that you are lovable, and for me, loving you is an everyday thing, as easy as breathing. Finding love isn't like finding a needle in a haystack, so that you should be surprised when you find it. It's not like some treasure hunt. You have to stop thinking of your love life as a treasure hunt. Sara… you *are* the treasure."

Sara moved to Colum and kissed him, at first lightly, but then deeply. At that moment, Sara made the decision to give herself to him completely. As they both melted into the kiss, soon the one-half inch of clothing between them felt like far too much, and their craving to feel the warm electricity of skin on skin overwhelmed them until, before they knew it, the barrier of wool was starting to come down. They fell onto the bed, and kissed with such focus and intention that they almost didn't hear the door frame splinter under the boot of Bernard De la Croix.

The four horsemen burst into the room and pulled Sara and Colum apart, slapping a screaming Sara to the floor. Colum surrendered consciousness under the butt of Bernard's rifle and Sara screamed again when she saw his limp body slump down onto the floor. Sheriff Bartleby grabbed her by the hair and jerked her head to the side, while Blaise and Brant took hold of her arms. Bernard walked away from Colum, leaving him bleeding from his head on the floor. He walked slowly over to where the other three men were holding Sara. He looked straight at Sara.

"Well, boys... how long has it been since we had a lynching?"

"Too long," Blaise said enthusiastically.

The sheriff let go of Sara's hair. "Now boys, you know I can't be part of any such thing. So I can't join you, but you go on, and I'll look the other way."

The three brothers dragged a screaming Sara all the way down the stairs and through the lobby. The people who saw it turned their heads away. Once out in the street, they tied Sara's hands, and tied a rope around her waist. The other end of the rope was tied to the saddle of one of their horses and they rode with Sara in tow toward the nearest square. Sara could see which tree they meant to use. It was old, and big, and had several thick branches running horizontal to the ground, just waiting for a rope. She started to cry, and then she started to pray.

†††

As Jimmy waited for the party to begin, he took the opportunity to try to call his parents and warn them about the train. But he had no idea where they were in 1973, and although he tried several times, he couldn't reach them. So he waited until nine o'clock to make his way to Julian Street and the Williams house. He planned to arrive late because wanted the place to be crowded, so he could move among the people anonymously. As he wandered through the house, Williams entered the upstairs room where Wordman was waiting.

"Shit! You scared me." Wordman was agitated.

"Relax Professor. You seem to startle so easily. Is everything alright with you?"

"No. I mean, I don't know. I won't know until I see the man who's looking for me."

"Well, he just arrived. He's downstairs. Leather sport coat and mock turtle neck. Rather… inappropriate for an event such as this, I must say. Or any event for that matter, except perhaps a NASCAR gala."

"Wait a minute. I don't have to see him. I know who that is. Look, Williams, you have to help me get out of Savannah. I'm a very important man. Very important. That guy in the leather coat must not see me here. If he does… things could go badly. I need to get to Athens right away. Dammit, I shouldn't have stayed here this long. I have to go right away."

"Alright, alright. What do you need from me?"

"Could you get me a car?"

"Yes, I can arrange for that. But I can't do it until tomorrow, so you might as well enjoy the party tonight. The most important thing is to avoid a scandal."

"Where's your phone?"

Williams showed Wordman to another room with a telephone, and then went downstairs to rejoin his guests. Wordman racked his brain to remember the number, and then tried to make his voice sound young. "Dad? It's me, Donny." When he heard his father's voice, Wordman almost couldn't stay on his feet. He looked around for a place to sit down, but there was no chair within the span of the telephone cord, so he ended up just leaning against the wall.

His college days came flooding back to his memory, and Wordman could vaguely remember a time when he was idealistic, when he thought his father was the most honorable man he knew. Images of the accident came back to his mind as well, and the whirlwind aftermath of police, lawyers, and his father's influence making it all go away. It was actually a bit eerie, he thought, how the consequences of his actions had dissolved into the air in a matter of a day or two, and after that there was this vacuum, this void where guilt should have been. Wordman remembered having a conscience then, but telling himself that this must be how the game is played, and how it would be ungrateful to those who saved him if he didn't make the most of the opportunity. And from that time on, whenever he allowed people to manipulate him, he just told himself that it was opportunity knocking – until the day came when he was the one doing the manipulating. That was the day he knew he was a success. "Yeah, I'm okay. But I need some help. I got into a little trouble... no I'm in Savannah. Yeah... look Dad, I'm real sorry to ask, but could you send a couple of your guys down here to pick me up and take me back to school? No... tonight. Yeah, I'll give you the address..."

Jimmy hung around the outskirts of the party looking for Wordman. Eventually, as the party began to thin out, he went out the back door into the garden. He hoped he could stay out of sight while still looking in through the back windows. Wordman didn't want to come downstairs so he wandered into a guest bedroom and lay down on the bed. He fell asleep hearing his father's voice in his head, and he dreamed of his parents. He could see his father, looking as he did in the 1970s. He had a smile on his face. "We're real proud of you, Donny. Real proud." Then Wordman saw his father put a gun in his mouth and pull the trigger. Wordman awoke with a start and sat up in the bed, trying to catch his breath.

"Wordman!" Jimmy walked into the guest room and drew his gun, pointing it at Wordman's chest.

Wordman stood up. "Stop right there, AG-nello."

"It's *Ahn-yello*."

"Whatever." Then Wordman dropped his attitude and decided to appeal to Jimmy's reason. "You have to let me do this. I'm doing a good thing. I'm saving that girl's life."

"Sorry, Wordman. You can't undo what you did. You have to face it. Anyway you can't go back in time to change the past without negating the reason for going back in time. If you don't have the accident, you never get in the time machine. It's a paradox. At least that's what Sofia says. It just doesn't work."

"A paradox? Are you trying to school me? I won't even *try* to explain it to you, but all you need to know is that I know what I'm doing. Anyway it's worth a try. If you stop me, you're participating in her death. You're killing her!"

Jimmy took a deep breath, and took his eyes off of Wordman for a split second. For one slim moment he felt sorry for Wordman. Jimmy knew what it was like to have regrets, and to live a life of looking over your shoulder, always worried that someone will find out who you are – what you've done. And in that moment of compassion, Wordman was able to pull Sofia's gun out of his coat pocket and point it at Jimmy. Wordman's gun hand was shaking, which made Jimmy nervous. "Nice try, Wordman, but my orders are to bring you back alive or leave your dead body here. It's up to you."

Then Jimmy heard the clicking sound of two pistol hammers being pulled back on two guns behind him. He slowly turned around, keeping his gun pointed at Wordman. "What the… Fat Paulie G.? Is that you? Geez, you're... skinny. What the hell are you doing here? And who's this mook?"

Paulie's associate squinted at Jimmy. "Fuck you."

"Okay, fine," Jimmy shrugged. "I'll just call you Mook."

"Who the fuck are you?" Skinny Fat Paulie didn't wait for an answer from Jimmy, but spoke to Wordman. "Who the fuck is this? And who the fuck are you? Where's that brat kid Donny?"

Wordman had completely forgotten that when his father's men arrived they wouldn't recognize him. "Uh... Donny's good. I'm his... uncle, or... second cousin, really. This man is the problem. I need you to take care of him."

"We don't know you from Adam, pal, and we don't clip a guy unless Mr. S. says so."

"Look, *pal*." Wordman thought fast. "The senator told you to come down here and pick up Donny, right?"

"Yeah."

"Well how would I know that if I wasn't working for him, too?"

"Okay."

"And anyone who's pointing a gun at me should be considered an enemy of Senator Wordman, right?" Jimmy tried to protest but the thugs were convinced.

"So what do you want we should do with him?"

"I'll tell you what." Wordman thought for a moment. "Take him to the cops. Tell them the senator says he's insane and needs to be locked up in the mental hospital for observation. Tell them he might be a danger to himself and others."

Jimmy was in shock. *What are Chicago boys doing working for Wordman's father? What's the connection? They didn't recognize me because in 1973 I was only four years old. But they must have thought Wordman looked enough like his father to pass for family. Shit, I can't go back to the loony bin.*

Fat Paulie G. pointed his gun at Jimmy while Mook took Jimmy's gun and pulled a pair of handcuffs out of his jacket pocket. Jimmy made his move, rotating out of Mook's grip, only to spin around head first into Paulie's meaty fist. Jimmy was stunned just long enough for Paulie to put him in a headlock while Mook put on the handcuffs. Paulie didn't let up on the headlock, though. He held on until Jimmy passed out.

Wordman put Sofia's gun back in his coat pocket. "After you take him to the cops, meet me at the Antebellum Club. It's just off Bay Street." With that Wordman walked out of the room, down the stairs, and out of the house.

When skinny Fat Paulie G. and Mook arrived at the Antebellum Club, they gave Wordman the cold shoulder. Wordman tried to get them to drive him to the college in Athens, but they refused.

Paulie always spoke for both of them. "Am I your fuckin' chauffeur? Do I look like I'm wearing a fuckin' chauffeur hat?"

"No, but my fa- I mean, Senator Wordman would be very appreciative if you would do me this favor and get me to Athens."

"Yeah, well, we called him, and he never heard of you. He wants to know where his son is, and if you don't tell us, we're gonna take you for another kind of ride."

"Look fellas, there's no need for threats. You can trust me. I'm family."

"So was Fredo."

Wordman was starting to get the feeling he wasn't getting out of Savannah with these guys, so he decided to take Jim Williams up on his offer to get him a car. "Fine. Never mind. I'll get there myself." Wordman turned to leave.

Paulie moved into Wordman's path to prevent him from walking away. "Where's Donny?"

"He's at school. Go ahead and call him if you don't believe me. But when you ask him why he called his father from Savannah, don't be surprised if he was too drunk to remember it."

Wordman walked out of the club and left the two thugs to enjoy the funky music without him, while he made his way back to the inn.

Later, Jimmy awoke to a pounding headache, a blinding light, and a body that he couldn't move. He soon realized that he was wrapped tightly in a sheet, like a mummy, laying in a hospital bed in the middle of an all-white room with bright lights shining on him. He struggled to free his arms and legs, but the sheet was wrapped too tightly around him.

"Stop fighting it."

Jimmy looked around and tried to focus his eyes on the shadow standing over him, but the overhead light was too bright in his eyes. He could only make out a white coat, and a bald head. "Who are you?"

"I'm your doctor."

"You're not my doctor! Where am I? Why am I wrapped up like this?"

"Now, don't you worry about a thing. I'm here to take care of you. Your friend Doctor Wordman is only looking out for you by placing you under my care."

"He's not my friend, and he's not a medical doctor! Let me out of here!" Jimmy struggled against the sheet.

"Now, now. I know you're confused, and you're suffering." The doctor prepared a syringe. "I'm just going to give you a little shot for the pain. You know, morphine is a great pain-reliever. It makes you feel so much better, and takes away all the pain. It's made from the same stuff as heroin. Of course, this is actually heroin."

†††

"What are you doin' here, barber? This is no concern of yours."

Sara looked up, and through her tears she could see the root doctor, Socrates, standing nearby. Suddenly the De la Croix brothers were startled by old Annie Flax the Boo Hag. She ran straight up to them and screamed gibberish at them. She waved her walking stick in the air and jangled her bracelets in their faces. Then, when they were sufficiently freaked out, she ran off. In the moment it took for them to regain their composure, Socrates walked up to them shaking his head. "Tsk, tsk, tsk, oh that *is* a shame. The hag has put the mouth on you gentlemen. And I'm sure you know, when a person is rid by a hag, he's likely as not to get real sick, or worse."

The three brothers looked at each other. They had heard the rumors about the first fever victims and were deathly afraid of being infected. Blaise shouted, "Shut your mouth old man!" But Brant said, "No wait, he's that witch doctor. He can help us. Tell us what to do, old man!"

"Well, I can help you, but it won't be easy. And it will cost you."

Bernard took a step toward Socrates. "How about we pay you by not putting this rope around your neck?"

"Alright, alright. If you want to break the conjure, I'll chew the root for you, but I'll need some dirt from a preacher's grave. I suggest the yard behind the Episcopal Church." The men looked at each other. "Well, you'd best go now, before the sickness comes on."

The brothers looked at Sara. "We can finish this later." They dropped the rope and got on their horses.

Socrates called out to them. "Now I need a sack of dirt for each of you. I'll be waiting right here when you get back."

The men rode off and Sara fell to her knees crying. Then she felt a hand on her shoulder. It was Esther, bending down to help Sara to her feet, and trying to help put her dress back together.

Socrates walked up to them. "I have no intention of being here when they get back, so I'll just be on my way."

Esther looked up at him. "Thank you Socrates."

Sara looked up and tried to wipe her eyes. "Thank you." Then she looked in the direction where the Boo Hag had walked off muttering her gibberish. "Is that woman ill?"

"The Boo Hag?" Socrates thought for a moment. "They used to try to feed us things not fit for people. Cotton seeds and other trash, hopin' to find a cheap food for slaves, hopin' we could live off what they were fixin' to throw away. Imagine, thinkin' what's poison to white folks might be okay for black folks to eat. That woman there is old Annie Flax. Her real name is Anna Felaxis. And when she was a little girl, they fed her all kinds of poison to see if folks like us could live off it. Now the poor old woman's not right in the head."

Then Sara's eyes widened. "Colum!" She got up and started running back toward the hotel, and Esther followed as close as she could. The sun was going down and the last of the day's light was dimming. Sara found her way to the hotel and ran up the steps without stopping. Then up the staircase and into the room where she had been locked up. Colum's blood was still on the floor, but he was nowhere to be found. Sara ran down the stairs as Esther was coming into the lobby. Not knowing what else to do, Sara ran into Crown's office with Esther following. The office was empty, and Sara looked around desperately. On the desk, she saw Crown's dueling pistol. Without even thinking about it, she reached out, and picked it up.

"Put that down, little lady."

Sara spun around to see Sheriff Bartleby and deputy Ronan coming into the office. She looked to Esther, who backed away from the men, off to the side near the poker table. Sara was trapped, with her back against Crown's massive oak desk. But she still had the gun in her hand. She raised it and pointed it right at the sheriff. She had no intention of going back to that tree.

The sheriff kept walking toward her and held up his hands. "Now, now, little lady. Put that gun down."

"Don't take another step." Sara's voice quivered.

The sheriff stopped for a moment. "C'mon now, you don't want that gun to go off, do you? You're not a killer." The sheriff took one step closer to Sara.

Sara raised the gun a bit more, her hand shaking. "I said stay back! Don't come any closer."

The sheriff took another step, and then slowly took another. "Now listen here, we both know you're not going to shoot me." He took another step.

Sara steadied the gun by holding it with both hands. She raised the gun to aim at Bartleby's head. "Not another step!"

As the sheriff took another step, he said, "Just give me the gun, little lady. You're not going to shoot me. You're not going to shoot me." He reached out to take the gun from Sara.

Sara exhaled, and a thought flashed through her mind. *I will not be your victim.* Then she pulled the trigger, and the sheriff didn't live to see the world's next moment. One little bullet, not much bigger than a pomegranate seed, and Sara Pugliese was a killer after all.

Esther almost fainted. As Sara regained her composure after the blast of the pistol, she turned the gun toward the deputy. But he just took a step back, and sat down in one of the poker chairs. He tipped his hat to Sara, and looked toward the door. Sara kept the gun aimed at him while she and Esther ran out of the office and into the lobby. From there they ran outside, where both women looked around in a panic, realizing that they were at the other end of town from any safe place to hide. And even if they went back to the log cabins, that would be the first place anyone would look for them.

Sara looked down at the gun in her hand, and threw it to the ground. "The boarding house!" She started running in the direction of Bryan Street with Esther following. Mrs. Lillibridge's boarding house was close by, so it didn't take them long to get there running at top speed. They burst in through the door without knocking.

"Oh my!" Mrs. Lillibridge was startled, but happy to see Sara safe and sound. "Come in, come in."

Sara moved out of the front parlor and away from the windows, and Esther followed. They sat down to catch their breath, and Mrs. Lillibridge went into the kitchen to get them some sweet tea. After a moment of silence, both Sara and Esther started to cry, and hugged each other. Mrs. Lillibridge appeared with two handkerchiefs, but didn't say anything. She just put the two glasses of tea on a table and left the room.

Sara tried to stop herself from crying, but could only speak between the sobs. "I have to get out of here. I can't be here. I have to get out of here."

Esther did her best to stop crying, and she took Sara's hand. "Sara?"

"Yes?"

Esther hesitated, twirling a lock of hair behind her ear. "I need to ask you something."

"What?"

"When you leave Savannah… will you take my Rosie with you?"

"What?!"

"Take her with you. If she stays here, it won't be long before she's… Oh!" Esther couldn't hold back the tears. "I thought she would be free. I thought she would be free."

"Esther, I… I don't know if I can. I mean, I understand, but I just don't know if I can. I don't even know how I'm going to get back home. And now Colum is missing."

Mrs. Lillibridge came into the room and tried to lighten the mood. "We sure could use some rain here." Sara and Esther looked at her, and she knew her attempt was futile. "Well you're right about one thing, Miss Sara. You can't stay in Savannah."

Sara thought for a moment. *Even if I knew where Colum was, we don't have the time machine. And even if we had it, the damn thing is so glitchy we can't rely on it. I can't put my hopes in that wooden box. I just have to face the truth. There's no way to go home. This is it. I'm stuck here. What do I have to go back to anyway? My family is a fraud. I have no idea where I come from, so what does it matter where I go from here?* Sara looked at Esther. "Okay. I'll take her with me. I'm going to get out of Savannah, and I'll take her with me."

Tom Kennedy poked his head around the corner and looked into the room. "Where will you go?" The women all looked at him. "I'm sorry, I didn't mean to eavesdrop. It's just that I'm leaving town myself. I've already stayed longer than I should have, with fever season now upon us. I'm going back home, to Illinois. If you don't have anywhere else to go, you can come with me as far as Hanover, and then go on back to Chicago. I wouldn't mind a few traveling companions, and I have already acquired a wagon."

"When are you leaving?" Sara thought Chicago sounded as good a place as any to go, and it was familiar territory, even if it was a century before she was born.

"Tomorrow, after I settle an obligation with Mr. Gleason. I have a small monetary debt I owe him, and I promised I would meet him at his church to repay him before I leave town."

"We have to find Colum, but hopefully that will be enough time. We'll meet you at the church tomorrow."

"It's the Methodist church. Mr. Gleason is directing the choir for the service there. Now, I must be off to finish my packing."

Sara turned to Esther. "The Methodist church? The minister there is a friend of Crown. I don't know if we can risk going there."

"There will be a lot of people," Esther said thoughtfully. "You can stay out of sight long enough to meet Mr. Kennedy."

Mrs. Lillibridge reassured Sara. "Don't worry about the Reverend. I'll speak to him."

Sara looked Esther in the eyes. "Can you have Rosie ready to go by tomorrow morning?" Esther nodded. "Then meet us at that church. Mrs. Lillibridge, can I impose on you to allow me to stay here tonight? I'm afraid I can't pay you."

"Oh never mind that, dear. You're welcome to stay one more night, I suppose."

Colum slipped in and out of consciousness for a while, until he finally came to, and forced his eyes open. He panicked a little when he couldn't see anything, but soon his eyes adjusted to the lack of light. He could see very little of his surroundings. Dark wooden planks and ropes. He could hear the sound of water slapping against wood, and he could feel everything swaying. *I'm on a boat.* And then he realized the worst part of all. He was in chains. Shackles bound his wrists and ankles, and a chain kept him attached to the wall. Before he even had time to consider the gravity of his situation, he heard voices coming toward him.

"In two months' time we'll be in England, then we continue east from there."

When Colum heard this, he panicked. He pulled at the chain that bound him to the wall, and clawed at the shackles on his wrists. But it was futile. A large shirtless man opened a hatch and came down the short staircase to where Colum was in chains. He could see the fear and confusion on Colum's face, and he just laughed. "Well, Mr. I-Don't-Give-A-Shit-What-Your-Name-Is, it looks like you are now a sailor. But don't worry, we'll be back here at this port in no time at all. Not more than a year or two at the most. And now that we've shoved off, it's time for me to show you how you're going to earn your keep around here."

CHAPTER 6
TUMBLIN' DOWN

On Sunday morning it finally rained. Sara had waited for Colum to turn up, and even asked around a bit with the help of Mrs. Lillibridge, Daisy, and Margaret. But Colum was nowhere to be found. Sara suppressed fears of a worst case scenario and hoped that Colum would show up in time for them to leave town together. But she could not delay her own escape any longer. The reality that she had killed the sheriff was like Damocles' sword hanging over her head, and it was simply too dangerous to stay in Savannah. In addition, she was committed to the idea of taking Rosie away, and getting her away from Crown. She put on the borrowed dress and gathered her things, all the time listening for a knock at the door, hoping to hear Colum's voice. For a long moment, she held the small prayer book that Harriet had given her. She ran her hands over the leather cover, and held it close to her chest before tucking it into her purse. She left the boarding house after the church service began to make sure she would arrive when no one would see her. Everyone would be inside, and she could meet Esther and Tom Kennedy outside the church and they all could be on their way.

Sara walked quickly to the Methodist church, trying to stay under the trees and out of the rain as much as possible, and trying to stay inconspicuous. When she got there, she waited alone around the corner of the building. After a while, she started to worry that no one was coming. She wondered if she had missed them, and a moment of panic was soon averted when she finally saw Esther walking slowly toward her, holding Rosie's hand. In spite of the rain, Esther didn't hurry. She just strolled along with her head down, looking at Rosie. When they got to the church, Esther walked Rosie to a semi-dry place under a tree, and knelt down to face her daughter. The raindrops on her face hid her tears.

"Where are we goin' mama?" Rosie's smile was full of anticipation.

"Not *we*, my sweet child. But you're gonna be free. You're gonna be free of this place, and free of these people who want to use you up."

Rosie's smile left her face. She couldn't understand what her mother was saying, but she knew that her mother was torn up inside. "Are you sending me away? Don't send me away, mama. I promise I won't be no trouble, I'll be good." Rosie's little body bounced up and down as she tried to deal with the fear and confusion, and the oncoming tears.

"Oh, you *are* good, child. But you aren't safe. Not here. You're goin' someplace safe. Miss Sara will take you."

"But you can come, too, mama."

Sara walked up to Esther and Rosie, struggling to hold back her own tears. "Yes, Esther, you can come too. We'll go to Illinois, all of us together."

"No, girl. I'm already used up. Besides, if I go, Mr. Crown will come looking for me. But if I stay, maybe he won't go after you and Rosie. Maybe I can…"

Sara whispered so Rosie wouldn't hear. "But he'll hurt you."

"No. If Rosie is safe, he can't hurt me. Only way he can hurt me is if he gets Rosie."

"That's her, chief! Her name is Sara Resonator." Esther looked up, and Sara turned around to see Dickey-Jim Crown standing with the chief of police and two officers. Crown spit a mouthful of chewing tobacco on the ground.

Chief Anderson put his hand on his gun. "Sara Resonator, you are under arrest for the murder of Sheriff Bartleby."

Sara looked around quickly and took off running in the only direction she could - right into the church. Chief Anderson drew his revolver and pointed it at her back, but he couldn't pull the trigger. She burst through the doors, making everyone in the congregation turn to look. Esther followed her in with Rosie, but when she saw that all eyes were on them, she took Rosie off to the side behind the last row of pews. The choir stopped singing, and Solomon Gleason turned around to see why. Sara saw Gleason, and thinking he was her only hope, she ran down the aisle toward him, and threw her arms around him, causing the congregation to gasp and mutter. As Crown and the police came in, Reverend Meyers walked down the aisle to meet them. He ignored the police and spoke directly to Crown. "Mr. Crown, why are you interrupting my worship service?"

"Reverend, did you not see that fugitive enter your church? It was not I who interrupted the service, but her!" Crown pointed at Sara dramatically.

The Reverend could see that Gleason was protecting Sara. "And just what has she done?"

"Well, nothing less than *murder* our beloved Sheriff Bartleby, in cold blood." The congregation gasped again.

The Reverend was silent for a moment, and it was clear to everyone that he was considering his options. He looked at Sara, cowering behind his choir director. He looked at chief Anderson and the police officers. "Well, sir, far be it from me to obstruct justice. If she is guilty of such a crime, then she must be arrested and accept the consequences." The church was silent, except for a few quiet sobs that escaped Sara's lips. The police moved toward the front of the church, but the Reverend stepped in front of them. "However… this is a house of God, and we are in the middle of worship. By law, this is a sanctuary. You can arrest her after the service. But not during worship. Not here in God's house."

Crown sputtered, "What?! Are you opposing me, Reverend? No one opposes me! Why would you risk my friendship for a negro girl? What would be the point? We will still arrest her as soon as the service is over. We will wait outside so she cannot leave without being arrested. She *will* face the consequences. She *will* be hanged!"

"Mr. Crown, I know for a fact that your departed mother was a devout Episcopalian. Do you not fear God? Do you not fear that there may be consequences to *your* actions?"

"Do not bring my mother into this, Reverend. And to answer your question, I do not believe in any God, at least not one who cares in the slightest about people and what they do, or even listens to their prayers, let alone answers them. Such ideas are pure superstition, and weigh a man down, like barnacles on a ship." More gasps from the congregation, and at this chief Anderson and his men took a step back away from Crown, and started to look uncomfortable.

Reverent Meyers remained calm. "Well, sir, I do believe in God, and I've come to believe that if I'm right about God, then I've been wrong about a great many other things, and I've made many mistakes that cause me to fear God's anger. In this very church I have preached that it is God's will that some men own and enslave other men. But now I think that conviction – though I held it dearly not so very long ago – was false. And the progress our society has made has convinced me to change my opinion on what is the will of God."

"Progress?! Let me tell you, Reverend. Gatling guns and ironclad ships – that is progress. Not this... this... destruction of our very culture – a culture that once was civilized and honored things like nobility and the legacy of the genteel."

"So you say. But nevertheless, this is a sanctuary, and you cannot arrest anyone in my church."

Chief Anderson took Crown's arm and gently pulled him toward the door, and Crown stormed off, shoving the doors so that they opened with a bang, and bounced back, almost hitting Anderson as he followed Crown out. The congregation could hear Crown barking orders to the police as he walked down the steps to the street. "We will stand at the exits, and arrest her the moment she leaves this building."

†††

Jimmy struggled in the sheet as the doctor approached with the syringe. Then he saw another shadowy figure enter the room.

"Well, look at you, all rolled up like a big joint. I guess you spent too much time in Jamaica."

Jimmy recognized the voice, and squinted, forcing his eyes to focus, to prove to himself what his ears already told him. "CHRIS!"

"In the flesh."

"Chris, get me out of here! And watch out for the syringe!"

Chris walked toward the doctor, who backed away. He swung the syringe at Chris, but Chris dodged it and threw a round kick into the doctor's stomach. The doctor grabbed his gut as he stumbled to the floor. Then he picked himself up and ran out of the room. Chris turned back toward Jimmy, but Jimmy moved his eyes toward the floor.

"Bro. Check your shoe."

Chris looked down to see the syringe sticking out of his Converse. Chris looked closer, and then laughed. "Heh, heh – between the toes." He pulled out the syringe, and then helped Jimmy get out of the sheet.

Jimmy still could barely believe his eyes. "What the hell are you doing here?" he had so many questions he could hardly spit them out. "How did you get here, I mean, now?"

"No idea. But look, there's something you should know. Sara never made it to Jamaica. Something went wrong and she ended up... well, here. But a hundred years ago. Colum and I were going back to get her, but, *again*, something went wrong. Dude, I just materialized all by myself – without the time machine – under the bleachers at a Savannah State football game. The hometown Tigers thought it was in very poor taste for the visiting team's band to play *Marching Through Georgia*."

"Well, I'm glad I didn't leave Sara behind in Kingston. So how did you find me?"

"I was so disoriented when I arrived that people thought I was drunk and called the cops. They brought me here to the hospital, where I spent the night. This morning I was told – guess what – they had somebody else with the same last name who had just been admitted to the psychiatric ward, and would I like to visit him?"

"Well, I'll be a *deus ex machina*."

"No shit. Science's failure is God's opportunity. Now let's get the hell out of here."

Jimmy and Chris ran out the door, looking down the hall in both directions to see if anyone was coming. A door was opening at the end of the hall to their left, so they ran to the right. They pushed through a security door, setting off an alarm, and ran out into the parking garage. Jimmy grabbed Chris by the shoulder. "Wordman is here – but he doesn't know you're here. That's our advantage. So we have to make sure they don't see you. Let's split up – you go, and I'll hang back and get them to follow me. After I lose them, we'll meet up. One hour from now, at the Sixpence Pub. It's on Bull Street. Now go!"

Chris ran off, and Jimmy waited until the doctor and two security guards came through the door, and then he ran in the other direction, away from Chris. Before long, he had outrun them, and he circled back to make sure they weren't still following. It took a while to walk from the hospital back into the heart of town, and Jimmy and Chris took different routes. Along the way, Chris walked through a depressed part of town. A homeless man was sitting on an overturned bucket next to a shopping cart full of junk. The man looked down to avoid eye contact with Chris. "Sir, could you help me out? I would sure appreciate it if you could spare some change."

Chris almost said no without a thought, but it occurred to him that if his grandfather were in the same situation, he would give the man some money. Chris looked around to make sure it wasn't some kind of ambush, and then he reached for his wallet. *Gone! My wallet's gone! Damn, the cops took it. It's probably still at the hospital.* Chris looked back toward the hospital, but there was no going back for it. *Good thing I left my ID back in New York. But all my money!* Chris looked at the homeless man. "Sorry man, I'm broke." He mindlessly put his hand in his pocket, and he felt a bill. "Wait a minute." He pulled out the bill and looked at it.

Abraham Lincoln stared back at him. Putting everything in perspective, at this moment Chris wasn't so worried about getting stuck in the past. He was just happy to be alive. He handed the five dollar bill to the man, who thanked him profusely.

As Chris walked away, he remembered Dublin, in 1742, when he saw Handel give his last coin to a beggar. And he remembered Colum giving away his change outside the Harp and Whistle. *Hmm. God's opportunity.* Then his thoughts drifted to Willow, and the morning after their wedding. *I'm married. I have responsibilities now. Hmm. I guess I am taking after Gramps after all. Not as a musician, though.* Chris remembered a conversation he had with his grandfather when he was very young.

Gramps, what's your job?

I'm your nonna's husband.

No I mean your REAL job.

That is my real job. Being your nonna's husband is the most important job I have. And it's for life. Other jobs come and go, and that's okay. The other jobs are secondary. But a man's most important job is to be a husband.

Hmm. I don't need to be anything else but Willow's husband. I just need to get back to her. That's all that matters now.

Wordman found himself running for his life. The two Chicago thugs were chasing him, running full speed with their guns drawn. Wordman reached into his coat pocket to look for Sofia's gun, but it wasn't there. He kept on running, stumbling along, and tripping over dead flowers and broken down trees. He was running through the Colonial Park cemetery, and now he had to jump over open graves, and run around the tombstones. It was getting hard to keep going, and not being able to run in a straight line was slowing him down. Fat Paulie was gaining on him. Wordman looked behind him, and tripped and fell. When he pulled himself up he saw something that made him stop. It was a brand new headstone, and the name chiseled on it was his own. He read the inscription. *Here lies Donald Wordman. Selfish Bastard, Irresponsible Hedonist, Mean Drunk, Foolish Gambler, Shameless Cheater, Coke Head, Porn Addict, Spineless Coward, Unrepentant Murderer, Immoral Liar, Fucking Racist, and All-Around Asshole.* Wordman couldn't believe what he was seeing. He rubbed his eyes, and woke up.

When Jimmy and Chris found each other at the Sixpence Pub, it wasn't open yet. They went around to the side of the building to stay out of sight. Chris was excited. "So you said Wordman is here? How do we catch him?"

"I don't know. There are only two places I know for sure he goes. One is the disco, but that's not open now. The other is this rich guy's house. Williams. I say we go there and see if he shows up."

"You got it, bro. Let's go."

Jimmy looked at Chris. "*You got it bro*? You sound like you're trying to talk like me. Are you trying to talk like me?"

"No, man. I'm just…whatever."

"Look Chris. Don't imitate me. You don't want to be like me. Be like your dad. At least you have a dad. Why are you trying to be like me?"

"Geez, Jimmy."

"Forget it. Never mind. We have to move so we don't miss Wordman. And I want to catch that bastard so I can try to contact my parents before we leave here."

"Speaking of that, how are we going to get back? We don't have the time machine."

"Yeah, I know. We're going to have to put an ad in the paper and hope Sofia and Armando see it."

Chris followed Jimmy as they made their way to Williams' house. They moved through a neighbor's yard to stay behind a row of hedges. Wordman was in front of the house talking with Williams, and they were standing next to a Cadillac. Jimmy and Chris moved as close as they could to try to hear the conversation, but their movements attracted some unwanted attention.

"What the fuck? Didn't we put you in the hospital?" It was Fat Paulie, holding a gun up to Jimmy's head.

Paulie pushed the barrel of the gun against Jimmy's neck, while Mook stood over Chris. Jimmy didn't respond verbally. He tapped Chris on the shoulder, which made Paulie look at Jimmy's left hand. This meant he wasn't looking at Jimmy's right hand, and before he knew it, Jimmy had reached up and grabbed the gun, pulling it forward toward the ground. He pulled Paulie down by the arm and rolled over on him, guiding the gun until it was pointed at Mook, and he put his finger over Fat Paulie's finger and pulled the trigger twice. Paulie was shocked to see his partner die right in front of him, but Jimmy didn't give him time to think about it. He put an elbow in his face, and then spun around, wrenching the gun out of Paulie's hand and pointing it at him. Paulie fell backwards, then struggled to his feet and ran off between the houses. Jimmy kept the gun pointed at him until he was out of sight.

Jimmy lowered the gun, and then looked at it. "Son of a bitch! This is *my* gun. I hate that people keep taking my gun." He stepped over the dead mobster and walked around the hedge into the open, pointing the gun at Wordman.

Chris' mouth hung open. *Wow. He just shot that guy, without even thinking about it. Look at him. He's dead. Just lying there dead. Good thing Willow isn't here – she would hate this.* Chris followed Jimmy around the hedge, looking back at the dead body on the lawn.

"Hold it right there, Wordman! I can't let you leave Savannah."

"What are you going to do, Jimmy? Shoot me?"

"If I have to, but I'm hoping it doesn't come to that. You can see that you wouldn't be the first person I've killed. But I want you to come back with us and take responsibility for your actions."

"If you just let me go, I can undo it. I can save that girl. Then we can all go home." Wordman motioned for Williams to go inside and call the police.

"The time machine's not there, Wordman. I sent it back. You can't get back without us."

Wordman's face fell as he searched his mind for some hope of a plan B.

Jimmy kept the gun pointed at Wordman as he walked up to the Cadillac. They keys were in the ignition. "Get in." Wordman started to get in the back seat. "No, wait." Jimmy pulled out the keys and tossed them to Chris. "Open the trunk." Chris opened the trunk, and Jimmy walked around the front of the car toward Wordman. He motioned toward the trunk. "Get in."

"What?"

"You heard me. Get in the trunk."

Wordman reluctantly got into the trunk of the car, and Chris closed it. Jimmy and Chris got into the car and sped off, just as the sound of police sirens approached. With every bump they hit, they could hear Wordman yelling in the trunk.

Chris was worried. "Dammit Jimmy, we gotta get outta sight. You killed a guy back there, and now we just stole a car."

"Best we can do now is head out of town, and try to make our way to the newspaper office."

"Do you know where that is?"

"No, we're going to have to do the unthinkable."

"What's that?"

"Stop and ask for directions."

Jimmy drove the car out of town, turning in random directions, until he was sure no one was following them. They pulled into a gas station to get directions, and soon they were headed toward the offices of the *Savannah Morning News*. They parked in the back by the loading dock to keep the car out of sight, and to keep anyone from hearing the yelling man in the trunk.

As they walked up to the classified ads desk, Chris whispered to Jimmy. "Say it's a three-legged horse."

"What?"

"A three-legged horse. Say you're selling a three-legged horse. That's what Sara did."

So Jimmy and Chris placed a classified ad for a three-legged horse. Interested parties should inquire of the Resonator brothers of Savannah, Georgia.

"We need a place," Jimmy whispered to Chris. "We need to know where the time machine will materialize, and it would be nice to know when." Then he raised his voice to speak to the clerk behind the counter. "Are there any concerts coming up here in town?"

"Are you kidding?" The clerk looked at Jimmy like he was from outer space. "Johnny Mercer is back in town. He's playing a concert at the Savannah Theater. Here's the flyer. Says they're recording it for a live album."

†††

The shirtless man unlocked Colum's shackles and took him up the short staircase into the sun. As the man rapidly listed off all of Colum's new duties, Colum was not listening. He was squinting to try to force his eyes to adjust to the sunlight, and desperately looking back toward the shore. The ship was just pulling up anchor and starting to move out of the bay. Colum noticed a man waving his arms on the shoreline. It was black man, holding a bow and arrows. Then to Colum's surprise, the man set an arrow and pointed the bow right at him. Colum froze as the man released the arrow. Colum could see the arrow flying straight towards him, almost as if in slow motion. The arrow stuck hard into the shirtless man's chest, and now the archer on the shore was yelling, "Jump!" So Colum jumped - over the side and into the water. He could feel the sting of salt water on his head wound as he swam for his life. When he stopped swimming for a second and looked back, there was no sign of the shirtless man, and the ship just kept on moving out of the bay. Finally, Colum made it to the shore, and John Brown reached out his hand and pulled Colum up onto dry land. Colum stood up, then fell to his knees.

"Get up, boy. No time to kiss the ground."

"Thank you. Thank you. How did you...? Thank you."

"When you disappeared, I reckoned there was only one place you could have ended up. Shanghaied. Now c'mon. Miss Sara is waiting for you."

John Brown took Colum to the Methodist church, where Crown and the police were waiting outside. They walked right past them, and went up to the door of the church. Brown said goodbye to Colum, shook his hand, and then headed for the woods. Colum turned and looked back at a fuming, pacing Crown. "Mr. Crown, we have a saying in Ireland. If you come up in this world, make sure you don't go down in the next. Men like you – after they're gone, they're forgotten by everyone but the devil. You think you're so important. But you're ridiculous. You come from old money and call yourself a self-made man. But you can't have it both ways. Someday maybe the people of this town will tell you to your face how pathetic they think you are. Maybe that day is today."

As Colum entered the church, the Reverend was just finishing up his impromptu sermon. "And so I ask the good people of Savannah, and of this congregation, to forgive me. I have been listening to the wrong people. But today, the Lord brought me face to face with a choice. I could choose to be loyal to a man who is not my friend, and who doesn't even know the meaning of the word loyalty. Or I could choose to be loyal to… well, let me tell you whose face I saw in my mind. It was my colleague, the Reverend William Campbell. That's right, the preacher at the Baptist church. Now he may be a negro, but he is also my Christian brother. And if I were to take the side of men like Crown, an admitted atheist, I would betray my brother. Blood may be thicker than water, my friends, but baptismal water is thicker than blood. And though it may cost me, in worldly terms, it is my decision that we will offer this poor girl a safe haven for as long as it takes to protect her from persecution. Since they cannot arrest her while this service of holy worship goes on, we will extend the service – all day, and into the night if needed – until the Lord presents us with some guidance on how to protect her." The congregation broke into applause, and the applause became clapping, which then turned into a song. Reverend Meyers nodded to Gleason, indicating that he should keep the music going.

Once the sermon was over, Sara and Colum couldn't hold back any longer, and they ran to each other and hugged and kissed. The women of the congregation fanned themselves and looked away. Some of the men fumed at the sight of a white man kissing a black woman, and they wondered if their pastor had betrayed them. A few walked out.

After a while, the choir ran out of songs they had prepared, but the energy in the congregation was at a peak. Gleason got the choir's attention and whispered to them. Then he turned to the congregation. "Ladies and gentlemen, allow me the indulgence of presenting to you a hymn of my own composition. The choir has rehearsed it, and although we did not plan to present it to you today, I would like to offer it now." He turned back to the choir, everyone standing tall and at the ready. When the song began, the people of the congregation were very pleased with it. Then the excitement grew, as the music swelled, and the people heard something they had never heard before in that Methodist church. They heard the harmonics of the Resonator materializing. It appeared right in the middle of the church, at the front of the aisle.

A few of the women fainted, and a few others screamed. The auto-pause worked perfectly, and the large wooden crate just sat there, front and center, as everyone in the church stared at it in silence, on the edge of panic. Colum jumped up to the pulpit. "Please don't be afraid. I know this looks very strange to you, but everything is all right. This… box belongs to some friends of ours. Believe me, I know how frightening it can be to see this thing appear like that, but it's okay, really. It's not evil, or anything like that, I promise."

The Reverend moved over to Colum at the pulpit. "What is it?"

"It's our ride home," Colum said. He ran over to the crate and opened the trap door. But when he looked in he remembered that only one person can fit inside. He stopped, and turned around to look at Sara, who was walking up to the crate slowly. "How can we both go back?"

Sara thought for a moment. "It doesn't matter. I'm not going back."

"What?"

"I made a promise. To take Rosie to Illinois. If I just escape, nothing changes here, she's still in danger."

"But you don't belong here."

"How do you know where I belong? If I go back, I'm alone. If I stay here, I'm doing something. I'm part of something."

"But Sara…"

"You go. You should go. You have a family, you have your brother and sister, your dad, you have the Agnellos. You have something to go back to. I don't."

"Sara, I can't go back without you. I can't lose you again. I have nothing to go back to if I don't go back with you."

"It doesn't matter. Only one of us can go back anyway."

"Well, if they know about Mr. Gleason's hymns, I suppose one of us could go back, and then we could ask Mr. Gleason to play more of his hymns until the machine comes back here, and then…"

"What if it doesn't come back? What if they only have a recording of the one hymn? What if the other hymns were already performed years ago? What if something goes wrong? And something always seems to go wrong."

"You can't stay here, in this time – it's too dangerous."

"I'm not afraid. I've almost died already, and anyway no one lives forever. I don't matter, Colum. What matters is bigger than me. What matters is freedom… and Rosie… and… not being a victim. No matter what, we can't take Rosie back to our time, so I'm taking her to Illinois. I'm keeping my promise. I want to make sure she has a life. So you should go back without me, so you can have a life, too."

"No. I want you in my life. If you're going to Illinois… so am I." Colum reached into the Resonator to push the button and send it back to the year two thousand with no one inside.

"Wait!"

Colum stopped and pulled his hand out of the crate, turning to look at Sara.

"Okay. If we're gonna send it back empty, we should put a note in it."

Gleason got the choir going again, while Sara and Colum composed a note to send back to Sofia and the others. The congregation sang rather tentatively as most of them couldn't stop looking at the wooden crate over their sheet music. Reverend Meyers composed a letter of his own, addressing the envelope to the Reverend William Campbell of the Baptist church. Then he sent Tom Kennedy out the side door to hand deliver the note immediately.

Sara read her note out loud to Colum one last time.

Sofia,

Colum and I are alive and well here in 1876. But we can't come back right now. We have to keep a promise first. We're heading to Illinois, and expect to be in Chicago by September. Maybe you can pick us up there. We have not seen Chris, and we suspect that he never arrived in this time. We hope to see you again, but if we can't get back, please don't blame yourself.

Sara

Colum placed the note in the time machine and pushed the green button. The Resonator's computerized randomly generated melody clashed with the choir's song for a moment, and then the time machine was gone. Sara and Colum looked at each other, wondering if they had made a terrible mistake, but neither one said anything. They got up from the floor where the crate had been and took a seat in the front pew, happy to have a moment just to sit and take a deep breath, and think about what to do next.

†††

When Jimmy and Chris came out of the newspaper office, they saw that the trunk of the Cadillac was open, and a man in overalls was standing next to the car with a crowbar in his hand. He saw them coming and called out to them. "Hey, is this your car?"

"No. Nope. No."

"Weirdest thing. I hear this guy yelling and kicking from inside the trunk. So I open the trunk, and he doesn't even thank me, he just runs off." The man pointed in the direction that Wordman ran.

Jimmy looked at Chris, then shrugged his shoulders. "That *is* weird." Jimmy nodded for Chris to follow him, and he led him off in the direction of the shortest path out of the man's line of sight. Then they circled back to where the man had pointed, and headed off to follow Wordman.

Before long they came to some railroad tracks, and their path was blocked by a slow moving freight train. While Chris was looking toward the back end of the train to see how much longer it was going to be before the path was clear, Jimmy was looking toward the front end of the train to try to figure out how long the train had been there. "C'mon." He ran alongside the train, and then headed for the first open boxcar and jumped up, pulling himself inside. Then he helped Chris up, and they both moved farther into the boxcar, away from the open door. "Well, now it's official. You're a hobo."

The train moved along slowly, but Jimmy was confident that Wordman was on that train, just farther up toward the front. Since there was no way to move from car to car, the only thing they could do was wait until the train stopped and hope Wordman would get off. They crouched down and watched out the open door in case Wordman jumped before the next stop. Soon the train came to the Savannah station. It didn't stop, but it did slow down, and Jimmy and Chris could see Wordman running away from the tracks. They jumped from the boxcar and followed him into the terminal. There they saw him kneeling on the ground and holding his chest. He was gasping for air.

"Help me... someone help me... I can't... breathe... I don't... have... my pills."

Jimmy and Chris started running toward Wordman, but a railroad security guard got to him first and called for an ambulance. So they got out of sight quickly and watched from a distance. There was nothing they could do but watch as a crowd surrounded Wordman, and then an ambulance arrived. Wordman was put on a gurney and taken into the ambulance. The doors were closed and the ambulance drove off.

Jimmy whispered to Chris. "I really don't want to go back to that hospital."

Chris walked over to the security guard. "Hey, that guy was a friend of ours, did they say what hospital they're taking him to?"

Before the guard could answer, his radio crackled with a flurry of static and urgent yelling. "What? Say again? What the hell? Looks like your friend isn't going to any hospital. He just jumped out the back of the ambulance."

"Did they say where?"

"On Bay Street. He ran into the warehouses."

Jimmy and Chris were both anxious to stay out of sight, since they were wanted for stealing Williams' Cadillac, not to mention the dead thug on Williams' neighbor's lawn. They got a cab from the train station to the warehouses at the riverfront. Then they started looking for Wordman. Some of the warehouses were abandoned, and a few of those were open and accessible, either through broken doors or open windows.

"We'd better split up." Jimmy drew his gun and checked the magazine. "You go right, I'll go left."

"I don't have a gun."

"Well, if you see him, come and get me. Don't try to grab him yourself. We'll get him together."

Chris and Jimmy separated and started walking through the abandoned warehouses. But Wordman was nowhere in sight. He had found his way into the basement of one of the warehouses, and was working his way through the boiler room. He could hear Chris on the first floor above him, so he kept walking deeper into the maintenance tunnel. All alone in the dim light, Wordman started feeling sorry for himself. *Those assholes just won't give up. I don't understand why they won't let me save that girl. But even if I could warn myself and prevent the… there's no fucking time machine to get me back. Unless they're lying about that. But even if it's still there, I would have to get back to Jamaica with them on my tail. They're just not going to let up. I can't get back without them, but even if I do, they'll know everything. I'm fucked.* He had a sudden urge to pray, but he fought it, stubbornly refusing to be the atheist in the foxhole. *It's better if I don't go back at all.* He looked around him. He was surrounded by broken down machinery, and a lot of old building materials, but not much more. Wordman kicked a box, sending its contents flying across the concrete floor. He kicked at some paint cans, and then picked up a metal pipe and started swinging it, smashing everything he could. His frustration radiated through him like the shock of each impact vibrated through the pipe. Above him, Chris heard the noise. He thought about going to get Jimmy, but he didn't. Instead he followed the noise down the stairs to the basement. As he crept along he wondered what would be worse, getting stuck in the past, or dying in the past.

When Wordman's hands were raw from swinging the pipe, he dropped it at his feet in despair. As he looked down he could see the mess he had made, including a small lake of paint and paint thinner. In a moment of desperation, Wordman stepped back and leaned against a wall. He sighed and took out his lighter and a pack of cigarettes. After lighting one he took a long drag, and then held it in his hand and just looked at it for a moment. *They said these things would kill me*. He threw the cigarette into the paint thinner, and slumped down into a heap, leaning up against the wall. Wordman closed his eyes as the warehouse basement glowed with an orange light.

After a couple moments, the increasing heat forced Wordman to open his eyes. For one second, when he threw that cigarette, he had sincerely intended to sit there and burn to death, but now that it was about to happen, he wanted to avoid it at all costs. He jumped up and looked for a way out, but there was too much fire and smoke between him and the door. There was no going back, so he turned and ran farther into the tunnel. By now the whole building was in flames, and a piece of the ceiling came down on Wordman's head, cutting a gash into his forehead. It hit him so hard, he fell to the ground, and had to wipe the blood from his eyes so he could see enough to pick himself up. He was having trouble breathing, and he wasn't sure if it was the smoke getting into his lungs, or if he was having chest pains again. Deciding that it was both, he started to panic. *This is it. I'm going to die here.* But he pushed on deeper into the tunnel. He hoped that there would be a way out, but it soon dawned on him that he had walked too far in that tunnel to still be under the same warehouse. He couldn't know where the tunnel would lead, but he hoped it wasn't a dead end.

Jimmy circled back to the place where he and Chris had split up. There was no sign of Chris, but when Jimmy looked in the direction he had gone, he saw the smoke rising from one of the warehouses, and the flames reaching out from the windows. "Shit! Chris!" He ran toward the burning warehouse.

The tunnel was filling with smoke, and Wordman crawled along in the darkness. Rats ran past him, brushing against his hands, causing him to recoil and slowing him down. He wanted to get off the ground, so he tried to pull himself up along the tunnel wall. The smoke was choking him, but he pressed on, hoping he could move faster if he stayed upright. He felt along the walls and soon he got the sense that the tunnel had widened. He gasped for air and grasped for hope. Then he could feel something on the tunnel wall. Metal protruding out from the wall. Iron rings attached to the wall at regular intervals. Wordman hung onto the rings and pulled himself along, coughing and gagging all the way. His knees started to buckle, and he hung onto the iron rings to keep himself up. Then he realized what the rings were for. *Slaves. Jesus Christ.*

In the dark and smoky haze Wordman was startled to see the shape of a man. He jumped back, and slipped, his feet flying out from under him, but he hung onto the rings. The man seemed to be hanging on to the rings as well. Wordman turned and he could see another man on the rings, on the other side of him. *Slaves!* Wordman tried to move away from them, but he couldn't. He was just as shackled as they were. Now he could see that all around him were the shadows of slaves chained to the wall. They were groaning and crying, not for themselves, but for their loved ones whom they would never see again. Wordman tried to close his eyes and put his back up against the wall.

In spite of himself, Wordman opened his eyes, and there, standing right in front of him, was the young woman he killed that night in college. At first she was standing in the same position she was in the crosswalk when he ran the red light. But then she turned and looked right at him – right into his eyes. To his horror, she spoke to him. "Twenty-Seven!" Wordman felt nauseous. "Twenty-Seven!"

Wordman screamed, "What? Twenty-Seven what?"

"Twenty-Seven years since you took my life! Twenty-Seven Christmases for my family to grieve!"

Wordman screamed again. "Go away!" He closed his eyes and yelled as loud as he could. He yelled for as long as he could. He yelled until the yelling was a combination of screaming and crying. He exhausted himself yelling, so that by the time the light came in, he was too spent to notice. The staff of the bakery above him had heard his screams and opened the door to the tunnel. They dragged Wordman out into the fresh air, a bloody whimpering mess.

†††

Sara and Colum quickly noticed that the church was silent, and all eyes were on the place where the Resonator had been just a moment ago. Several people ran out of the church in fear while the rest stared with their mouths hanging open. They could not reconcile what they had just seen with anything in their experience. Sara stood up and spoke to the congregation. "Please don't be afraid. You're not in any danger. That thing is gone now. Don't worry about it." She gave a desperate look toward Gleason, hoping he would get the music started again, and after fumbling around with some sheet music, the choir started singing, though a bit tentatively. Eventually, the people joined in, and the music was back in full swing.

The side door opened, and Tom Kennedy crept in and exchanged whispers with Reverend Meyers. The Reverend nodded and called Esther over to join their huddle. Sara and Colum looked at each other. Then Esther took Rosie's hand, and motioned for Sara to follow them into the sacristy. Once again, Esther knelt down to her daughter's level. "Now you do what Miss Sara tells you. Don't be no trouble to her, treat her like she's your mama."

"No, mama. You're my mama!"

"I'll always be your mama, child. But sometimes a mama has to do a thing she don't want to do. But she does it because she loves her child more than she loves herself."

"No! I don't want to go! I want to stay with you!" Rosie's tears got in the way of her words.

Sara walked over to Rosie and took her hand. "Rosie, honey... you have to come with me if you want to live."

Esther stood up and turned to Sara. "And you have to trade that pretty dress for my old one."

Once Esther and Sara had switched dresses, Esther put on a scarf and they emerged from the sacristy into the church, still wiping the tears from their faces. On the Reverend's instructions, the whole congregation filed out the main doors, along with Esther wearing Sara's borrowed dress. As Crown and the chief pointed at Esther and yelled to the other officers, Sara, Colum, and Rosie moved toward the side door with Tom Kennedy. When the officers all ran to the front of the church where Esther was disguised as Sara, the real Sara, along with Colum and Rosie, climbed into Kennedy's wagon and sped off around to the back of the church and then north on Jefferson Street. By the time Crown and the police caught Esther and realized they had been duped, Kennedy's wagon had a head start of several blocks. The wagon raced up Jefferson, seven short blocks, and by the time the police were on their horses and in pursuit, the wagon was turning left onto Bryan. Then around Franklin Square and up to the Baptist church. Tom pulled on the reigns and Sara, Colum, and Rosie jumped from the wagon and ran into the church. Tom took off with the wagon, and the police arrived just in time to see the church doors close behind their fugitives.

But Crown hadn't gone with the police. He held on to Esther's arm, and as soon as the police were away, he punched her in the face. She fell back, but he tightened his grip on her arm. Esther looked up at him and mumbled, "My people and I were sold into slavery, and delivered up for destruction, slaughter, and extinction. But you have no real power, and you will not be able to undo what you have done to offend God my king. You are the enemy of Savannah!" Then Crown released all of his rage onto her fragile body, and beat her mercilessly, and he kept on beating her, even after she was dead. The church members were sickened by the sight, and some of the women among them urged their husbands to make Crown stop. But their fear of him caused them to hesitate, and they could not save Esther. Eventually, when Crown let go of Esther's body, a few men of the congregation grabbed him, and as he fought them, a few more joined in, until Crown was subdued. The men took him to the jail, and he was thrown into a cell.

Chief Anderson and his officers walked up the steps to the Baptist church, but they were met by Reverend Campbell before they got to the door. "May I help you gentlemen?"

"Now, Reverend, don't pretend you don't know that a group of fugitives just ran into your church."

"I don't know anything about any fugitives, chief. All I know is that my congregation is in the middle of a service of holy worship, so if you have business with any of them, you'll have to wait until the service is over. This is a sanctuary, holy unto God."

"Really?" The chief sighed. "All right, then. We'll wait out here until the service is over. Just like we did at the Methodist Church. But I'm warning you, Reverend. The Methodist preacher is going to be in some big trouble for helping them escape so you'd better not get any ideas. We won't fall for any tricks again. You can be sure of that. We'll be right out here, waiting. We'll be right here when the service is over. There's nowhere they can run. We can wait all day if we have to."

"You do that." Reverend Campbell closed the doors and locked them, as the congregation belted out *Give Me That Old Time Religion (It's Good Enough for Me)*. As Reverend Campbell was coming down the aisle toward the front of his church, members of his congregation were already opening the trap door in the floor. Campbell approached Sara and Colum, as one of the church members handed them candles. "This tunnel is from the Underground Railroad. You can only take it so far, but then you'll need to get into the other tunnels. It's very important that you stay to the right until you're under Hangin' Square."

Sara interrupted him, "How will we know we're under Hangin'… um, Hanging Square?"

"You'll see a place where the wall's broke through. Go through there, and you'll be in the basement of the courthouse. Be very quiet. Take the tunnel to the left. Soon you'll be in the slave pens. Look for the iron rings on the walls. Just keep goin' all the way to the river. When you come out, Mr. Kennedy will be waiting there with his wagon. We'll be praying for you. And we'll keep the service going until you're long gone."

"Thank you, Reverend." Sara took Rosie's hand, and led her down into the tunnel.

"Yeah, thanks." Colum followed, and Campbell closed the trapped door.

Sara, Rosie, and Colum walked along in increasing darkness as the sounds of the congregation singing faded behind them. The candles flickered as the air got more and more stale. Soon it was hard to breathe, as the staleness of the air gave way to a horrible stench. Colum gagged as he and Sara took short breaths, letting in only the smallest amount of air with each breath. Rosie coughed, and Colum offered his handkerchief, which she held over her mouth. As they walked along, the air became increasingly unbearable, and the three starting holding their breath as long as they could before inhaling again. Rosie was losing her valiant fight to keep from crying, and Sara started to think about turning back. She tried to speak quietly to Colum, but only a cough came out at first. "If this keeps getting worse, we could suffocate."

"The Reverend wouldn't have sent us down here if it was a dead end."

Both Rosie and Sara were holding their noses now. They kept going for what seemed like a very long time, holding their breath as long as they could, always staying to the right, but often looking back and wondering if they were past the point of no return.

Sara was getting very nervous. "I think we should go back."

"Go back to what? The cops? We can't go back. They'll hang us both."

Rosie remained silent as the tension was threatening to become an argument. But then the flickering candlelight revealed a hole in the wall up ahead.

Sara started running to the opening. "The courthouse! C'mon!" She stepped through the wall and took a deep breath as the merely stale air of the courthouse basement felt like fresh air compared to the air in the tunnel. She helped Rosie though the hole, and then Colum stepped through. The basement was dark, but they could hear voices above them. Then they could hear the sound of a door opening, and light poured down the stairs. Sara and Colum looked at each other, and then looked around the basement, searching for the entrance to the other set of tunnels. The only way out, other than up the stairs, was through a large steel door. Colum opened the door, and the screeching of the hinges echoed off of the basement walls. Sara grabbed Rosie's hand, but Sara tripped and fell, and the skin of her legs skidded on the rough concrete floor. Someone was coming down the stairs. Colum helped Sara to her feet and Rosie, Sara, and Colum ran through the door, closing it behind them.

They went through into the tunnel, but Sara had lost her candle, so they had to go slowly to see where they were going. Colum's single candle seemed to create more shadows than light, and they were constantly startled by their own silhouettes. They moved along slowly, listening behind them for anyone who might be following. When they stopped for a moment, Sara rested her hand on the wall, and she felt cold iron. She looked, and there in the candlelight, was an iron ring attached to the wall. She realized what she was holding on to, and quickly pulled her hand away. Then she was overcome with emotion, and collapsed in tears and sobs.

Colum ran to her. "C'mon Sara, we don't have time for… We have to keep going." Colum pulled her to her feet, but she was unable to walk. He put his mouth close to her ear. "Rosie needs you now, Sara. If we don't keep moving, she'll die here." Sara's crying dwindled. She grabbed onto Colum's shirt and pulled herself up, her face meeting his, and she kissed him, hard. She kissed him like she was going to the gallows. And then she grabbed his hand, and took Rosie by the hand, and she started walking farther down the tunnel.

†††

Jimmy searched for Chris, but couldn't find him. All he could do was hope that Chris wasn't in the burning warehouse. When the police arrived with the fire trucks, Jimmy had to get out of sight. He walked away from the warehouses, and ended up on a familiar street. He saw the Marshall Hotel, and decided that was a good place to lay low and figure out his next move. But as he approached the hotel, he could tell that it was all closed up. He ran up to the door, but it was boarded over.

A concerned neighbor peeked over the fence. "May I help you?"

"No, thanks. I just... I was hoping to go in here, but it's all boarded up."

"Has been for almost twenty years."

"What? No, I stayed here just last night."

"Not here you didn't."

"Yeah, I did. This is the Marshall Hotel, right?"

"Yes, but I'm telling you it closed back in the fifties."

Jimmy felt a chill run across his shoulders, so he decided to walk away. He made his way to the Six Pence Pub and went in and sat in the back, in a dark corner where he could have a Smithwicks and think. After a while, Jimmy could see the waitress and bartender looking in his direction as they talked, and he worried that they knew he was wanted by the police. He started planning his escape, but soon the waitress came over to Jimmy's table by herself. "Do you need anything else?"

"Not right now, no. I'm fine, thanks."

"Um... this is going to sound strange, but... are you... Jimmy the Fist?"

Jimmy's heart sank into his stomach. *How could they know? I was only four years old in 1973. What the hell?*

The waitress could see the distress on Jimmy's face. "I'm sorry, I know that sounded crazy. But this guy left a note for someone named Jimmy the Fist, and you kind of fit the description – and he said you'd order a Smithwick's - but I'm sorry, I'll leave you alone."

"No, wait. I'll take that note."

The waitress handed Jimmy the note.

Hey Jimmy, I have Wordman. I've got him at the riverfront right now, come if you can. If not, I'll see you at the concert. Chris.

Jimmy breathed a sigh of relief. He looked up the waitress. "Thanks. This was for me after all. But do me a favor. Don't go telling anyone this 'Jimmy the Fist' stuff. It's just a bad joke."

The staff of Matthew's Bakery was surprised to see Wordman in the tunnel, but they were even more surprised when Chris came out after him. Chris was able to convince them that Wordman was a disturbed psychiatric patient who got away, and Chris was a relative trying to take him back where he would be safe. The bakery workers didn't want to have to deal with Wordman themselves, so they were happy to turn him over to Chris, after he borrowed a roll of duct tape, as he told them, "to keep this poor fellow from being a danger to himself and others." Wordman was so shaken that he didn't put up a struggle, or say anything at all, until Chris had walked him away from the crowd of people that had gathered.

Once out of sight, Chris dragged Wordman toward the river where they could hide in the alleyways below the warehouse walkways. Chris gave Wordman a few punches in the arms to keep him malleable, then sat him down on the ground. "One move, and I'll kick your ass."

Wordman sighed in despair. "Who cares?"

"Yeah, that's right. Who cares? Nobody cares about you, you asshole. It's because of you I'm stuck in the past again, you *fuck*!"

Wordman could sense the tension in Chris' voice. *They don't have a plan*, he thought. *Or they don't have a way back.* "She's bored with you, you know."

"What?" Chris wrapped more duct tape around Wordman's wrists.

"Your wife, what's her name?"

"Willow."

"Right. Willow. She's totally bored with you, I can tell."

"Oh, you can tell? You can tell what my wife is thinking? Look, just leave her out of this. You don't get to talk about my wife!"

"All right, I won't say anything more. But I would think you'd want to know."

"Fuck you."

"I'll bet she had all these big dreams, of an exciting life in the twenty-first century. She probably thought you were some big deal back home, and look at you. She ends up married to a wanna-be rock star and college failure."

"I said, fuck you. So shut up."

"Do you even have an income? Can you support her? I'll bet she wishes she didn't marry you, so she could find someone better now that she's living in the modern age."

"Shut the fuck up!"

"Okay, okay. Sorry I brought it up. I was just thinking, if she's going to leave you, wouldn't you want to see it coming?"

Chris was beside himself. "God dammit!"

Wordman was watching Chris carefully, and as soon as Chris took his eyes off of him to look down at the roll of duct tape, Wordman lunged at Chris head first, knocking him back. Wordman tried to run, but his hands were duct-taped together, and Chris was too fast for him. Chris caught up with him, and tackled him to the ground, throwing a couple punches at his head to soften his resolve. After Wordman surrendered, the secret fear that he might be right led Chris to throw one more punch before pulling Wordman to his feet and dragging him back to where he was sitting on the ground. Now Chris took the roll of duct tape and wrapped Wordman's feet. Wordman wiped the blood from his nose onto his sleeve.

"Okay, now I guess you're going to *have* to sit still. And you're not going anywhere until it's time to go to the concert." Chris looked around and thought for a moment, and then he dragged Wordman into an abandoned boat house and duct taped him to a support beam. "You wait here. I'll be back. Just need to go to the pub."

Chris had gotten to the Six Pence before Jimmy did, and when Jimmy didn't show up, he decided to leave the note and get back to Wordman, to make sure he didn't get away again. On the walk back to the riverfront, Chris had time to think. *Wanna-be... Failure... Why am I spinning my wheels? Why is nothing working for me? I thought when I came back from the eighteenth century things would be different. I gave up living in the past, but I still don't have a future. Not even a plan for a future. Why can't a guy have a dream come true? Is it because the dream is selfish? I don't think so. It's not like I have to be a star. It's not about the applause. I don't need to be rich and famous. I could be happy with rich and anonymous. Heh, Heh. I crack me up. Seriously, though, it's about the music. I just love the music. Shit... God, just get me home, and I'll do whatever you want.*

Chris found Wordman right where he left him. The duct tape was twisted a bit where Wordman had tried to free himself, but he hadn't gotten anywhere. "I told you I was going to kick your ass." Wordman didn't say anything.

"Chris!" It was Jimmy. "Oh geez, am I glad I found you."

"Yeah, me too."

"Hey, enough with the 'Jimmy the Fist' stuff, okay? I don't go by that name any more."

"Sorry, cuz. It seemed funny at the time, but I've been thinking. We just gotta get home. I just wanna get home."

"Me too. I think this concert thing is going to work. We just have to lay low until it's time." Jimmy looked around. "This is as good a place as any."

Chris and Jimmy sat in silence watching over a duct-taped Wordman. After a while, Jimmy spoke up. "You did good, Chris. You got the job done. You didn't do what I said, and come and get me, but then if you had, he might have gotten away."

"Thanks."

Jimmy looked at Chris. "You know, it's different now. Between me and you, I mean."

"Yeah?"

"Yeah. Used to be, you were the kid, and I was almost more like an uncle than a cousin. But I came back, and you're all grown up. Then you went through that ordeal, and you come back a married man. And Willow's great, and I would say I'm proud of you, but it feels like that's something people say to someone who's not their equal. I don't know, it feels more like we're equals now."

"I'm strangely comfortable with that."

"I tried to contact my parents again. From the pub."

"Oh yeah?"

"It's four years before the… train thing, give or take. And nobody knows where they are. I can't believe I can't find them. It's like, I'm here, and they're alive right now, and I can't reach them to save them."

"I'm sorry man."

Wordman spoke up, with contempt and sarcasm in his voice. "It's like you told me. You can't change the past."

Chris put a piece of duct tape over Wordman's mouth.

†††

Sara found herself crawling on her hands and knees, as the tunnel closed in around her. The tunnel was getting smaller and smaller, until she had to scoot herself along the ground to fit through. She started to worry that she might get stuck, or that she might come to a dead end and not be able to turn around. As she pulled herself along the ground, the tunnel kept on getting smaller, and soon she was in a hole not much bigger than a couple feet in diameter, and the tunnel was tilting downward. Her elbows bumped the sides as she pulled herself along, and now she had to twist her shoulders to make it through. It was getting tighter, and darker, and harder to breathe. She struggled to turn her head to look back, but Colum and Rosie were not in sight. Sara could see that the tunnel behind her was too narrow to turn around, and she could not back up. She was committed to going forward, and her only hope was that somewhere up ahead the tunnel would widen again. She pushed on, but the hole got even smaller, and now Sara's shoulders were scraping the sides. The air was thin and full of dust, and her breathing was labored, and she could feel the blood rushing to her head. She turned to get one arm in front of her head, but it got pinned against her side. She was stuck, and she started to panic. Her breathing got faster, and she was starting to hyperventilate. She moved her body to try to free her arms, but it only made her more stuck. She couldn't shove herself backward, and she couldn't force herself forward. Then Sara could feel the tunnel above her starting to come down in pieces on her head. Her body started to shake as she struggled against the sides of the tunnel, as her head started to spin. Sara was certain she was about to die. And then she opened her eyes and woke up tangled in a blanket in the back of Kennedy's wagon, looking up at the stars.

As Sara lay there trying to slow her breathing, she remembered coming out of the tunnel at a tavern on the riverfront. She remembered that Kennedy was there with his wagon, and she remembered helping

Rosie into the wagon and all of them speeding off toward the edge of town. And now it was night, and they were on their way to Illinois. Sara could hear voices a short distance away. She sat up, and looked to see Tom Kennedy talking to a man she didn't know. She woke up Colum.

Colum rubbed his eyes. "I dreamed about my mother again. But this time, my dad was with her."

Sara pulled Colum up to a sitting position, and jumped out of the wagon. They walked over to Kennedy and the other man.

Kennedy introduced them. "Miss Sara, Mr. O'Connell, this is Mr. Theodore Meves, former owner of the Curiosity Shop in town." Meves tipped his hat. "Mr. Meves is also a pass forger. Before the war, free negroes needed a pass to travel – official papers. Mr. Meves is providing us with the papers we need to get out of the south. For a small fee, of course." Kennedy smiled at Meves, who smiled back.

"Well, the Curiosity Shop no longer provides an income. A man's got to provide for his family." Meves handed the papers to Kennedy and walked away into the trees. Sara walked back over to the wagon by herself and leaned up against it. She thought about Harriet, and a sense of peace washed over her. She let go of everything she once thought of as home, and set her mind on getting Rosie to Illinois.

It took two weeks to get to Atlanta on that wagon, avoiding the authorities all the way. In Atlanta, the group was able to board a train for Illinois. Tom Kennedy's uncle had given him enough money to get the four of them to Hanover, where Tom brought them to his family's farm.

Dickey-Jim Crown was taken from his jail cell, ranting and raving like a lunatic. And that's exactly what he was taken for. The good people of Savannah turned on him, and sent him to the psychiatric wing of the hospital, where he was wrapped in a sheet to keep him from throwing a tantrum. He was yelling and screaming so much that Dr. Richard Arnold brought him to an unused basement tunnel and left him there to cool off. But Dr. Richard Arnold was infected with yellow fever, and became bedridden and died before he could figure out what to do with Crown, and in fact he never even filled out the paperwork for Crown to be officially admitted. Dickey-Jim Crown lay alone in that hospital bed in that basement tunnel next to the morgue until the bricklayers came to close the entrance to the tunnel. He lay there, starving and too dehydrated to call out, as he heard the sound of the tunnel entrance being bricked over, one brick at a time. Brick by brick, he self-righteously held on to his convictions until the moment finally came when his resolve was broken and he decided to pray. But it was too late - the bricklayers finished their job, and as their muffled voices faded away, Dickey-Jim Crown was left to the silence of his own regrets. The man who once was considered the patron of Savannah had become a permanent fixture of its substructure while the town of Savannah moved on into the future without him.

Esther was buried in the Catholic cemetery. Fr. Murphy, the priest, took care of the arrangements, and the members of the Catholic, Methodist, and Baptist churches took up collections for the expenses.

They collected enough for a beautiful headstone. It said, *Here Lies Esther, Devoted Mother. She gave her life so her daughter could live.*

†††

Jimmy looked at his watch. "It's time. The concert is just over an hour from now. Let's go."

Chris pulled the duct tape off of Wordman's mouth and feet, and dragged him along as Jimmy held his gun to Wordman's back. They made their way south along Abercorn Street, and soon they came to Reynolds Square. There they walked under a large tree, thick with Spanish moss. The tree was old, and big, and had several thick branches running horizontal to the ground. As they pushed through the hanging moss, Wordman made a desperate move, hoping Jimmy wouldn't shoot him in the back. He jumped backward into Jimmy's gun hand, knocking Jimmy back for a moment, and then tried to run for it. But Chris shoved him into the tree so that he fell to the ground at its roots.

Jimmy pointed his gun at Wordman. "Wordman, I could shoot you right now, and we could go back to our time, and there would be no consequences for me. I literally have a license to kill. And you would be dead, and no one would even bury you, let alone mourn you. I'm trying to spare your life. Why are you fighting me?"

"Why are *you* fighting *me*?" Wordman was so angry and frustrated, he was spitting out his words. Chris noticed that a small crowd was gathering, and he started worrying someone might call the police. Some of the people started talking among themselves, wondering if they should help the man who was being held at gunpoint. But Wordman sputtered on. "Why won't you let me untangle myself from this thing? Why are you against me? I'm going to be president! You want me on your side! Why throw that away all because of some stupid bitch walking across the street at the wrong time? I can't believe all this is happening because of one dead ni-."

"No you don't!" Jimmy shoved the gun in Wordman's face. "You don't get to pretend you're more important than she is. No. By rights I should shoot you in the head right now – or better yet, run over you with that Cadillac. But I'm taking you back to face your shame. An anonymous death here and now would be too good for you."

The people who had gathered heard what Wordman said. They heard that he was about to use the N-word, and they decided he wasn't the good guy after all. Then Jimmy flashed his TIA badge, and they realized that Wordman wasn't a victim, and they just walked away and went back to their own business.

Jimmy grabbed Wordman by the collar and pulled him to his feet. He pushed him to keep going, and on they marched, all the way to the Savannah Theater. When they got there, Jimmy had to hide the gun, and Chris took the duct tape off of Wordman's hands. They both took Wordman's arms and led him inside the theater.

Once inside, Wordman saw Jim Williams and called out to him. "Mr. Williams!"

Jimmy and Chris looked at each other, not knowing what to do. Williams saw Wordman, and started walking toward him. But he stopped when he noticed the gash on Wordman's forehead, and when he saw Jimmy and Chris, he backed away, and turned to go and call the police. Jimmy whispered, "Our cover's blown. I sure hope Mercer plays the hits first."

"You know that's not how it works." Chris' voice was full of sarcasm. "He'll play the stuff off his new album first, and force everyone to sit through the whole concert before he gets to the favorites. For all we know he could even wait until the encore to play the songs that are going to get us home."

As Johnny Mercer took the stage, Jimmy and Chris walked Wordman around to the back stage door. A large bouncer stopped them, but Jimmy pulled out his TIA badge and waved it in the air quickly. "FBI. We just need to look backstage for a few minutes. Nothing to worry about, we promise not to disrupt the concert." The bouncer hesitated. "If you don't let us in, then we *will* have to disrupt the concert. Do you want that to be your fault?" The bouncer stepped aside and opened the door.

As soon as they were back stage, Jimmy pulled out the gun again and pointed it at Wordman while Chris duct taped his hands. Jimmy whispered, "Here's how this is gonna go down. We wait here for the time machine to show up. Chris, you go back first. That way, if anything goes wrong after that, at least you make it back. You've got a wife, after all. When you get back, get my TIA colleagues to come and be ready to take Wordman into custody the minute he arrives. He'll be the second to go. And then I'll go last. Got it?" Chris nodded.

Fortunately for Jimmy and Chris, Johnny Mercer decided to give the people what they wanted and he played his biggest songs first. He started off with *I Wanna Be Around*. Jimmy and Chris couldn't know it, but Sofia had found the live recording from this very concert. The time machine honed in on the performance, and the wooden crate materialized right there next to the green room. There was no time to waste, since the police were surely on their way by now. Chris got into the crate, and pushed the button, and in a few moments he was back in Willow's arms.

Mercer's second song was *Something's Gotta Give*. The time machine materialized again, and the auto-pause kicked in as the crate waited for its cargo. Jimmy shoved Wordman through the trap door, and duct taped his feet so he wouldn't be able to try to make a surprise escape when he arrived back in the year two thousand. In a moment, Jimmy was alone, as the police walked through the audience toward the back stage door. Mercer played his third song, *Moon River*, from *Breakfast at Tiffany's*. Jimmy held his breath, waiting for the crate to appear, but it didn't. The police were speaking to the bouncer.

Johnny Mercer started talking to the audience, and Jimmy's mind raced. *Hurry up, Mercer, you're killin' me, here.* The audience was loving the banter, and Mercer explained that now he wanted to perform one of his earliest songs, *I'm an Old Cowhand from the Rio Grande*. Jimmy's heart sank. Mercer started the song as the back stage door opened and the police officers filed through. But the Resonator appeared just in time, and Jimmy got in as quickly as he could. As he closed the trap door, he looked out at the police officers running toward him. "Buh bye." And he pushed the button.

†††

The time came for Sara to say goodbye to Rosie. The Kennedys had agreed to take her in and raise her as their own, since they were still grieving the loss of their other children. Rosie seemed at peace about staying on the farm. She sensed that she would be safe there, but Sara was a bit uneasy. She knelt down to talk to Rosie. "Rosie, I have to go on now. Mr. O'Connell and I are going to Chicago, but the big city is no place for you. This will be a good place for you."

"Miss Sara, do you think my mama will be alright without me?"

"I know she never wanted to let you go. And I know she loved you so much that she wanted you to have a better life than you would have had back in Savannah. Don't you worry about your mama, God will take care of her. You just do what she wanted – you have a good life. You live and be free."

"Okay Miss Sara."

"Rosie, I want you to have something. It's very important, okay?"

"What is it?"

Sara reached into her purse and dug to the bottom. She pulled out the small prayer book, looked at it one last time, and handed it to Rosie. "This prayer book was a gift to me from someone who is very important to me. She's strong and peaceful, and these prayers gave me strength and peace. I know you can't read them all yet, but someday you will, and I hope they give you strength and peace. Promise me you'll take good care of this book, and learn to read it."

"Okay Miss Sara." Rosie took the book and held on to it tightly. She had never owned anything as fine or as expensive as that book, and Sara could see that she already treasured it. Sara and Rosie said their goodbyes, and Sara turned away, wiping the tears from her face. She walked over to Colum, who took her hand, and the two of them walked in silence to the Kennedys' carriage. Tom drove them to the train station, where he bought their tickets to Chicago. He saw them safely on the train, and then went back to the farm.

When Colum and Sara arrived in Chicago, they stood on the train platform, and Colum said what they were both thinking. "Do you think they'll be able to send the time machine back here for us? Or are we here for good?"

"I don't know, Colum. And to be honest, I don't even want to think about it right now. Even if they could come up with a song to send it back here, how would we find it? It could pop up anywhere in the city, at any time. And even if we found it, it only holds one person."

"Well, in case I wasn't clear before, I would rather stick with you than go back by myself."

"Thanks." Sara squeezed Colum's hand.

"So… what do we do now?"

CHAPTER 7
LEE AND MOLLY

Fergus had procrastinated as long as he could, but he knew eventually he would have to come downstairs. He had had another dream, and as he awoke he called out something – he wasn't sure what – but he was sure the whole house heard him. As he came down the stairs, his father gave him a sympathetic look. Fergus said, "This time everyone else was going fast except me. You and Colum and Willow, and the Agnellos – they were all going so fast, but I was going slow. I couldn't keep up with everyone, and all I could do was watch as all of you got farther and farther away and I stayed behind."

"It's alright, son. Just a dream. Dreams aren't real." Patrick walked into the kitchen to refill his coffee cup.

Fergus followed him. "Do I have to go to work today, Dad?"

"Are you sick? If not, you work."

"Maybe there's something I can do here. You know, without having to ride in the car."

"Well you can ask Gus about that, but you would just have to ride in the car tomorrow. You can't avoid it. You have to get used to it."

"Jaysus, what I wouldn't give for an Irish breakfast."

Patrick came into the living room and looked at the picture on the mantle, just like he did every morning. It was a pencil sketch of his wife in a silver frame. Gus and Colleen had made a donation to the police widows' fund on the condition that they get a sketch artist to sit down with the O'Connells and come up with a picture of Mary. Then they bought a silver frame for it, as a wedding gift to their new daughter-in-law Willow. Ever since August, Chris and Willow were living in Chris' room, and Patrick and his sons were living out of the guest room, though more often than not Colum slept on the couch. The house was crowded, but no one seemed to mind too much. It was just assumed that the O'Connells were not ready to go out on their own, and without social security numbers and bank accounts it was just easier for them to stay with the Agnellos. The fact is, with most of the younger generation in New York, the house seemed kind of empty.

Gus walked up to Patrick quietly, not wanting to disturb his moment with the picture.

Patrick looked down at the cup of hot coffee in his hand. "Gus, I can't tell you how grateful I am for the way you've taken care of me and my family."

"Well, now that you mention it…" Gus scratched his head. "If you want to thank me, you could, maybe… wash your clothes. I mean, you wear the same clothes every day – not that I care, but you know, Colleen mentioned it."

"Don't throw me under the bus!" Colleen was yelling from the kitchen.

Gus continued. "Well, the truth is, she's not the only one. And also take a shower."

Patrick sighed. "I guess I'm that old dog that can't learn a new trick."

"The old dog has to learn some new tricks to survive in the twenty-first century. Look, you learned how to use a cell phone. If you can do that, you can get used to the idea of fresh clothes and a shower every day."

"Every day?" Patrick looked back to the sketch of his wife. "Mary, you wouldn't believe this world." He thought to himself, *I don't belong here. But the boys need me.*

Gus nodded toward the leather chair to get Patrick to look in that direction. There was Monica, sitting in the chair with her eyes closed, with ridiculously huge headphones on. "Ever since Sofia burned that CD from the old recording of my father playing the blues, she listens to it every day."

Patrick smiled. "If I had a recording of Mary's voice, I would listen to it every day, too. Now I can't even remember what her voice sounded like. Isn't that terrible?"

"That's life, my friend. But life goes on. And you're here, and you're alive. And that's good."

Colleen came into the living room and tapped Monica on the shoulder, then motioned to her that it was time to go. The two of them were heading to morning Mass, and then grocery shopping. At the store, they decided to get some fresh flowers for the house. Lost in the task of picking out flowers, they didn't see the two men walk up behind them.

"I like flowers… 'cause they smell good."

Colleen turned around to face Dante and Vince. Dante rolled his eyes at Vince's weak opening line. "Please excuse my associate. He ain't as cultured as you are, as is obvious by your impeccable taste in floral arrangements. A rose of another color would still smell like a rose, right? Dat's Shakespeare. You're Mrs. Agnello, am I correct? I guess you're both Mrs. Agnello, no? Heh, heh."

Colleen took a step back. "Yes – can I help you?"

"Oh, no ma'am. You see we're friends of your husband, and we just wanted to say hello, and, uh, wish you a, uh, you know, to have a nice day, and all dat."

Vince spoke up. "Yeah. Have a nice day."

Colleen took another step away from the men. "Well, my husband isn't here with me, but I'll tell him you said hello."

"Yes, you do dat."

"You do dat," Vince echoed.

"One other thing." Dante moved toward Colleen. "If you don't mind, you would be doing me a favor if you could give your husband a message for me. You see, he gave us a thing dat was supposed to have a thing, but the thing he gave us ain't got the thing we wanted, and we were just hoping you could let him know dat the thing didn't have da thing, and we're still looking for da thing. Okay?"

"Okay."

Dante adjusted his pants and leaned on the florists' counter. He slowly picked up a scissors and ran his fingers over the length of it. "You know, Mrs. Agnello, da human body is a delicate thing. Da soul, you see, is lighter dan air, and it wants to float up, up, and away – like dis foil balloon here. But da body, it holds da soul down, like dis weight at de end of da ribbon. But all it takes is for something hard and sharp, like dis scissors here, to push into some soft part of da body - so easy it would slide right in – and da soul will float away, just like dis balloon." Dante made a pushing motion with the scissors, and then cut the ribbon on the balloon. Colleen and Monica watched in silence as the balloon floated up, past the fluorescent lights and into the rafters of the grocery store. "Well, have a nice day."

Vince echoed. "Yeah. Have a nice day." And the two men walked out of the store.

Monica muttered, "*Cazzo vai via stronzo.*"

Gus was fuming. He was so mad he ran out of swear words and sputtered as he tried to think of even worse things to say about Al Tallone and his crew. Colleen was starting to wish she hadn't told him. "Okay, but calm down. It doesn't help if you get so mad."

"They threatened you. My wife – and my mother! They've crossed a line now, God dammit."

Patrick was also furious, and wanted more than anything to express his gratitude toward the Agnellos by helping to defend them. "I told you we should get more guns. These men… have you seen the news reports on the TV? Have you seen the things they show? That could happen to… that could happen here!"

Gus sighed. "Pat, you've got to cut back on watching the news. Anyway, they're not coming here. I'm going to put a stop to this."

Colleen was worried. "What are you going to do? These are dangerous people."

Patrick was not to be deterred. "She's right, Gus. We gotta show these fookin' dagos…"

"Jaysus, Dad!" Fergus rolled his eyes in embarrassment. "The Agnellos are dagos."

"Stop saying 'dagos,' will you?" Gus was getting flustered.

Colleen put up her hands. "Jesus, Mary, and Joseph. Everyone, please! Alright, now let's just all calm down."

Monica was fighting tears and muttering to herself. *Questa é la goccia che ha fatto traboccare il vaso! Debbiamo rendere pane per focaccia.*"

Colleen put her hand on Monica's arm. "Not now, Mama."

"Ah!" Monica threw up her hands and walked away.

Gus was pacing. "And that little shit Corona. Thinks he's so tough. He's a stooge."

Colleen walked away toward the kitchen. "Gus, honey, try not to worry about it. Now, I have some soda bread in the oven I need to check on."

"Try not to worry? You're making Irish bread?" Gus looked at Patrick. "Do you believe this?"

All the tension made Nero nervous. He hunched his shoulders and his ears drooped as he walked slowly out of the room.

†††

Sara opened her eyes and sat up on the hard wooden bench of the Chicago train station. "I dreamed of a bird flying high in the air. And the bird's name was Rosie." She looked around but Colum was nowhere in sight. "Colum?"

Colum came around the corner. "I'm here. I just went over to the ticket booth to ask some questions. Look, there's a big map of Chicago on the wall over there."

"Colum, we're going to run out of money very soon. What are we going to do? We're never getting home, are we?"

"I'm going to find a job, and we're going to get a place to live, and we're going to get married."

"Whoa, slow down there, Mr. Olden-Days-Man. I never said I would marry you, I never even said I loved you." Colum's face fell. "Yet. I mean yet. I never said I loved you *yet*. I'm not saying I don't. But this is all moving too fast for me. I mean, look at us – we're kind of an unlikely couple for 1876."

"Sara you have to trust me. Yes, this is 1876. That's a century after my time, sure, but it's a century before your time – and I daresay it's more like what I'm used to than what you're used to. If we're going to survive here, you have to let me take the lead. I know you're used to living on your own, but here, in this time, a woman on her own is a woman in danger."

"I can take care of myself."

"Oh really? Can you get a job in 1876?"

Sara thought about it for a moment. "Well I didn't say were weren't gonna stick together."

"Daisy gave you her aunt's name, right?"

"Yeah, her mother Nellie is from Chicago, and she still has a sister here, Mabel Kinzie."

Colum was thinking. "Maybe that's a place to start. Maybe she can help me find a job."

"How do we find her?"

"I'll go ask the ticket agent. Be right back."

Colum went off around the corner, and Sara was left alone with her thoughts. *Did he just propose to me? How did I get to be in this place? One thing I know, I'm sure as hell not going to be an orthodontist. This whole thing doesn't make any sense. He's a mess, he's disorganized, he's naïve, all the things I'm not. It's crazy. But he's all I've got.*

Colum returned with a somber look on his face.

"What's wrong?"

"Well, the good news is they have a directory of everyone who lives in Chicago."

"Is there bad news?"

"The ticket agent told me they had to completely redo it because there was this huge fire a few years ago. Hundreds of people died, and about a third of the houses burned down. So they had to start over. I mean, not just the directory, they've had to rebuild the city."

"Yeah, the Chicago fire."

"You heard of it?"

"Oh, yeah, everyone's heard of it. You don't have to be from Chicago to know about the Chicago fire."

"Oh, so that's why they named the football team the Chicago Fire. I get it now."

"Yeah, but you mean soccer."

Colum rolled his eyes. "Well, the guy over there was pretty surprised I didn't know about the fire. But it's just so sad."

"Was Mabel Kinzie in the directory?"

"Kinzie, Mabel. Widow. Guess what street she lives on."

"Uh, Kinzie?"

"Yep."

Soon Colum and Sara were standing in front of a large house on Kinzie Street overlooking the Chicago River. They both took a deep breath and walked up the steps to the front door. Colum banged the knocker, and before long a young woman in an apron opened the door.

"Yes?" The young woman looked Colum and Sara up and down, and took a step back, closing the door a bit to make the opening smaller.

Colum looked at Sara, and then spoke. "Excuse us, but is Mrs. Kinzie at home?"

"I'm afraid she is not accepting visitors. And she does not welcome solicitors."

"No, we're not selling anything, we're friends of her sister, Nellie Gordon."

A rather large woman pushed the servant aside. "You say you know my sister, do you? Prove it."

Colum and Sara looked at each other. Colum couldn't think of anything to say, but Sara had a thought. "Hello, ma'am. When we first met your sister, she slid down the banister of her home, and, if you'll forgive me for saying, she used the words 'damn' and 'crap'."

"Come in!" Mabel Kinzie stepped aside and waved her maid away. She walked into her parlor without looking back, and Sara and Colum stepped into the house and followed her. Once in the parlor, Mabel turned around and looked at Sara with suspicion, but motioned for her and Colum to sit down. After the introductions, Mabel was anxious for news of her sister, and although she remained a bit gruff, her demeanor improved perceptibly.

Eventually, Colum got to the point. "Mrs. Kinzie, we've just come to Chicago, with only the clothes on our backs. I was wondering if you might have some advice on where I could find employment."

"Refugees, eh? You two married? It's alright, we're very progressive here in Chicago."

"Uh, no, we're not married. But I am hopeful that one day…"

"Not married? Well, we're not *that* progressive." Mabel looked Sara up and down. "But, if you know Nellie, I guess I can trust you. At least until I can write to her. I could use another maid. Have any experience?"

Sara sat quietly for a moment. *I have lots of experience. Just nothing that would make me qualified to be a maid.* "No ma'am, I don't. But I will work very hard, and I'm very organized."

"Organized is good. I could use more of that around here." She looked at Colum. "As for you, you're in luck because there are a lot of building jobs right now. Are you skilled?"

Colum was enthusiastic. "Yes, ma'am."

"Good. She can stay here in the servants' quarters, but you will have to take your unmarried self out of here until you make an honest woman of her. Go down to the water tower and wait there – people who want work stand around there until someone hires them."

Mrs. Kinzie didn't waste any time putting Sara to work – or putting Colum out of the house. Before he knew it, Colum was walking down the street, hoping he was going in the right direction, and wondering what Sara was doing in that mansion. He followed Michigan Avenue north and soon he could see the water tower ahead of him. When he got there, he joined a group of men standing around hoping to find work for the day.

As it turned out, it was not easy to find a job. The few men who came by looking for laborers wanted certain building skills that Colum didn't have. One showed some interest in Colum, but when he asked him his name and found out he was Irish, he was no longer interested. It was late afternoon and Colum was getting hungry when another potential employer showed up. But this time, the other laborers muttered to themselves and walked away. The man approached Colum. "Need work today, son?"

"Yes sir."

"I need a man to help me rebuild my barn. Burned down in the fire."

"Yes sir, I can do that."

The man squinted at Colum. "You don't know who I am, do you?"

"No sir, but I've just come to Chicago from… from the south."

"Don't worry, son. I can tell by your speech you're Irish. So am I. The name's O'Leary. Patrick O'Leary."

"My father's name is Patrick."

"Then he must be a good man!" Colum and Patrick O'Leary shook hands.

Colum noticed that the other laborers were staring at him. "Mr. O'Leary, if you don't mind me asking, why don't those men want to work for you?"

"I'm not well liked in Chicago, truth be told. That barn you're going to help me rebuild? That's where the fire started."

Colum helped O'Leary clear the space for a smaller version of the old barn. But before they could start any construction, the sun had set. Colum was ready to keep working by lantern light, but O'Leary slapped the dust off his hands and stuck out his right hand to shake Colum's. "We'll call it a day and get started first thing tomorrow. Be here at eight."

"Yes sir."

"Now come on up to the house for your wage." O'Leary led the way, and Colum followed him.

"You rebuilt your house already?"

"No, the house didn't burn. The wind pushed the fire the other way, thank the Lord. Colum O'Connell, this is my wife, Catherine."

"Ma'am."

Catherine O'Leary nodded to Colum. "Nice to make your acquaintance Mr. O'Connell. Thank you for helping my husband rebuild our barn."

"I'm just happy to have a situation." Colum held out his hand as O'Leary counted out one dollar and eighty cents. Colum looked at the coins. "Sir, I know from talking with the other men this is a full day's wage. But I barely worked a couple of hours."

"Call it a good faith gesture. For a fellow Irishman."

"Thank you, I'll be ready to go at eight." Colum paused. "So how did the fire start?"

"Well, that's a story in itself," Catherine began. But she was interrupted by her husband.

"Now Kate, no one wants to hear your fanciful tale."

"It is *not* a fanciful tale! I saw it! I saw that thing."

Mr. O'Leary shook his head. "Colum, folks are saying that our cow kicked over a lantern. But Mrs. O'Leary here believes that's not the whole story."

Mrs. O'Leary was adamant. "That cow was spooked, I tell you. Spooked by that big wooden crate."

Mr. O'Leary ignored her and spoke to Colum calmly. "There was no big wooden crate."

Mrs. O'Leary stomped her foot. "There was indeed. I saw it. Others saw it too." She turned toward Colum. "We were having a little show in our barn. Mr. Westendorf was playing some of his songs, and the house was too small for the audience, so we moved the performance into the barn. Right in the middle of one of the songs, all of a sudden there was this ruckus, and that box appeared. It spooked the cow, and the cow kicked at it. Then it was gone. But the damage was done. We barely got out alive."

Colum's voice became shaky. "You saw a big wooden crate, that was there… and then it wasn't?"

"Just appeared out of thin air, and then disappeared again, sure as I'm standin' here now."

"You don't know where it is now, do you?"

"It's gone. It's nowhere. Never seen again. And that was five years ago."

Colum ran all the way back to Mrs. Kinzie's house. When he was still half a block away, he started shouting, "Sara! Sara!"

Sara opened a second floor window and called down to him. "What? You got a job?"

"Yes, but more than that. Can you come down?"

"I'll ask Mrs. Kinzie if you can come in."

Sara and Colum sat across from each other in the parlor, as Mabel Kinzie chaperoned, her pinky extended on the hand holding her cup of tea. They were self-conscious about their conversation with the widow listening in, but Colum was so excited he couldn't contain himself. "The you-know-what was here." Sara raised an eyebrow. "The *Resonator*. It showed up five years ago, and then disappeared. Mrs. O'Leary saw it."

Mabel scoffed at the name O'Leary. "That woman still claims it wasn't her cow's fault."

Sara refused to let herself get her hopes up. "So maybe it was here and maybe it wasn't. But it's not here any more, right? So how does that help us?"

Colum thought for a moment. "I don't know. But it was so close."

"Five years isn't close, Colum."

"But I was standing right there. In the O'Leary's barn."

The widow Kinzie put down her teacup. "You were in the O'Learys' barn?"

"Well, in the place where it was. Mr. O'Leary hired me to help him rebuild it. Which reminds me, I have to be back in the morning, and I don't know where I'm sleeping tonight. I have a dollar and eighty cents. Is that enough for a room?"

Mrs. Kinzie frowned. "A hotel room costs two dollars. But I'll give you the twenty cents, and take it out of Sara's wages. And I suppose I can't send you to bed hungry. I'll see what we have in the kitchen."

When Mabel went into the kitchen, Colum whispered to Sara. "The time machine was here. They must be trying to find us. They were just a few years too early, that's all. The crate materialized right there in the O'Learys' barn. Mrs. O'Leary says it spooked the cow, and that's what started the big fire!"

Both of Sara's eyebrows went up. "Well, if we ever see Sofia again, let's not tell her about that. Hey, wait a minute. The time machine runs on music. So what music was playing in the barn?"

"They were having some kind of concert in there. Some guy named Westerhoff."

Mrs. Kinzie overheard as she was coming back into the parlor. "Are you speaking of the composer Thomas Westendorf?"

"Yeah, that's his name."

"Ah. I know of him. Very sad. He hasn't written anything in years, and they say that now he just sits alone in his house doing nothing. I'm afraid that people say he's quite mad."

Colum cleared his throat. "Mrs. Kinzie, do you suppose you could introduce us to him? We'd like to talk with him, and see if he saw anything, uh, strange that night in the barn."

"I don't know him personally, but apparently the O'Leary's do. Perhaps you could ask them for an introduction."

Colum stayed in a nearby hotel, newly rebuilt since the fire. He was up early the next morning and at the O'Learys' house by eight. He didn't want to seem too anxious by leading with the question about Westendorf and his music, so he worked with Patrick for a while and tried to bring the conversation around to the night the fire started. "If you don't mind me asking, sir, it sounds like you don't agree with Mrs. O'Leary about the cow being spooked."

"I don't like to talk about it. That night changed everything. We even considered leaving Chicago."

"I'm sorry." Colum was silent for a while. "I only ask because I'm interested in the music of this Westendorf fellow."

"I don't go in for it much, myself. That's why I wasn't there in the barn at the time. But Mrs. O'Leary has corresponded with him some. She says he hasn't written any music since that night. She says he was spooked as well."

Over lunch, Colum asked Catherine about Westendorf, and she confirmed what Patrick had said. "However, I wouldn't say he's mad. More... melancholy. But the rumors of him keeping to himself and staying home alone, I'm afraid those are true."

"I want to meet him. Could you introduce me?"

"I could. In fact, hearing from an admirer might be just what he needs. I'll send him a note, but you will have to go to his home. He won't come out to meet you."

At the end of the day, Colum held out his hand to receive one dollar and eighty cents from Patrick. *I'm going in the hole by twenty cents a day. This can't go on.* Then he walked to the Kinzie house and knocked on the door.

The widow answered the door herself and looked at Colum for a long time without saying anything. "You care for her, don't you?"

"I do. Very much."

"What are your intentions?"

"I plan to marry her."

"A white man in love with a negro girl. Your life won't be easy." Mabel shook her head. "Well, I suppose that's what we fought a war for." She stepped aside to let Colum in. Then she reached over and smoothed out Colum's hair. "A combed head sells the feet, my boy." She walked Colum into the parlor and then walked away and into the kitchen. Colum sat down and waited for what seemed like a long time.

Eventually, Sara came into the parlor. "I think Mrs. Kinzie just had *the talk* with me."

"Which talk is that?"

"Oh, never mind."

"Sara, I think there's a chance that we can get back home. I mean, you know, to the year two thousand. And when we do, I want us to be a couple. I don't mean to pressure you, we can take our courtship at any pace you think is right. I just want us to be together."

"Colum, I don't think we should get our hopes up. This may come to nothing, and we may have to make a life here. But whether we're here or back home, I can't make any promises to you right now. Those things you said before - about me being 'one of the good ones' – that hurt. And I just don't know you well enough yet to know if I can really trust you."

Now it was Colum who was hurt. To think that Sara might not feel that she could trust him was a devastating thought. "How can I prove to you that you can trust me? That I meant that in the best possible way? That I'm not really a racer."

"You mean racist?"

"Right. What did I say?"

Sara chuckled and smiled a bit. "Let's just take it one day at a time. As long as we're here in this time, we're going to have to stick together anyway."

"That reminds me. I'm going to need another twenty cents."

Sara worked for Mrs. Kinzie, and Colum worked for Mr. O'Leary for two more days, as Mrs. O'Leary set up a meeting with the composer Thomas P. Westendorf. On Sunday, they both had the day off. Sitting in St. Patrick's church that morning, Colum got to thinking about how much he missed his father. Then he started thinking about his brother, and sister. Sara noticed his eyes were getting watery. "Are you okay?"

"Yeah, fine. Somethin' in me eyes."

Sara felt a tinge of jealousy that Colum had a stable family to miss. Her anger toward her parents and their impending divorce meant that on some level she didn't want to go home. Missing them was out of the question. She felt she had no one. No family at all. No ties to anything. Then it occurred to her that Colum wanted to be that for her. *Why? What does he see in me?* She remembered what he had said about her being a treasure, and she took his hand and held it, interlocking her fingers with his.

After Mass, Sara and Colum walked to the home of Thomas Westendorf. Although he was expecting them, he took a long time to answer the door. When he did open the door, he looked like he had not gotten properly dressed in weeks. He was polite, but unenthusiastic, as he invited them in. The dust was visible on the velvet chairs as Sara and Colum sat down in Westendorf's living room. Westendorf just looked at them, and waited for someone to speak. Sara took the lead. "Mr. Westendorf, thank you for seeing us."

"Please, you may call me Tom. There's no point to formality."

"Okay, Tom, um, we wanted to ask you about the night… the night of your concert in the O'Learys' barn."

"Oh. I'm sorry, I have nothing to say about that."

Colum sat forward in his chair. "Please Mr., uh, Tom, please we need to know if you saw what Mrs. O'Leary says she saw. A large wooden crate, maybe?"

"I told you I have nothing to say about that! Really, the nerve of you people coming in here, into my home, and dredging up the memory of that terrible night! If I had known that's what you wanted to talk about, I would never have agreed to this inconvenience. Now I think it's time you go."

Neither Sara nor Colum got up from their chairs. Sara was about ready to give up, but Colum persisted. "Look, Tom, no one is blaming you for the fire. No one is saying you're mad. We believe Mrs. O'Leary's story. We think there *was* a big wooden box that appeared out of nowhere and then disappeared. And I'll bet it even had some numbers painted on the side in red paint, right?"

Westendorf's face went white. He got up from his chair and turned away from Colum and Sara. He took a few steps and then turned back to look at them. "Follow me." Westendorf walked slowly, talking to

Sara and Colum who followed behind him, but without looking at them. "After that night, I found I couldn't motivate myself to play any music at all. I couldn't even rehearse, let alone write anything new. What I had seen that night weighed so heavy on my mind, that I just couldn't concentrate. I closed up my music room." Westendorf led Sara and Colum up the stairs to the second floor of his house. "My inability to play or compose lasted for almost four years. And then, things got better for a while. I actually started to think about playing, and I opened up my music room again, and played a few of my old songs. It felt… good." He took a key out of his pocket and approached a door at the end of the hallway. "Then, about a year ago, I wrote a new song. It's called, *I'll Take You Home Kathleen*. But when I played the finished version…" He turned the key and opened the door. In the middle of the room sat the time machine, covered with dust.

Colum let out a whoop, and turned to give Sara a big hug, but she was in shock, just staring at the wooden crate, hardly believing her eyes. Colum turned to Westendorf. "You mean it's been here for a year?"

"Yes. I wish it wasn't here. But I've been too afraid to touch it. Even if I could move it, it wouldn't fit out the door. So I just locked the room up again, and haven't gone back in. Until now."

"Tom, I can't tell you how… well, I can't tell you. But you don't have to be afraid, and you don't have to stop writing music. I know what this is, and I can get rid of it for you."

"I would like that. I surely would."

"All we ask is that you leave us alone with it for a while, and when you come back later, it will be gone, and all will be well. Can we count on you to do that?"

"What have I got to lose?"

"Okay, we can start right now. But you have to go. Go ahead."

Westendorf left the room, and closed the door behind him. Colum turned to Sara with a huge smile on his face. "We're going home!"

Sara folded her arms. "We? It only fits one person, remember?"

Colum looked at the Resonator, and looked back at Sara. "Well, okay. You go back first, and then Sofia can use a different song to send it back here again."

"No, Colum. It's been sitting here for a year. And Tom hasn't written anything new since then. Even if Sofia uses another one of his songs – and we don't even know if that would work – it would come back over five years ago, and who knows where. Oh, dammit, it's like… having it here is worse than not finding it at all! I mean, if we can't use it to get both of us back, how would we ever decide who goes back first? If the other person gets stuck here, then that person is stuck here – and the one who does get back has to live with that for the rest of her life."

"Her life?"

"You know what I'm saying."

Colum paced around the room. "I refuse to believe that we could have this time machine sitting right here, and we can't use it." He paced and thought for a while longer. "Look, remember when Sofia came back to my time and kicked Chris in the stomach, and then Jimmy came back to get her? Oh right, you weren't there. Well, when Sofia got in the crate and went back to her own time, she took the dog with her."

"So?"

"So you can be the dog!"

"Excuse me?"

"I'll get in, and then you get in and sit on my lap."

"Um, in case you haven't noticed, I'm a little bigger than Nero."

"I know it will be a tight fit, but we have to try. I'm getting in." Colum crawled into the time machine, and then held the trap door open for Sara. "C'mon, get in."

Sara hesitated for a moment, but then started trying to climb in. Her knees and elbows were all over Colum. "This is not working, I'm getting out." But Colum grabbed her, and pulled her through the trap door. Her head bumped on the edge of the opening as Colum pulled her farther into the Resonator. The glass ball banged against the side, and some of the chimes sounded. Inside the crate the sound was deafening. "Dammit, Colum!"

"Sorry. Just twist yourself."

Sara's head hit the top of the glass ball. "It's no use, I can't sit on your lap because my head is too high. We can't be touching the glass at all or it won't vibrate."

"Okay, spin around." Colum grabbed Sara by the sides and turned her body. She pushed his hands off of her and turned herself around, hitting the glass ball and creating a terrible cacophony inside the crate. She and Colum both winced, but she kept twisting her body until she was sitting on Colum's legs facing him, with her legs wrapped around him. Her head just barely cleared the top of the glass sphere. Colum was face to face with Sara. He smiled and said, "Okay, now make yourself as small as possible."

"Story of my life."

"I mean you have to hold onto me." Sara put her arms around Colum. He put his arms around her and they struggled to keep from touching the sides of the glass ball. But every time they moved off of one side off the glass, the other side touched. For one moment, it seemed as though they were right in the middle, not touching the sides. Colum reached around Sara and pushed the green button. The crate seemed to vibrate, and the computer generated melody played, but then it stopped and started like a skipping record album. Sara's elbow was touching the side of the sphere, and the time machine was not going anywhere. Sara realized that she was touching the side of the glass and pulled her arm in tight to Colum, and the music continued. But now Colum's knee hit the glass. As the computerized melody faded, both Sara and Colum felt their hearts sink. They had gotten their hopes up and now it seemed as though their hopes were about to be smashed. They responded to the feelings of despair by instinctively holding each other tight, and when they did, the time machine vanished from 1876. When it materialized back in the year two thousand, and Sofia opened the trap door, she was surprised to see Sara and Colum locked in a passionate kiss.

†††

The flight back to Chicago from New York seemed like closure. Sofia and Armando, Chris and Willow, Sara and Colum, all breathed a sigh of relief as the plane touched down at O'Hare in a cold rain. Only Jimmy stayed behind in New York to tie up loose ends in the aftermath of Wordman's arrest, and to assist the TIA in securing the Resonator for eventual dismantling. And of course, he hoped to get another chance to use the Resonator to try to contact his parents in the past and prevent them from riding any trains.

Donald Wordman was finally behind bars. The reunions had been tearful and a little messy, but that was all behind them, and now as the plane pulled up to the gate, everyone anticipated getting back to a life that would be something close to normal. Fergus immediately took Colum to see his new favorite film, *The Boondock Saints*. Colum dragged Sara along, and she agreed because it would postpone her having to decide what to do next. Sofia got right to work on her newest project, the Lucidator, even though her doctor had put her on unofficial bedrest. And Gus wasted no time in talking Chris into coming with him to work, in hopes that this time Chris might come around to seeing the advantages of going into the family business. But Chris was showing his lack of interest by moving slowly as he got ready for what he called, "bring your musician to work day."

Gus called up the stairs, "C'mon, let's go!" Chris reluctantly appeared at the top of the stairs, but Gus looked him over with a disapproving face. "You couldn't wear something nicer than that? You look like one of those *grungy* musicians."

"You mean grunge? What's wrong with this? Your guys wear jeans and flannel shirts."

"Yeah, but they're not the owners of the company. I deal with other people who run businesses. You have to dress for success."

"I'm dressed as a successful musician."

Eventually Gus stood with Chris and Fergus in his half-built building, looking out from the open frame over the skyline of Chicago. Gus was standing close to the edge, but Chris kept a little farther back away from the precipice. "Someday, son, all this will be yours."

"Dad..."

"Now don't make any hasty decisions about what you do or don't want to do with your life. You don't have to decide now. Just think about it. In the meantime, what do you think about the design of this space?"

Chris sighed and decided to play along. "Well, um, it seems okay, but there are a lot of these poles blocking the view. Can't you just make it all open?"

"Yeah, we could do that. If our plans for this building included having it fall down. These are load bearing posts, Chris. C'mon, even Fergus knows that." Fergus shrugged and nodded.

Chris just said nothing and hoped that his father would see that he was proving Chris' point - that this career wasn't for him. Gus walked to the construction elevator and Chris and Fergus followed. When they got to the ground floor and exited the elevator cage, four men were waiting for them. Al Tallone and his two goons Vince and Dante, along with another man wearing a sheepskin coat and a Rolex watch.

Gus walked right up to them and stopped in front of the man in the sheepskin coat. "Jocko."

Giacomo "Jocko" Scolio was the *capo*, the boss of Chicago's north side. He was a weasel of a man, for whom the phrase 'honor among thieves' had no meaning. Beyond ruthless, he was irrational and unpredictable, and that made him dangerous, even to his friends. Many wondered why he wasn't taken out a long time ago when he was a cocky soldier. But now he was the boss, and he was the most dangerous kind of mobster – the kind who didn't believe in anything.

"That's 'Mr. S.' to you." Vince was brown-nosing.

Jocko looked Gus up and down, nodding his head. "You're lookin' good Gus. How's the family?"

Gus gave a look in Chris' direction, and suddenly became very self-conscious that Chris was there to see this meeting, hearing this conversation. "Never mind them. What do you want?"

"Where are my manners?" Jocko walked over to Chris and put out his hand. "You must be Christopher. You can call me 'Mr. S.' Your father and I go way back – we're old friends in fact – did he ever tell you about me?" Chris shook his hand without saying anything. "Well, I must say I'm a little hurt by that Gus, after all we've been through together." Jocko put his hand on Chris' shoulder and squeezed it. "You ever need anything, you just come ask Mr. S., okay?"

Gus was squirming in his own skin. "Jocko, what do you want?"

"Well, Gus, what I want is to get paid the money that's owed me. But there's a problem, you see, because the person that owes me this money has now relocated to a new home in a federal prison, and he is, shall we say, out of reach."

"What does that have to do with me?"

"I will tell you what it has to do with you. It was your son here who put Mr. Wordman in that prison." Jocko squeezed Chris' shoulder harder. "It's too bad. We had high hopes for him. Thought he would follow in his father's footsteps, or even surpass him. But, what the fuck - we can get another puppet. What I can never get is the very large sum of money he owes me for his many addictions. However, there is a way that you can make it right."

Gus looked away from Chris. "I gave you the computer."

"There was nothing on it."

"Then she must have erased it. It's gone. Look Jocko, you have to leave my family out of this. They're civilians."

"I let you walk away once. Don't make me regret that. Speaking of walking away, where's that nephew of yours, Jimmy?"

"Jimmy? Nobody knows. No one's seen him in years."

"Bullshit. I happen to know he's back in town, and I'm going to want to see him, too. So if you see him, you should probably say your goodbyes. Now I need those plans, and any equipment you have. I need that shit now, and I'm not a patient man. That time machine is going to pay everyone's debts. Once I have it, I walk away, you walk away, and you live in peace."

"Everyone's debts? Even Jimmy's? I give you the machine, you leave Jimmy alone?"

Dante's face turned red. "No fuckin' way."

Jocko put up a hand to silence Dante, then thought for a moment. "Yeah… you get me that machine, I will tell Mr. Corona here to let go of his grudge with Jimmy." Dante gritted his teeth as Jocko turned to walk away. As Gus turned toward Chris he could see several south side street gang members standing around the construction site. In spite of the cold, they were standing with their track suit jackets open so Gus could see the guns in their sweatpants. Gus stopped in his tracks, and then moved closer to Chris.

Jocko turned back as he was getting into Al's car. "Don't worry about them, Gus. They're with me." The four men sped off in Al's Lincoln, spitting gravel up into the air, and in a moment the street thugs were gone, too, and Gus, Chris, and Fergus were left standing in an empty construction site. Gus wondered if having Chris go into the family business was going to be too dangerous.

In the car, Dante was fuming. Eventually his anger grew until it was greater than his fear of Scolio, and he spoke up. "Skipper, you gotta let me take care of Jimmy. I've been waiting a lot of years to settle accounts with him. He betrayed you, too, you know. But with me it's personal."

Jocko turned toward the back seat to look at Dante. "As far as I'm concerned, you vouched for him, so this is on you. You're lucky I don't take it out of your skin."

Dante got suddenly nervous. "I've never been disloyal to you, Boss. Never. He was. He betrayed us. He has to be punished."

Al could see in the rear view mirror that Vince was rolling his eyes. Jocko didn't respond to Dante. Instead he changed the subject. "I need a meatball sandwich." Al turned the car around and headed for the deli.

At the Agnello house, there was more Irish soda bread and brown bread than the family could eat, even with most of them home from New York. Colleen was pushing the bread, even between meals. Fergus looked at a half-eaten piece of the Irish bread, and then set it down on the kitchen counter. "I can't believe I'm saying this, but we should go out to an Italian restaurant."

Patrick raised his eyebrows. "I can't believe you're sayin' that either."

"We just have to make sure we sit where we can see the door. I mean so our backs aren't toward the door."

Gus looked at Fergus with a skeptical glare. "No restaurant tonight, we're eating here. Sauce is already on, can't you smell it?"

When the table was set, everyone gathered around the table to figure out who was sitting where. Gus took a step back and looked over the group with a smile. "We're gonna need to get a bigger table." Colleen looked at him and smiled as she brought out the large bowl of pasta and set it on the table. Once everyone was seated, and grace was said, then the silence set in – that silence that Chris loved so much, when everyone was eating. The bread was soft and warm, the Lambrusco was flowing, and Nero the cockapoo was nosing around under the table waiting for a handout. His efforts were soon rewarded in the form of a piece of meatball from Monica's hand.

It was Colleen who finally broke the silence. "So… are you ready to talk about it?"

Chris, Colum, and Sara looked at each other, and Chris spoke for them. "Not really Mom. It's still kind of swirling around in our heads, I think. I mean, we appreciate that you asked, and we'll talk about it eventually, I promise." Willow squeezed Chris' hand, and smiled at Colleen.

Sofia spoke up. "Well I don't want to talk about it, or hear about it. I just want to fucking forget it."

Colleen scolded, "Sofia! Language!"

Colum turned and whispered to Fergus, "How come she doesn't tell us to mind our fookin' language?"

Sofia rolled her eyes. "Jesus Christ, Mom, who fucking cares? We're all adults here."

Gus started to get angry. "Sofia, what's gotten into you?"

Chris smirked. "Armando's seed." Fergus and Colum almost choked on their rigatoni with laughter.

"Alright that's enough." Gus pretended he didn't think it was funny.

Sofia was on the verge of tears. "You don't get it. People are dead – in the past." Sara stopped eating, and instinctively looked around to see if anyone was looking at her. "And who knows if they were supposed to have children, and descendants, and there's no way of knowing how much damage was done. All of this is my fault, because I built that God damn time machine."

Armando put his hand on Sofia's arm. "It's not your fault, honey. Nobody blames you. And anyway, there's nothing you can do about it now, so try not to let it bother you."

"Try not to let it bother me. That's like saying, 'Don't think about pink elephants. Are you thinking of pink elephants?' Again, you people don't get it. If I could do something about it, I would *do that* – it wouldn't bother me because I could fix it. But it's the very fact that I *can't* do anything about it that bothers me. When you say that it's like you're saying it would be better to be bothered when I can do something about it, but that makes no sense. It makes no sense!"

Armando felt defensive. "Okay, but Jimmy and Chris caught Wordman, and now he's in prison. So that's kind of a happy ending, right?"

"I hope they execute him." Everyone was surprised that Colleen would say such a thing.

Gus thought maybe she was joking. "Really?"

"Yeah, really."

Monica said, "The Church is against the death penalty."

"I know, Ma, but some people have disqualified themselves from the sanctity of life – murderers, terrorists, and I think that should include rapists, child molesters, and people who drive drunk and kill people. He's a murderer. If they kill a killer, they're doing society a favor."

"But what about the soul of the executioner? The best way to overcome your enemies is just to outlive them."

"Well, Ma, I can agree with that." Colleen and Monica clinked glasses, and at the same moment, the doorbell rang.

Chris got up to answer it. When he opened the door, Jocko Scolio was standing there in his sheepskin coat, with Al and Vince standing behind him. Jocko reached into the door and put his hand on Chris' shoulder. "Well, Christopher! Good to see ya! We just stopped by to say hello to the family, you know, now that everyone's back in town." Jocko pushed past Chris and walked into the house, and Al and Vince followed. As Jocko entered the dining room he took off his coat. "Oh I am so sorry to interrupt your nice family meal here, but, as long as we're here, I don't mind if I do. Pull up a couple of chairs, boys." Jocko sat down in Chris' chair, leaving Al and Vince to pick up living room chairs and bring them in. As they maneuvered their chairs to the table, scratching the walls along the way, Jocko said, "Scoot down a bit there, make room for our new guests. This is Al, and this is Vince, and you can call me Mr. S. I'm an old friend of Gus. It is so nice of you to invite us."

Everyone at the table could feel the tension, but Jocko and his men seemed to revel in it. They helped themselves to large helpings of pasta, licking their fingers and slurping the wine. "So Gus," Jocko mumbled with a mouth full of meatball, "where's Jimmy?"

"I told you, he's not here. I see you don't have your dog Dante with you."

"Normally I would be offended if someone were to insult one of my associates, but in this case…" Jocko shrugged his shoulders, and Vince chuckled. "Dante does not have - how shall I say it? - the social skills to attend a nice dinner with a fine family such as yours. He's just so unpredictable. Flies off the handle at the smallest things, and he really goes mental if he thinks he's been betrayed, or lied to. This is such a nice family. I only hope that nothing tragic should befall such a fine, fine, family."

Colleen gave Gus a look, but he looked back at her with a helpless expression. The three mobsters kept on greedily eating their pasta, and flashing creepy smiles to everyone at the table. When Colleen got up to go into the kitchen, Sara and Willow followed. Once out of earshot, Sara and Willow went over to Colleen and started whispering.

"Who are those guys?" Sara asked. "What was that about a tragedy befalling… Was that a threat?"

"I don't know," Colleen confessed. "I've only seen one of those men before. If Gus knows them, it was from before he and I met. But they seem dangerous."

Willow balled up her fist. "I'd like to give those bastards a piece of me mind."

Colleen grabbed Willow's fist, and held it between her hands. "Oh, honey, no. That would only make it worse."

"You can't punch first and confess later." Monica had come into the kitchen. "Not in this day and age."

"Ah, that's okay," Willow said as she relaxed her hand. "All those times I went to confession for punching a man, I was never really sorry. Except with Christopher. That's how I knew he was special. When I hit him, I felt bad. With the others, hitting them felt good. But I wasn't punching just them. I was punching every man who ever made a woman cry. I was punching the men who took my mother away." Colleen squeezed Willow's hands and held on tight.

"Maybe I could talk to them," Sara offered. "When they leave, I could follow them out, and then see what they're really after."

"No, Sara, it's too dangerous. I may not know these men, but I know what kind of men they are."

"But I want to help. I feel like your family is..."

"I know, Sara. I know what that feels like, to want to help fix something, and even to have a reputation as a fixer, and other people rely on you to fix things. But then the day comes when you can't fix something, and it all goes sideways." Colleen wiped a tear from her eye. The tension was starting to get to the younger women, too, so they all silently agreed they had better return to the table. When they got back into the dining room, the "guests" were gone.

†††

Sara found herself walking home late, heading toward her apartment in the city. She wondered why she had gotten herself into this situation, having to walk so far in the dark. Soon she started to feel like she was being watched, and then she was certain she was being followed. In the shadows, she could see the figure of a man up ahead of her. He was waiting for her. She turned around to run but two more men stepped out into her path, and she ran right into them. They grabbed her, and pushed her to the ground. One man had a large, course rope, fashioned into a noose. He climbed on top of her, and put the noose around her neck. Sara tried to scream but she was having trouble breathing. All she could do was inhale as hard as she could to try to get enough air. The rope was around her neck, and the men were laughing. She tried to see who they were, but her vision was blurry. Sara woke up in a sweat, clutching the cushions of the red corduroy couch in the Agnellos' basement.

When Sara told Sofia about her dream, it only made Sofia more intent on finishing the Lucidator project, so that she could try to alleviate the bad dreams everyone was having. "Sara, it's bad enough that you refuse to go home. I mean, you're welcome to keep sleeping on our couch, but you can't avoid sleep altogether."

"Yeah, but it's not like I would get any rest. Every time I fall asleep I dream I'm being attacked. I'm tired all the time, no matter what I do. And I'm starting to feel really… sad about it. About everything."

"Sara, when this whole thing started, I didn't want you to get into the time machine. I didn't want you to travel through time because I was afraid for you. But now look at you." Sofia was feeling the effects of her pregnancy, and getting emotional. "Not only did you travel through time, and come back, but you saved a little girl's life. You're a hero. Try to live on that, while I work out the problem."

"Yeah, I could save others but I couldn't save myself."

"What the hell does that mean?"

"Nothing. Sorry. I'm just rambling."

"Shit, Sara, is there something you're not telling me? Why haven't you gone home? Have you even talked to your parents since we got back?"

"Never mind. It's nothing."

As Gus tried to figure out how to keep his promise to deliver the time machine to Jocko Scolio, the family noticed a steady stream of college students coming to the house. They would go down into the basement, and come up an hour or two later, each with a new twenty dollar bill in their hands. Periodically, the family would send someone down to see what Sofia was doing, but all they could see was a bunch of college students with wires stuck to their heads, watching videos.

One evening, the rest of the family cornered Sofia and pressed her to tell them what she was working on. At first, Sofia got defensive, but then she relented. "Oh, fuck," she sighed. Gus and Colleen looked at each other and wondered if it was a bad idea to push her for answers.

Sofia sighed again, this time with a condescending eye roll. "Like I told you before, it's called the Lucidator, and it records dreams."

Chris smiled and nodded his approval. "Cool. But how do you record dreams? I mean, sometimes people don't even remember their dreams."

"There's this thing called an oscilloscope. It gives a graphic representation of changes in voltage over time... Um, look, the *simple* version is this. Oscilloscopes are used to analyze video signals, like on a TV set. The video image is turned into waves on the scope. But that means you can also turn the waves from the oscilloscope back into a video image. I've been using volunteers – hooking up sensors to the part of their brains that interprets visual signals. They watch a video, and I record the brain waves on the oscilloscope. Then I compare the readout from their brains to the readout from the video image they're watching at that same exact moment. By doing that, I hope to be able to convert one signal into another. And I should be able to take the brain waves from a sleeping person, and convert those brain waves into the visual images they were seeing as they dreamed. I record the brain waves while you sleep, and end up with a video tape of your dream. Well, just the visual. No audio."

"I'm impressed," Sara said. "But just because you can see our dreams, how does that make them stop?"

"I think that once you watch the tapes of your dreams, you can deal with the anxieties that are coming out in your sleep, and the dreams should go away. Might require some therapy, but it should work."

"So what happens next?"

"I've done the preliminary work of gathering the control data – the brain waves from the volunteers – and I've done the comparisons to create a computer algorithm to make the conversion from brain waves to video signals. Now I just have to record some brain waves from a person who isn't watching a video – someone who's actually dreaming."

"I'll volunteer," Chris said.

"No, thanks but I'm starting with myself. If I do get video images, I want to be able to at least check them against my own memories of the dream, if I have any – memories, that is. Anyway, I'm hoping that way I'll know if the images are really from a dream."

Sofia went to bed that night with several electrodes attached to her head. In the morning, two of the electrodes had come off, and Sofia had no memory of any dreams, but there was a recorded signal. She ran the signal through the computer algorithm and waited for it to finish rendering. As she was about to push the space bar on the computer to play back the dream, she hesitated, then got up and locked the door, just so she wouldn't be interrupted by curious family members. This was her dream, after all, and she couldn't be sure it wasn't going to be embarrassing if someone saw it. The image was blurry around the edges, like a kind of tunnel vision, but Sofia could recognize her home. But she could tell from the furniture and décor that this was the home many years before, when Sofia was a very little girl. It was dark in the house. She could see the cat they had back then. She could tell that in the dream, little Sofia was walking through the house in the middle of the night. She watched from her own point of view as little Sofia walked to the kitchen. Then she saw her mother, and smiled at how young Colleen looked. She must have been about the same age that Sofia was now. Little Sofia hid in the kitchen and watched Colleen come into the living room. There, she saw her mother carrying a duffle bag, and quietly walking out the front door. And that was the end of the dream. *That's weird. Not much of a dream. I wonder where mom was going in the middle of the night.*

    All the rest of that day, Sofia worked on a wireless system that would receive a person's brain waves from a short distance away. This would avoid the problem of the electrodes coming off in a person's sleep. That night, she waited until very late, when Chris and Willow were asleep. She crept into their room, and pointed the tiny parabolic dish at Chris' head. *Heh, heh. Do robots dream of electric sheep? Heh. I hope whatever is in his dream doesn't get him in trouble with Willow.*

    The next morning Sofia announced to everyone that they were about to see what Chris was dreaming the night before. Chris wasn't happy, but was too curious to put up much of a fight over it. Everyone gathered around the computer monitor, and Sofia started the recording. Just like before, the edges were blurry, but the center of the image was clear enough to make out objects. Unlike before, the colors seemed off, like the hues on the monitor were set wrong. Sofia fiddled with some settings, but nothing helped. The image seemed to be an open field, with flowers and trees. A butterfly came into view. The point of view seemed very low to the ground, and the image started to bounce and follow the butterfly. Chris was racking his brain trying to remember having a dream like this, but Colum and Sara looked at each other and started laughing out loud. Sara was laughing so hard she could hardly speak. Colum choked out the answer between fits of laughter. "It's the dog! You recorded Nero's dream!" Everyone else burst out laughing, as Sofia muttered a long string of swear words.

Willow finally got her laughter under control and said, "Nero was sleeping on the bed with us."

Colum said, "Well, we know it works on dogs!" Everyone had laughter tears in the corners of their eyes.

That afternoon, Gus noticed Fergus looking at a catalogue. He had stopped on a page with sheepskin coats. This made Gus just a little angry. "Fergus. Didn't I tell you to trust me? You wanna be like him? You wanna be a thug?"

"I don't know what I want to be. But I know what I don't want to be. I don't want to be afraid of anyone. We were afraid back in Ireland. I want it to be better here. These bravos, they have money, and power, and they're not afraid of anyone. Maybe if you can't beat 'em, ya join 'em."

"Fergus, sometimes I don't get you. Hell, you talk like everything is hopeless, but yet you work like anything's possible. You're a good man, a hard worker. I don't want to see you lose that… that goodness. But you've gone from only wanting to be Irish, to wanting to be… too Italian, if that makes any sense."

Fergus was confused, and a little repentant. "I know, I know. Jaysus, I should be happy here. I have a job, and a place to live.

Compared to our cottage back home, this place is a fookin' palace. But I'm *not* happy here. Even when we're not being threatened. Time was, I knew who I was in the world. The world seemed so much smaller then. Now it's too big, and I'm smaller than ever. Colum doesn't even need me anymore. I guess I should be happy that life is easier now. I should be happy to just kick ass and relax."

"You mean kick *back* and relax?"

"Right. What did I say? Anyway, sometimes I think about going back."

Chris came into the room. "So you wanna go back to Egypt, eh?"

Fergus tilted his head at Chris with a confused look on his face. "Maybe a good retreat is better than a bad stand."

"And the devil you know, is still the devil."

Gus shook his head. "Alright you guys, your clichés are making my head spin. Fergus, look at your mother." Gus pointed to the sketch on the mantle. "She wouldn't want you to go back. Sure you'd be a bigger fish in a smaller pond, but you'd still be afraid. Your mother wouldn't want you to go back to that persecution. It is like a kind of slavery."

Fergus was starting to feel defensive. "Even slaves have a purpose. Maybe a slave with a purpose is better off than a free man without one."

"Oh, no you don't!" Sara came into the room. "First of all, no slave ever had his own purpose – only his master's purpose – and that was never more clear than on market day, and anyone who goes back to slavery is... well, that's just a slap in the face to every single slave who couldn't get out."

Fergus felt self-conscious. "I know. Believe me, I wouldn't really go back, even if I could. Too many troubles in Ireland."

Colleen chimed in. "Oh, I know all about that." The others looked at her. "Well, you know... when I was a kid. I heard about it. Fergus, you think there were troubles in Ireland in your time, but it didn't get better. Not for a long time. Not really until just recently."

Later, as Sara wandered aimlessly through the house, she was feeling a little guilty for giving Fergus such a hard time. She walked from room to room, hoping for someone to talk to, but not really having anything to say. Feeling tired, she went down to the basement to take a nap on the red corduroy couch. She decided to listen to some music, so she put her headphones on, and put on her favorite CD by The Cure. Colum came down the stairs and startled her. "Oh, it's you."

"Yeah, it's me." He had a big smile on his face as he went in for a kiss.

Sara held him back. "Colum..."

"Uh oh."

"No, it's not like that. I'm not going to say anything like, kissing you was a big mistake, or anything. I don't have any regrets."

"Nor do I, my love."

"Okay, see there, uh, you have to stop calling me 'my love'."

"Why? I love you."

"Yeah, I know. But I'm not ready to, um, return the favor."

"Look, I thought I explained, I know racism is wrong. I've been on the receiving end of discrimination, remember. And if I'm not acting right, by twenty-first century standards, I mean, just tell me and I'll change my behavior."

"Colum, I don't want to change you, really. You're a great guy, just the way you are. But I'm not sure I'm ready to be that committed to any guy. It's not you."

"Are you giving me the *'it's not you, it's me'* speech? You know we had that in the eighteenth century, that's how old that is."

"No, that's not what I'm saying. I guess I just don't trust my instincts when it comes to men. I thought Maurice was the one. But he wasn't serious. Maybe that's it. He seemed safe because he was funny. And then you came along, and you made me laugh, so you seemed safe, too. But ever since Savannah, you're more serious. Not that it's your fault. We're all a lot more serious than we used to be."

"So let's be serious together."

"I wish it were that easy. But I think there's something else. I think… maybe… you're not really comfortable with the fact that I'm not a virgin. I keep wondering if you're looking at me, feeling sorry for me, or judging me. Like you're going to save the poor ruined girl. You know, in this world, it's weird that you *are* a virgin."

"Yeah, well, from what I've seen of the modern world, if I wait for a virgin, I'll be waiting for a very long time."

"That's not helping your case."

"It's okay, really. I accept you as you are. I'm ready to have a twenty-first century courtship."

"No you're not. And anyway, the twenty-first century doesn't start until next year."

"We almost made love in Savannah."

"Well, *that* would have been a mistake."

"Why haven't you gone home to see your parents?"

"They're not my parents."

"They're not?"

"Well, they adopted me, but…"

"Didn't they give you a good home to grow up in?"

"Yeah. But that was then. Everything's different now."

"Sara, if you have something you need to work out with your mother and father, you should do that. Maybe that's what's getting in the way of… of us. For all you know, if you don't talk to your parents, you could end up alone forever."

"Maybe you're right. And maybe you're not. But I think we need to take a break until I figure things out."

Colum was visibly saddened. "No, I don't want to be on a break. You saw what happened to Ross and Rachel."

Sara took Colum's hands in hers and looked him in the eyes. "I'm sorry Colum. I like you, I really do, but it's like I said. I just can't make any promises about the future right now." She thought to herself, *How can I figure out where I'm going when I don't really know where I'm from?*

Soon Sara was next door, standing at the front door of her house. She hesitated, with her hand on the door handle, and then she slowly turned the handle and went in. Her first instinct was to call out, *Mom! Dad!* but she couldn't bring herself to say those words. So she walked through the house silently until she was suddenly face to face with Peter.

"Well, well. Look what the cat dragged in. Nice of you to visit. Since you've been back for a week. Our house not good enough for you any more?"

Sara took a deep breath. "I have something to say to you."

"Okay, shoot."

Don't tempt me, Sara thought. Suddenly she realized just how angry she was with her parents. She knew her anger at them wasn't really justified, so she took a moment to calm herself. Then she looked at Peter and said, "If you and mom get divorced, it'll be like I have no family."

"Oh, come on."

"No, don't interrupt me. Let me get this out."

Peter sighed and leaned against the kitchen table. "Okay. Go ahead."

Sara took another deep breath. "What do you see when you look at me?"

Peter hesitated. "Look, Sara, I don't know what I'm supposed to say here."

"Exactly." Sara looked down at the floor. "It's like I don't know who I am – and if I don't know who I am, how can anyone else? It's like I have no identity." Sara didn't wait for Peter to respond. She simply turned and walked out of the house, making sure the front door slammed hard behind her.

†††

Chris found himself seated in the first car of the roller coaster. He grabbed on to the safety bar and pulled it down over his head, locking it tight on his lap. He held on to the bar as the coaster pulled away from the loading station and moved out onto the track. As the roller coaster moved toward the incline, Chris could hear the chains pulling it along, and then that familiar ratcheting sound as the car was pulled up the incline toward the top. Chris held on tight as the ratchet sound grew louder and the coaster picked up speed, moving higher and higher up the incline. He could see the top of the hill, and the place where the track went over the peak and down the first drop. But as the roller coaster ascended, it kept picking up speed, and when it came to the top of the hill, it jumped the track, and just kept going up, up, up, and into the clouds. Chris could see the roller coaster track beneath him, and then he could see the whole amusement park far below him. He knew that soon what went up would have to come down, and he feared the fall would kill him, but all he could do was hang on as tightly as possible. He kept looking down as the speed of the coaster slowed to a stop, and it finally ended its ascent, and started falling. Chris could see the pavement rushing up toward him as the roller coaster reached terminal velocity and hurdled toward the ground. Just before it hit the cement, Chris woke up.

Chris realized he was alone in the bed. Willow was already up, working at the dining room table. She was making wreaths out of dried flowers, hoping to sell them for some extra spending money. When Chris came downstairs, Patrick and Fergus were there with their morning coffee mugs, mindlessly watching Willow work.

Chris came into the dining room. "Working on your wreaths?"

"You can see that I am."

"Yeah, I know. That's just something people do – you know, say the obvious as a way to start a conversation when they come into a room. How many have you sold so far?"

"Just a few."

Fergus took a sip of his coffee. "How much do you sell them for?"

"Ten dollars."

"How much is that in shillings?"

Chris chuckled. "Yes, and when you calculate the exchange rate, please factor in the two hundred and fifty years of inflation."

This annoyed Fergus. "You know you'll never make enough money with those to make any kind of difference. Everything costs so much here, you think a few extra dollars will make you safe?"

Willow didn't look up from her project. "Not trying to be safe, Fergus. Just trying to be frugal."

"Well, I'm proud of you, daughter," Patrick said. "Your mother taught you to make those, and by bringing that skill here, you're bringing her here, too. Even if there's no money in it at all."

"Well, I hope there *is* money in it," Chris said. "We could use all the money we can get. Willow always wants the newest things." Willow stopped working and gave him a look. "Ah, the folded arms. The timeless stance of the annoyed wife."

"It's the annoying husband that's timeless, my dear." Willow smiled to herself and went back to focusing on her wreaths.

Patrick laughed, but the impending argument was also making him a little uncomfortable. "I would quit before you make it worse, son. And if you're worried about money, you might need to look at your own contribution."

Chris was hurt by Patrick's comment, and was starting to feel as though he now had two fathers to bug him about getting a real job. "Aren't you people supposed to be all old-school 'men are the head of the household' and all that?"

"Sure, every marriage starts that way." Patrick thought for a moment before going on. "But then, after a while, the woman turns it around, and you don't even know it's happening. And you don't fight it because… well, you're happier when you don't fight it. You're gonna find that a marriage grows, like a person, or like a tree. A marriage isn't like a house. A house, you build it, and then you live in it, and by the time you move in, the house is done, and it's not gonna change much.

But a marriage, grows, and changes. You gotta be ready for the changes, because like a tree, if it's not growing, it's dying."

"But a man's gotta have his own life, right? He's gotta be able to follow his dreams?"

Patrick chuckled. "What dreams? When I was your age, my dream was to live to be my age. Son, I don't mean to play the role of your father, but I am your father-in-law, and I have to think of my daughter. What makes you think you deserve to do whatever you want for a living when most people just have to work hard for a living? Most people feel lucky when they can do what they want on the bookends."

"You mean weekends?"

"Right. What did I say?"

Chris pressed his point. "I heard this expression once. 'Do what you love, and you'll never work a day in your life'."

Patrick frowned. "Well, I can tell you we didn't have that expression in Ireland. For us it was, do what you have to and if you're lucky you'll survive to see another day in your life. It's a nice thought, but only a very few people get to live like that. And if it were true, who would pick up the garbage or clean out the sewers – who would love that enough to choose to do it? But without those jobs, the world would be full of garbage and shite."

"Yeah, I get that. I mean, that's why the best jobs don't always pay that much. Unless you're famous, musicians don't make much money because people are going to do it anyway. But I think I would be miserable all my life if I had to work at a job I hate."

"Son, that's what life is. Miserable. But with enough little miracles along the way to make it all worthwhile."

"But don't you think life should be better than that?"

"Not in my experience. And I need to know you'll do whatever it takes to take care of Willow."

"I'm sittin' right here." Willow chimed in without looking up from her work. "No need to talk about me like I'm a child."

Chris was getting defensive. "Okay, but if we're not going to be so old-school, why is it all on me to get the hard job and you do your crafts and go off on your own to who knows where for hours at a time?"

Gus walked into the room and joined in on the conversation. "Christopher, in my experience, women go off on their own and don't tell you where they're going. Happens all the time. And I don't hate my job. I like what I do. I don't *love* it, but I like it well enough. It's… satisfying. You don't have to love what you do, but you can like what you do and not be miserable. Problem is, I don't see how you can do what makes *you* happy, and still have security. Don't get me wrong, I want you to be happy. But it's more important to provide security for your family."

Now Chris was feeling ganged up on. So much so, that when the entire family went out for dinner that evening, he stayed behind, claiming that he wasn't feeling well. Sofia also stayed behind to keep working on the Lucidator.

Chris was sitting on the floor going through his CD collection. He had decided to make room for some new CDs by separating out a few that he could get rid of. After a while, he noticed that it was more than a few CDs going into the charity box, and most of them were from his collection of 80s music. He almost took them all back, but then decided it was okay. He was done with them. As he was deep in thought over letting go of so much of his 80s music, he heard the sound of breaking glass in the kitchen. "You okay, Sof-? Need some help?" When no answer came, he decided to get up and take a look.

Coming into the kitchen, he saw a man in a ski mask walking toward him. The window of the back door was broken, and the door was open. Chris yelled at him, "Get out!" The man came toward Chris, but Chris didn't wait for him. Chris closed the distance between them quickly and used a front thrust kick to shove the man back toward the door. Chris hoped that would be enough to make the intruder head for the door and run out, but the man in the mask picked himself up off the floor, and looked around the kitchen. Then he lunged for the knife block, and pulled out the biggest knife, waving it in Chris' direction. Chris took a step forward, faking a lunge toward the man, and the man took a step back. It was enough for Chris to reach for the knife block and grab one of the handles. Chris pulled out the knife sharpener. The intruder laughed at Chris for drawing the bladeless tool from the block. But the laughing stopped when the metal shaft of the knife sharpener came down hard on his hand, breaking the hand and forcing him to drop the knife. Then before he could react, the knife sharpener came up again and cracked him across the face, breaking his jaw and cheekbone, and sending him flailing backward. Now the intruder in the ski mask crawled as fast as he could toward the door, and stumbling to his feet, ran out into the night.

Chris locked the door, and quickly became aware that Nero had been barking the whole time, and yet he was nowhere in sight. Chris ran to the basement to make sure Sofia was safe. But when he got there, he was shocked to see that her workroom was in a shambles, and she was gone. "Sofia! Sofia!" Chris ran through the house calling her name. *Oh shit – that whole thing with me in the kitchen was a diversion.*

As Chris finished his search of the house, Jimmy arrived at the front door, and came in to see the look of panic on Chris' face. "What's wrong?"

"Jimmy! Sofia's gone. They took her."

CHAPTER 8
REDEMPTION SONG

"We have to move fast." Jimmy said it with a cold determination as he dropped his bags on the living room floor. "How long ago?" Nero stood with his ears back and teeth bared, barking in the direction of the front door.

"Just now," Chris said, looking around desperately. "They were *just* here."

"Let's go." Jimmy ran to his Mercury, and Chris followed. In a moment they were well over the speed limit as they raced off in the direction of the nearest major intersection. While Jimmy drove, Chris was left with the terrible job of calling the family at the restaurant to tell them Sofia had been taken. Jimmy and Chris drove around in a spiral pattern looking for some sign of the kidnapper's car, but they never found any. By the time they gave up and went back to the house, everyone else was there, pacing the floor and letting their worst fears get the best of them.

Armando was beside himself. "They must have seen that she's pregnant! What if they hurt her? What if they hurt the baby?"

"We have to call the police," Gus said. "Maybe the ones who arrested her last summer will feel guilty and help us now."

"I've already made some calls," Jimmy reassured him. "I've got people on it. But until they make a move and contact us, there's not much we can do. We have no idea where they took her."

Sofia had done her best to fight off her kidnappers, but she was seven months pregnant and there were two of them – and one of them was Dante Corona. She got a couple good shots in before they grabbed her, but Dante hit her with a backfist across her face, and the shock of it made her stop fighting, realizing that if she kept resisting them they could hurt the baby. They sat her down in a chair while Dante stood over her and Al went through her equipment with a photo of the receiver, hoping to find it, or at least find something they could take with them. But in the end they ran out of time, and just took Sofia. As they drove away from the Agnello house, Sofia was in the back seat of Al's Lincoln next to Dante. Al drove with one hand on the wheel and the other on his groin where Sofia had kicked him, and Vince sat in the front passenger seat moaning from the pain of a broken hand, jaw, and cheekbone.

After a few minutes of driving, Al's anger boiled over and he slammed on the brakes. He turned to Vince. "Shut the fuck up!" Then he got out of the car, and opened the trunk. "Put her in." Dante grabbed Sofia's arm, pulled her out of the car, and made her get into the trunk. Once she was locked in the trunk, he sped off again and headed for the nearest hospital. He stopped about a block away from the emergency room, and turned to Vince. "Tell them you fell off your bike."

"He's wearing a suit," Dante said.

"Did I ask you?"

As soon as Vince was out of the car, Al sped off, bouncing Sofia around in the trunk as he made no attempt to miss the potholes in the road.

Finally, the panic at the Agnello house was interrupted by the ringing of the phone. Gus went to answer it, but Jimmy stepped in and motioned for Gus to let him take the call. He picked up the phone, hesitated a moment, and then said, "This is Jimmy Agnello. Who is this?"

"Well, hello Jimmy. We've been looking for you. You know who this is, and you know why I'm calling. With a certain friend of mine under the watchful eye of the feds, the plans for that machine will no longer do us any good. So I want the machine."

"Al the Frog. It's been a long time. The machine's not here, it's in New York."

"Well, that's not my problem."

"You have my cousin. She's pregnant."

"No shit."

"If you hurt her…"

"Look Jimmy, you know how this works. We hold on to her for a while, until you give us the thing. If you don't give us the thing, we have to hurt her. It's not personal, it's just business. We hurt her until you give us the thing. If you still don't give us the thing, we have to make her suffer. And then if you still don't give us the thing, somebody has to die. Maybe just the baby, but the longer you take to give us the thing, the worse it gets." Al didn't wait for a response, he just hung up.

Jimmy hung up the phone and turned to face a desperate family. "It's Al and his crew. They want the Resonator. They say they'll hurt her if they don't get it." Armando clenched his fists and gritted his teeth as he fought to hold back his tears. Colum and Sara tried to comfort him, while the others tried to process the situation and figure out what they should do. Gus went to Colleen and they held on to each other.

Meanwhile, Sofia sat duct taped to an old office chair on wheels. The tape pulled at the stubble on her ankles and chaffed her lips, and course rope burned her wrists. She looked around the room, her eyes wide with fear for herself and her baby.

Dante could see her eyes moving quickly in every direction. He puffed out his chest and adjusted his pants. "Yeah, take a good look around. You're in da middle of nowhere, in a house we can just burn to da ground - with you in it - if we need to."

Sofia mumbled something threatening but unintelligible through the duct tape.

"Yeah, keep making threats. You'll be dead as a pancake soon with dat attitude."

Al leaned against the back of a torn up couch and rolled his eyes. "You know, Vince is out of commission. It's gonna take months for that shit to heal up." He walked over to Sofia and put his face up to hers, looking straight into her eyes. "Your brother fucked him up real good. Somebody has to pay for that."

Dante shook his head. "Vince is a fuckin' fanook. Can't take care of himself in a fight. I don't know why you even keep him around, he's so useless. Long as you got me, you don't need him."

"Shut up you dumb fuck. Let's not air our family laundry in front of the company. Anyway, he's a good earner, that's what counts."

"Hmpf. Earner. Fuckin' pussy."

Al rolled his eyes and walked out of the room. Dante looked at Sofia. "I'm da one who gets shit done around here."

Colleen crossed herself and whispered, "Jesus, Mary, and Joseph."

Jimmy noticed that she wasn't crying. She was thinking, and pacing with her arms folded. The look on her face was the look of someone who has built up an edifice of strength, but its foundation was crumbling under the weight of it. "Why do you fold your arms that way, without crossing them?"

"Oh, I just do that so I don't wrinkle my sleeves."

"I see..." Jimmy thought for a moment. "Okay, look we have to find Sofia, and we have to do it now. I don't mean to make this feel worse than it already does, but the PTSD alone could be devastating, so we need to end this now. There's no way we're getting the time machine moved here in time, even if I could get the TIA to release it to us, which they won't. But... the guy Chris fought off is probably at a hospital. I'm going to check the hospitals around here to see if I can find him and... help him with his suffering."

Monica walked over to Colleen and Gus. She pulled Colleen away from Gus to talk to her privately. She squeezed Colleen's arm and whispered, "*Tu fai qualcosa.*"

When Jimmy got into his Mercury, Colleen was already in the passenger seat. Jimmy looked at her and tried to think of something to say that would make her get out of the car and stay at home, but coming up empty, he just said, "When I go in, you stay in the car. Now point me in the direction of the nearest hospital." Then they drove off. No one in the house had noticed that Colleen was gone until she and Jimmy were well out of their subdivision. Now Colleen's strong exterior was starting to crack. Jimmy didn't look at her, but he could hear her stifled sobs. "Tissues are in the glove compartment."

Once at the hospital, Jimmy parked and went into the emergency room, and walked up the admitting desk. "I'm looking for a friend of mine. Broken hand, maybe broken jaw. Paying cash. He may be disoriented, and I'm worried about him."

The nurse at the desk looked up at him. "Yeah, he's here. Wouldn't give us his name, though, so if you can help me fill out the paperwork, I'll let you see him."

Jimmy smiled. "Oh, thank God he's here. We're all so worried. Yes, please let me see him, and I'll give you all the information." The nurse led Jimmy to an ER bay and pulled the curtain back. There was Vince lying in the bed. When he saw Jimmy his eyes got very wide, but with his broken jaw he couldn't say anything, he could only mumble and grunt. Jimmy squinted at him, and then turned to the nurse with a smile.

"Could I have a couple minutes alone with him?" The nurse nodded and walked away, and Jimmy closed the curtain. Jimmy moved in close and whispered into Vince's ear. "Listen you piece of shit. Ever heard of Jimmy the Fist?" Jimmy took Vince's broken hand in his and squeezed. Vince moaned in a low growl and his eyes rolled back in his head in agony. "I got all day. But you don't. Now I'm going to put a pen in your good hand, and you're going to write down the address where your friends are keeping my cousin, and I'm just going to hold your other hand here for moral support." Jimmy squeezed again, and Vince almost passed out from the pain. But eventually, Jimmy had a piece of paper with an address on it, and he snuck out before the nurse could see him.

Jimmy ran to his car and opened the door, but before he could get in, he heard the voice of Al. "Hold it right there, Jimmy." When Jimmy looked to see where the voice was coming from, he saw that Al was pointing a gun at him. Al pulled back the hammer. "Sorry it has to end like this, Jimmy. You earned a lot of respect in your time. But a rat's a rat. And now you're in my way."

BAM, BAM... BAM

Al Tallone jerked backward from the impact of two bullets to the chest, and then he slumped forward, and the third bullet hit him right in the top of the head. He was dead before he hit the ground.

Jimmy turned around to see who the shooter was. "Aunt Colleen?"

Colleen calmly picked up the three brass shells from the pavement and put them in her pocket. Then she turned the gun around and handed it to Jimmy. "Just like riding a bike."

"This is my gun! Where did you get this?"

"I took it from the glove compartment while you were inside the hospital. Did you get the address? Let's go." They left Al lying dead in front of the ER and squealed out of the parking lot. In a matter of minutes they were in the city and heading for a very run-down part of town.

Jimmy had a thousand questions for Colleen, but he figured he already knew pretty much everything she would ever tell him. "So… Molly Malone, huh?"

"Fight fire with fire."

"I can't believe that was you."

"I can't believe you didn't recognize me."

"Well, in my defense… blond dreadlocks?" Jimmy slowed the car down and drove past the abandoned house where Dante was guarding Sofia. They parked a half block away and got out of the car. Jimmy handed the gun back to Colleen. "Truth is, I'm better with my hands." Colleen took the gun, but her hands started shaking as they approached the house and they could hear Sofia screaming in pain. They ran through the small front yard and up to the front door.

Dante was yelling, "Shut up! Shut the fuck up!" Sofia was still screaming. Jimmy kicked in the door and he and Colleen ran into the house. They could hear that the voices were coming from the basement.

Jimmy went down the stairs first, with Colleen right behind him, covering him with the gun. Jimmy yelled out, "Dante! Get away from her!"

Dante was startled to see his old protégé along with a woman holding a gun. "Jimmy? What the hell? Look I didn't touch her. She just started freakin' out, so I took the tape off her mouth and she's been screaming ever since."

Colleen kept the gun on Dante as she moved toward Sofia. Moving her eyes back and forth between Dante and Sofia, Colleen could see that Sofia's water had broken. "She's going into labor! She needs to get to a hospital!" Jimmy took the gun and kept it pointed at Dante while Colleen got Sofia free of the duct tape and rope. "It's okay, honey. You're okay, the baby's going to be okay. We just have to get you to the hospital. C'mon."

Jimmy moved toward Dante, pointing the gun at Dante's head. Dante backed away. "I should clip you right here, Corona. You came at my family. You crossed the line. In fact, I think the world is better off without you. You have disqualified yourself from the right to live. When I kill you, I'll be doing society a favor."

"Jimmy." Colleen's voice remained calm. "Don't become what you hate. Believe me, I know how hard it is to come back from that. Why do you think I go to Mass every day? Because I'm holy? I go to Mass every day because I'm not. Killing to save lives is one thing, but if you kill when you could just as easily walk away, that's cold blooded. Don't do it."

Jimmy thought for a moment, and the urgency of getting Sofia to the hospital overshadowed his other emotions. He scowled at Dante. "Al's dead. If I ever see you again, you're next." Jimmy kept the gun pointed at Dante, and backed away and up the stairs, following after Colleen, who was helping Sofia walk, and struggling to get her to the car. The two of them were able to get Sofia onto the back seat, and Jimmy hit the gas while Colleen tried to keep Sofia calm by talking to her.

"You're safe now, honey. We're away from that place, and we're going to a hospital. They'll take good care of you and the baby."

Between contractions, Sofia tried to talk. "They want the Resonator. Who were they? Mom, did you have a gun?"

"Never mind that, just relax, we're almost there."

Armando Fernandez Jr. was born two months premature. Both mother and baby were stressed, but ultimately healthy. In the hospital waiting room, the family finally had time to breathe and try to mentally process all that had just happened. Colleen approached Gus tentatively. "Gus, who were those men – I mean, how do they know you?"

Gus looked down at his hands. "I'm so sorry, Col-. They were people from the old days. From an old life, before I met you. Back then, I wasn't always… honest in my business. I took some shortcuts. They were trying to blackmail me to get the time machine, but I guess they got impatient. I'm so sorry that I didn't tell you about this stuff from before we met. I feel terrible that I kept this secret from you."

"Well, uh, you know, we all have things in our past we're not proud of. I can forgive that."

"But the good news is that after you and Jimmy left, that Al Tallone called again, and I told him off, in no uncertain terms. I told him I didn't care if people knew about me, all I wanted was my daughter back and if he didn't set her free I was going to go to the cops with everything I know about their crew. He hung up on me, but he got the message. I don't think Al is going to bother us any more."

"I think you're right, honey. I don't think he'll bother us any more. I'm proud of you, you did good."

"So how did you and Jimmy find Sofia?"

"Um, well, we ran into Al at the hospital, and we got the address. Like you said, he got the message."

"That'll teach him to mess with the Agnellos."

Back at home, everyone was exhausted. The O'Connell men fell asleep in front of the television, and Jimmy found Colleen puttering around the kitchen. He walked up to the kitchen island across from her and reached into his pocket. He took out the switchblade knife that Colleen had given him in Jamaica when she was only twenty-three years old. "I guess this is yours."

"Keep it. I gave it to you."

"I gotta know."

"I can't tell you."

"At least tell me how you got into it."

Colleen hesitated, looked at Jimmy, and then sighed. "Well, in 1968 I was a hotheaded Irish girl, mad as hell about the troubles in a homeland I'd never been to. Back then, there were groups here who supported what was going on over there. Groups that met in the back rooms of Irish pubs in the city."

"You mean, the IRA?"

"What about the IRA?" Gus had come into the kitchen looking for a beer.

Colleen didn't hesitate. "I was just telling Jimmy that he really needs to starting planning for his retirement now."

Gus grabbed a Peroni from the refrigerator and shut the refrigerator door. "Yeah, that's probably a good idea." Then he walked out of the kitchen.

Jimmy leaned in and whispered, "You were in the IRA?"

"Almost in. But I was approached by your... I was approached by an agent who wanted me to be an informant for them, giving them information about IRA connections in Chicago. At first I said no."

"What changed your mind?"

"When they killed Bobby Kennedy."

"The IRA killed him?"

"No, no, he was Irish. No, I just mean... first they killed Martin Luther King, and then Bobby Kennedy, and I realized I was on the wrong side – the side of violence. And yes, I see the irony now. But I knew I had to be on the right side. Within a year I was an asset for the CIA."

"What about the CIA?" Gus had come into the kitchen looking for a cookie.

Without missing a beat, Colleen said, "I was just telling Jimmy about the time I spent in California at the Culinary Institute of America. I got an A in knife skills." She winked at Jimmy.

Jimmy smiled. "I'll bet you did." Gus walked out of the kitchen with his cookie.

"So anyway, to make a long story short, I was a field agent by the age of twenty, and I was considered a pretty good 'fixer,' but I was only in it for about four years because I met Gus, and we fell in love, and got married, and I retired. A year later, Sofia was born."

"Geez, what a story. Actually kind of sounds a little familiar."

"I know, Jimmy. I know more about you and your story than you think I know. But maybe we'll get to talk about that someday. Not today. The truth is, I've always lived in fear that my past will come back to haunt me – and hurt my family."

"So obviously Uncle Gus doesn't know."

"No, and we have to keep it that way." Colleen smirked. "Don't make me regret that I didn't shoot you in Jamaica."

"Does anyone know?"

"Yeah, actually your nonna knows. But she's the only one. Which reminds me, I need to get to confession."

"Nonna knows? Ha, she can really keep a secret."

"Look Jimmy, this is no small thing. I remember being your age, and I remember thinking it was so cool. But here's what nobody tells you – I mean tells you so you really know it – but I'm telling you. You can never undo what you do. You can never go back in time to a point where you don't know what you know. You might really want to un-know something, but not even a time machine can do that. You can't change the past, you can only confess it and hope for forgiveness. But look, it's not too late for you. You don't have to be stuck in the shadows forever, you can come out – back into the light."

†††

Jimmy found himself in his old room. The wind was howling outside the frosted window, and Jimmy was hurriedly going through all the drawers in his desk and dresser. He went through all the socks and underwear, throwing everything out onto the floor, and when the drawers were empty, he pulled them out and turned them over. He tried as hard as he could to remember what he was looking for, but he couldn't remember, so he just kept looking, hoping that he would know it when he found it. Then he started to worry that whatever it was, someone else might find it first. Someone else might find it and know his secrets. *Oh my God, I killed a man. What if they find out? What if they find his body? What if they come for me?* He looked down at his hands, and he was handcuffed. Someone was chasing him, but he couldn't run. His legs crumpled under him, and he tried to crawl into a wheel chair, but the moment he pulled himself into the chair, he couldn't move at all. The door burst open and several men with guns started firing. He could feel the bullets penetrating his body, but he was trapped and there was nowhere to go. Then he awoke to the sound of birds singing outside his window. He dragged himself out of bed, and went to the window and looked out. The trees were starting to bud, and the sun was shining. It was going to be warm, sunny spring day.

This was the day that Jimmy had agreed to play a club gig with a reggae band called *Snare On Three*. They did classic reggae, along with reggae versions of popular songs like Toto's *Africa,* the Beach Boys' *Without You,* and *Vehicle* by the Ides of March. Jimmy was subbing in for their regular lead guitarist, and he had offered to let Chris sit in and lead one song during their set. When Chris woke up, there was a peace offering from Gus sitting in his room. A brand new electric guitar, with a red ribbon around the handle of the case. There was also a tag tied to the handle. It said simply, *Christopher, I'm proud of you. Dad.* Chris didn't waste any time tuning it up and practicing with it.

"What's that?" Willow rubbed her eyes.

"It's a new guitar. From my dad. Can you believe this?"

"That's nice, dear. By the way, I need to get a few things today, can I have some money?"

"You're going shopping?"

"Just a few things."

"Remember tonight is the reggae gig. You don't want to miss that."

"I won't miss it. I'll only be gone for the afternoon."

"The whole afternoon? Where do you have to go for the whole afternoon? In fact, I still don't know where you go most of the time when you're out and about." Willow didn't say anything. "Anyway, we really don't have the money for you to go shopping. What did you do with the twenty dollar bill I gave you?"

"I put it in the offering. They were taking that second collection for the orphans."

"Oh, man. Willow, it's nice that you want to give our money to the orphans, but we're gonna be orphans if we can't support ourselves. We can't live with my parents forever."

"Don't tell me not to be generous, Christopher. Just because we don't have a lot doesn't mean we can't be generous. If you can't be generous, you're not a success, no matter how much money you have. You want to be a success, you have to practice generosity on the way up, or it won't come naturally later."

"Okay, then be generous with me and tell me where you go when you're gone every day."

"I don't have to tell you where I am all the time."

"I'm your husband."

"Christopher, do you remember what I told you when we started courting? Courting is not owning. 'Tis the same with marriage. Marrying is not owning. You don't own me."

"I'm not saying I *own* you, but I think I deserve to know where you're going all the time."

"I just like to walk around."

"You like to walk around? Where? You can't just… walk *around*! It's not safe. I have to take care of you, but I can't take care of you if you don't let me."

"I can take care of myself."

"God dammit, Willow, then what do you need me for?!"

Willow took a deep breath, and looked right into Chris' eyes. "In all the years in that cottage, I never, ever heard my father raise his voice to my mother in such a way." She put on her robe and walked out of the room, leaving Chris sitting on the floor with his new guitar, staring dumbfounded at the doorway.

This was also the day that Sofia was finally able to bring the baby home, and in spite of all the confusion and newness of diapers, wipes, and a combination car seat/stroller, Sofia could still see that Willow was upset. When the commotion died down, Sofia held tiny Armando Jr. out to Willow. "Would you like to hold him?" Willow didn't say anything, but gently took little Armando in her arms. "Willow, you seemed upset when I came home. Is everything okay?"

"The movies lie."

"Okay. I'm sure that's true, but what do you mean?"

"The movies tell you marriage is a happy ending. But that's a lie. It's not the end of anything. It's just the beginning of a woman's troubles."

"Oh. Christopher. Yeah, I get it. Remember I lived with him most of my life. He's a pain in the ass. But I don't think anyone could love you more than he does."

"He's loving the life out of me. He's such a tighty-whitey with money…"

"You mean a tightwad?"

"Right. What did I say? But the worst part is that he feels like he always has to watch over me, and know about my every move."

"Oh, honey, welcome to my world. Try being married to an intelligence agent. Armando is so over-protective, he's actually kind of paranoid. To him, there's an enemy behind every tree, under every rock, and if he had his way I would stay home all the time, just to be on the safe side. It's stifling. But you know, you're going to have to tell him eventually. I mean, to be fair, some of this is coming from the fact that you have a secret."

"It was so much simpler back in Ireland."

"Simpler, yeah. But maybe not better, right?"

"I don't know. I always wanted to choose me own path, and that hasn't changed. I want to have me own money, and be me own person and have me own destiny, so I'm never dependent on anyone. I suppose I want to be a man." Willow chuckled.

Sofia laughed along. "Well in this time you don't have to be a man to do all that."

"Then I guess I'm in the right place. Or time."

"You're not having second thoughts about marrying Chris, are you?"

"No. I mean, I've had my doubts, but when we thought we lost him… you know, to the outer darkness, well that banished all doubts. I want to *have* a husband. I just don't want to *need* one."

"From what I hear you were always way ahead of your time."

"I was. But now… here… it feels like I'm falling behind."

Chris stayed in his room most of the day, and never said goodbye to Willow when she left to go shopping. He practiced with his new guitar, but none of the original songs he was working on were ready to perform for an audience. Nero walked into the room and Chris set down the guitar to pet him. "Hey boy, how's my pooch? Who's a good dog? Who's a good dog? You are." Chris scratched Nero's ears. "You know, I never did get to talk to Gramps. And Jimmy's no help. I feel like I'm right back where I started. Can't put a band together to save my life. Dad still wants me to go into construction. But… he did buy me this awesome guitar. He must have really asked around to find out what to get. He wouldn't have known about this guitar on his own. Where do you think Willow goes every day? Shit, maybe Wordman was right. Maybe she regrets marrying me, and she's out looking for something better. I don't know, buddy. So far it seems like dogs are better than wives."

Jimmy and Chris arrived at The Wild Hare early to set up. Some of the other members of the band were coming in, and Jimmy introduced them to Chris. The audience was relatively small, since *Snare on Three* was the opening act, and it wouldn't get really crowded until later. But it was exciting for Chris to sit backstage as Jimmy played with the band. They did an assortment of Marley tunes, both Bob and Ziggy, as well as some covers. As it got closer to the time when Chris was going to do his song, he started to get nervous. He hadn't played with a band since his own band broke up, and memories of the last open mic made his fingers tremble. The band did a particularly whimsical reggae rendition of

Heart's *Dog and Butterfly*. Then Jimmy went to the microphone. "I'd like to bring out my cousin Chris Agnello, who's going to lead us for a song. Everybody give a shout out to Chris!" The audience made a little noise, but not much.

Chris came out and plugged in his new guitar, and stepped up to the mic. The band launched into a reggae version of the song *Corner of the Sky* from the musical *Pippin*. Chris nailed the vocal part, but his nervous fingers flubbed a few of the chords. The audience response was polite but not enthusiastic. Chris left the stage to wait out the rest of the show in the green room.

When the set was over, Jimmy went right to Chris. "You did great!" Jimmy was trying to encourage Chris while the band packed up their gear. "Your mom and dad are out there, and Sara, and the O'Connell guys came too."

"Not Willow?"

"Well, I didn't see her, but she might be out there."

Chris sighed. "I don't know why this is so hard. I just want to make people happy with music, but it's making me miserable. I can't do it alone, and I can't get a band together. It's a catch-twenty-two, like the universe is against me."

"Don't personify the universe, and don't blame the universe." Jimmy put his hand on Chris' shoulder. "Look Chris, maybe the reason it's so hard is because you're pushing in a direction that not natural for you. I mean, you're an introvert, and you're trying to be in the spotlight. It's kind of counter-intuitive, you know?"

"Whatever."

"Look, I don't know what you're so mopey about. You played the gig, you did great. Enjoy it. I'm heading down to see the family, so don't hang around here too long."

"Alright. I'll be down there in a few." Chris took the strap off of his guitar and started putting the guitar into its case. When he looked up, he was staring right into a large pair of surgically augmented breasts. To his surprise, the breasts spoke to him.

"You're Chris, right? You played that one song?"

"Yeah, that's me."

"I'm Crystal." She stuck out a fake-fingernailed hand for a loose handshake.

Chris stood up and shook her hand. "Hi. Chris Agnello."

Crystal didn't let go of Chris' hand. Instead she put her other hand over Chris' and held on. "I thought you were really great. You have such a beautiful singing voice."

"Oh, thanks."

Crystal took a step closer toward Chris and moved her hand up his arm. "You know, when you were up on that stage singing, and I was watching you, I was thinking, I really want to get to know you better, you know. Like I felt like we have this… connection, you know?"

"Yeah?"

"Yeah. I really think so." Crystal put an arm around Chris' waist and moved in close. "You wanna get out of here? I just can't keep my hands off you." She whispered her hot breath into Chris' ear. "I have a van parked right outside the stage door. What do you say you and I go out to that van, and lock the doors, and steam up the windows?"

Chris hesitated, as his thoughts swirled like a tornado in his head. Then he brought up his left hand so Crystal could see his wedding ring. "There's a part of me that would love to go out to your van with you. And I'm sure you can guess which part that is. But as you can see from this ring, I already have enough drama in my life. No room for more. Sorry. But thanks for the offer." Chris picked up his guitar case and walked away to catch up to his family.

Crystal shrugged and walked out the back stage door to the van. She went around to the driver's side window and held out her hand. "Nobody's ever turned me down before."

"Well, don't cry over spoiled milk, there's a first time for everything." Dante Corona put a hundred dollar bill in her hand, and she turned around and walked away toward the bus stop.

Sara finally worked up the courage to go back home – to walk next door and see her adoptive mother, Nancy Pugliese. She got as far as the front door, but then stopped and rang the doorbell. She hoped no one was home. Nancy came to the door and was surprised to see Sara there. "Sara, honey. What are you doing at the door? Why didn't you just come in?" Sara stepped inside. "Oh, we miss you here, with you staying at the Agnellos' all the time. Let me look at you. My God, I almost didn't recognize you standing there at the door."

"That's because I'm a different person than I was before… when I was here before."

"What's the matter, Sara? Tell me, I'm your mother." Nancy tried to stroke Sara's hair, but Sara pushed her hand away.

"You're not my mother."

Nancy had never heard Sara say those words before. "Well, um, I know that I'm not your *biological* mother, but I raised you. Doesn't that make me a mother to you?"

"Yes, you raised me. You raised me as a Pugliese. But now you and dad are splitting up, and so what does that name even mean any more? Especially since it wasn't really ever my name to begin with. And now it's like… it's like I'm always chasing after peace of mind, but I can never quite get it. You… and him… you're not really my people. And who I am, it's like my whole identity has been a fraud. I'm not a Pugliese any more. I mean, I guess I never was." Sara didn't wait to see the reaction on Nancy's face. She calmly walked out the door and back to the Agnello house.

Nancy was devastated. Sara was her only child, and now there was nothing to do but watch her walk out the door. There were no words she could say in response to Sara's renunciation. All she could do was stand alone in an empty house and cry silent tears.

✝✝✝

The time seemed to go by slowly. Sofia spent her time nursing her baby, the Lucidator. And also taking care of her actual baby, Armando, Jr. Although she was often exhausted after a long day full of feedings and changings, Sofia would stay up late so that she could test the Lucidator on sleeping members of the family. The velocity stress dreams continued, but now Sofia felt she was close to a way to make them less disturbing and get rid of the associated headaches. She believed that time travel produced a kind of post-traumatic stress disorder, and that the only way to relieve it would be for people to confront their dreams and process them in their waking conscious mind.

When she used the Lucidator on Chris, she saw visions of the Irish countryside, with green fields and rolling hills. She saw a blurry image of a broken down abbey, and flashes of a woman's fist coming straight toward Chris' point of view. When she used it on Willow, there were visions of her mother Mary, but the O'Connells were disappointed that the images were blurry and too hazy to see her face. Sofia used the Lucidator on Armando, and she saw her kidnapping from his point of view, but ending with her death. She had to take a break from the project for a couple days after seeing that one. Then she used it on Jimmy (against his wishes) and she saw images so dark and disturbing that once again she had to put the project aside for a while and work on her PhD project, the FTL Transmitter.

Eventually, the family confronted her over dinner and asked about how the "dream catcher" project was going. Sofia had put off talking about it as long as she could. She crumpled up her lips and thought for a moment. "The problem is that some of the dreams are caused by anxiety – we're literally dreaming of what we fear. I think having traveled faster than the speed of light just heightens that stress.

But some of the dreams are memories." She thought about her own dream of her mother sneaking out of the house with a duffel bag. She looked at her mother and wondered whether that was a fear or a memory. "And I suppose maybe a lot of the dreams are a combination of both." She put her hand on Armando's leg. "Armando dreamed that I died."

Armando's eyes got watery. "Well, in my defense, you were abducted and we didn't know what was going to happen to you. And here I am, an agent, and I couldn't protect you. I left you here alone, and they took you, and I didn't even help get you back."

"It's not your fault, honey."

The others all chimed in with assurances that Armando should not blame himself, but it didn't make him feel any better. "How do we know something bad won't happen again? There are dangerous people out there – jealous people who want to steal what other people have worked for rather than work themselves. Evil people who want to destroy what you've built rather than build something themselves. I feel like counting my blessings just makes me afraid someone will try to take them away. You know, I used to want to be on the front lines confronting our enemies, but we have a baby now, and if it's going to put my family in danger, then forget it. In fact, I've been meaning to tell you, I don't think we should go back to New York. I think we should move back here permanently."

Sofia nodded. "Okay. We'll stay here. That'll make Mom and Dad happy, right?"

Monica, Gus, and Colleen all smiled and nodded.

Sara stayed with the Agnellos and no one complained about the crowded house. Colum loved having her around. He had no idea what she was going through, but he tried to be a source of strength for her, that is when she wasn't pushing him away. Sofia suspected that something was bothering her, and after many days of watching Sara's behavior, she finally decided to ask her about it. She found an opportunity when Sara came up to the bedroom to see the baby. "You wanna hold him?"

Sara nodded and took Armando Jr. "He smells good."

"Not at the other end. Listen, Sara… It seems like something is bothering you lately."

"Well, you know, I *was* stuck in racist land for a while."

"Yeah. That must have been so scary, I'm so sorry that happened to you. It just goes to show how dangerous that stupid time machine is. Nobody went where they were supposed to go. Well, I guess Jimmy did, but Chris almost d- um, we almost lost him. That thing has to be dismantled before it can cause any more trouble. I mean, I was always against using it for profit, but that's small potatoes compared to what it could do to the time continuum. Anyway, I'm sorry. You were saying?"

"No, I don't really want to talk about it."

"Are you sure? I mean, we love having you here, but… why are you here, when your house is next door?"

"Well… that whole family thing… with me being their daughter… that's not really going to work out any more."

"What? What happened?"

"I can't talk about it. But you know, I came back from Savannah, and I thought about going back to that house, and it's like, I don't feel like I belong there any more."

"Really?"

"Yeah. And I don't know who I am, coming from there. I've been really trying to figure out who I am – I mean really *who* I am. Who do people say that I am? Do they see me as a black person, or a woman, or a black woman? There's got to be more to it than that."

"Wow. I wish I knew what to say. It sounds like you want to be part of something bigger. But without losing your individuality."

"Yeah, but it's like I don't know who my people are. And it's not the Puglieses. I told my mo-… I told Nancy that I'm not a Pugliese any more."

"Holy shit, Sara, that's huge. But… I guess it's your right to name yourself."

"Yeah, I mean look at how most African Americans got their last names. From their owners."

"So what's your new last name going to be?"

"I don't know. I guess I get to pick one. I need to put some thought into that."

"How about O'Connell?" Sofia winked.

"Okay, let's not get ahead of ourselves."

"So is this what's been bothering you?"

"Well, that… and… and I don't think Willow likes me, and she's your sister-in-law now, and-."

"What do you mean?"

"She's been giving me the stink eye ever since I went to Jimmy and Chris' reggae show and she didn't. I think she thinks I went to see Chris, but I actually went to see Jimmy."

"Do you still have a thing for Jimmy? I thought you were with Colum?"

"Yeah, the thing with Colum is off and on. It's just that Jimmy…"

Willow poked her head in through the bedroom door. "Can I come in?"

"Yeah, sure." Both Sofia and Sara motioned for her to come in and sit down.

Willow looked down at her hands. "I'm sorry, I wasn't trying to hear your conversation, I promise. Well, not at first anyway. Sara, please forgive me for being mean to you. It's not because you're… you know, it's not that at all, in fact my family was against slavery… oh, when I think about it, it makes me cry." Willow started to cry, and pulled out an eighteenth century lace handkerchief to dab her eyes. "It's just that it hasn't been what you would call marital bliss with me and Chris lately. And I know he used to have a crash on you."

"You mean a crush?"

"Right. What did I say?"

Sara took Willow's hand. "Willow, I'm not interested in Chris, I promise. I love you both – together – and I want us to be friends."

Sofia put her hand over Sara and Willow's hands. "Not friends. Sisters."

"Yes, sisters," Sara agreed. "And anyway, I have enough man troubles without adding another one into the mix."

Willow looked into Sara's eyes. "Sara, if we're sisters... oh, my, it just occurred to me that none of us have ever had a sister before. And we almost lost you both," Willow started to cry again, and all three of them hugged. "So... so if we're sisters, can I give you some advice?" Sara nodded. "My mother once told me, don't show your skin to a person who won't cover it."

"What's that supposed to mean?"

"I don't think Jimmy is the man for you. He's not one to settle down."

Sofia smiled. "I think you're right. Willow, I can tell you see into people."

Sara looked at Willow and smirked, "You just want me to date your brother."

"I do at that," Willow admitted. "But I think he's worthy. And since we left Dublin, he's truly become a man. He practically begged Sofia to let him go in the time carriage and find you. He wouldn't take no for an answer, and he knew he was risking his very life."

Sara nodded. "He certainly stepped up in Savannah. I'm sure I could love him. And I *think* I could improve him." She winked at Willow.

Sofia laughed. "Well what man doesn't need a bit of improvement?"

"I can tell you your brother does," Willow said. "Every time I bring up the subject of our future, he becomes silent and seems like he wants to get away from me."

"Yeah, I hear that. But in my brother's defense, I think he's scared he might not be able to provide for you. He's dreading going back to school in the fall, but I heard him talking to the dog the other day and he was saying something about, What good is it? Just because you get a degree, it doesn't mean you're going to get a job. Stuff like that."

Willow smiled. "Well, I suppose he's all I've got."

"No, you've also got us," Sofia said, taking Willow and Sara's hands. "We'll help you straighten Chris out."

All three of them joined hands and Sara said, "Let's all work on our men together."

Gus walked by the room and saw the three young women holding hands. "Well, there's a formidable triumvirate."

Sofia rolled her eyes. "Triumvirate means three *men*, Dad."

†††

The Democratic National Convention came and went, and Donald Wordman was disgraced and under indictment, so he did not get the nomination for president. Instead, Vice President Al Gore was nominated to run against George W. Bush. Sofia, Willow, and Sara started going to Mass more often with Monica and Colleen, and Chris started going to the gun range with Jimmy. But Jimmy was restless, and wanted to get back to New York to use the time machine again before it was destroyed. He struggled to figure out how to save his parents, when all his prior attempts had been unsuccessful. And he was uneasy about the apparent lull in the dangerous adventures of the Agnello family. One day he found Sara sitting alone in the living room reading. "Sara?"

"Yeah?"

"How long do you think it takes for a broken cheekbone, jaw, and hand to heal?"

"I don't know. A few months, maybe. Why?"

"No reason." Then Jimmy yelled up the stairs. "Chris! Let's go! If we wait too long it gets too crowded and we won't get a lane." Chris came down the stairs, and the two of them drove off to the gun range.

After about an hour of practice, they came out of the range to find someone leaning on Jimmy's Mercury. He had spikey hair with a lot of gel in it, and he was wearing a multicolored leather jacket with a large 8-ball on the back. He didn't look up, but just unwrapped a piece of gum as Jimmy and Chris approached the car. Jimmy was annoyed that someone would be leaning on his car. "Um, can I *help* you?"

"Hi Jimmy." The man looked up and reached into his jacket pocket.

Jimmy was visibly surprised. "Shake. Long time."

"Yeah. Long time… They sent me here to kill you, Jimmy."

"I know."

"But I'm not gonna do it."

"I know." Jimmy broke into a smile, and then a laugh, and the two men hugged.

"It's good to see you Jimmy."

"Shit, bro, it's good to see you, too. Chris, this is a friend of mine, from the old days. Goes by the name of Vanilla Shake."

Chris was confused. "You mean, like Vanilla Ice?"

"No, not fuckin' like Vanilla Ice." Shake was annoyed.

Jimmy laughed. "Shake was a rapper at the same time as Vanilla Ice."

"I woulda been huge, too. Like the Sinatra of my time."

"Complete with financial backing from the outfit," Jimmy added.

"But that fuckin' Vanilla Ice stole my career. You know, I had a song on the radio in 1990. It was called *Daddy's Girl* – maybe you remember it?"

Chris hesitated. "No, sorry. But it sounds kind of creepy."

Jimmy laughed. "Yep. That's what everyone else thought, too." Shake frowned. "But hey, Shake - I was your biggest fan."

"And my best friend. Actually, after the rapper thing tanked you were my only friend. So no way I was gonna whack you. But they sent me so I thought I'd come by and say hi, and make sure you knew about the contract out on you."

"Yeah, I know. Thanks. So, what? You're a fixer now? Last time I saw you, you were a bouncer at Faces."

"I went from bouncer to muscle. Now they want me to do these clean-up jobs. But it's not for me."

"Careful how you tell them that. Do me a favor – tell them you did the job – tell them Jimmy the Fist is dead."

"You know I will. Take care Jimmy."

"Take care, Shake."

†††

Chris found himself back at his grandfather's funeral. He was trying to walk up the aisle between the folding chairs, to say his last goodbye to Gramps, but he found he couldn't make any progress because he encountered one obstacle after another. *Chairs in the way... Bumped into Sofia... Sara laughing at me...Tripping over flowers... Bumped into Mom... Dad yelling at me... Falling down... now crawling along the floor, pulling at the carpet to move forward...* After what seemed like forever, Chris was finally able to claw himself to the front of the room. *Jimmy won't let me get by...C'mon Jimmy, let me go! Let me get to Gramps... Oh no! The casket is closed... I'm too late! I'm too late...* Chris tried to open the casket. He struggled and strained, but it was locked. Then he saw his grandmother. She turned to him and said, "Let go, Chris... he will do it for you..." Startled, Chris let go of the casket, and it opened on its own. Gramps was opening it from the inside. Chris turned to his grandfather, weeping openly. *Gramps! Gramps! I love you! Don't go... I need you!* Rocco opened his eyes, which should have surprised Chris, but it didn't. Rocco smiled. *Gramps... tell me what to do!*

Rocco spoke lovingly. "Be my legacy."

"I've been trying, Gramps, but I can't get a band together. I was gonna quit, but I don't want to disappoint you."

Rocco smiled at Chris. "Oh, Christopher, don't dream of the applause. Just remember the joy."

"What does that mean?"

But Rocco didn't answer. The casket lid slammed shut, and Chris woke up in a sweat.

Chris looked to Willow's side of the bed, but she was gone. So he patted the bed to get Nero's attention, and the dog jumped up. Chris started petting the dog. "Who's a good pooch? Who's a good boy? I saw Gramps again, buddy. He spoke to me this time. But I don't know what he was talking about. 'Remember the joy.' Hey today is Sunday. That means spaghetti. Maybe you'll get a meatball, eh?"

When Chris came downstairs after a long hot shower, there was a message for him. Colleen handed him the piece of paper. "She said it was about a music performance or something. I think they want you to play."

"She?"

"She didn't say her name, but it was definitely a she."

Chris dialed the number on the paper. "Hi, this is Chris Agnello. You called me, so I'm returning the call."

"Hi Chris, it's Crystal. Remember me? We met after you played that reggae show."

"Uh, yeah, I remember." Chris looked around to see if anyone was listening, and then whispered into the phone. "You remember I'm married, right?"

"Yes, Chris, I remember. Although I have to say you hurt my feelings."

"What's up, Crystal?"

"Well, I have this friend who's a music producer. He's putting on an all-ages show today, and they had someone cancel on them. So I convinced him to let you play. All you have to do is come down to the club with your guitar. The house band already knows the song. This could be your big break, Chris. Important people will be in the audience. Music industry people."

"Uh, yeah, that sounds great. When is it?"

"It's today. Two o'clock. It's at the Lyons Den, on Irving Park Rd. Come in through the back door."

"Wait, Crystal. I don't think I can do it."

"What? Why not? You shouldn't miss this chance."

"No, I know, I mean… to be honest, it's just that we've got Sunday dinner with the family, and I don't want to miss it. I know that sounds lame, but that's just the place I'm in right now. Thanks for thinking of me, but it just doesn't feel right for today." Chris didn't wait for Crystal to protest any more or even say goodbye. He hung up the phone, and sighed heavily.

Later that day, Christopher Agnello crossed himself, and looked around the table. Monica… Gus… Colleen… Jimmy… Armando… Sofia… He loved that moment of silence when everyone was eating, and the food was so good that no one talked. As he savored the moment, it occurred to him that it had been over a year since he came back from the eighteenth century, and six months since he returned from the 1970s. The whole time travel thing might have seemed like a dream, except that the proof of its reality was staring him in the face as he continued scanning around the table. Patrick… Fergus… Colum… Sara had made sure to sit next to Colum, and he didn't seem to mind one bit. And next to Chris was his bride, Willow. He turned and smiled at her as he shoveled rigatoni into his mouth. She smiled back, still wearing his grandfather's crucifix.

Nero was going from chair to chair, nuzzling each chair's occupant in the hope of getting a meatball. After several attempts with no results, he decided to go for the sure thing, and went over to the high chair where Armando Jr. was dropping food onto the floor. Sofia was handing bits of pasta to her son, as Armando Sr. looked on proudly. The infant was wearing a sauce-stained t-shirt that said, *Embrace the Chaos*. Sofia turned and kissed her husband, and didn't care who saw it.

It was Gus who eventually broke the silence. "Pat," he said, "Tomorrow we have to go over to the phase three site and sign off on the work so far." Patrick nodded confidently. "Then I need you to-."

"Oh, Gus," Colleen interrupted. "Do we have to talk about work at the table?"

"I guess not," he said, giving up more easily than he would have in the past. "But I do want to say something." He raised his glass of Lambrusco. "Sometimes... even a man of few words... has to say... I'm very grateful that God brought my children back to me... and even more, I got a daughter-in-law!" He gestured toward Willow. "And a son-in-law." He gestured toward Armando.

"And a grandson!" Colleen chimed in.

"And a grandson, of course." Gus acknowledged. "And... now I don't have to do everything myself, because I finally have three managers I can trust..." He gestured toward Patrick, Fergus and Colum. "...because they're family. Salute!"

Everyone raised their glasses and said, *Salute*, or *Sláinte*, but it was all mostly drowned out by the clinking of glasses.

Colum raised his glass. "On behalf of the O'Connells," he began, "I want to say thank you as well... you saved us... and the life we have here is a life we never could have imagined..." he thought he was going to say more, but the words didn't come to him. "So... we are also very grateful."

Before anyone could clink their glasses again, Monica spoke up. "So, good. We're all thankful. So we're all going to Mass."

"We're all going to Mass!" Gus agreed, and the glasses clinked.

As it happens many times with a big family, the Agnellos, the Fernandezes, and the O'Connells could not get their act together and get going early enough on this particular Sunday, and so they missed all three morning Masses. The Sunday evening Mass was the last chance of the weekend, so the pasta dishes were left for later, and the group piled into the Suburban and the minivans, and made their way to St. Cecilia's church. There, the Agnellos were surprised and happy to see Jimmy go forward to receive communion, something they hadn't seen him do since he left home over a decade before.

Sitting in the pews, Colleen gave Monica a knowing look. They had succeeded in getting the whole family back to church. Monica held her rosary tightly, and told God that now she could die happy. But instead of the voice of God, in her mind she only heard the voice of her son. *Ma, you're not going to die soon… you're in perfect health.*

That evening, when everyone was together, Jimmy stood up. "I have something I have to say," he said, getting the group's attention. They all got silent and looked at him expectantly. "It's time for me to leave," he announced.

What? Why? Everyone protested in unison.

"My job here is done," Jimmy said with a hint of sadness. "I have loved every minute of being with all of you. But I have to go back to Rome. There's a girl waiting for me there."

When everyone finished saying their confused goodbyes to Jimmy and started going to bed, Jimmy started packing. Later, when the house was quiet, he went into Gus' office and picked up the phone. He hesitated and looked upward as he tried hard to remember the number he wanted to call. Then he dialed, and waited while the phone rang and rang. Just as Jimmy was about to hang up, someone answered, and Jimmy heard a voice he hadn't heard in over ten years.

"This is Frank."

"Frankie Stamps, how the hell are ya?"

"Who the fuck is this?"

"Aw, Frankie, I'm hurt you don't recognize my voice. It's Jimmy."

"Jimmy? Jimmy the Fist?"

"I haven't been called that in a decade."

"No shit, where have you been?"

"Away. And I'm leaving again in the morning. But I thought maybe we could meet and catch up before I go. Can you meet me at the restaurant at seven?"

"Sure Jimmy, I'll see you then."

At seven o'clock the next morning, Jimmy stood in front of 932 N. Rush Street, staring at a Starbucks coffee shop. Frank walked up and stood next to Jimmy, both of them facing forward, just staring at the Starbucks.

"Frank, what happened to the restaurant?"

"Gone."

"Well, I can see that. And where's Faces?"

"Gone."

"Geez, does anything stay the same?"

"You've been gone a long time, Jimmy."

"What about that girl of yours, what was her name, Fia? Yeah, Fia Miferi? She was hot."

"Uh, she is now Mrs. Franco Bolli, thank you very much."

The two men laughed, then hugged, slapping each other's backs. "Let's go inside."

They sat at a small table in a corner near the back. "So... Jimmy the Fist."

"Enough with that. It's like I told you, I don't go by that name any more."

"So were you in witness protection?"

"At first, yeah. Then... other stuff. What about you? Did you ever become a made guy?"

"Nah. I was more use to them as a buffer, so it wasn't in the cards. And I'll tell you I'm glad. You know once you're in, you owe them. I gotta think about Fia now."

"Yeah, it's tough. For a long time, I didn't have any connections. Nobody to put at risk. Now, it's like I got this whole family. That's why I gotta leave. Plus, I got some shit to do in New York."

Frank reached into his jacket pocket and pulled out something shiny. Jimmy looked closer. It was a pinky ring with diamonds in the shape of a horseshoe.

Jimmy smiled. "Hey, that's your ring! How come you're not wearing it? Ha - I always thought that ring was so cool."

"Jimmy, I got a confession to make."

Jimmy's smile left his face as he looked toward the door to see if he was being set up. "What is it?"

"This isn't my ring. It's yours."

"What?"

"It belongs to you. It was your grandfather's ring. Your mother gave it to me. Told me to look out for you, and when you got older, to give it to you."

"My mother? You knew my mother?"

"Jimmy, do you have any idea who your mother was?"

"What do you mean?"

"She was the daughter of one of the New York bosses. She was a friggin' mafia princess. So she gives me this ring, and I can't say no because, well, you know, but you were just a little snot-nosed shit at the time, so I figured, what the hell. I started wearing the ring, and it became my good luck charm. And now, well I'm sorry I never told you."

"Wait, what? My mother was... what?"

"And if I never said it for real, I'm sorry for your loss. Your parents, I mean."

"Yeah, thanks. So who was my grandfather? Do I still have relatives in New York?"

"Only in the cemetery. Which is where you're going to be if you don't get the hell out of town. You know there's a contract on you, right?"

"Yeah, I know. Do you know who's behind it?"

"Well, you're old karate teacher Dante Corona is the muscle, so I assume it's coming down from Mr. S. You gotta watch out for Corona, Jimmy, he's fuckin' oobatz. He has no sentiment for the past, so don't even think of counting on that. He's got paranoid delusions of grandeur, like he thinks he's the center of the whole operation, but the rest of the crew, they don't even want to be around him because he's losin' it like some fuckin' Mexican jumping bean, all over the place. You know he's not even Italian."

"He's not?" Jimmy put on the pinky ring and looked at his hand approvingly.

"No. He always said he was southern Italian, but he's really just southern. He's from Savannah, Georgia. His mother was somebody's gumar, that's why they call him Il Bastardo, but he changed his name to Corona to sound Italian. His real last name was Crown, or some shit like that."

Jimmy laughed. "Oh, that figures. Well, I just need to have a talk with Jocko."

"No, Jimmy. You'll never get to him. His soldiers will kill you before you get anywhere near him."

"Well, if I can get done what I want to get done in New York, I think everything will be okay. Then I can wrap this shit up and get back to… well, you know, wherever it is I'm going."

"Yeah, I get it. You don't have to tell me. But I'm on your side, Jimmy. In spite of the ring thing, I've always had your back, just like your mother asked me to."

"Thanks, Frankie, I appreciate it."

"Listen Jimmy. You're not like Dante, no matter how much he taught you. He's a sadist and a psychopath – you're a person. Don't lose your humanity – don't become like him."

"Goodbye Frank. And thanks for not asking me if I was a rat."

"Never crossed my mind."

Colum found himself sitting in front of a roaring fire in a pub. He was surrounded by a large group of thugs, thieves, pirates, and gangsters, drinking beer and talking with them. He was telling them everything he was thankful for, and giving them the names of all the important people in his life. One of the gangsters said, "Well they're really in danger now!" and the entire pub erupted into laughter. Then Colum woke up feeling extremely ashamed and vulnerable. He realized he was running late and decided to skip the shower and dress for work.

Willow handed sack lunches to her father and brothers as they walked out the door to catch up to Gus, who had already started up the Suburban. As Colum took his lunch she whispered to him, "Colum. Remember, a combed head sells the feet."

"Yeah, so I've heard. Wait, did Sara say something about me?"

"No. I don't know. Just, you know, make yourself presentable when you're around her."

Colum sighed and walked out the door. Willow held on to her father's arm to hold him back while Fergus followed Colum out. "Dad?"

"Yes, my daughter?"

"You told me once that you're proud of me."

"That I am. That I am. You're a fine young woman."

"Why have you never told the boys you're proud of them?"

"Because it might make them let down their guard. You and Christopher have each other. But they don't have anyone but me. And this world is a hard place. I need to be hard on them so they'll be strong, to harden them against the violence of the world. I won't be around forever, you know."

"Yes you will."

Gus beeped the horn, and Willow kissed her father on the forehead and pushed him out the door.

Jimmy was on the morning flight to New York. His plan was to try again to use the Resonator to find his parents in the past, warn them about the train accident, and hopefully save their lives. But now he also had a new mission. He was going to connect with his roots, by paying his respects at his grandfather's grave. Now that he knew who his mother was, and who her father was, he wondered if his family connections might help him with his problems in Chicago. When he got off the plane, he went right to the airport pay phones and started calling the Catholic churches in Brooklyn until he found out where his maternal grandfather was buried. A cab ride later, he was standing in front of the grave of the grandfather he never knew, Fortunato Patrono.

Jimmy was so lost in thought that he didn't notice two men hiding in the tress, and circling around him. He didn't hear them as they approached him from behind. By the time he sensed their presence, they already had their guns pointed at him. Jimmy sighed. "I must be losing my edge."

"You must be some kinda fuckin' idiot comin' here. Now hand over the piece."

Jimmy took out his gun and handed it over to one of the men.

"Hey, do you see that? Do you see what he's got on his hand?"

"The ring. And look who's grave he's standing over."

"Holy fuckin' shit. Who the fuck are you?"

"My name's Jimmy Agnello. Our friends in the midwest call me Jimmy the Fist. My mother was Angela Patrono." He gestured toward the grave. "I'm his grandson."

The two men looked at each other. "What do we do?"

"Orders are to clip him on sight."

"You wanna be the guy who clipped Patrono's grandson?"

"Hell no. Anyway, we can't clip him here, he'll fall right on the old man's grave."

"Let's take him back with us. We can double check the orders haven't changed. Then we can clip him and dump him somewhere else."

The two men made Jimmy get into their car, though he didn't resist. They drove him to a house in Brooklyn and pulled far into the driveway and stopped the car behind the house. Jimmy was told to get out and walk through a side door and down a flight of stairs into the basement. There they made him sit in an uncomfortable old chair while they kept their guns pointed at him. He waited for a while, not knowing what to expect, and then he heard the footsteps of someone coming down a different flight of stairs, from inside the house. He could barely see in the dim light of the basement, but he could make out the figure of a very large man walking down the stairs, leaning from side to side as he walked, and relying on the railing so much that it creaked. The man walked into the small circle of light produced by the single bare bulb hanging from the ceiling. "I hate fuckin' stairs. And I hate anyone who makes me walk up and down the fuckin' stairs. What is this?"

The two men who had brought Jimmy there looked at each other. Neither one wanted to be the one to speak, but eventually one of them did. "Boss, this is the guy our friends in Chicago said was going to be a problem. We were gonna just clip him and be done with it, but we noticed he was wearing the old boss' ring – look."

The large man looked annoyed. "Anyone can have a ring like that."

"But he was standing over Mr. P's grave, and he claims to be Patrono's grandson."

The large man looked at Jimmy for a long time. "Yeah, I see it. Looks like his nonno. What's your story, kid?"

The more quiet of the two soldiers now found the courage to speak up. "Says *he's* Jimmy the Fist."

The large man smiled. "So Jimmy the Fist is the old boss' grandson. That's rich. You can put away the pieces fellas. Nobody's gettin' clipped today. Chicago can go fuck themselves. Look, uh, Jimmy. Sorry about the inconvenience, but we didn't know who you were. You don't make trouble for us, we got no beef with you."

"Thanks." Jimmy stood up and put out his hand for a handshake. "But I still have a problem with our friends in Chicago. I need someone high up to put the word out for them to leave me and my family alone."

The large man shook Jimmy's hand. "I wish I could help you. But there's only one man who has that kind of pull – Don Pella. But he's not here. He's retired, living in Miami."

"If I'm willing to go down there, can you get me a meeting with Mr. Pella?"

"I can make a call, tell him you're coming, but I can't promise he'll see you. He's a very private man in his old age."

The time machine would have to wait. Jimmy made a quick stop at a music store to pick up an acoustic guitar, then he was on the next plane to Miami. Getting off the plane, he was hit with a hot wave of humid air. He stopped walking for a moment and let it wash over him, smiling at the feeling. The blazing sun made him squint as he walked to the car rental office. Soon he arrived at Don Pella's house on Bayshore drive, overlooking the ocean. Jimmy pulled up to the house, and walked slowly up to the door, carrying the guitar. *Am I crazy? I could be walking into a trap.* Jimmy looked around. *I've come this far. No turning back now.*

The doorbell was a series of chimes that seemed to go on forever. A sixty-something year old woman came to the door dressed to go out on the town, and she stood there waiting for Jimmy to speak.

"Um, hello, I'm Jimmy Agnello. I have a meeting with Mr. Pella."

"Yeah, he's expecting you. Come on in. I'm Vera, by the way. His wife." She picked up a leather handbag from the table in the foyer and looked inside for her keys. "I'm just on my way out."

"Nice to meet you, Mrs. Pella."

"He's out on the lanai."

"I'm sorry, I don't know what a lanai is."

"Back patio, by the pool."

Jimmy slowly wandered through the enormous house, self-conscious and feeling like he shouldn't be there. But after a few wrong turns, he could see the pool through the large windows, and eventually he found his way to the lanai. There was a wrinkled old man, sitting in a lawn chair, watching a soccer game on an old television set, which was also sitting on a lawn chair. "Mr. Pella?"

"Who's asking?"

"Jimmy Agnello. Our friends in Brooklyn told you I was coming?"

"Jimmy the Fist. Your reputation precedes you. Sit down."

Jimmy sat down on the edge of a pool lounger as Don Pella groped around under his chair, searching for the TV's remote control. He muted the television, and took off his sunglasses. He looked at Jimmy for a while, and then nodded slowly. "I knew your grandfather well. Considered him a friend. What can I do for you?"

"Well, sir, to be honest, I'm having some trouble with our friends in Chicago. They think I ratted them out, and there's a contract on me. Now I could just disappear, but they're coming after my family."

"I'm sorry kid. I can't get involved in their business... Is it true? Did you rat them out?"

"No. But I did disappear just when the shit was hitting the fan, so I don't blame them for thinking I did. My other grandfather had just died, you know, my dad's father."

"Well it doesn't help that your old man was a fed."

"I'm sorry, he was a what?"

"Ha. You didn't know. Oh, yeah, real Romeo and Juliet, your parents. Capo's daughter falls for G-man. Real shitstorm that caused. Too bad about them. I'm real sorry for your loss. But like I said, I can't get involved."

"Well, if you could just hear me out, there's more to the story. You know that guy who was running for president, the one they indicted? Donald Wordman?"

"Yeah, what about him?"

"He was working with the Chicago outfit. Owed them a lot of money, in fact. But he's a real piece of shit. Involved in all kinds of things you wouldn't approve of. Turns out he got the Chicago crew involved in child sex trafficking. Helping our friends in the midwest smuggle young girls into the country by flying them into small airports in the middle of nowhere and getting around the security. I mean, look, I don't judge our family history, I get it. The system failed our people when they came over as immigrants and so we created our own system. Our thing. But we have our honor, and we have lines we won't cross, and nobody in the old days would allow anybody to hurt kids."

Pella thought about what Jimmy was saying for a while. Then he shook his head. "I'm retired. It's a new world. I can't keep up with whatever the fuck these babbos are doing any more."

Jimmy sighed. "Okay. There is one more thing you should know. But it might be hard to believe."

"You're treading on my patience."

"Just one more thing, I swear." Jimmy hesitated, and Pella tilted his head and gave him a *get on with it* look. Jimmy took a deep breath and spoke quickly. "My cousin invented a time machine. The Chicago crew is trying to steal it, and if they get their hands on it they're gonna go back in time and screw up a lot of things for a lot of people."

"Are you fuckin' oobatz? Or maybe you think I am. 'Cause if that's the case, I'm about to get real offended real quick."

"No sir, I know it sounds crazy, but it's true. And if the Chicago crew can go back in time, they can whack anyone they want, and take anything they want. Including New York."

Pella was silent for a moment. "And I'm supposed to believe you 'cause what?"

"Let me prove it to you." Jimmy opened his guitar case. "I'm going to play a song I wrote." Pella looked truly annoyed. "It's a song I've never played for anyone before, and it's really, really bad."

"Then why are you gonna make me listen to it?"

"You'll see, I promise." Pella shook his head.

Jimmy began to play his song, and it was terrible. The words didn't make any sense, and the chord structure was a musical mess. But only about half a minute into the song, just as Pella was about to yell for Jimmy to stop, the music got louder, and the harmonics started ringing. Pella covered his ears, and the Resonator materialized right there on his lanai. And as if that wasn't shocking enough, the trap door opened and Jimmy poked his head out from inside the wooden crate. He looked at a very confused old mob boss and said, "Hey Mr. Pella, it's me Jimmy. I came here from a little while in the future to prove to you that everything I'm telling you – that's me over there with the guitar, but to future me that's past me – everything I'm, uh, he's telling you is true. You can't afford to let the Chicago crew get their hands on this time machine. Okay. Gotta go now. Bye." Future Jimmy pushed the green button, and the crate vanished.

    Pella was stunned for quite a while. He looked at Jimmy, and he looked at the place where the time machine had materialized. Then he looked back at Jimmy. Then he closed his mouth. "Okay, I'll make a call. See what I can do. But I can't promise anything."

    "That's all I can ask. Thank you." Jimmy packed up the guitar and started walking back through the house toward the front door.

    Pella called out after him, "Jimmy." Jimmy turned around. "Hang on to that pinky ring – it's good luck for you. If you weren't wearing it, you'd be dead now."

    Jimmy went right back to the airport and caught the next plane back to New York. He used the Resonator to go back to Mr. Pella's lanai, but before he could use it again to try to save his parents, he got a call that made him hurry back to Chicago.

Gus, Patrick, Fergus, and Colum were making the rounds of construction sites to do inspections and see if everyone was on schedule. Their last stop for the day was a relatively new site where the cement company was pouring concrete for the foundation of an apartment building. As they stood over a foundation block mold full of wet cement, Jocko Scolio walked up behind them along with Dante and Vince. When they turned around and saw Scolio and his men, they were backed up against the foundation block mold.

Gus knew that these were the men who had kidnapped his daughter. His face turned red. "Get out. Get out of here!"

Scolio shook his head. "That's not very nice, Gus. Where's your sense of hospitality?"

"Hospitality? Your goons have come uninvited to my house one too many times. Now get out!"

"No Gus. We have all kinds of unfinished business. We still have no time machine, no Jimmy the Fist, and no revenge for our fallen brother, Alphonse Tallone. Not to mention just general loose ends to tie up."

Patrick took a step toward Vince. "Face all healed up asshole? Our boy Chris did a nice job on you, didn't he?"

Vince mumbled, "Fuck you," and pulled out his gun.

"Enough!" Scolio put up a hand to silence Vince. Then he saw Gus looking around to see if there was anyone nearby to help. "Hey! Quit lookin' around. Look at me when I'm talkin' to you. Ain't none of your spic teamsters around to save you."

"Listen you asshole, my grandson is a spic – I mean, Hispanic. Shit."

"Yeah, well maybe we'll have to pay him a visit, too, like we did his mommy. Then we'll bury his grandpa somewhere where nobody will ever find him. It'll be like he never existed."

Patrick's anger boiled over, mixing with his loyalty to the Agnello family, and he lunged at the group of thugs. As he moved toward them, Vince pulled the trigger and shot Patrick in the stomach.

The sound of the gun shocked everyone. Gus and Colum were stunned for a moment, trying to process what they had just seen, trying to clear away the fog of denial in their minds.

Colum yelled, "No!"

Fergus jumped toward Patrick and tried to grab him as he fell backward into the trough of wet cement. "Dad!"

Colum was filled with rage, and made a move toward Vince, but Gus stepped in and grabbed him, holding him back. Then both Gus and Colum turned to try to help Fergus pull Patrick out of the cement, but Vince walked toward them, pointing the gun at them. Dante laughed sadistically and picked up a two-by-four from the ground. He used the end of the two-by-four to push Patrick farther down into the cement. Colum started screaming unintelligibly at Vince and Dante, as Gus held him back again, and Vince put the gun right up to his head.

Patrick's eyes were wide with fear and pain as he sank into the cement. He reached up and grabbed Fergus' shirt. Fergus tried to pull him out of the trough, but he only pulled himself down closer to Patrick, who looked into his eyes. Patrick struggled to speak. "I'm proud of you boys."

Tears were streaming down Fergus' cheeks. "We love you Da – oh, Christ don't take me pa from us!"

Patrick pulled on Fergus' collar. He reached up and grabbed Fergus' face with his cement encrusted fingers. "Son, look at your father." Then he turned Fergus' face to look at Gus. Gus was surprised by Patrick's words, and he let go of Colum and turned toward Patrick.

Colum shouted, "No! Dad!"

Patrick strained his neck to see Gus and he reached up and grabbed Gus' shirt. "Gus, look at your son," and he nodded toward Fergus. Then Dante shoved again with the two-by-four and Patrick's body went down into the wet concrete. His mouth filled with cement as he tried to say, "Mary." Then he was gone.

"You fookin' bastard!" Now Fergus lunged at Dante and Gus had to hold him back as Colum cried over the block of hardening cement that concealed his father's body.

Gus held up his hand toward Vince. "Don't shoot. Don't kill these boys. You've taken enough from them, please! We'll do whatever you want!"

Scolio remained calm. "Now that's more like it. That's the kind of respect I should get from people like yourself. So here's what I want. I want Jimmy to deliver the time machine to us within the next twenty-four hours, or we will become regular visitors to your home and your family. Do I make myself understood?"

Gus was out of breath. "Yes. Yes."

Jimmy came home as soon as he could after he got the call. When he arrived at the Agnello home, everyone was crying. Everyone except Fergus, who was mostly staring into space, but every so often he erupted into bursts of energy, yelling at Colum to "gear up" like the *Boondock Saints* and avenge their father. "C'mon Colum! What would Connor and Murphy do?"

Colleen tried to calm him. "Fergus, I'm so sorry for your loss. We all loved your father. But revenge is… well, it's like drinking poison and hoping it kills your enemy. If you go after revenge, you'll only get yourself killed, too. You have to think of your sister now. You must know the Irish saying, 'the man who plans revenge should dig two graves'."

Fergus just retreated back into himself and into more staring off into space.

Chris was with Willow, who was inconsolable, and Sara tried her best to comfort Colum, as he sat on his father's bed holding Patrick's tool belt. Sara kept her arm around Colum as he silently took one tool at a time out of the belt and held it, and looked at it.

Armando was pacing the floor, sputtering angry words of frustration. When Jimmy came in, Armando and Sofia went to him right away to try to talk about what they should do next. They went into Gus' office and closed the door so the others wouldn't hear their conversation. Armando was beside himself with grief – but also with fear. "There's no way we can protect everyone. I wish I had been there, but I couldn't be there. And if I was there, I couldn't be there every day, I mean we can't be everywhere every day. And we can't count on the cops, they're not going to follow everyone around every day in case something happens. What if something happens to Sofia or Junior, and I'm not there? What the hell are we going to do?"

Jimmy tried to get Armando to stop pacing and sit down. "Alright, 'Mando, try to calm down. This is a terrible thing, but we still have like, twenty hours before anything else happens." Jimmy tried to think of what to do next, but in the absence of any good ideas, his thoughts drifted to the fact that he was not able to try to save his parents again, and there wasn't much time left before the Resonator was going to be dismantled. "Okay, they want the time machine, right? But once we destroy it, they won't have anything to go after. Except of course getting rid of witnesses. Shit." He thought for a while in silence. "So we have until tomorrow afternoon to get ready for whatever it is that's going to go down. But whatever we do, it has to be something that ends this once and for all. Like you said, 'Mando, we can't go on living in fear. And it's only a matter of days before the TIA is going to destroy the time machine."

Armando scratched his head. "I still think it's a bad idea to destroy it. You never know if it might come in handy someday."

"No," Sofia was adamant. "You've never actually travelled through time, 'Mando. It doesn't really work that well. Most people don't end up where they plan to."

"But maybe there's a way to use the time machine to get us out of this. Maybe we could even save Patrick."

"I've been trying like hell to save my parents," Jimmy said, "but no luck."

"Yeah I've been thinking about that," Armando replied. "You say they died in a train accident, but then you went back and prevented that accident, and then it turned out they died in a *different* train accident."

"Yeah, I did that a few times, and I prevented all those train accidents. But my parents are still dead. I don't get it."

"Why is it always a train accident? Why not a car accident, or plane crash, or something else?"

"What do you mean?"

Sofia said, "I get it. If you can't prevent their deaths because of some time travel paradox, like it's their time to die, and the universe won't let them live on, it wouldn't have to be train wrecks. It could be anything."

"Okay, don't personify the universe. But I see what you're saying. But so what?"

Armando scratched his head again. "Something doesn't add up. If you prevented the accidents, your parents should be alive. What is it about train accidents?"

"I don't know," Jimmy said. "And it sucks because with trains, it's not like a plane or even a ship, where you have a passenger list and you can see who was actually on board. With a train, anyone can buy a ticket with cash, get on and get off, and so you don't really know who was on it when it crashed."

"That's it!" Armando jumped up from his chair and started pacing again. "Nobody knows for sure who was – or wasn't – on those trains when they crashed. So if someone was going to fake their own death, they could wait until a train crashes, and then leave some sort of clue that makes everybody *think* they were on that train. Everyone would think they were dead, but no one has to find a body."

Jimmy was disturbed. "Are you saying you think my parents faked their own deaths?"

At that moment the office door opened. Jimmy looked toward the door. He felt as though his heart stopped for a moment, as he thought he recognized the two people who came into the room. His voice cracked as tears welled up in his eyes. "Mom? Dad?"

CHAPTER 9
THREE LITTLE BIRDS

Michael and Angela Agnello shut the door behind them and held their son Jimmy for a long time. Everyone in the room cried. After a few minutes, Colleen came in, smiling. She looked at Jimmy and said, "You didn't give me much choice. I couldn't let you keep risking your life going back in time looking for them."

"You knew?" Jimmy didn't know whether to be grateful to Colleen for setting up this reunion, or angry with her for keeping this secret all these years. "You knew they were alive all this time?"

"Jimmy, you have to understand, it broke my heart to see you hurting over this. It really did. It broke my heart for your father's grief and your nonna's, too. I've felt so guilty for so many years."

Michael spoke up. "Son, don't be mad at your aunt Colleen. She was only doing what had to be done, to save our lives, and to keep you safe." He turned to Colleen. "And it was *not* your fault."

Jimmy looked to his mother, who still could not speak from the emotion of it all. "But where have you been?"

"Where haven't we been?" Michael answered. "Europe, mostly. A few times we got to see you in Italy."

"You were there? Oh my God, you were right there?"

Colleen smiled, "Yeah we saved your ass a couple times, too."

"What? What do you mean 'we'? What do you mean?"

Angela stroked Jimmy's hand. "I see you got the ring."

"Yeah… Mom." Jimmy's voice cracked again. "And I visited my grandfather's grave, your father. And I met a few of his old friends." Michael and Angela looked at each other with concern. "Don't worry, they all think you're dead. Wait a minute, if you didn't die in a train accident, where did all the money come from that kept showing up in my bank account?"

Michael shook his head. "Don't ask."

"Well," Angela said, "you have your grandfather to thank for that."

Sofia finally gathered her thoughts and was ready to join in on the conversation. "So, you're my Uncle Mike and Aunt Angela. But, does my dad know you're alive? And what about Nonna?"

"Nobody knows but us here in this room," Michael answered. "We're afraid that telling them might put them in danger. Or give your nonna a heart attack."

Sofia shook her head. "Oh, geez she's gonna freak when she finds out. She might be really pissed at you. I mean, Gramps was never the same after he lost you."

Michael's head drooped and he let out a heavy sigh. "Yeah, I hated having to put the family through that. But it was either fake our deaths, or die for real."

"Not only that," Colleen whispered to Jimmy, "if we were to tell Gus that his brother and sister-in-law faked their own deaths, it would raise questions about my involvement that I don't ever want to answer. Do you understand? He can never know about my past."

"I get that," Jimmy said. "But I'm sick to death of lying to my family. I mean, what if people find out anyway, then they'll never trust me again."

Angela hugged Jimmy again. "Honey, we have to go now. This is just a bad time, right now. This house is in mourning, and we can't draw attention to ourselves. But we'll see you again before we leave town, and we can talk. You must still have a lot of questions, and we'll try to answer them all. But not now."

"Okay, Mom."

As Michael and Angela got up to leave, Armando stood up and offered his hand to Michael for a handshake. "It's great to meet you, sir. I guess I'm your nephew-in-law."

Michael smiled. "Oh, I know who you are, Armando. We've been watching you and Sofia, too. Let's talk later… about your future."

"Yes sir."

Colleen ushered Jimmy's parents out the back door without anyone else seeing them.

†††

Jimmy found himself at Faces, the night club on Rush Street. He was talking with Dante Corona, who was adjusting his pants and giving out advice. Jimmy was leaning against the bar looking down at his shorter mentor. "Jimmy, always assume da worst, and you'll be ready for anything. Me, I don't trust nobody, not even another made guy. And I'm not just being an empty glass guy, I'm being relativistic. The only way to survive is, just assume everyone is your enemy. You wanna be tough? You wanna be muscle? You got no friends. You hear me? No friends. No family. It's you, and your fists. That's all you got. Jimmy the Fist. That's who you are, from now on. Jimmy the Fist." Jimmy woke up yelling, "You're not my father!"

As soon as he shook off the daze of sleep and got his bearings he had an oppressive feeling that time was flying and he was losing his grip on the situation. The twenty-four hours would be up soon, and he didn't have a plan. When he came downstairs, all of the O'Connells were still in bed, exhausted from their grief. Jimmy went into the kitchen where he found Gus, Colleen, Armando, and Sofia already talking about what to do. But they knew that it was going to have to be up to Jimmy, since Scolio wanted him as well as the time machine. As he walked in, he could tell they were talking about him because they stopped their conversation and looked at him. He didn't look at them, but starting making himself an espresso. "Look, I know what you're thinking, and you're right. I have to deal with this. Even if we could give them the time machine, they wouldn't be satisfied without getting me, too. So I have to face this head on. As someone once told me, fight fire with fire."

Gus was already frustrated by the situation, and his frustration was growing into anger. "Dammit, Jimmy, you can't put yourself in danger. My brother, God rest his soul, would never forgive me if I let anything happen to you."

Colleen, Sofia, and Armando all looked at each other.

"Don't worry," Jimmy said calmly. "I have no intention of giving myself up to them. We're going to have to come up with some kind of deception. Like maybe I buy us some time by giving them an empty wooden crate."

Gus shook his head. "No, I tried that with the computer. It only postponed the inevitable, and you're not going to fool them with an empty box."

Sofia said, "Yeah, he's right. You'd have to give them something that at least looks like technology."

Armando looked at his Velcro watch. "We don't have time for that. We don't have time to build some fake time machine."

The phone rang. Everyone looked at each other, but no one moved toward the phone to answer it. Jimmy was the only one standing, so he shrugged his shoulders and answered the phone. "Agnello residence."

The voice on the other end of the line said, "Time's up."

"What? We still have, like eight hours."

"Okay, will you be ready to deliver the thing at five pm today?"

"Yeah. I'll have it for you then. Meet me at the construction site. Same place you killed Patrick O'Connell."

"Fine. No tricks. No cops. No feds. We know where you live, and more importantly, we know where your family lives. Sofia… Sara…

Willow... like three helpless little birds, and we can get to the nest any time we want."

Jimmy hung up the phone. "We have to end this."

Colleen voiced what everyone was thinking. "Why did you agree to meet them? You don't have anything to give them."

"I had to move the meeting away from the house, so they wouldn't come here. I had to think fast, and that's all I could come up with. Now we have eight hours to figure out what to do."

Gus spoke up, "Well, we'll call the cops. They can be there waiting for those bastards when they show up."

"Uncle Gus," Jimmy said with a sigh, "That construction site is in the city. I think you know as well as I do that in this city, you never know who's bought. If we call the cops, and the wrong person gets wind of it, that'll make it worse."

"What about the FBI? Can't you use your connections to get them involved?"

"Yeah, they said no feds, but let me make some calls and see what I can do. I'll get to work on that."

The house was very quiet that day. Everyone was still processing their grief, and they all felt the dark cloud of the mobsters' threats hanging over them. Jimmy made a point to speak to everyone one on one, and tell each of them that he had the situation under control. The fact that he was handling it alone made Gus and Colleen worry, but they couldn't think of a better idea that wouldn't put more people in danger. Jimmy reassured them that he had contacted the FBI, and they were going to be on the scene. Even though Jimmy had nothing to give Scolio and his men, the FBI would arrest them before they could take any action. Still, the whole extended family watched the clock as it slowly counted down toward five pm.

At four o'clock, Chris heard the Mercury fire up and drive off. He went to Gus and asked, "Where's Jimmy? Did he leave?"

"Yeah, he left," Gus answered. "He said the FBI agents are going to get to the construction site early, to set up their stake out, or whatever. So he wanted to get there to meet them."

"He went alone? No one's going with him?"

"No, son, and you're not going either. The more people who go, the more people are put in danger. Just let the FBI handle it."

As his father walked away and went into the kitchen, Chris looked around. Sofia and Armando were upstairs with the baby. Fergus, Colum, and Willow were in the basement talking about their dad. So Chris went into Gus' office and took the old .45 out of the safe and checked the magazine. Then he took the keys to Armando's car from an end table in the living room, and he started toward the front door.

"Where are you going?" It was Sara.

"Jimmy's alone. That's not good."

"What do you think you're going to do? Is that a gun? Jesus, Chris. If the bad guys have guns, and the good guys have guns, how are the good guys any different?"

"The good guys practice." He turned and walked out the door.

"Wait! Wait, Chris. Don't do this. You could get yourself killed, and then what? You make Willow a widow, right after she lost her father? You want her to be alone in this world? Please don't go."

"I have to. Someone's got to have Jimmy's back." Chris walked toward Armando's car as Sara tried to keep up with him.

"Okay, I get it. You want to make sure Jimmy's okay. Um, but you know, the FBI is going to be there, so they'll have it under control."

"What if something goes wrong?" Chris opened the car door and got into the driver's seat.

"Yeah, what if something goes wrong, and you get killed?"

"Jimmy will have my back, and I'll have his. Two guns are better than one."

"Oh, shit." Sara was getting desperate. "Look, Chris, um, can you at least promise me you'll just hang back and stay in the car? You can watch and see that everything goes okay, but don't interfere, okay?"

"I can't promise. But I guess I can just watch at first to see how it goes." He started the car. Sara opened the passenger side door, and got into the passenger's seat. Chris looked at her, confused. "What are you doing?"

"I don't know. I guess I'm coming along to talk you out of getting involved. Willow isn't here to stop you, so I'm doing it for her. Someone's got to have *her* back."

Chris shrugged, put the car in gear, and pulled out of the driveway.

When Jimmy arrived at the construction site, the FBI agents were not there yet. He got out of his car and walked around the side of the building foundation, but then he realized that Jocko and his men were already there, snooping around in the construction trailer. *What the hell? Why are they here an hour early?* Jimmy tried to sneak back to his car, but the thugs saw him, and came out of the trailer, and stood near his car. Jimmy started to panic just a little. *Shit. My gun is still in the glove compartment.*

Jocko Scolio looked at Jimmy and shook his head. "Well, Jimmy. I see *you* here, but I don't see no time machine."

Jimmy knew he had to stall for time until the FBI arrived. "It's not five o'clock yet."

"Yeah, well, we thought we would come over a little early and make sure you weren't planning to try anything funny. And we thought while we were here, we might as well take what we came for. But it's not here, is it?"

"No, it's not."

"Is it going to be here by five o'clock?"

"Yeah, it's on its way. I've got some teamsters bringing it over here in an SUV."

Dante was glaring at Jimmy in silence, grinding his right fist in his left palm. No one said anything for a moment, and then two black SUVs pulled in. Scolio and his men immediately knew something was up, and when the FBI agents saw that the mobsters were confronting Jimmy, they put their flashing lights and sirens on. Scolio said, "You're gonna regret this, rat." He nodded toward his men and they ran off in the direction of their car. They disappeared around the back of the construction trailer and a moment later the car came squealing out from behind it, toward Jimmy, throwing up gravel in its wake as it picked up speed. Jimmy jumped out of the way, and the car took off into the street, with the two SUVs full of FBI agents in pursuit. When the gravel dust settled, and the FBI was gone, Jocko and Vince walked out from behind the trailer and once again blocked the path from Jimmy to his car.

"I told you you're gonna live to regret that. But not for long."

Armando's car pulled up on the other side of Jimmy's car and came to a hard stop. Chris got out and started waving his father's old gun in the air. "Back off, you fuckers!"

Sara shrieked, "Chris! Stop!" She stumbled out of the car and ran to catch up to Chris.

Chris took a stance and pointed the .45 at Jocko and Vince. "I swear to God I'll kill you both."

Jimmy yelled, "Chris! Don't do this. They both have guns. I don't have mine. That's two against one. You shoot one of them, the other one shoots you."

"But they killed Patrick."

"I know, but we can't fix that here and now."

"Yes we can. I bet I can get two rounds off before either one of them draws a weapon."

At that moment, Vince opened his jacket and made a move toward his gun. Chris aimed the .45 at Vince.

Jimmy kept pleading, "What if you can't? What if you miss? Chris! Think before you do this. It's not your job to fix this. I've got this under control. This is not for you. Stop, and think... Remember... Number five, track ten."

"What?"

"Album *Number 5*, track ten."

"Are you talking about Steve Miller's album, *Number 5*?"

"Yes."

"Track ten. The last track on the second side. *Never Kill Another Man*."

"Right. What does he say? If you can, if you can get through life, without killing another man. Because once you kill, you can never again be a person who hasn't killed. It changes you, and I don't want that to happen to you. Chris, that's a club you don't want to belong to."

Chris stared at Jocko and Vince for a moment, and then lowered the gun. Jimmy's voice got calmer. "Okay, hand the gun to Sara, okay?" Chris let his shoulders drop, and turned the gun around to hand it to Sara. Sara took the gun and crossed herself, thinking, *Where the sign of the cross is, evil is weakest*. As soon as Vince saw that the gun was pointed away from him, he pulled his pistol from its holster and took aim at Chris.

BOOM, BOOM... BOOM

Vince jerked backward from the impact of a bullet to the chest, and then he fell flat on his back, dead.

Jimmy watched Vince hit the ground, and then turned to see who had pulled the trigger. "Sara?"

Sara shrugged and said, "What the hell, I'm already in the club." Then she pointed the gun at a stunned Jocko.

Jimmy turned to look at Scolio, afraid he might be drawing a weapon, but he wasn't. He just stood there staring at Vince's body, fuming with anger. He looked up at Jimmy. "That's two of my men. Two."

"Actually three, Jocko. There was that punk sidekick of Fat Paulie."

"That was almost thirty years ago."

"I have a time machine."

"Well, now your time is up, smart ass. My friends are here."

Two cars pulled into the lot, a wildly-painted Mitsubishi Lancer with a huge spoiler and neon lights underneath, and a similarly customized BMW X3 with spinning wheel hubs. Two men got out of each car, wearing track suits and gold chains, carrying pistols tucked into their sweatpants. The four street gang thugs walked up behind Jocko and stood with their arms crossed. Jimmy was still too far from his car to get to his gun, and he couldn't protect Chris and Sara who were on the other side of his car. The three of them had one gun, and they were facing four guns.

"Hello Jimmy." The voice came from behind him.

Jimmy turned around to see who was speaking to him, and he saw four men in suits walking up behind him. At first, his heart sank because he thought he was being surrounded by more of Scolio's men. Then he recognized the two men who had found him at his grandfather's grave. He turned back to face Scolio and smiled. "Looks like my friends are here, too."

In one smooth and effortless move, the four men from New York reached into their jackets and drew their pistols. The street thugs' arms were crossed and it took a second for them to untangle their own arms to try to get to the guns in their pants, but before they could, four shots rang out, all at the same time, almost as though it was only one shot that was heard. Four bullets from four New York guns, and four gang members were shot in the face. And then Scolio was alone, standing in the middle of four more dead bodies. The men from New York put their guns away and walked over to Jocko Scolio.

One of them shook his head. "Street thugs, Jocko? You're using street thugs? That never would have happened in the old days. I guess organized crime isn't as organized as it used to be."

Then the man from New York nodded to Jimmy and said, "Our friends in New York told me to tell you, you and your family are under their protection now. No one will hassle you any more."

All Jimmy could think of to say was, "Thanks."

The four men took a confused and protesting Jocko Scolio, and they put him in their car. They drove him to the steel mill, broke in, and walked him up onto the catwalk above a vat of molten steel. When Jocko realized what was about to happen, his knees buckled, and he couldn't walk. But that didn't save him, because a moment later he "fell" into the vat, and his body was dissolved in the liquid metal before he could even let out a scream.

Jimmy, Chris, and Sara arrived back at the Agnello house to a very relieved family.

"I just wish I could have been there," Fergus said. "I wish I could have seen him die. Sara, thank you for avenging our father."

Sara was a bit embarrassed, and pretty shaken up by the whole thing, and she just looked down at her feet. Jimmy spoke for her. "Yeah, Sara did what she had to do, but it was pretty intense there for a while. I wondered if any of us were going to get out alive." Sara was disturbed by the fact that Jimmy could talk about it so matter-of-factly. Even though he admitted he was scared, Sara realized that this kind of thing was a regular part of the world he lived in, and she knew she did not want to be a part of that world. At that moment she knew with certainty that Jimmy was not the man she wanted for herself at all.

Willow ran to Chris and hugged him hard. She looked over Chris' shoulder at Sara and mouthed the words, *Thank you.*

Colleen came up to Sara and put her hand on Sara's shoulder. "Sara, honey. We're all very grateful, and proud of you. And I hate to interrupt your hero moment, but… there are some people here who want to talk to you." Sara looked around. "They're in Gus' office. Go ahead."

The door to Gus' office was closed. Sara walked over to the door, and looked back at Colleen.

"Go on. They're waiting inside."

Sara opened the door and peeked in. A black couple she didn't know was sitting on the love seat, holding each other close. Sara closed the door behind her. "Hello."

The woman said, "Sara?"

"Yes."

"Sara… I'm your mother." Tears ran down her face.

"What?"

The woman nodded, then did her best to speak through the emotion. "Yes. I'm your mother. And this is your father."

The man said, "Hello, Sara."

Sara sat down on a chair and started to cry. "What? Really? How did you find me?"

Sara's mother was now too emotional to speak, so her father answered. "The woman who adopted you. Nancy. She found us, and invited us here to meet you. She said it only took her three days to find us. Oh, I'm Joe. Joe Anderson. And I'm your father. And this is… well, this is your mother, Minnie Anderson. Well, Miriam, really, but everybody calls her Minnie."

"I… I can't believe this. I have so many questions, I don't know where to start."

Minnie reached out and put her hand on Sara's knee. "I know you must want to know why we gave you up for adoption. It's okay to want to know that. But it wasn't because we didn't want you. You have to know – it was long before we were married. We were just so young, we were only in high school. We loved you from the moment you were born, but we were just kids. We thought we were doing the best thing for you." Sara embraced her mother, who hugged her back, and her father put his arms around the both of them.

When they released from the group hug, Minnie noticed the scar on Sara's palm, where she had cut herself on the cemetery wall in Savannah. "Oh, you have a scar here."

"Yeah, I've been through a lot recently. But I think everything's gonna be okay now."

"We hear you're going to be an orthodontist."

"You know… actually, no. I haven't told anyone this, but I've decided not to be an orthodontist. I think I want to be a pediatric dentist. A children's dentist."

"That's great. We're so proud of you."

"Thanks. It's been rough, trying to figure out who I'm supposed to be. It's like you have to know where you're from before you can know where you're going."

Joe nudged Minnie. "Give her the…"

"Oh, right." Minnie reached into her purse. "Before I give you this, I need to tell you a little story. It has to do with your… let's see, your great-great-great-great-grandmother. She was the first free woman in our family." Minnie took from her purse a very old photograph. "This is a picture of her, taken in 1935, when she was seventy."

Sara took the photograph and looked at the old woman in the picture. She looked into the face of her own ancestor. "What was her name?"

Minnie smiled. "Her name was Rosary Kennedy. But folks called her Rosie."

Sara almost completely broke down. She started to weep, and it was all she could do to contain herself.

Minnie tried to console her, while she looked to Joe with a confused expression. "There, there, honey. It's okay."

Sara tried to talk through the sobs. "Rosie? Really? Her name was Rosie?"

"Yes. And *her* mother's name was Esther, and she gave her life so Rosie could live and be free." Sara was speechless, as Minnie reached into her purse again. "And this is for you. It was Rosie's, and it's been handed down from mother to daughter from that time to this, and ever since I got it, I dreamed that one day I would find you so I could give it to you, my daughter." Minnie's hand came out of the purse, and Sara saw the small leather prayer book, looking very old and very worn, but it was the same prayer book that she had given to Rosie.

Sara took the little book and held it tight in her hands. She ran her fingers over the worn, cracked leather, just like she had done when it wasn't so worn or so cracked. She held the book up to her face, closed her eyes, and touched it to her cheek. Under her breath she whispered, "Rosie."

Minnie took Sara's hands in hers and looked into her eyes. "I want you to know, when I got pregnant with you, lots of people told me… they told me to go to a doctor and 'take care of my problem,' but I knew the story of Esther and Rosie, and I knew that a mother should be willing to give her life to save her daughter, not the other way around. So in a way, Rosie saved you."

Sara cried some more, and then the three of them hugged in silence for a while, until Colum opened the door and stuck his head in. Sara saw him and smiled, then she jumped up from her chair and pulled him into the room. "Mom, Dad, I want you to meet Colum. My boyfriend." Colum smiled like he'd never smiled before.

Joe looked Colum up and down. "A white boy, huh?"

Colum put out his hand to shake Joe's. "Who's white?" He tugged on his dark hair. "I'm black Irish."

Joe laughed. "Well, then it's okay," and he shook Colum's hand.

When they came out of the office, the rest of the family was waiting in the living room, looking with anticipation at the newly reunited family.

Sofia said, "Well…?"

Sara thought a moment and answered, "I am an Anderson. I'm Sara Anderson."

†††

It was difficult for everyone as Sofia tried to explain to Fergus, Colum, and Willow that the time machine could not be used to prevent their father's death. Going back in time to change the past – if it could be done – would negate the need for that particular trip into the past, and without the need for that trip, no trip would be made, which means the past would not be changed. "It's what we call a temporal paradox, and I'm so sorry, but there's no way around it, at least none that I know of. The sad irony of time travel is that you could accidentally change the past, and even screw up the present and future, but you can't intentionally change the past. The only way to go is forward. To move on."

Monica spoke up, her Italian accent making her words sound almost like a song. "The past is just memories – good and bad. Keep the good ones, let go of the bad ones. It doesn't matter where you've been or what you've been through, it only matters that you're moving in the right direction. It's time to think about the future."

When the day for Patrick's funeral came, it was sunny and warm, but with a light rain. The house was quiet as everyone got dressed, and Nero walked around going from person to person, collar medals jangling and tail wagging, trying to cheer everyone up. Chris was with Willow in their room, they were sitting on their bed, and he was holding her as she quietly wiped her tears on her lace handkerchief. Chris took her hand in his. "Willow?"

"Yes?"

"Never mind. It's not important right now."

"What? Talk to me. Christopher, you have to talk to me - not to the dog - but to me."

"My Gramps told me once that his most important job was to be Nonna's husband. I want to be like that – so being your husband is my most important job, whatever else I do. But I feel pretty lost about whatever that other job might be. Just promise me you'll stick with me while I figure it out."

"Of course I will, you moron."

"Okay, you've been spending too much time with Sofia."

"Are you talking about me?" Sofia stuck her head through the doorway.

Chris gave Sofia a dirty look. "Your protégé just called me a moron."

Sofia laughed. "Oh, honey, I get it. But usually wives don't call their husbands 'moron.' Maybe once in a while when they really deserve it." Sofia winked at Willow. "Have you told him?"

"Told me what?"

"Oops."

Chris looked at Willow. "What?"

Willow looked away to avoid eye contact with Chris. "I meant to tell you sooner, I did. But I was afraid you wouldn't approve."

"Tell me what? Approve of what?"

"What I've been doing when I'm out and you don't know where I am." Chris started to fear he wasn't going to like hearing the answer to this mystery. Willow stalled. "Like I said, I'm sorry I didn't tell you sooner. Everyone said I should tell you."

"Everyone? You mean everyone else knows except me?"

Gus came into the room. "So you finally told him?"

Chris' frustration was starting to come through in his voice. "No, she hasn't told me, but apparently everyone else knows."

"Relax," Gus said. "It's good."

Willow held Chris' hands tight in hers. "I've been going to school. I got my GED, and then I started community college. I like math. And I'm taking accounting."

Chris was relieved but still a bit confused. "That's all it is? Well, that's great. But why didn't you want to tell me?"

Sofia answered for her. "Don't give her a hard time about this, Christopher. She's an eighteenth century woman trying to find her place in the new millennium. She was afraid you'd tell her not to do it."

"Why would I tell her not to go to school? Wait a second, who's paying for this?"

"And, there it is," Sofia said. "See, this is exactly the reaction she was afraid of. And it's not as though college has been a great experience for you. Anyway, the tuition is being paid by an anonymous donor, and we're not supposed to know who it is, but his initials are Cousin Jimmy. And if you tell him I told you, I'll have to k- um, I mean, just don't let on that you know."

"No, you're right. It's good." Chris and Willow embraced, then kissed.

"That's my cue to leave," Sofia said, walking out the door.

But Gus didn't leave. Chris and Willow sat there on the bed looking up at him expectantly. Gus paced the floor for a moment. "Christopher, Willow, I have a proposal for you. Just hear me out, and then you can decide if this is something that's for you. I've decided to build a new building, to house the offices of the Agnello Construction

Company. It's going to be all brick, with our family name on the side, built right into the brick. Now I really only need a single story, but it seems a shame to have my name on a one-story building. I mean it should be higher up there, you know. It should be a strong, imposing building, like a fortress. So I'm going to build it two stories, at least, and put the offices on the second floor. And I was thinking, the first floor would be the perfect place for a business that would generate more income for the family. So I thought for a while about what kind of business we could have, and then it came to me, we could have an Irish pub. And I want you two to run it. And it can have live music on the weekends – the real traditional Irish music. So... what do you think?"

Chris nodded slowly. "Yeah... I think that might be..."

"I'll do the books," Willow said excitedly.

Gus looked at them seriously. "I think you're ready to run a business."

Chris looked down. "I don't know."

"I was talking to Willow." Gus winked at Willow and Chris looked up to see him smiling. Gus slapped Chris on the back, and started walking out of the room. Then he turned around. "One more thing. Christopher, that means you're off the hook for taking over the construction business – are you okay with that?"

"Yeah, Dad. I'm very okay with that. Thanks."

Gus walked to the guest room and found Fergus alone. He had just finished getting dressed. Gus knocked, and then walked in and stood in silence for a moment. "Fergus?"

"Yes, sir?"

"Fergus, I don't know if this is the right time or not, but I want you to know I'm proud to have you as part of my family."

"Thank you. You've done so much for us, we're very grateful."

"Well, it was your father's dying wish that I take you boys on as though you were my own sons, and I'm happy to do that. You'll always have a place at our table, you don't ever have to worry about that."

"Thank you. There's no other table we would rather sit at."

"You know, Christopher is not going to be the one to take over running my business when I retire."

"Oh?"

"That's right. So I want you to be the one. I want you to be my right hand, from now until I retire, and then you will take over running the family business. And there will always be a place for your brother, too, of course."

"I'm sure I don't know what to say… except that, I accept."

"Good. So it's settled, then. Good." Gus walked out of the room.

At the funeral Mass, Father Graziano read from I Thessalonians, chapter 4: *We do not want you to be unaware, brothers and sisters, about those who have fallen asleep, so that you may not grieve like the rest, who have no hope. For if we believe that Jesus died and rose, so too will God, through Jesus, bring with him those who have fallen asleep.* In his homily he said, "We Christians know how to grieve. Oh, we do grieve – but ours is not a hopeless grief, it's a hopeful grief. Because we know that heaven is a reunion."

After the homily, Gus got up to give the eulogy. "I will always remember my friend Patrick as a born builder. To be a builder is to put your faith in the future. Building things is an act of faith in the future, and an act of hope. To be a builder is to reject destruction. Oh, sure, sometimes you have to dismantle something to build something better. But in this world, it's so easy to feel hopeless. Sometimes it feels like every little battle is won by fear, or despair. And I won't lie to you, sometimes Patrick was a bit overwhelmed by fear in this violent world we live in. But even when fear wins the battle, hope wins the war, because in the big picture, Patrick chose hope, because he chose to keep building."

When they arrived at the gravesite, the rain stopped, and a huge rainbow arced over the committal service like a canopy. The burial required a crane because Patrick's body was still in the block of cement. It was decided that removing his body from the cement would risk damaging his remains so much that it would become disrespectful, and then his casket would just have to be put in a cement vault anyway, so he was buried as he was, concrete block and all. As the crane lowered the block into the grave, the weight of it almost made the crane tip over. Everyone watched in horror as the crane's back wheels lifted off of the ground for a second, and then settled back onto the grass as the concrete block was lowered down to the bottom of the grave. Everyone breathed a collective sigh of relief, and then in the silence that followed, Colum blurted out, "Last night I dreamed he had just moved to Phoenix." The tension of the crane almost tipping over, combined with Colum's ridiculous outburst caused Fergus to start to giggle. Then Chris, then Jimmy, and the giggling became a feedback loop of laughter among the men. When Colleen started laughing, the women joined in and the laughter was fully contagious. Even Father Graziano laughed. The laughter was mixed with tears and hugging, and it seemed the perfect ending to the service.

Before going home for the party, Willow asked to see Father Graziano privately.

"Will you hear my confession, Father?"

"Of course, Willow. What's on your mind?" The two of them sat down on a bench away from the rest of the family.

"Forgive me father, for I have sinned. It's been several months since my last confession."

"Okay..."

"I lied to my husband. Well, I didn't lie, really, I just didn't tell him something when he asked me. I told him... okay, I lied."

"Mm hmm."

"I feel so bad, I wish I could undo it."

"Well, that's the thing about sin, Willow. Once it's done you can't undo it, no matter how much you might wish to. But the good news is, you can make it right and receive forgiveness and reconciliation. Have you told him the truth?"

"Yes."

"Willow, everyone has regrets in their past they would like to erase, but you can't erase them. You can only cover them in the present with good works to make the future better. St. Peter wrote, *love covers a multitude of sins*. Love leads to reconciliation and it makes us want to be better people. The remedy for the past is not in the past, Willow, but in the present, and in the future."

When Willow and Father Graziano stood up and walked back toward the family, Chris was there waiting for Willow. Father Graziano put his arms around the two of them. "Chris, Willow, remember what I said at your wedding? Marriage is not a master and servant relationship. That doesn't work for long. And it can't be two masters fighting it out for control. That doesn't work at all. A marriage has to be two servants, serving each other. That's the only way it works. You have to be equals. Not one person taking care of the other, but partners taking care of each other. Partners. Now go be a team."

The celebration of Patrick's life lasted late into the night, complete with the singing of Irish songs. As the party was winding down, Monica started going around to everyone and giving them things of hers, telling them that she wanted them to have these things when she was gone, so she might as well give them now. She gave away her rosary, her prayer cards, a pair of earrings, some rings, and an onyx jewelry box. Gus said, "Ma, you're not going to die any time soon. You're in perfect health."

†††

Jimmy sat on the back deck of the Agnello home, trying to enjoy a few rays of sunlight on one of the last warm fall days. He was listening to his Ziggy Marley box set with headphones on, eyes closed and sunglasses on, oblivious to the world around him. Nero sat on the ground next to Jimmy, and every time Jimmy would stop scratching his ears or petting his head, Nero would paw at Jimmy's hand to get him to start up again. With the headphones on, Jimmy couldn't hear Dante Corona creep around the side of the house with a knife in his hand. As Dante approached Jimmy, Nero growled, and then barked. Jimmy opened his eyes just in time to roll off of the lawn chair as Dante lunged at him, sticking the knife through the back of the chair. In the split second that the knife was caught in the webbing of the chair back, Jimmy grabbed the hand holding the knife and punched Dante in the bicep of the same arm, causing him to drop the knife and take a step back.

Dante looked at Jimmy with surprise. "I taught you that move, mother fucker."

"Yes you did. You taught me a lot of things. Including how to be an asshole. And now you're here to kill me?"

"You betrayed the outfit, Jimmy."

"I'm no rat. I never flipped."

"Bullshit. You took the feds' protection."

"You know nothing about that time in my life."

"I was there, Jimmy."

"You were blind. You were only into what you were into, and oblivious to the rest. You played the wise master like you were Caine from *Kung Fu*, but it turns out everyone thought you were a joke. I don't know why I idolized you, but I was a fool. All those nights at Faces… you're walkin' around like you own the place, and I'm following you around like a fuckin' puppy. But at least I danced. Come to think of it, you never danced. Why is that?"

"Hmpf. Dancing. I was too busy getting blown, or doing blow."

"Yeah. That's the difference between you and me, Dante. I never wanted my head clouded up with that shit."

"Yeah, well I got pretty tired of everybody singing your praises right in front of me." Dante took on a mocking tone. "Jimmy's so great. Jimmy's so cool. Jimmy's so tough. Dante, you're good, but Jimmy…"

"Listen, Mr. *Crown*. You're just a poser bastard who's living in the past. Get over yourself and walk away right now while you can."

"Oh, no. Not this time. Even if you didn't betray the outfit, you betrayed me. This is your last day on earth."

"You would fight to the death over something you could easily just walk away from? There's no shame in it, everyone else who saw you humiliated is dead."

"So maybe I'll replace them. Maybe I can be the capo. Once I kill you, that is."

"Look if you come after me or my family, our friends in New York will not be happy with you."

"Fuck them. I've never been weak before. Not gonna start now."

"No mercy in this dojo, eh? You did see *The Octagon*, right? You know how that ended?"

"I coulda been like a father to you, Jimmy. I coulda been the father you didn't have. But you disrespected me. Or at least I coulda been like an uncle, I coulda been there for you, like my uncles were there for me."

"I hate to tell you this, bro, but they messed you up, big time."

Dante lunged at Jimmy and took a swing at his face with a jab, cross, left hook combination. Jimmy was fast enough to step out of the way of the jab and block the cross, but the hook connected and sent Jimmy reeling off to the side. Nero barked at Dante, as he lunged for the knife and picked it up.

Jimmy got to his feet and reached into his back pocket. He pulled out the switchblade that Colleen had given him in Jamaica. He pushed the button and the blade swung out and locked into place with a hefty *click*. Jimmy turned the knife around in his hand so the blade extended from the bottom of his fist and he took up a fighting stance.

Dante lunged with his knife toward Jimmy's ribs, but Jimmy blocked Dante's arm with the blade of his knife, cutting a deep gash in Dante's wrist. Dante reeled back in pain and grabbed the wrist with his other hand, then turned and surprised Jimmy with a spinning back kick. This knocked the wind out of Jimmy and pushed him backward. Jimmy stumbled and fell backward onto the grass. Nero was barking continuously at Dante now. Jimmy thought to himself, *I need to end this, quick. Somebody's going to hear Nero barking.*

Dante took a step toward Jimmy as he lay there on the ground, but Jimmy kicked Dante in the knee, causing him to stumble and fall backward. In a second, both men were back on their feet, shaking off the pain, and facing off.

Jimmy threw a couple jabs and then landed with an elbow solid on Dante's cheek and eye. Dante stumbled backward and Jimmy stepped to the side where Dante's now swelling eye couldn't see him, and yoked him in the throat. Dante choked and sputtered, and then lunged at Jimmy with his knife in an overhead strike position. Jimmy leaned inside the arc of the knife, and was able to catch Dante in a headlock, but he wasn't ready for Dante's old-school judo sweep and takedown. Jimmy slapped the grass to break his fall but he hit the ground hard, and it knocked the wind out of him again. Both men lost track of their knives in the fall. The next thing Jimmy knew, Dante was on top of him, punching repeatedly, while Nero barked anxiously. Dante picked up his knife. Jimmy put up his hands to protect his face, and grabbed the wrist of Dante's knife hand with both of his hands and held on tight. Jimmy couldn't use his hands to strike at Dante without letting go of Dante's knife hand, so he had to take the punches on his arms and head that were coming from Dante's other hand. Dante was merciless as the blood from Jimmy's nose and face sprayed wildly. Jimmy's mind raced as his thoughts kept going back to his family in the house. *This is bad. It's not just me. If I lose... if I die here... everyone in the house could be next.*

Jimmy absorbed the blows and bided his time to try to catch his breath. He counted Dante's punches to find the rhythm, but he was hyperventilating and starting to get light headed. Soon Jimmy started to get desperate as he felt he was about to pass out. He waited for the next punch, and then in one last surge of energy he let go of Dante's knife hand with his right, blocked Dante's punch, countered with a palm strike up into Dante's face, and then locked up Dante's arm in his own. He used the arm to pull Dante off to one side, and then rolled over, pulling Dante off of him and rolling over to get on top of Dante. Dante tried to fight back from the bottom, but Jimmy wasn't taking any chances. He put Dante in an arm bar, and broke the arm. Dante yelled out in pain, and Jimmy took the opportunity to get on his feet, kicking Dante in the kidneys so he couldn't get up.

Dante tried to pull himself up, but Jimmy kicked him again. "Stay down! Don't get up, or I'll keep kicking you."

"You fuckin' kid, I made you!"

"You made me? I thank God I didn't become like you, you psychopath."

Dante pushed Jimmy's kicking foot away and struggled to his feet. He lunged at Jimmy, swinging his knife toward Jimmy's head, but Jimmy stepped to the side, dodged the arc of the knife, and swiftly moved his own knife up and into Dante's chest. The blade slid between the ribs and Dante's lung collapsed, sending him to the ground.

Dante gasped for air. "You can't stop me. I'll just come back. You thought I was gone before, but I came back. I'll always come back. I can get to you when you're not expecting. I can get to your family. I'll kill them all, one by one, and then kill you last, and there's nothing you can do about it."

Jimmy put his foot on Dante's neck. "You're not leaving me with any options here, Dante."

"Fuck you."

"Goodbye, Dante." Jimmy put his weight on Dante's neck until he heard it snap, and then Dante spent his last seconds in the realization that his brain could no longer tell his lungs to breathe, or his heart to beat. And then he was dead. The whole fight had happened so fast - in just a matter of seconds - by the time everyone in the house came out to see what Nero was barking at, all they found was a panting, bloodied Jimmy standing over the body of Dante Corona.

In the weeks leading up to Wordman's trial, Sofia was able to make the Lucidator work, and everyone took turns sleeping under the small parabolic antenna of Sofia's new invention. As they all watched the video recordings of their dreams, they were able to talk about them and process their memories and their anxiety. Eventually the headaches and nightmares subsided. Colum stopped watching so much television and started working on his GED, with plans to go to school to become an architect. Sara even stopped carrying around so many self-defense devices, and she moved all of her belongings to her apartment near the dental school and started sleeping there.

†††

Donald Wordman found himself trying to look into his bathroom mirror, but the mirror was so dirty that he could not see his reflection. He tried to clean the mirror, but he found he was too drunk to get the job done. He wiped at it with his hand, and then his sleeve, but his attempts just made the mirror more dirty. Finally, he took a towel and tried to clean the mirror, and he was able to wipe the dirt away from a small spot in the middle. When he looked into the mirror at that spot, he saw his reflection, but his face was distorted, dirty, monstrous. He tried to look away, but he couldn't. He noticed that the face in the mirror was not looking back at him. Then, all at once, the monster in the mirror looked right into his eyes, causing him to jump back from the mirror, and he awoke in a sweat. At first, he was relieved that it was only a dream, until he remembered that he was sleeping on a cot in the Manhattan Detention Complex.

A cool breeze blew across the island of Manhattan as Jimmy, Armando, and Sofia arrived in New York for Wordman's trial. As the guards walked Wordman into the courtroom, he looked defeated, and the scar on his head was visible to everyone. The prosecutor set up the case with his opening statement, pointing at Wordman. "This man had everything. He came from a wealthy and powerful family. But that wasn't enough, because he took something from another family, something they can never get back. He took a daughter, a wife, and a mother. He wanted to be our president, he wanted to uphold the law. Now he must be judged by the law, and accept the consequences of judgment under the law. He was supposed to be a scientist, but science without morality is a deal with the devil."

When Sofia was called to the witness stand, a large TV monitor was rolled out on a cart, and turned to face the jury. The prosecutor addressed Sofia, "Please state your name for the record."

"Sofia Agnello Fernandez."

"Ladies and gentlemen of the jury, Ms. Fernandez has invented a way to record the visual images of people's dreams. Ms. Fernandez, can you please tell us what we are about to see on this video tape?"

"I've recorded the dreams of the defendant, Dr. Donald Wordman. I've captured the images of a recurring dream made up of his own memories, which his subconscious is struggling to deal with. What you're about to see on this video is from Dr. Wordman's own point of view – it's what he saw the night of the accident, when he hit and killed Mrs. Tanner."

"Objection!" The defense attorney stood up. "Dr. Wordman's guilt has not been proven."

The judge sighed. "Sustained. The jury understands that our expert witness should have said he *allegedly* killed Mrs. Tanner. Proceed."

The bailiff started the video tape, and the jury watched with awe and disgust as the images showed the point of view of a college-age Wordman, looking through his car windshield. The car was speeding and swerving, and the images were going in and out of focus as the view shifted back and forth between windshield and dashboard, radio and beer can. At the last moment, the jury could clearly see the face of the young woman who was killed that night, as Wordman's car ran the stop light and plowed right into her, running over her and continuing on without even stopping. The tape ended and no one said anything. The whole courtroom could hear the sobs of Donald Wordman crying into his hands. He was judged, not only by his actions, but by his own vision of what he had done, as he was made to sit there while images of his crime were played out for all to see. A few minutes later, he confessed to everything, saying that taking responsibility for the woman's death would be worth it if only the dreams would stop. The jury didn't take long to convict him of aggravated vehicular manslaughter, and when it was all over he was led out of the courtroom in chains.

✝✝✝

Gus came into the house from the garage carrying a grocery bag full of Italian bread. He handed it to Colleen, who was watching over the sauce, and then he went into the living room. "Isn't Sara coming to dinner?"

Monica was under the headphones listening to the CD of Rocco's blues band. She could see that Gus was talking to her, so she took the headphones off. "What?"

"Sara – isn't she coming to dinner?"

"She's already here – upstairs with Colum."

"Wow, that's funny, I could have sworn she wasn't here. I mean, the magazines aren't perpendicular to the edge of the coffee table, and the ottoman isn't even with the chair. It's like she hasn't been here at all."

"She's not straightening things so much any more, I guess."

Gus yelled up the stairs. "Let's go, time to eat."

As everyone gathered and took their seats around the table, Colleen came in with the huge platter of pasta. "See, Gus. It's a good thing you bought this bigger table. Who would have ever guessed we would need to put this many people around our table?"

As Chris and Willow came to the table, Willow straightened Chris' tie and gave him a kiss.

Colleen frowned. "Oh, 'Mando, do you have to wear the gun to the table."

"Sorry, Mom, FBI issue." He smiled and looked over at Jimmy, who winked at him.

Chris crossed himself and looked around the table. Monica... Gus... Colleen... Jimmy... Armando... Sofia... Armando Jr., and an empty chair for Patrick. Chris thought about the way life goes on. *One life ended, and another one begun.* He continued his scan around the table. Fergus... Colum... Sara... Joe and Minnie Anderson, and Uncle Mike and Aunt Angela. And next to Chris was his bride, Willow. He turned and smiled at her as he shoveled rigatoni into his mouth. She smiled back, still wearing his grandfather's crucifix. Monica noticed her husband's crucifix around Willow's neck and smiled.

Monica picked up her butter knife and clinked it against her wine glass. Everyone stopped talking, and Monica took a breath. "This is what matters. The people around the table. The world changes, but what's important stays the same. I used to think I was old, but getting my boys back, that makes me feel young again. And some of you were born two hundred years before me!" Everyone laughed and clinked glasses.

Chris turned to Monica, "So, Nonna, is this where you tell us we all have to go to Mass?"

"No. I'm going to Mass, you can come if you want to."

"Nonna, you trust us to decide for ourselves?"

"Trust you? No, I trust God."

Sara broke the bread and passed it as Fergus stood up to make a toast. He lifted his glass and took a deep breath. He had a lot of things he wanted to say, but all he could get out was, "If God sends you down a stony path, may he give you strong shoes." Everyone chuckled as they said *Salute*, or *Sláinte*.

Jimmy took the opportunity to make his announcement. "I hate to be the one to break up this table, but now I really do need to get back to Rome. I have a job, and a girlfriend, both of which have been very patient with me as I put them on hold to be here and help… you know, fix things. So after we make our last trip to New York to dismantle the time machine, I'll be going on to Rome. But don't worry, I'll keep in touch, and I'll visit for the holidays."

"No you won't!" Gus said. "Because we're all coming to Rome to visit you!"

Everyone smiled and sounded excited to think of a family trip to Rome. Jimmy looked down and noticed the diamond horseshoe pinky ring on his hand. "I was going to say that I was feeling lucky to be at this table. But it's not really luck, is it? It's love, I guess. It's family. It's not science or technology that fixes what's broken – it's people – people putting their faith in God and in each other. Bob Marley said something to me when I was in Jamaica. He said 'money can't buy time.' That's so true. Money can't buy time."

EPILOGUE

Sofia finally completed the FTL transmitter, and with it, her PhD. Using lasers as carrier waves, Sofia was able to send a directional beam to the exact place where the earth was in orbit on a particular date in the past. She and Jimmy used the transmitter to send the messages back in time to themselves, including Jimmy's messages to Sofia when she first built the receiver. Then they sent the plans for the time machine. For a moment they thought about not sending the plans, but they quickly realized that if they never sent the plans, Fergus, Colum, and Willow would never have been brought to the present. Jimmy suggested that they include a warning with the plans, but deep down they knew it would never be received – it was apparently lost in the first moments of reception, when Sofia was trying to figure out how to save such a large file on a 3.5 inch floppy disc. After sending the plans back in time, Sofia deleted the files and burned the printout, destroying any trace of the plans in the present.

At last it was time to dismantle the Resonator. Jimmy, Armando, and Sofia met a TIA team at the loft in New York, and for a while they didn't really know where to start. It seemed a shame to destroy it, but it was now officially classified as a weapon of mass destruction. In the end, it didn't matter how they took it apart, since the goal was simply to make sure it could never be used again. Sofia, to her own surprise, wasn't very upset about having to destroy her work. She never really considered it her own, since she never set out to invent time travel, and the plans did not originate with her. Finally, she said, "You know, it never worked that well anyway." And so she supervised the destruction of the Resonator, first removing all the components that could be repurposed, and then barking orders at Jimmy and the TIA team as they tore it down, and took it apart. Essential components were melted or smashed, and the rest was scrapped. It only took one day, and at the end of that day, the Resonator was reduced to a pile of garbage. As they drove from the loft to the airport, Armando looked up at the twin towers of the World Trade Center. "I can't help but think we shouldn't have destroyed it. What if something terrible happens and we need it?"

Sofia put her hand on his knee. "Honey, trying to change the past is a waste of the present."

✝✝✝

Gus stood on the curb looking up at his new building. Built into the brick were the words, AGNELLO AND SONS across the front. Gus smiled and nodded his head approvingly. Then he turned and looked at Fergus, who was standing next to him. Fergus was admiring the cufflinks that Gus had given him. "You know," Gus said, "you're all my sons now. You and Colum, and even Armando. It's not Agnello and Son, it's Agnello and Sons, because we're all one family now. Agnello, O'Connell, and Fernandez." Fergus nodded, and looked to the sign over the first floor door of the building: PADDY O'CONNELL'S PUB.

Inside the pub, Chris was playing some traditional Irish songs with an impromptu group of local musicians. He looked out over the audience and scanned the faces. Sofia was feeding her son as Armando held him on his lap. Colum sat next to Sara, who was admiring her new engagement ring. Willow was listening intently to Chris, and Chris was having the time of his life. He thought how much this was just like the pub in Dublin, where he realized that this feeling is the reason he wanted to be a musician in the first place. Then suddenly he remembered the words of his grandfather in his dream. *Remember the joy… Don't dream of the applause. Just remember the joy.* And he thought to himself, *This is it. This is how I'll be your legacy, Gramps.*

†††

Wordman was startled by the sound of the prison's lights-out bell. He never could get used to that, even though he knew it was coming at the same time every day. He lay on his cot and sighed as he folded down the corner of a page in his copy of *Atheist Delusions* and set it on the floor under the bed. He had come to appreciate the low-tech world of the prison as a kind of long term sabbatical from his blind faith in science. The lights went out, and Wordman closed his eyes, and prayed.

HISTORICAL NOTES

William Kennedy left county Monaghan in Ireland and came to the United States with his wife Mary Ann (Cournahan) Kennedy and their children in the year 1872. Three of their children, Mary, Sarah, and Willie, died in the fall and winter of 1874. Their son Thomas died in 1884 at the age of 21. He is buried next to his sisters and brother in Hanover, IL, in the Old Log Church Cemetery.

Both Solomon Gleason and the Rev. Edward Meyers died in the yellow fever epidemic in Savannah in the summer of 1876. However, Solomon Gleason was able to get his remaining children out of Savannah, and they survived. Joel Harris, editor at the *Savannah Morning News*, went on to write the "Uncle Remus" stories.

Juliette (Daisy) Gordon was the founder the Girl Scouts. Her home in Savannah is still a pilgrimage site for Girl Scouts who come from everywhere to visit. An important part of the Girl Scout motto is, "to help people at all times." Her mother, Nellie Kinzie Gordon, was from Chicago.

You can read the autobiography of a former slave named John Brown. It's called, *Slave Life in Georgia*. To find out more about the hauntings in Savannah, read the books by James Caskey and Robert Edgerly.

I hope that the good people of Savannah will recognize my love for their beautiful city in the pages of this book. The use of historical characters and locations is meant as an homage to Savannah and its people.

The same goes for the beautiful island and people of Jamaica, and my love for Reggae music. Bob Marley passed away in 1981, at only 36 years of age. It is said that his last words to his son Ziggy were, "Money can't buy life."

CPSIA information can be obtained
at www.ICGtesting.com
Printed in the USA
FFOW04n1910100816
26671FF